The Last IN LINE

One

Freya Cortez bounced on her heels outside The Ruby Room's double doors; her sleeveless, sunny yellow dress, with its nipped-in waistline, doing a piss-poor job of keeping her warm. Late summer in Melbourne, Australia, could be fickle, and lately, the nights held a constant chill.

"How'd things go with the rep?" Crystal loomed to her right, tall, dark, and slender, dwarfing Freya's significantly shorter and rounder physique—probably a good thing, since she'd hired the woman as the bar's bouncer.

"Well enough."

Wednesday nights at the burlesque club weren't usually all that busy, but business had picked up. Freya looked over the small huddle of people still trying to get into her venue, despite the time nearing midnight.

"Just well?" Crystal's voice somehow still held a bored, dull edge, as if very little ever impressed her.

After years of being knocked back, followed by six-months of planning now that they were in, the bar's inclusion in the Live Wire Festival *was* reason for excitement. And that inclusion was what brought Freya to the club on her night off tonight. More planning. More prep.

"Okay, better than well." She shrugged, still downplaying things.

The festival rep she'd met earlier had been impressed with the weeknight atmosphere and the flow of patrons.

Now, four people waited in line, and she whispered for Crystal to admit these last patrons, then lock the doors to anyone new. Her voice held a subtle croakiness from much yelling over bawdy music while talking to that rep. Though with any luck, last drinks would be called in the next hour or so, and then it would be time to go home. She'd rest her voice soon.

A young woman in front of Crystal dug around in her purse for ID, only to drop the hot pink clutch.

Crystal's bored tone returned. "I'm not getting that."

To be fair, Crystal's skin-tight leather pants and five-eleven frame meant Freya was closer to the ground, and therefore the better person to help.

She crouched and began collecting stuff off the pavement, sparing Crystal the long, tight-panted journey down. That said, Freya had her limits too, like collecting the loose tissues floating about; though the rolling pink tube of lipstick and blue pen she could do.

Someone huddled down beside her, the warmth from their hand crossing hers in the cool night and drawing her gaze to a set of soft blue eyes. Varying shades of stone and sky held her attention for a beat too long; for some reason, she imagined gentle waves atop a wintery sea within those pupils. An irrationally dreamy thought, especially for her.

Her eyes narrowed of their own accord. She knew this guy. One of her regulars. Knew those shaggy, surfer curls kissing his brow, and those broad shoulders paired with his tall physique, a tad on the slender side.

Yes, she knew. Some sort of tech millionaire, or maybe that was his brother, or something along those lines… Unlike his queue of admirers at The Ruby—mostly her own staff—she pretended not to notice.

She gave him a small nod and extracted a case of mints from his long fingers. "First drink's on me. Just tell the bar staff the door woman sent you."

A smile pulled at his lips and sent a small thrill of electricity through her tummy.

Small, yes, but still enough to compel her back to standing.

She turned away from him, offloading the breath mints on to the bag dropper, catching the jittery movement of her own hand as she did so. *Screw that.* Surfer guy might have had an unintended effect on her, but she wasn't above flirting out of pure retaliation.

She turned back around, intent on delivering some witty one-liner, only to find someone else standing in his place. Someone who stank of sweat and cigarettes and had a dirty blond buzz cut. *Not the surfer guy at all.* This guy's blue eyes didn't conjure the ocean, unless she counted the turbulent sinking sensation dragging at her belly. No, all she got from this guy was a flat, leering stare.

She offered him a weak smile anyway, and then turned to go back inside the bar, pausing at the low grumble she *thought* she heard, one that sounded something like, "Where's *my* free drink, bitch?"

A distant whisper in the back of her brain warned her, a whisper that had saved her life once before. She'd owned The Ruby Room for years now, had worked other bars for years before that. She knew a creeper when she met one. The Leerer had positioned himself up against her on purpose. He'd wanted to touch her. Expected she'd shrink away.

Well, he wouldn't get what he wanted. Not from her.

She spun around, ready to ask him to repeat those words, partly so Crystal would hear and keep him out of the bar. But he spared her that trouble, already marching down the street, past the closed stores with their blackened windows, fists clenched at his sides, taking with him his downright *off* energy.

Or at least, so she thought.

She pushed past Crystal and back into the bar. This night was turning out too long and weird for her liking. Time to go home. She crossed the darkened space, with its red-tinged lighting and boisterous patrons, only to catch sight of one of her bar staff clutching his hand.

Blood poured from his enclosed fingers, a glass having shattered in his grasp. She picked up her pace and came at him with a clean wad of paper towels from the counter, ordering him and the bar manager to the back where the first aid kit lived. No way would that employee be returning for his shifts any time soon, so she tended bar till the manager returned, then stayed back even longer to rejig the week's roster.

By the time two a.m. rolled around, and like an idiot who didn't know better, she exited The Ruby Room alone, her attention buried on the stack of fresh messages on her phone. She'd already ambled a few meters from The Ruby's doors, when a sick sensation surged through her tummy, urging her to stop.

No.

The feeling was less *sick*, more *off*.

The feeling offered a premonition, or maybe a warning; she jerked up her chin, but too late. The Creeper from earlier stared at her from across the sidewalk, his back against a banged-up blue van. The super wide pavement meant she stood closer to him than the bar, too far to double back inside, with zero chance of anyone in The Ruby spotting her.

She could scream.

Would anyone inside hear her over the music?

That only left running forward, toward him. Sure as shit not an enticing option, nor was running to her car since she didn't have one. The Creeper didn't even bother to give her a typical, sleazy scowl or an uptick of his lip to spell out his ill intentions. What he offered was worse—a flat stare, soulless and as dead as a long-departed snake.

His hand rested over his crotch, its placement by no means an accident. She darted her gaze to the rusted blue van behind him, his foot pressed against the open door's edge. An aching silence made a coldness rush her body. The sharp night air cut down to her bones.

He would grab her. He would shove her into that van, and no one would see.

A sob broke from her lips. Any second now, the terrified tears would start—a big feat since she pretty much never cried. The Creeper pushed away from the van and took a step toward her, not even giving her the credit of being quick with this attempted kidnapping.

His slow and snake-like movements gave the impression he'd done this before. *Gotten away with this before.* He tipped his head to one side, and the wrinkles over his cheek bones settled, as if he savored the expression on her face. Her open fear.

A loud crash sent more ice through her veins, and she startled as The Ruby Room's doors burst open. The Creeper's expression turned hard, and his stare flicked off her to a point in the background. Modern jazz fused with dance, The Ruby's door always slow to draw shut. Next came the crack of laughter and a jovial male voice calling goodbye to his friends.

Her heart sprung to a wild and racing gallop, the sudden ray of hope twisting another sob through her chest.

Fuck this guy.

He wouldn't get her tears.

She spun around to whoever had just left The Ruby. The millionaire surfer!

The guy already powered away from her, his hands jammed in his pants pockets, his rapid and fading footsteps like claws digging into her heart.

Well, fuck him too.

"Hey, Marcus!" Her voice wobbled, but rang true enough; whether surfer guy liked it or not, she'd make him part of this showdown. "Where are you going?"

Her entire twenties had been spent yelling at people from across noisy bars, so she had friendly yelling down to an art form. Of course, surfer guy's name probably wasn't Marcus, so he didn't turn around, though for the literal life of her, she couldn't remember what his real name was.

"Hey, asshole!" She took a risk and ran after him. "Marcus, are you fucking drunk again?"

This time he did stop, and he spun around, a single brow raised, as if to say, *Who you calling an asshole?*

She caught up to him, plastering on her biggest fake smile and looping her arm through his. "You weren't just about to leave without me, were you?"

She fluttered her eyelashes, hoping the over-dramatic approach would tip him off enough to play along; though her frothy blond curls, Betty Boop dress, and their earlier eyeballing probably only worked to make her look like some kind of psycho-clinger, hoping to nab herself a millionaire pretty-boy.

Maybe when this whole thing was over, and if she got out alive, she would find a moment to puke at that idea.

Surfer guy frowned down at her arm on his. "Who's Marcus? My name's Max. What's wrong with you?"

His cool British accent caught her momentarily off guard, since she'd seen him so many times and never once swapped a single word. But now, she narrowed her eyes, a voice inside her head screaming, *Fucking catch on, you sun-affected doofus!*

But she held onto the charade, because her life depended on it, and gave a bright, air-headed giggle.

"Oh, shut up, you big dope." She gave Max's arm a playful smack, though the space between her shoulders burned with The Creeper's stare.

If Max dropped her, The Creeper would swoop in.

Her leg muscles felt weak, and a pain dug into her gut. Maybe it was time to lose the bimbo act. The man she clung to didn't seem all that quick on the uptake.

So, she rested her head to his bicep, making it seem from the outside that she might be his girlfriend, all while dispensing her situation's harsher truth.

"Please. Just play along, okay?"

$$\mathcal{T}wo$$

MAX REGRETTED HAVING ROLLED up his shirt sleeves the moment the woman who'd latched onto him dug her nails into his arm, dragging him into a brisker walk.

He tried to tug his arm free, eager to return to his luxury apartment for a decent night's sleep, before an ocean swim first thing in the morning, then his flight to Ibiza tomorrow night. But hell, for someone a whole foot shorter than him, this woman had one heck of a grip.

He peered down at her, her wide-eyed, chestnut-colored gaze meeting with his. "Play along with what?"

He swore she mumbled the words, "Just look."

Her suddenly pale cheeks sent a chill down his spine; he'd only ever seen this woman hyper-focused on whatever it was people who worked at bars did. The mere change in her, plus those mumbled words, made him peer over his shoulder in search of her problem.

Icy-blue eyes connected with his, that creepy-ass stare attached to a long, lean, somewhat scruffy-looking dude walking about ten paces behind them.

Instinctively, Max picked up speed. "Holy shit!"

On size alone, he'd probably smash the weirdo in a fight, but hell, there was no accounting for what kind of added strength or weaponry came with being a deranged kidnapper. *Kidnapper.* Was that even the right word for someone clearly more into stealing fully grown women?

Focus. For once in my life, could I just bloody focus?

Yes, right. Focus. Don't make this woman regret trusting him, even if he was the most unreliable choice for a hero in all of Melbourne.

His heartbeat thundered, and he lashed his hand around the scared woman's waist—a performative and real show of support. He wasn't clever. He wasn't *anything*. All his advantages came from pure, unexplainable luck.

Still, this woman's actions showed hard-to-match bravery and intelligence; at least for this moment, he'd try to level up.

He kept his stride long and fast, and she panted, her hips bumping into him as if keeping up wasn't all that easy. A quick glance over his shoulder revealed The Stalker in hot pursuit, albeit at an ambling, stalkerish pace.

Max held a hand out to the woman. "Give me your purse."

She frowned up at him but did as told.

"What the fuck are you doing?" The woman's voice came out as a low growl as he stopped and turned to face the screwball trailing behind them. "Are you stupid or something?"

Maybe he should have been insulted, but at least she said out loud what most people implied to him in silence.

The Stalker stopped ten paces away, his deadpan stare working over Max.

Max put on his best deranged smile but slipped a hand into the woman's purse, hinting The Stalker wouldn't like what might be inside. "Are you all right there, mate?"

The Stalker took the bait, his gaze flicking down to the purse and narrowing for a beat. He lifted a hand and scratched the back of his dirty blond head, grumbling something about, "Fucking hipsters," before turning in the opposite direction, literally stalking away.

Max held onto the woman beside him and made sure she didn't go anywhere just yet.

"That could have gone a whole other way." Her unimpressed tone fell short of the enthusiastic relief he'd aimed for. "What was your plan if he'd pulled out a knife or something, and all you had in your hand was one of my tampons?"

The Stalker retreated some more, and Max handed over her purse, turning in the direction of his car. "Yeah, well, he didn't. Aren't you lucky?"

"*Me?*" She followed beside him, a good thing since he wouldn't have to insist she do just that, anyway. "I'm pretty sure that nutter had plans for you, too, buddy."

He stopped at a corner and peered back in the direction they'd come from, seeing nothing but the flash of red taillights from the busy street, cutting through the quieter one they'd turned down. "Look, is your car nearby? I'll walk you over and wait until you drive away."

Her cinnamon stare darted across his face, and she shook her head, her thick, platinum blond curls kissing her light olive cheeks. "I don't drive. I mean, I know how to drive, I just don't have a car."

She jutted her chin forward, drawing attention to the line of her neck and a small tattoo on the crest of her left shoulder, one of a thinly drawn sun and a cat dancing beneath its rays.

He forced his gaze back to her challenging stare. That stare, daring him to protest her lack of car—even though her chest still rose and fell in the wake of her earlier panic—and he had no intention of making this moment any more difficult.

"Do you need a lift?" Cold tension spread through his muscles, the lingering set of her jaw making him fear she might say no. Then again, could he blame her? "It's a leap of faith, I get it, especially given what you just escaped, but I'm parked a couple of blocks up. If a ride is too much, then you can even just sit a minute and catch your bearings. We can leave the door open, if that would feel safer for you. Or, I don't know, maybe I could call you a cab?"

Her pupils grew darker. She didn't say anything, didn't even hint whether she liked his plan or maybe contemplated kicking him in the shin and running for dear life.

He rubbed the back of his neck with an open palm. Nothing he had to say seemed right. Yet another thing he should be used to, even though he wasn't. "I'm sorry. I just don't want to leave you here alone."

She pulled her attention from him and extended her hands with palms turned down in front of her, the ends of her delicate, red-tipped fingers shaking.

He tensed, his own hands curling into fists at his side. He wanted to step forward and pull her in for an embrace. But even he wasn't dim enough to think that a good idea.

She doesn't know me. She can't know that not every man is out to hurt her.

Over his last few months frequenting The Ruby, he'd watched this woman pour drink after drink with unbroken proficiency, never shaky or unsteady, but this… *this* was a story he'd heard his female friends recount far too many times. A story of being followed, harassed, and threatened.

He should have believed them. He *did* believe them.

Only believing and experiencing were two very different things, and he'd swum amongst their same fears tonight.

"I'll call the police first." Her crisp voice snapped his focus back to her face. "I got his license plate number, and I won't sleep tonight knowing he might move on to another woman."

He wanted to ask if she'd manage to sleep tonight anyway, but the question seemed too personal, so he gave a quick nod instead. "Yeah, sure. If you think you're up to it."

"The bar will have footage of me leaving with you. If something happens, they'll know who you are from your past visits. Do you understand?"

Despite her hard tone and warning, and the joyful scent of sunshine and tangy mandarin floating from her skin, she wrapped her arms protectively around her waist.

He gave another nod, slower and smaller now; his understanding of what he'd stepped into earlier, and what it meant to her, sinking even deeper.

"Good." She unwrapped her arms, a woman with a new mission. "Then show me to your car."

Freya ended her call with the emergency dispatcher under the reassurance a police patrol would be on the lookout for The Creeper. Hopefully they would find him. She couldn't imagine how she'd ever leave The Ruby alone until then.

She shot a quick message to Crystal, asking her to check the security cameras for anything that might be helpful to the police. Now that the immediate danger was over, as well as her phone call, the ache in her shoulders rose to the forefront of her mind.

She sank back into the soft leather seats inside Max's stationary car, succumbing to exhaustion and the need to let go, taking in her surroundings—the pristine white and wood trim, the crisp scent of pine and mint, along with an unmissable Tesla badge in the center of his steering wheel.

Yes, the guy had money. And he sat in the driver's seat, silent and staring ahead, as if maybe the whole Creeper incident bothered him too.

Well, she had kind of dragged this poor man into her nightmare, so his silence was expected. She cleared her throat, all of a sudden overwhelmed and needing distraction. "Umm… Nice ride."

He nodded ahead, eyes narrowed, before turning back to her. "Are you okay?"

She nearly flinched at how easily he disregarded her attempt at small talk. Still, she held eye contact, not wanting to lie about her shaken state while also not wanting to stir discussion about what had happened.

She wasn't okay.

Nowhere near okay.

But he'd been at risk back there too, and he'd done *more* than enough to help her out of a bad situation. Whatever she felt now wasn't his problem. So, she set about doing what she did best, what the performers at her bar did all the time, *faking it till she made it.*

"I'm sorry for taking over your night back there. For what it's worth, thanks."

His lips curled with a sheepish smile, a smile so unassuming, her own lips yearned to mirror his expression. "I was just a prop, remember? You mostly helped yourself."

"You could have refused to play along. You could have decided The Creeper was too creepy and ditched me mid-escape." She ran her attention over his fitted, light-blue shirt, a light blue that highlighted the turquoise flecks in his eyes. A thin, silver swirl peeked through his open collar, a pendant shaped like a wave, which made sense given his whole surfer deal. "So… umm… Honestly, thank you."

He held her gaze but said nothing, so she peered down and twisted the silver ring on her pointer finger—funnily enough, shaped like a swirly kind of wave too, though with a chunkier design and a deep-set ruby pressed into the center. The whole thing looked mysterious and witchy.

And speaking of witchy, she'd learned at a young age to trust her intuition—intuition born from having to predict who could be trusted and who would hurt her. Maybe that's why she'd had that sick sensation wash over her before she'd even spotted The Creeper waiting.

Why she'd taken one look at Max and known he would at least try to save her.

Her heart quickened a little, and a subtle warmth swept over her skin. Despite this guy's "innocent dope" vibe, she'd watched him in passing at her bar for months and had only ever thought of him as a "good patron".

He kept patient during delays and slow orders, all while his cashed-up friends got snappish. He never groped or harassed her staff, a bare minimum of respect, but one so many failed at on a regular basis. And then there was his habit of stacking the empty plates on his table, making it easier for her wait staff to clear the area, even as he thanked them for every small assistance, furthering his thanks with genuine and engaged conversation.

Every time he visited, the crack of laughter could be heard from across her bar. As much as she tried to stay out of employee gossip, it was near impossible not to notice how many of her staff held not-so-secret crushes on him.

If she had to guess, Max hadn't grown up with money; he sure as hell didn't act like it, anyway. And now, as much as she'd avoided any kind of adoration, she'd just become the latest member of his fan club.

"I'm ready to go home now." She flicked her gaze over his face, to the masculine cleft at the center of his chin, to those sparkling blue eyes; her breath settling with a strong certainty she hadn't just jumped from the clutches of one dangerous man and into another's.

This one can be trusted. His small kindnesses add up.

"You're okay with me driving you?"

His long fingers curled around the steering wheel, but his attention stayed on her.

She gave a quick nod, recalling the few times she'd watched him focus that attention on other women at the bar, before eventually leaving with those women on his arm.

The engine started, and a distinct flutter worked its way through her tummy. One she knew well. Most women would not do what she was about to do, not after the near horror she'd just escaped... but then... she wasn't most women.

Her back catalogue of fucked-up experiences ran deep and wide. Enough for her to know she'd eventually recover from The Creeper's attempt to destroy her.

Even though it was clear Max had an unintended way with women, he had something far more interesting going for him.

Despite how easy his life seemed from where she sat, he still had compassion, his emotions so clear she could pretty much reach out and touch them, a rare enough combination to make her want some of that. *Some of him.*

Irrational, right? But her childhood had taught her everything she needed to know about survival, while adulthood had pushed her to thrive, to take her pain and turn it into something amazing. She *knew* pain. She also knew how to make it go away.

She could overcome another person's attempt to steal her joy and find an escape, just as she had tonight. She'd find that joy again, and in this case, pleasure.

All she had to do was convince Max to help her one last time.

Three

MAX PULLED his car over to the front of a double-story brick townhouse on a small lane just off the heavy trafficked main road of Brunswick Street. He nodded out to a giant mural of a man, fist raised high and dressed in head-to-toe white, except for a gold jacket. "You have Freddie Mercury painted on your house?"

For the first time since this encounter, the woman beside him broke into a brilliant grin, the ruby of her lips no match for her hickory eyes, shining with their own unique brilliance. "I painted it myself. And he's joy personified, so why not?"

Max laughed at her statement but also her reaction—and the way his heart jolted at the pure exhilaration in her smile.

He shut off the engine and slumped back in his seat. He'd gotten this woman to safety. All he had to do was walk her to her front door, and his night would be over. He could go back to his multi-million-dollar apartment and the moonlit ocean just outside.

But first, he'd keep her talking and double-check she was truly all right. "You know, I doubt many people get through 'We Will Rock You' without at least tapping a foot along."

She gave a shrug, the light bronze in her eyes still glittering. "It's a classic, but I'm more into the flamboyance of 'I Want to Break Free' or the layered harmonies in 'Somebody to Love'. Freddie knew how to be completely himself. I admire that. He was bad in the best kind of way, you know?"

"I have a feeling you wouldn't be far from that yourself."

She lifted a brow but didn't respond. To be fair, he wasn't all that sure where that response had come from or if it had been all that appropriate.

Still, he struggled to pull his focus off what seemed to be a constant light behind this woman's expression. Constant, now there wasn't some crazed predator hunting her down, anyway. That smile hid a childishness, an unrestrained radiance, like a sunbeam personified… or something.

He chuckled to himself, at the way in which he'd suddenly waxed poetic about a woman he'd only technically just met.

"What?" She narrowed a glare at him, though that smile still held, her thick platinum curls overwhelming her yellow polka-dot headband and hugging her doll-like cheeks. "What is it? Why are you laughing?"

He chuckled again. First because he'd likened this *woman* to a child, then the sun, and now a doll, which, with her killer curves, sensuous red lips, and Marilyn Monroe-inspired attire—complete with off-the-shoulder, polka dot, vintage pinup dress—she most certainly was not!

But second, because he now had to deflect his true reason for laughing.

"Nothing." He brought his closed fist to his lips and cleared his throat, unable to pry his thoughts off how he'd now decided those curves were less "killer" and more "divine" like a goddess. A *goddess?* Jesus-bloody-hell, he needed to get his mind together. "Umm… I just found it interesting how you've clearly not overthought your feelings on Freddie Mercury, that's all."

She beamed again and twisted toward him, his heart panging hard. "You saying I'm weird? I'm *not* weird."

"You totally *are* weird." He jabbed a finger at her house. "I bet you're hiding a Freddie Mercury shrine in there, complete with a life-sized cardboard cut-out and preserved finger you probably scavenged right out of his grave."

She threw back her head and gave a full-on witch's cackle, hands clapping as though she attempted to stem the laughter. "Hiding? You're more than welcome to come inside and have a look for yourself. I have no shame about my altar."

"You're joking, right? You don't actually have an—"

His shoulders locked under a suddenly rigid posture. Surely, she wasn't really inviting him in? But damn it, he wanted to throw himself at the offer either way.

Get a grip. The woman just had the fright of her life. She's being friendly. She doesn't want me. Now open her door and let the poor darling out.

He shifted in his seat and pressed a button on his door console, the one that released the locks on his car. "Well... good to know. I bet you're tired. I should let you go."

But she didn't move, and neither did he.

He just stared out to the cobblestones edging the lane and the black asphalt center bathed in pale-white street light.

"Max?"

He turned at his name, her dark lashes rising and falling, her gaze moving around his face in a way that made his heart want to throw itself against the front of his ribcage.

Like she, too, wanted to stay for a moment longer.

Piss off, you dope. She probably just wants to say thank you, then be on her way. Go on then, just say goodbye already.

And still he said nothing.

As much as he wanted to congratulate himself on his heroics tonight, he deserved a hard kick in the groin for also having noticed the way her yellow dress supported her ample breasts, or how the nipped-in waist didn't hide the slight bump of her tummy, a bump he found inordinately feminine and fucking sexy.

Hot lust burned through his body. Well, maybe he deserved to burn. Or maybe he was just human, and she all raw and unabashed woman made for physical worship in any other circumstances.

Dude, these are the bleeding circumstances. Say. Good. Bye!

"Seriously"—her light jovial smile returned, albeit a little slower this time and tinged with an unreadable focus—"do you want to come inside?"

His jaw slipped loose, and he tried to coax out words that just wouldn't come, his mind working double-time to decide what her invitation might mean.

Eventually, he decided to cut his lumbering brain a break and just ask. "You mean, as in…"

"As in, I'm not ready to be alone, and I figure I at least owe you a drink."

Righto, then. His posture dropped, and he couldn't decide whether to be disappointed or relieved, but he shook his head and pushed on with the farewell either way. "You don't owe me anything."

He wanted to jump at the offer, to at least grasp at some kind of connection with this woman whose name he'd stupidly forgotten to ask. But what he'd done for her tonight, not leaving her to fend for herself in the face of trouble, didn't deserve a reward.

Or a drink.

Definitely not a chance to heat up his dating life.

She extended her hand to her door and pulled the handle, only to fall short of actually leaving. "If it'll make you feel better, consider it another favor to me, but you're coming in for that drink."

He frowned, prepared to argue with her, but by the time he opened his mouth to do just that, she'd already slipped out, her keys jangling in her hand.

His hand worked on autopilot, unlatching his seatbelt, while his moronic legs chased after her. He waited. She punched in the code to a barred gate leading to a small courtyard and her front door.

He followed her into her house where she flicked on the lights. Beyond the entrance, a cozy, white kitchen with a gray marble counter greeted him.

"So…" He made a show of peering around the bright dining area just up ahead, this woman's home all "urban arty", with its white walls and various indoor plants, and in a trendy part of Melbourne. Whereas he'd invested almost everything he owned into upgrading his multi-level apartment into the eco-efficient apex of city-coastal living. "I might have been mistaken when I decided you were one of the bar staff at The Ruby Room."

"What gave me away?" She dropped her purse on a tiny table by the front door and sauntered into the kitchen. A giant painting of a half-naked lady—little more than a thick, black outline and a few solid splashes of color—graced the side wall.

He forced his attention from the semi-nude and back to the *actual* woman standing before him, a small knowing smile twisting her lips. "Even if you rented, this place isn't exactly within a bar worker's budget."

She gave a light shrug and pulled a tray of ice from the freezer. "Maybe I have five other house mates hiding upstairs, and we share the costs. Or maybe my money is inherited. Or maybe I have a more lucrative side-hustle, and bar work is merely a passion project."

"Or maybe it's all the money you save not driving a car?"

She laughed at that one. "I don't *need* a car. Not in this pocket of Melbourne. I have trams and buses, trains and cabs. Plus, this house is just blocks away from the bar."

She turned her full attention to him, but he stood silent, not sure what to make of her evasive reply.

"Fine." She rolled her eyes and went about ripping a handful of mint from a plant sitting on the white marble counter. "I own The Ruby Room. Now, I'm having a mint gin and tonic since I've damn well earned one tonight. What'll you have?"

He paused, still trying to get his head around the fact she owned The Ruby, one of Melbourne's more eccentric but cool venues, much less that she threw the fact out there with zero celebration; unlike his friends, who loved to harp on about everything they owned or achieved.

And maybe that's what he liked about this woman because, despite what his friends thought and his own tendency to blow money on travel and parties and renovating, his bank account wasn't a bottomless pit. He had money, yes, but unlike most of them, his was new and not inherited. He had no "bank of mum and dad" to fall back on. Since ceasing his work at Tiluma, the tech company he co-owned with his brother, his financial flexibility wasn't as crash hot as it used to be.

"No gin for me. I have to drive home soon."

"Right."

She turned to a cabinet behind her and pulled out two short glasses.

Both landed on the counter with a loud clink, followed by the bottle of gin. She gave him an upturned grin. "You sure it's a no for that drink?"

He moved closer to the mint plant, its cool and peppery scent helping to ground him. And goodness knew, he needed all the grounding he could get to escape the familiar sense that, as always, he was just a few steps behind everyone in the room. Or in this case, the one other person in the room.

"Okay. Yes, to the drink." Anything to distract from the sinking knowledge that, as little as he knew about this woman, she seemed to have so much more going for her than he did. "Business must be doing well."

She dropped a slice of lime into each glass and slid one over to him, her direct stare seeming to see right through his mindless prattle. "How do you figure that?"

"It's a Wednesday night, and the place was busy. In fact, The Ruby is always busy lately. And then there were the new posters for the Live Wire Festival and the "Help Wanted" sign in the front window. Things can't be too bad if you're hiring, right?"

She tilted her head to one side, her luminous curls shifting to expose the long tendon down the side of her neck, as well as that delicate sun tattoo. "Oh really, you noticed I'm hiring?" Her gaze made a show of looking him up and down, hinting she'd caught him admiring her neck. "I wouldn't have picked a flashy guy like you to be interested in a bar job."

A broken chuckle slipped from his lips, and his heart jolted. *Damn.* He couldn't tell if she was giving him attitude or flirting, or maybe even both. He'd always been terrible at picking up these things. Case in point? This woman embodied all that he found attractive, and he had no clue how to move things along with her... or even if he should.

And because he wasn't exactly the smoothest guy ever, he often waited for women to approach him. And the women who usually did approach him, the ones who assumed he'd be interested, were similar to him, in that they were all tall and athletic and with decent access to "the bank of mum and dad".

When it came to hooking up, he didn't often get what he wanted. But given the way his nerve endings tingled, he sure wanted this woman.

He sipped at his drink, suddenly thankful for the liquid courage in his hand. "Me, work in a bar? That wouldn't go well."

"Why not?" She leaned a hip against the counter, seeming far more comfortable in his presence than he was in hers. "People seem to like you. That's more than a decent start."

He tipped his glass her way, heartened she'd noticed his presence in the past. Then again, she had no idea about his people skills, or lack thereof, and how his odd-ball behavior had gotten him booted from the company he'd helped start. "*Some* people like me. My former co-workers would say otherwise."

Since he'd left Tiluma, all he really had was travel, parties, and working on his apartment.

She raised her drink to him in a playful *cheers*. "Well, Max, consider me *some* people. Suddenly, I seem to like you, too."

Her attention flicked down his body again and back to his face, her cheeks maintaining their subtle blush, but nothing more than that. Like she had no qualms about checking him out or the potential repercussions of her words.

His mind snapped to the painting of the topless woman again, then the loud mural outside, along with her adoration of Freddie Mercury's ability to be completely himself. Except perhaps, her adoration had more to do with recognition. A recognition of who she was. A woman completely herself.

And this woman was *not* the damsel in distress he'd assumed, though true enough, she had needed him at least for a few minutes there. She was someone with an innate ability to survive, not the type to fumble on tough decisions. Someone who ran headlong into conflict and, unlike him, didn't bungle the hard stuff with her weird sense of humor.

In other words, she was his complete opposite. His perfect kind of woman. And probably why this encounter wouldn't lead anywhere.

He drew a steadying breath. "You know my name. What's yours?"

The least he could do was to stop referring to her as *this woman* in his head, perhaps even say hello the next time he saw her at The Ruby.

She smiled and placed her drink down on the counter next to his, the action drawing her closer to him. "Freya. Look, I'm not going to lie. I'm still shaken up about what happened earlier, so I'm not likely to get any sleep tonight." She rounded the counter and paused just in front of him. "So if you're in any way interested in staying here tonight, I'd like that. I'd like that very much."

Heat crept through his body, starting at his chest and filling up space from his head down to his toes; all while his skin prickled, the hairs along his arms and at the nape of his neck standing on end.

There she went again, running headlong while he scrambled to keep up.

He wanted so much to believe she meant that she wanted him, but he'd read so many people wrong in so many other scenarios, not just the sexual kind, and he wasn't taking any chances. She'd already met one creep tonight.

"I'm happy to crash on your couch if that'll help you feel safer."

Though maybe he should just stick to his original plan and go home, get a decent night's sleep, jet off to his holiday, and forget any of this ever happened.

Freya's eyes glittered, and she drew closer, bringing her scent of tangy, sweet perfume wafting over him, her body's full curves just dangerous centimeters away.

"I don't want to feel safe." She pulled the sheer yellow scarf she used as a headband from her hair, shaking out her curls. "I want to feel *you*."

Her hair, her scintillating words, that low and husky whisper, eviscerated his already unstable ability to keep his thoughts in check, drawing from him a desire to reach out and bunch his fingers through her wild locks.

But even with his compulsion to touch her, she was the one to reach out first, to touch *him*, her palms landing on his chest, only to slide up his pectoral muscles, finding a home at the side of his neck. "And I sure as hell don't want you sleeping on my couch, Max. I want you in my bed."

Four

FREYA'S not-so-subtle seduction landed right on target, Max's breath catching in sync with his dilating pupils. Watching his reaction sent an electrified thrill up her spine.

He'd given all the signs that he wanted her—his lingering stares, his long pauses hinting that he played his advances carefully—when she didn't need careful. While toying with him had been fun, she preferred to get on with things and put the poor guy out of his misery.

A comforting heat radiated from his neck into her hand, and she extended her thumb to stroke the edge of his well-defined and only slightly stubbled jawline. The tips of her fingers curled instinctively, and she pulled him down to her, his lips parting a split second before their mouths collided.

A small blaze took light in her lower belly, and his hands found the small of her back, dragging her in, as if his body awoke right along with hers. The possessive gesture made her press into him more, her lips drinking him in, the tension from earlier draining from her body. *Just what she'd wanted.*

It'd been a hell of a long time since she'd felt this enlivened at a man's touch, and it wasn't as if she didn't have access to men. Max's kiss made her heart pound and her mind clear. She was supposed to be the one leading this thing, but he left her feeling needy and weak.

A sigh rolled through her throat, and her hands balled at the thin blue material of his shirt. She pulled him back with her a few paces before his movements stiffened, and he pried his lips away. "What are you doing?"

She peered up at him and gave a sweet smile, stroking her knuckles over his front, hoping to offer more reassurance, only to feel the distinctive brush of hard, rippling abs.

A manic laugh threatened to break loose at her indiscriminate good luck—at the joy of her senses returning to her body after a particularly shitty night. Though dealing with the occasional creeper was almost part of her job description, the one she'd encountered had gotten closer and creepier than most.

But a night with Max would fix her woes. She was almost certain of that.

"Let's take this upstairs." She took his hand and turned to leave, but he tugged her back, halting her journey.

"You had a scare tonight. One that involved a man trying to kidnap you, and God knows what else." Max frowned, his attention dropping to the floor, the blue of his eyes turning stormy. "And now you have me, another man, in your house and—"

She gave him a narrow side glare, a warning that he sounded painfully close to judging her decision-making skills. "Are you planning to kidnap me?"

"What? No. Of course not!"

"And are you saying no to having sex with me?"

He went still for a beat and then shook his head. Quiet.

"Good. Then let me decide how I feel about tonight, okay?"

His shoulders eased down a couple of inches, and he gave a steady nod. She reached out and grabbed his hand again, commencing the journey through her house. The stairs creaked as she pulled him along, catching a glimpse of him through a mirror at the top, his attention snagging on yet another of her painted nudes.

She hooked her teeth over her lower lip and held back a smile. Perhaps now he'd pieced together just how much the human body didn't faze her. She owned a burlesque bar, for hell's sake, and had zero shame about giving or receiving pleasure, with no time for any judgmental asshat who expected *any* woman to hide her general enjoyment of sex.

And she loved sex.

She loved that sex could defuse almost every form of stress she encountered.

She loved the play between connection and power, how sex made her feel about her body, so alive, so free, so divine and human all at once.

Her bedroom door lay open, and she got within stepping distance before her world spun and tilted. Max pushed her back to the wall, only to rain down a whole storm of kisses on her. Like he'd wanted to do that all along but only now found the courage.

Well, welcome aboard, handsome stranger.

She laughed at the pleasant surprise, at him stepping up and taking charge. Maybe her provocative paintings had stoked his enthusiasm, or maybe he'd just needed time.

His tongue brushed over hers, hot and demanding, a rush of adrenaline cascading through her body so that she gave in to his direction, allowing him to back her into her room.

She pushed into him, alerting him to the expanding need within her, making it clear she would give as hard as she got. Even if her lips hurt from the force of their kisses, and her limbs already trembled. She still wanted more. Wanted to taste him. To run her nails over every inch of his body.

A light thud sounded from his foot hitting her bedframe, he stumbled back, dragging her down with him onto the mattress, her forehead crashing forward and into the bridge of his nose.

"Holy shhhh"—he whipped a hand over his face and hissed—"my eyes are watering."

She couldn't help it; knew she should ask if he was okay, but burst into laughter all the same. He lowered his hand and pressed his forehead to hers, continuing the rain of kisses while laughing hard himself.

He now sat on the mattress's edge with her on his lap. Occasionally, she'd pull back to witness the sweet, lop-sided smile tugging one corner of his mouth higher than the other, the innocence in that look making her heart surge.

She began releasing his shirt buttons, opening all but the last before he pushed her hands away, his long fingers entangling the thick dress straps at her shoulders and pushing them down over her arms until her dress bunched at her waist.

Her breasts overflowed her black lace bra, and he sucked in a loud breath, as if for a moment there, he forgot to breathe. The reaction filled her belly with a million dancing butterflies and the shock of never before feeling so desired.

And because of his reaction, she decided to take her fill of visual stimulation too, trekking her gaze over his open shirt, to the valleys and mountains of pecs and well-honed abs.

Holy Mother Goddess!

His body was remarkable.

The man was built like an athlete—lanky, toned—as close to a living god as she'd ever seen. From his brilliant blue eyes, to his golden waves, once again she couldn't believe her good luck. That and, how the heck had she missed all that gloriousness whilst walking past him every other week at the bar?

Her next words fell from her mouth, breathy and unplanned, "Holy fuck!"

"Yes." He gave a slow nod, his stunned blue gaze catching hers, like he too needed a moment. "Holy fuck."

His "Holy fuck" seemed aimed at her body more than his own, so she shuffled back, resolved to put on a slow show of stepping out of her dress, holding his attention until she stood before him in just the lower part of her underwear.

The act of watching him watch her lit sparks of pleasure throughout every nerve, igniting heat between her legs, her body wanting more. More touch. More action. More *him*.

And as if he knew, he slid off his shirt, where a thick scar sat at the top of his shoulder, one that only added a sense of intrigue, strength, vulnerability, stoking her desire.

She wanted to know how he'd gotten the scar, wanted to press her lips right there since he was physically perfect in every way except for this small chink in his armor, which somehow still increased his perfection.

Holy fuck again.

He removed his pants, revealing narrow hips balanced by strong-looking thighs. He *was* a god. A Nordic one, probably capable of launching lightning bolts from his magical pecs or something. Kind of ironic since her name, Freya, came from the Nordic goddess of fertility, love, and beauty.

Maybe this guy was made for her after all.

Well, just for tonight, anyway.

She copied his initiative and took off the last of her clothes, her underwear finding a place on an armchair next to her bedside table, before she reached into the top drawer, seizing a condom in its silver packet.

She handed it to him, his long and seemingly dexterous fingers curling around hers, while his gaze held hers again for another beat, drawing that same strain on her heart as earlier.

She pushed at him, pushed at that feeling, and made him sit back down on the bed's edge, straddling her knees on either side of his powerful thighs.

He rolled the condom down his length and things moved quickly from there, his hands finding her hips, guiding her so very slowly onto him. Her head lolled back while he became incredibly still and released a low groan.

Exquisite pressure grew within her. Despite the lack of lights in the room, the soft, white glow through the sheer floor-to-ceiling curtains was enough for her to witness his pupils expanding.

She couldn't help but trace a finger over his cheekbone, marveling at the way his eyelids fluttered shut at her caress. He leaned in, giving in to her a little, kissing her neck, while hot, heavy breaths brushed her skin and lifted his broad, powerful shoulders.

Fingertips dug into her hips, rolling her over him in a steady, rocking motion, the gentle rhythm fueling one desire after another, forcing her eyes closed until she lost herself to the rising swell through her chest and the heat swallowing her every fiber.

This was a celebration. Of bodies. *Of her body.* Of being alive. Something she'd learned never to take for granted.

She'd survived. When surviving hadn't always been a given. And yes, she had more curves than mainstream culture deemed acceptable since there was less money to make from women who simply loved who they were. But she'd long ago decided that mainstream culture could suck eggs. She had a body made for indulging in, experiencing, one that functioned for her every day and deserved gratitude.

And oh, speaking of gratitude...

She pressed her palms to Max's shoulders and gave thanks for this beautiful man, too. For the way he held her in place and let her take her fill of him. For the awe expressed through his eyes, like maybe a total stranger could truly see her.

A moan broke from deep within her chest, and she allowed the light waves of tingling to rise and spread from the place where their bodies joined, the room thrumming with energy. An energy so electrifying it effervesced from her toes, all the way through to the very tips of her hair.

Oh yes, she did love sex. Always had. *But this man.* He was something else.

Another moan tore from her, and she clenched around him. His hand slid over her hip, over her tummy, fingers soft until he cupped her breast, his thumb abrading her nipple enough to steal her breath.

He bucked against her, rewarding her loss of control with further pleasure, taking their exchange up another level. A rich chuckle rumbled through her, betraying just how much she enjoyed this unexpected end to her night.

She cupped her palms to his cheeks, allowing him to kiss her through her slow and shuddering climax; her long curls falling forward and acting as a curtain of intimacy around them.

His fingers bunched the hair at the back of her head, and he deepened the kiss, grinding into her, obliging her to ride him harder; her breaths turned ragged, heart near bursting. His tongue lashed hers, hungry, hard, until he swelled within her and found his own release.

Five

Max nudged the door to his apartment open, ignoring the ring of his phone and humming to himself, as the first refreshing glimpse of the ocean greeted him from his floor-to-ceiling living room windows.

He glided onward into his kitchen, the view opening up even more. Patricia and Tom, the married couple he hired to clean his apartment each week, stood at his counter, a red bucket of cleaning equipment beside them, blue wiping cloths and frosted spray bottles in their hands.

"Hey, Max." Tom folded his cloth and dropped it into the bucket. "Don't mind us, we're wrapping things up now and will be out of your way in a few minutes."

Max opened his fridge and pulled out filtered water in reusable glass bottles, extending one to Patricia and Tom. They both shook their heads.

Patricia dusted her hands against her checked work shirt. "Thanks for the offer, darl, but can't chat today. We've got to hurry off to pick up a present for the soon-to-be ten-year-old. Thanks to those extra clients you got us, we were able to scrape enough money together to get her that electric piano and lessons she's been begging for."

An instant smile hit Max's lips, and he leaned against the fridge. Honestly, his day just kept getting better.

"Oh hey, that's great." He took a sip of water, glad a few of his well-placed recommendations succeeded in getting Tom and Patricia some extra work. "And if you're stuck for things to do for her birthday, you just let me know, and you guys can host something here. Pool party on the deck, maybe?"

Tom's mouth dropped open, eyes lighting up, and he wrapped his arm around his wife's waist. "Thanks, mate, you're a good egg, you know that? We might just take you up on that offer, but in the meantime, we'll leave you to your day. Have a good one, okay?"

Tom picked up the cleaning bucket and led Patricia out the door. Max waited for the couple to leave before heading for his bedroom, eager to pack for his flight out to Ibiza tonight.

Unlike most of his friends, he packed his own suitcase because, sure, he *had* money but not enough to call his bank account a bottomless pit.

From the few years he'd worked at Tiluma, as well as the profit share he received each year, he'd dropped four-million on his apartment, not just the purchase but the renovation too—complete with upstairs energy-efficient gym, eco-friendly theater, and an indoor spa. Then there'd been his balcony. Meters upon meters of sparse terracotta tile transformed into a lush entertainment area, complete with two different garden areas, high-end furniture, and a solar-powered, heated pool for when he couldn't get to the ocean.

But still, he had to be careful. Since leaving the company four years ago, the yearly profit share was all he had, and so he needed to temper his spending, to live on, to keep up with his loaded friends—most of whom were "old money". So while he lived well, he couldn't afford a full-time maid or someone to pack his suitcase.

He had his apartment. He had his cleaners. He had his meal delivery service. And just enough left over to live and travel with.

And still far more than most. Remember that.

Yes, he appreciated that much, even if he did wish he had more to attribute to his last few years than tinkering on his apartment and bumming about on the beach. He did *want* a purpose, but finding one, much less committing... Well, that's where the spokes fell off all his nonexistent plans.

His phone rang again, and he pulled it out from his crinkled pants pocket—crinkled because those pants had spent the night crumpled in a pile on Freya's bedroom floor. His reflection in the window now showed his mussed-up hair and slightly puffy, sleep-deprived eyes. He looked about as crumpled as his pants. Crumpled, tired, but lighter than he'd felt in a very long time, despite his carefree reputation.

If only people knew the truth about me, huh?

He peered down at his phone, at his account manager, Elaine's, name on his screen, which only made the muscles on his face turn lax and his smile disappear.

He pressed the call-reject button, refusing to talk about money today. Not when he'd just returned from an amazing night with a beautiful, bold woman—a woman he wanted to reconnect with once he got back from his equally amazing holiday.

Hard pass on anything even remotely boring.

Elaine could call him when he got back from his trip.

He stuffed his phone into his pocket and strode over to his walk-in wardrobe, stretching to reach his suitcase perched on the highest shelf.

He set it open on the giant, cushioned bench in the room's center. There wasn't all that much to pack. Ibiza would be warm enough that he wouldn't be wearing much beyond swim shorts and maybe a light shirt during the days. Other than that, he really only needed a couple of outfits for the clubs at night.

A few clothes, followed by some toiletries, a phone charger, and some shoes went in his case. He wasn't all that careful about how he arranged things. Whatever he forgot to pack, he'd just buy when he landed on the island.

His phone rang. *Elaine again.* He hung up and abandoned his suitcase, distracted by the swim shorts in his hand and the ocean calling him less than a hundred meters away.

He threw the shorts onto the steel-gray, silk cover of his double king bed. Perhaps he'd eke out some time for a nap later, but right now he got changed, his stomach grumbling. There'd only been time to share a coffee and a light chat at Freya's before she'd taken an urgent call, one that stole her former brightness, and she'd pretty much shoved him out the door after that.

He'd left confused, concerned about whatever bad news had found her this morning. Heck, he hadn't even had time to get her number or ask about seeing her again. Still, he *would* see her again.

Maybe he'd find a few minutes mid-trip to order something nice and have it delivered to The Ruby Room, then check if she was okay or wanted to talk when he got back. He'd stay fresh in her mind, despite his absence, and lay the foundations to get close again when he returned.

He glanced at the clock on his nightstand, nearly midday. Breakfast could wait a little longer. The summer sun called outside, the water likely beautiful and warm.

He dipped into his linen cupboard for a towel, then went to the kitchen to refill his water bottle. The whole time, his damn phone kept ringing, making it clear it wasn't just the sun calling him today. Chances were, he wouldn't get any peace unless he spoke to Elaine.

"Hello?" he answered in the most droning, bored voice he could muster.

"Max, I'm glad you finally decided to pick up."

He frowned at her snippy reply, the hard tone not fitting for someone he was paying to keep track of his money. Then again, he had been giving her the run around all morning.

"Okay. Fine. I'm sorry." He rubbed his fingertips over the bridge of his nose, just wanting this call to be over already. "What do you need to tell me?"

"Oh, Max." She released a loud sigh. "Are you sitting down?"

"No." He dropped his hand, a sudden pit opening up in his stomach. "Why? What's happened?"

"Let's put it this way. If you're not already sitting down, do it now." She paused as if she expected he would do just that, but he didn't. He mostly froze, almost like what someone might do the second before a car ran them over. "Your life is about to change, and you're not going to like it."

Six

Freya's shoulders sagged at the scent of chicken broth from the food trolley some kitchen worker left parked beside her. That smell. The salty-savoriness. It made her heart twist and plummet. Not because she sat in a hospital per se, but because in her younger years, she'd preferred her hospital stints to her dispiriting daily home life with her mother and brother.

"How long has she been having problems?" The words grated through her throat, and she turned to the young female doctor sitting on a chair before her.

The quaint furniture in the small alcove and upbeat floral arrangement on the coffee table hinted that this place existed for the express purpose of delivering bad news.

"From looking at Ms. Branner's chart, years." The doctor peered down at her notes, her sandy blond bangs skimming her brow. "It's often the way with cirrhosis of the liver. A patient can hold on for quite some time until other organs also begin to fail."

Freya swallowed at the dryness in her throat. She'd always expected this day to come but never expected she'd care when it did.

From past, very brief conversations, she'd known her mother had health issues. As socially inept as her mother could be, she'd known better than to make a big deal of health stuff around Freya, much less expect any kind of sympathy.

"She's not going to make it this time?"

The doctor gave a slow shake of her head. "No. I'm sorry. That's why we called you."

The doctor's hushed tone and the deep wrinkle between her brow suggested she'd made the wrong assumption about how devastating this news would be; the only devastating thing about all of this was that it *should* have been devastating and wasn't.

When it came to Kerry Branner, the only emotion Freya had left was apathy. Apathy and a pure and necessary need for self-protection.

She sat a little taller, the reminder about self-protection kicking in. "Right. How long does she have?"

The doctor leveled an unmoving stare, almost like she needed a second to decide how she felt about Freya's flat tone and lack of tears. "We don't like to give predictions, but my general guess here would be weeks to months."

"So..."

The doctor drew a deep breath, then released a sigh. "From my experience, I'd guess about a month on the shorter scale, but the really stubborn ones—"

Freya scoffed out a jagged laugh, cutting the doctor off, even as a tear pricked the corner of her eye.

Hang on a minute, aren't I supposed to "not care"?

She dropped her attention to the flared hem of her moss-green dress, a dress she'd made herself because growing up poor meant learning to sew her own clothes. Something she mostly still did with her vintage-inspired wardrobe. Something her mother had taught her to do.

See, even bad relationships weren't bad all the time. Not all bad people were bad all the time either, which was one thing that made leaving them behind all the harder.

And while her mother had been busy turning Freya's younger years into a living nightmare, there'd also been evenings where she'd tried to help Freya with homework, even though she'd had so little education of her own to draw from. Or sometimes she'd slip Freya candy, or a five-dollar note for getting a good grade, or sometimes just because…

But even then, those moments never held long.

Which was why she and her mother didn't share a name. Miranda Branner, the name Freya had been born with, had changed to Freya Cortez.

She'd wanted little to do with her mother, even in name. She'd picked a new first name simply because she liked it, then kept the surname of the people who'd eventually come to raise her, her grandparents.

She closed her eyes for a second and pressed her fingertips over her sockets, her heart a mad flutter, while tension bunched the muscles at the back of her neck.

"I'm getting the feeling you don't want to be here?" The doctor's softened voice cracked through Freya's racing thoughts. Perhaps reluctant relatives weren't all that uncommon after all. "But Ms. Branner listed you as her next of kin."

Freya dropped her hands from her face. Even after living out the remainder of her childhood without her mother, a harsh breakup with a boyfriend in her late twenties had sent her searching for a sign that perhaps the world wasn't so bad. That horrible people changed. That redemption could happen for anyone.

And to some extent, when she did reconnect with her mother, things weren't as deplorable as she'd recalled. Only because she was an adult now, and her mother couldn't hurt her in the same ways she used to.

"I guess I would be her next of kin." In that she checked on her mother occasionally and had spoken with her long enough to track down lost family members rarely spoken of. She'd wanted to uncover how monsters were made, and for better or worse, she'd found her answer.

Her gut tightened and churned, but she forced a casual shrug. "My brother lives overseas, so that makes me the only one to deal with this stuff."

This stuff?

More like, "end of life" stuff.

Which was ironic really.

"Ms. Cortez. I understand if you truly can't do this, but your mother will need someone to be there for her, if for no other reason than to settle her affairs and handle the funeral arrangements. The state can step in with government appointed contractors, but that would complicate matters, not just for your mother but for you, too."

She took a moment to kill her desire to walk away now, nodding instead.

Despite what her mother had done to her, or maybe because of it, she'd developed strength, even when she didn't want to be strong, to compartmentalize her pain and get through the hard stuff.

Her involvement now was way more than her mother deserved, but still, some indecipherable force kept her in her seat.

Could she handle her mother's final affairs? *Yes.*

Did she want to? *No.*

Would she do it? *Yes, again…*

Fuck!

Because even with all the poison lingering between her and her brother, Clay, she didn't want to give him more things to worry about. His life hadn't panned out to the success he'd been groomed for, and his life in America wasn't something he'd be getting away from anytime soon. Besides, any bad blood between them wasn't his fault. Not really, anyway.

She urged the muscles in her face to relax and forced her attention back to the doctor. Her mother was the last and biggest piece of her past to shed, and as it stood, mere months would pass and then that shedding would occur whether she liked it or not.

She could do this. She knew she could. She would push through as always.

"It's okay. Just tell me what to do."

Max plonked himself down at his kitchen table, his gaze pinned to the azure sky outside his wide windows, his phone pressed to his ear. "Listen, Elaine, I appreciate you have a job to do, but could we hurry this along? I have important things to complete before my flight out to Ibiza tonight."

Important things, like go to the beach, have a nap…

"Yeah, about that." Her tone went flat, unimpressed with his spiel about his important things, like she maybe knew his things weren't all that important. "You're not going to Ibiza, Max. You're not going anywhere any time soon."

He reeled back, his shoulder blades pressing into his chair. "What? Why not?"

"So, remember that thing I warned you about months ago?" She let out a heavy sigh, the kind that gave the impression he'd worn her last nerve, and she thought of him as some kind of simpleton or something. Maybe she wasn't all that off-base. "Unless you have some cash squirreled away that I don't know about, there's no way you can afford Ibiza. It doesn't matter if your flights and accommodation are already paid up. Just the daily costs, while making no money, will truly ruin you."

"Oh come on, that's a bit dramatic, don't you think?" He let out a sound that resembled a scoff and a light-hearted laugh rolled into one.

"No, Max. It's reality. If anything…" She paused as though she needed a moment to weigh her next words. "You don't know, do you?"

The softer edge to her normally bristly voice had his pulse racing. He searched his brain for whatever it was he didn't know, but of course, as usual, he drew a blank. "What are you talking about?"

"You have no money, Max." Her voice rose across the receiver, almost as if she'd decided to just spit that bit of news before she chickened out. Either way, an instant coldness hit him square in the chest, and his entire world seemed to tip sharply to one side.

"In fact," Elaine's voice lowered again, "you have less than no money. Your account is overdrawn by five grand."

"Wait." He planted his feet to the ground and shot to standing, trekking his gaze around the room—at the bronze-embellished and designer furniture, the pristine white walls and clean modern design, as if any of those might hold the clarity he needed right now. Meanwhile, his fingers clawed into the edges of his phone. "I have no money? How? Why? How did this happen?"

"Let's be real, you knew this was coming. You knew, Max. I've been telling you for years to moderate your spending, that your profit share from Tiluma wouldn't maintain your habits forever. I told you six months ago the overblown budget for your apartment renovation was a bad idea. You've also been on five luxury, international holidays in that time, and your partying, with all the costs that come with it… Oh, and of course, there was the hundreds of thousands you spent on your car prior to that. This isn't something that comes out of nowhere, it's a pattern of behavior with you. I mean, it's only January, and your next Tiluma payout isn't until June, but you're already five-grand in debt. What's your plan? Because I'm not a miracle worker. There's nothing I can do for a client who won't take my advice."

Her takedown seemed to reverberate through the silence, as he took one full, long breath to keep from being sick. This wasn't *just* about the money. Elaine was right, this was about him, and why he made the decisions—or more precisely, indecisions—that he did.

All his life, he'd dodged trouble simply by waiting for problems to settle down on their own. Only occasionally did his dodging culminate in any actual consequences. And *never* this bad.

He raked his fingers through the front of his hair, tugging a little before letting go. The mild pain brought him back from the feeling he might dissipate into a billion tiny pieces and disappear altogether. Though, maybe that wasn't such a bad thing given how monumentally screwed he was. "So, what do I do? How do I get myself out of this?"

"I don't know, Max. Maybe for once in your life consider moderating your behavior like pretty much every other person on this planet?" Her joyless inflection returned, offering zero silver lining.

Then again, she *had* been warning him for years, but just like those final months at Tiluma, every warning in the world didn't stop him from messing up all the same. Really, he didn't deserve any silver lining.

"You're going to have to find another means of topping up your income. You know, get a job, sell off some assets. I see here your apartment is now worth four million, so sell that and downsize to something modest. Even then, you'll still be doing better than ninety-nine percent of the population."

Her dragging tone held an edge of condescension and a lack of sympathy, like his fall from elite-client status meant she no longer had to be quite as nice to him. Or maybe she judged him for screwing up something ninety-nine percent of the population would give anything to have.

He put the phone on speaker and laid it down on the table beside him, needing a minute to bow his head and cup his hands over his eyes. The sudden darkness matched the colorlessness of his mood because, right now, all he truly wanted to do was hide.

Yet again, he'd failed, and above all else, he really didn't want to give up the one thing he held any pride in, his apartment.

He'd poured his body and soul into renovating this place.

His sanctuary.

A thudding pain overran his brain, making thought nearly impossible, to imagine a life different to the one he loved and lived now. It sounded shallow, oh he knew that much, but without his money, he had little else going for him, his identity nonexistent. And if he had to fail, he didn't want it to be as ridiculous as this.

He wasn't regimented like his brother, which had no doubt landed him in this mess to begin with, and nowhere near as book smart or cautious as his sister, again, more qualities that would have helped right about now.

And the saddest part was, he hadn't always been so aimless or clueless.

And speaking of his sister, Sophie and her husband Orlando would be flying in from the UK to stay at his apartment in mere weeks. Where on earth would he put them if he lost his home?

He cleared his throat. The least he could do was end this painfully hellish phone call and let poor Elaine off the hook. "Thanks for the call. I'm sure breaking the news to me wasn't easy for you. Leave this with me, okay? I think I know someone who can help."

Seven

Freya stood in the hospital-room doorway, the semi-drawn curtains not allowing enough light in, while the cream-colored decor lacked in personality and somehow added to the weight of what she was about to step into.

She ran her fingertips over the emerald glass beads at her neck, stealing a moment for courage and not bothering to cover the nervous tell, even as she pressed her shoulders back and strode forward.

Four beds filled the room, though only two had people in them. Her mother lay in the farthest corner, her gaze lost on the cityscape through the window to her right. Her washed-out sandy hair sat in tangled waves around her head, and her blue veins glowed through now pale, thin, skin stretched over bony arms.

Freya paused, maybe holding onto some unlikely but persistent hope that her mother's dying days might have changed her; that Kerry Branner might find a sudden ability, or *willingness*, to be kind and accepting. To maybe apologize…

Get real. That's never going to happen.

Her mother's head turned, and her whiskey-colored gaze, a couple of shades lighter than Freya's, made contact. For the longest beat, her mother didn't react, her face an unreadable mask, though even that remained only half true.

The lines on her mother's face told their own story, scoring gouges along her cheekbones and deep trenches across her forehead. Those lines had existed for as long as Freya could remember, as if her mother had aged long before her time, the result of a lifetime spent trapped in mental warfare with herself and her demons.

"Why are you here?" Her weak voice held a distinct croak.

Freya's muscles pulled with instant tension, thoughts running through a list of appropriate replies any normal dying mother would offer a child. *"Oh honey, this must be hard for you too," "Come here for a hug,"* or maybe just a simple, *"Lovely of you to visit."*

"Your doctor called." She bit the sides of her tongue, vetting her usual need for brutal honesty. "She said you're not doing so well."

She didn't want to mention death, or that the doctor had in fact said her mother wasn't going to make it; because sure as rain, her mother wouldn't want to hear that, much less admit to being a mere mortal like everyone else.

In all her mother's years of using poor health as a means for attention, she'd also maintained the contradictory facade that death was for *other* people. Weak people. Certainly *not* Kerry Branner.

Her mother spat out a hollow laugh. "So what, you've come to look after me, then?"

Freya shook her head. As much as her mother couldn't confess to being susceptible to death, Freya wouldn't openly admit to caring. "Why, do you want me to look after you?"

She lifted a brow, daring her mother to acknowledge wanting help, but Kerry merely trekked her gaze down to Freya's exposed collarbone, right where her sun tattoo sat, before returning that same pointed stare over to the window. "No man wants a woman with scribble on her body."

The barb about Freya's tattoo left a dull ache in her belly, but she rolled her eyes, deflecting any signs of hurt. "Then you'll be glad to know there are an abundance of men who still want me."

She bit her tongue again, her thoughts flicking back to last night and how one particularly desirable man had wanted her numerous times, even going so far as to direct some of his kisses right onto her tattoo.

Her mother's attention stayed pinned on the outside, extending a sentiment that Freya was undeserving of any direct attention. So, nothing new really. "Don't be disgusting, Freya. Mark my words, no man will ever marry you." This time she did turn, but of course her eyes held a harder, darker edge. "And let me guess, you still pour drinks for a living?"

Freya clenched her toes in her black, leather ballet flats, mostly because her feet had a sudden and understandable urge to march her the fuck out of this room.

Hot emotions burned and bubbled through her abdomen and into her chest, like a rise of lava taking up more and more space, threatening to explode. She wanted to lash out, despite this being a quiet hospital ward, but her mother's slower movements and gray complexion came as a sign of physical fragility, and that too held Freya back.

Not long. Not long. I just have to grin and bear her. I've gotten through worse.

Easier said than done, though. Her mother knew full well she didn't just "pour drinks", that she owned The Ruby Room outright, and enjoyed a level of independence her mother would never know. Not that pouring drinks should have been a source of shame. But even in that sudden verbal demotion, her mother ran home one undeniable truth.

Nothing Freya did was ever enough.

Over the years, Freya had hoped each success would finally convince her mother to ease up a little and admit her daughter had done something incredible with her life. But those were her more irrational moments, and maybe the fact she'd crawled away from her shitty childhood and started her adult life with nothing, only to found a hugely successful business, could be reward enough.

"Not every woman wants to get married." She drawled on the words and took slow steps forward, her way of sticking her mother's rudeness back to her. "Certainly not me."

And certainly not since doing so would be dancing to the tune of her mother's fiddle.

Her mother dragged her cold gaze down Freya's body, like she hated the way her daughter showed an inappropriate lack of fear. *Good.* That hadn't always been the case. Far from it.

"You're over thirty. When are you going to grow up, Miranda?"

"My name's Freya. And the answer is never."

Her mother's dismissive laugh returned. "You're still going by that ridiculous name?" She shook her head in mock pity. "You just watch, Miranda. You'll regret not having children. You'll die old and alone and used up by every two-faced man you let touch you."

Freya's lip curled with her scowl. She wanted to point out how her mother was old and alone and very much dying, but even with all her mother had done to her, she refused to be dragged down. "Can you honestly say having kids turned out to be your dream come true?"

Her mother's gaze froze and then dropped, before a flash of fragility stole away the harsh lines from her face.

"One day you'll see, Miranda." She turned her head toward the window again. "I did the best I could."

"And that's why the state took us away from you?"

"You had more than I ever did."

"You think just feeding us every day makes you Mother of the Year?" Freya's tone rang flat, not from sarcasm now, but from the weight of her memories pressing down on her words. "And then there was the other stuff."

"Your father left. What did you want me to do?" Her mother's focus lashed back to Freya with an all-too-familiar look, her eyes watery with her barely contained temper. "Why don't you ever cry to me about him, huh? No one ever cares where the dads go, only that Mother Dearest keeps on going like she doesn't need the help. And then you were sick all the time—"

"Oh, don't you even start with that." Freya's heart clenched hard, the skin over her face suddenly too tight.

After all these years, she still couldn't relax around her mother, that and any mention of the past from this woman's lips sent her into a quick, defensive rage.

Actually, it wasn't even the mention of the past, so much as her mother had just fucking lied. *She'd lied.* She'd taken advantage of Freya's youth and innocence and blind willingness to trust, and now she tried to pass off all that horribleness as a figment of Freya's imagination.

Now she would never know what was more lies or another ploy to manipulate her. Or maybe her mother was just so damaged she believed the fabrications she spat forth.

Freya hiked the black, studded strap of her handbag higher onto her shoulder, her stomach churning because she wished at her age, after all these years, she didn't still want the kind of relationship most kids had with their parents.

A relationship where maybe she could say something and get a kind response back. Where maybe, just once, her mother would show proof of accountability; something akin to having evolved beyond blaming others or playing the victim.

Something where she acknowledged the hurt she'd caused.

Freya's phone rang, and she pulled it from her bag, glad for the distraction, though only so long as it took to answer the call and learn it was someone from the police.

She asked the person on the other end of the call to hold, taking a moment to refocus on her mother.

"I have to go. I need to take this call." She reached out and snatched her mother's house keys sitting on her bedside table. "I'm going to need these; you won't. And I want you to know, I'm only here to help settle your affairs and only because Clay can't do it. I won't burden anyone else with you."

She jangled the keys in the air and caught the sharp movement of her mother's face turning slack, startled, hopefully hurt. Freya turned for the door, taking the call and hiding a small jolt of satisfaction.

A cold consolation prize for the acceptance she'd ultimately always wanted and never received.

Eight

MAX STROLLED the familiar halls at Tiluma, the Edwardian building's open-air design the same as when he'd first viewed this place with Luke so many years ago. The same could be said of the bare brick entrance and modern gray carpets. Only now, a sickening, roiling feeling overran his former positive associations.

Since he wanted to believe he'd changed in those last four years, he refused to ask Luke to bail him out of trouble. He'd offer something instead, the one thing he still contributed to this company, the one thing he was truly good at besides swimming. *App ideas.*

For each idea the Tiluma board accepted, he got a nice pay out in exchange for signing over his intellectual rights. A pay out for just one or two good ideas would be enough to settle his current debt and then some. It wouldn't be enough to get him fully out of trouble, but it would buy him time.

He crossed the main corridor, thankfully not encountering any familiar faces, and took the elevator to the top floor. The building was no more than three stories, and the metal doors slid open with a happy ding way too soon for his liking. Still, he stepped out and turned left, anything but happy about being mere moments from his brother's office.

The air was a little too hot for him, and he rubbed a hand over the back of his neck, pausing before a frosted glass door. He didn't want to admit he'd messed up. *Again.* Didn't want to lose his home. Didn't want to add more to the overwhelmingly big pile of evidence already damning him as Luke's flaky little brother.

Losing his money had to be his biggest mistake yet, especially since Luke had handed him his wealth, and he'd screwed it up.

Still, he couldn't keep this news to himself forever, so he lifted his hand and tapped on Luke's door, thankful he'd at least had the rare foresight to call ahead.

"Come in."

He obeyed the muffled voice and twisted the door handle, entering to the sight of Luke at his desk, glowering at his computer and his fingers drumming over the keys. "Sorry, just one moment."

"Intense email?" Max smiled at his brother, but Luke typed for a while longer, silent, before clicking at his mouse and lifting his hand away with a certain kind of finality.

"Yeah, something like that. Anyway, what's up? I can't remember the last time you came all the way to the office to meet me."

"I've... umm..." Max peered around Luke's office, at the clean, white design, punctuated with the rich browns from his leather couch against the side wall and his walnut desk.

This company was born from Max's failure and Luke's guilt, a guilt Max would bet on profiting from once again. "I've, um, been toying with some new app ideas, and I wanted to pitch them to you."

Luke narrowed his green stare. "We're only coming to February, and the first lot of this year's apps are still in early development. You know it's way too early for us to take on new ideas."

"Yes, yes, I know." Max swatted his hand and half-flung himself into a chair opposite the desk, trying to appear casual in the face of Luke's deflection—trying to avoid having to admit the extent of his trouble. "But I have two cracker ideas that I'm really excited about, and you're going to love them. I thought, why not give you the early jump on what I have?"

He extended a giant smile, playing into his role as "flaky brother" once again, trying to throw Luke off asking too many questions.

Luke's eagle-eyed stare swept over him, before the skin over his cheekbones settled. "I mean, I'm happy to listen to what you have, but my hands are tied until the other team leaders are ready to field new ideas."

"Right…"

Max slumped back in his chair, veering his attention to his right, to a black bookcase filled with leather-bound tomes and a small array of healthy-looking indoor plants. For some reason, he wondered whether Luke took care of those plants himself or if he had his assistant do it.

A frowned dragged at his face, since he found it hard to imagine his six-foot-four ex-military brother taking the time to tenderly water what looked like some rather finicky plants. But then, Luke had a knack at being nearly perfect at everything, so maybe the possibility wasn't all that far-fetched.

Max cleared his throat, suddenly aware he'd gotten distracted. "Is there any chance we could expedite the new ideas thing, just this once?"

Luke blew out a hard breath and leaned back in his chair. "Max? Is something wrong?"

"Nothing I can't handle." He stared at the gray carpet, his chest prickling with heat.

He really didn't want to say more than he already had. Didn't want to hear the disappointment in his brother's voice or for him to interpret this meeting as Max asking for yet another bailout.

So, Max plastered on a smile and gave an easy shrug, holding his brother's gaze. "Though, I guess if you're really not interested in my new ideas, I can always pitch them to Ben Fink over at AmaziCorp. Maybe come back to you with whatever other ideas I come up with between now and when you're ready for me?"

"Now hang on a minute." Luke swung his weight forward, his elbows pitched into the desk. "Why would you go to AmaziCorp?"

His hardened facial features gave the impression of a man who'd just learned his wife had cheated on him, but Max shrugged again, muscles eased that at least, for this rare moment, he had the upper hand. "Why not? I have no exclusivity contract with Tiluma, and

AmaziCorp does joke apps too. You've said often enough that it's past time I find my niche in the world. Maybe this is it?"

Luke raised an eyebrow, though the tension in his jaw remained.

Max hated making stuff up, much less that this lie hurt his brother. But Elaine had been right too; he needed to put his finances first, which also meant utilizing what little skill he had. Maybe limiting himself to Tiluma alone wasn't in his best interest.

"You're right." Luke scrubbed his hand over the darker stubble on his chin, all while shaking his head. "Bouncing from one tech company to the next and shopping novelty app ideas is about as niche as you could get."

Max drew his eyelids into a tight scowl, holding silence over Luke's dismissive response, until a jolt of energy zipped through his body. He pushed his hands into his armrest.

"Well then." He shot to standing. "It was nice chatting, but—"

"Sit back down." Luke's voice boomed across the room, and he thrust a pointed finger at Max's chair. "I'm not done here."

Max startled before a firm rigidity took hold of his every muscle.

"Well, I am." And even with that, even with the compulsion to cuss and walk away, he didn't take a step. "I have things to do before my flight this evening."

"Sit. Down." Luke barked the order, remnants of his military past coming through. "I know something is wrong here. While I admire you not outright asking for me to help you out for a change, you need to damn well sit yourself down and start talking. *Now.*"

But Max couldn't find the ability to sit, maybe because sitting would mean talking, and for once in his life, he didn't want to do that.

"Okay, then." Luke stood, his stare piercing the space between them. "If you don't sit, I'm coming over there to shake the information out of you."

Max's knees buckled, and he plonked himself in his chair.

Luke gave a tight smile and followed suit. "Good."

In that moment, Max hated Luke, even though he couldn't recall ever hating his brother. Even in the months following the accident. An accident Luke, in a lapse of his usual perfection, had caused.

But right now, he did hate Luke.

He hated his ability to strong-arm every meaningful conversation they had.

Hated himself because, as always, he'd allowed his predictable pattern of life-wasting behavior to continue; as always, Luke saw right through his attempt to save face.

Hated his brother again because he couldn't simply let him save face, just this once.

"I overextended myself, okay?" The admission slipped from his lips, weak, hollow, and somehow still sharp enough to tear shreds through his insides.

The strain on Luke's face fell. "How?"

The lack of a judgmental glare shed a layer from Max's hatred.

"I..." Max tore his attention from his brother. "I don't know..." He released a sigh, and his entire posture sagged, taking with it his last remnants of anger, as if he'd run out of steam to hold on to it any longer. "I lost track of my spending. The apartment renovations ran over budget. I forgot about a few big bills that were due to be pulled from my account, and—"

"And let me guess"—Luke dipped his chin and sent forth a knowing look—"you also did a hell of a lot of partying, picked up the tab for your grifter friends a few too many times, and that flight you have to catch tonight is another luxury international holiday. Am I right?"

Everything about his brother, from his forward-leaning posture to his pointed stare, dared Max to lie, but they both knew Luke had a knack for finding shit out. So, Max peered down at the gray carpet and gave a silent nod.

Luke released a loud sigh and flopped back in his chair. "Jesus Christ." More silence, while Luke seemed to mull over what to do. "You're only halfway to your next profit share. How much do you have to last until July?"

Max cringed and hung his head lower. "Negative five grand. And... and there's a chance I might lose my apartment."

Luke sat bolt upright, the sharp sound of his movement sending Max's attention back to him. "How the hell did you manage that?"

"Like I said." Max shrugged. "Surprise bills..."

"Damn it. Max…" Luke's hands clenched in tight fists on his desk. "How long have I been telling you to set yourself up with a backup plan? You and I didn't exactly grow up loaded. We have no safety net. There's no excuse for frittering away money like you do."

"I know, Luke. I know." Max wrung his hands together, his shoulders rounding.

"But do you really?" A quiet moment passed while Luke's attention bore into Max in a lingering manner, suggesting he took a moment to piece together a game plan. "I can't help you out this time. I just can't."

But the softer edge to his tone said he wanted to.

Max blinked at his brother, absorbing the deep worry lines across Luke's forehead and the downturn of his lips.

"You know I'd still like you to." He grimaced, realizing with every passing second how unfair it was for him to keep asking for help.

"Life as you know it is over, Max." A rueful smile pushed at Luke's mouth. "I just hope one day we'll both look back and say this moment changed things for the better."

The words hit Max like a door slamming shut in his face. He couldn't conjure any kind of reply. Could no longer find it in himself to blame his brother, maybe because a deeper part of him knew just how right Luke was.

Max couldn't keep playing the victim game, even though he failed time and time again to find any other way.

His life *was* about to change, and the thought alone seemed to open like a gaping chasm inside of him. He wanted to be sick. He wanted to run. But with his finances tied up, even running wasn't an option.

Shit!

"Do you remember when you left Tiluma?" Luke's cheeks turned pale. "You promised you could survive well enough without my help. I thought you were doing okay. I thought…"

Max nodded to himself. He remembered that promise; had meant it at the time.

If only he hadn't been born the "dreamer" child in his family. The one with the wandering—or maybe empty—mind.

He had dreams, yes, but no way to see them through.

"I don't know how to get myself out of this mess, Luke." *So, I'm here hurting you instead.* "I don't even know where to start."

Luke pressed both hands to his face and growled into his palms. He either held himself back from his natural inclination to take on his brother's problems, or from a new tirade of swears in relation to Max's cluelessness.

"Okay. Let's start with your flight tonight." Luke dropped his hands, his voice settling into his no-nonsense CEO tone. "Knowing you, you bought the premium tickets, yes?" Max nodded, and Luke's shoulders dropped an inch. "Good. That means they're refundable."

"But—"

"No." Luke held up a finger, indicating Max should shut up and listen. "No, 'buts'. It's time to enter the real world and clean up your disaster. That means no holidays. No extra expense. Not for you. Not for a very goddamn long time, you understand?" Max opened his mouth to reply, but Luke just barreled on. "You call and cancel your holiday the minute you leave this office. Get back whatever you can from the airlines and hotels, got it? The money from the holiday alone will be far more than most people have when they fall on hard times. I'll loan you the five grand you owe, just so you don't get into any kind of legal trouble, plus an extra grand to tide you over. And that money is just what I called it, *a loan*. You will pay me back, understand?"

"But what if I can't?"

Luke crossed his arms and dipped his chin, peering up in a way that said, "You can't be serious."

In the next beat, he stood, and then wandered over to his office door, a sign this meeting was over and Max needed to leave.

"You want to know how you'll figure this out?" Luke opened the door and pointed to the hallway outside. "Because this time, Max, you have no other choice."

Nine

THE RETURNING tide crashed over Max's feet as he watched the twinkling body of water, his apartment building positioned behind him and across the street. He'd pulled himself out of the turbulent sea not fifteen minutes earlier, while thick gray clouds rolled in and the sun dipped lower in the sky. The wintery image wasn't all that unusual for Melbourne, the city known for its "four seasons in one day", including during the summer months.

With his hair plastered down from his swim, the occasional droplet slid over his temples and cold wind kissed his damp skin, that skin tightening and bumping in response. This day couldn't end fast enough, though the discomforting elements offered him a sense of camaraderie.

"You going to get sick sitting there like that." Miroslav, or Miro, as he preferred to be called, laughed and sat down in the sand beside Max; the man's thick Ukrainian accent so distinctive, Max didn't even need to turn to see who it was. A good thing really, since he couldn't find the heart to move much now that he sat here thinking.

He plucked a minor smile, mostly for Miro's benefit. "This is what we call tropical weather where I'm from."

Miro made a low *tsking* sound. "And where I am from, where you are from might as well be the Caribbean, and still, we call people crazy who sit wet on a cold day."

Max chuckled and tore his attention away from the waves, finally willing to look at his friend with the jovial dark brown eyes reflecting gray clouds ahead. "Inland Ukraine doesn't have any beaches."

"This is true, but beach swim or river swim is still a bad idea in cold. Anyway"—Miro jutted his chin at Max—"something is wrong with you, huh? You sometimes act like you have rocks in your head, but today you act like you got boulders."

Max scowled at his friend, his chest aching because he should have laughed at that joke, but instead he drowned in the painful truth. Maybe he *did* have boulders in his head, entire quarries and cliffs, even.

No matter which way he thought to spin the story of how his day had gone, he sounded like a bumbling and entitled fool. One who'd wasted a chance most people would do anything to have. How would he explain that even selling his apartment tomorrow wouldn't get him any real money for months?

And sure, he could get a bank loan against the apartment until then, but he really didn't want to do that, as much as he didn't want to ask his friends for help. Not if he wanted any chance of ever returning to his current social group.

Bad enough he'd cancelled the holiday, which might go unquestioned, but pair that with asking for money…

He'd never be seen the same way again, and social exclusion would be the only possible outcome. And if admitting his failure to Luke had sucked, well then, doing the same with Miro would be much, much worse.

The man had escaped the fall of the Soviet Union minus everything he'd ever owned, the teaching credentials he'd worked so hard to achieve virtually useless in a new country, unless he planned to study all over again.

He arrived in Australia with nothing but a small suitcase of personal belongings, suddenly unqualified and reduced to working multiple odd jobs, scrubbing dishes and as a factory hand. The professional loss had been nowhere near his fault. Yet, he'd worked himself to the bone until he'd scraped enough money to start his own café—the café attached to the ground floor of Max's apartment building.

Max peered down at his sandaled toes covered in grit and sea. Of all people, he had no right to complain to this man about cancelling a holiday, much less the stupid way in which he'd lost his money. "I'm just having some money issues. It's nothing to worry yourself about."

"Ahh." Miro clapped Max on the back, but the encouraging gesture didn't make Max feel any more deserving of sympathy. "You are worried, so now I am worried. You are my friend for a long time, and you teach me how to swim, remember? Now you tell me what is wrong."

"Nothing major." He straightened and stared out to the hazy horizon, pretending he was okay. "I just had to cancel my holiday, that's all."

"Oh yes, that would make anyone sad. But why exactly did you cancel? Your hotel double booked?"

The man had one of those sometimes useful, but hard to hide from, analytical minds.

"You're not going to let this go, are you?"

Miro threw back his head and laughed, the gathering wind whipping at his thick brown hair. "No. You are not giving the whole truth, so maybe now you could put us both out of our misery and talk?"

"Fine." Max scrubbed his heel in the sand, adding a shallow dent in the shoreline, the action a poor buffer to him sharing his lame story of woe. "I cancelled my trip because I made a stupid financial mistake, okay? Actually, that's not true either, it wasn't just *one* stupid mistake. I've made many. Over a long period of time. With a boatload of warnings in between… I just got back from negotiating a loan with my brother, just so I can pull myself out of debt for a few weeks. A loan I have no idea how I'll pay back. Even with his help, I'll probably still run out of money and have to sell my apartment."

"*Ouuff.*" Miro shook his head, blinking in an exaggerated fashion. "That is one mess you are in. Why did you not come out and tell me?"

"Because of all the people I know, you have the greatest right to take one look at my stupidity and call me a big, bloody moron."

"Ha! Because you know my story, yes?"

Max nodded, but Miro shook his head again. "No. My story does not mean I wish bad things for you. It does not make me not sad for your problems. If anything, maybe I am the best one to talk to, yes? I know what it is to start again."

"Thanks, but I don't expect you to fix this."

"Ha." Miro used the back of his hand to slap Max's arm. "You think I give you hand out? My head is not one full of boulders, remember?"

"That wasn't what I—"

"No, what I am saying is you give up too easy. You used to be a champion swimmer. A long distance one, too. You not give in easy then, but now you acting like a big sack of potatoes someone throw down stairs."

Max gave Miro a side glare. "What? Dude, you come up with the strangest analogies. Why would someone throw potatoes down a flight of stairs?"

Miro laughed. "I don't know, but my strangeness at least got your attention, yes? What I mean is, you need to pick yourself up, think of your life like you did your swimming."

"But I haven't competed in years."

Miro rubbed the heel of his hand between his brows, before using that same hand to smack Max playfully upside the back of his head. "You act dumb, but you really just making excuses, maybe because what you really are is scared."

"I'm not scared. It's just…" Max turned away to gather his thoughts, kicking more sand with his foot, the heavy weight of his past and current problems pressing down on him. "I watch everyone around me go about their lives so sure of what they're doing. They have *purpose*, while I have no idea what I want. All I know is that since I quit swimming, my passions consist of travel, parties, sex, and dipping into the ocean at any chance I get. That's all. And as much as anyone might yell at me, 'Just get on with it', I have no freakin' idea what 'it' is for me. Much less how I'm supposed to just pick any old vocation and find the will to invest my energy into a life I don't actually care about."

"Confused. Scared. Confused because you're scared. It is all the same thing. And maybe the boulders in your head are not so big that you cannot see you do nothing because you can. Well, could." Miro's eyes widened, and he leaned in slightly, pressing his point. "Your life is not normal, Max, and now you are closer to normal, you don't have luxury to hide behind. So now you do what normal people do, yes? You start something and hope it works."

Max stared at his friend a while, the advice sinking in, even though his mind drew nothing but blanks. "Where do I start?"

"*Yedrit' tvoyu...*" Miro followed his mumbled Russian with a smack of his palm into his forehead again. "I have to think of everything for you?"

"You're the one acting like my personal guru. Give me something to work with at least."

"Fine, since I am your guru." Miro took a deep breath and stared out to the ocean, his eyes squinting against the glare. "You already give me a list of your passions, so let's start there. First, I think probably you are too ugly to ask any ladies to pay for sex, so this option is not good."

Max squeezed his eyes shut and cringed at Miro's idea of humor. Meanwhile, Miro's lips split into a giant smile, before he near fell backward with laughter.

"Okay, I am sorry. Serious time now." Miro straightened, still chuckling. "Let us start with your other passions. What about swimming? You teach me, now you teach others."

Max's mouth fell open with an instant need to dismiss the idea, but then he forced himself to pause, to take a slow breath, and let the idea roll around in his head for a while. He wasn't exactly in a position to be choosy, and perhaps it wouldn't hurt him to "start something and hope it worked".

"I'm not sure beginner swim instructors make enough consistent cash to cover my current troubles, but maybe you're right, maybe it's a start. What else have you got?"

"Hmmm..." Miro frowned out to the bay. "I have no other ideas just yet. Maybe I take some time to think of more, though you the one who knows a lot of business people. Maybe someone is looking to hire?"

Max leaned sideways and nudged Miro with an elbow. "You, maybe? The café always looks full. Are you hiring?"

"You, work in the café?" He shook his head, slow and serious like. "No. No. No. You are fun for the customers, but I do not trust you with hot drinks."

Max actually found it in him to laugh at that one, and Miro shrugged, not even trying to cover his act of clear rejection.

The rushing ocean tugged at Max's focus, and he set about making his first decisions on how the rest of his life would go. Miro was right. He needed to start somewhere. And for the moment, that somewhere would be the site of the lowest hanging fruit—or in other words—jobs he could nab *right now*. Jobs to tide him over until he had a more permanent plan.

And Miro was right about another thing. Max *did* know a lot of people. In fact, he had a knack for making connections, but he didn't want to ruin those by asking for some entry-level job. Because again, social exclusion was something he wanted to avoid.

But there was one person he could *maybe* turn to. One encounter last night that had brimmed with potential, perhaps now in more ways than one.

He lifted his gaze to the darkening sky, the first star breaking through the city haze and a gap between the clouds. Any minute now, The Ruby Room would open. Not only would it open, but since his holiday had gone bust, he would be free to visit the one person he'd wanted to see all along. A person who exuded indescribable calm. A person he seemed to just *click* with.

A person who also just happened to be hiring.

Freya.

Ten

Freya stared in wide-eyed silence as she took a moment to decide whether she'd heard Max right.

When he first walked into her paper-crammed office, she hadn't noticed him, her mind buried deep in completing this week's payroll—her best attempt at forgetting her encounter with her mum and then the call from the police right afterward. Not only had Max's sudden appearance blindsided her, but the first few words out of his mouth outright short-circuited her brain.

"The job you have advertised in your window." He gave a weak smile, his blue eyes dimmed to gray. "I want to apply."

"Why? Why would you want to do that?" Her thoughts reversed to this morning and how she'd practically shoved him out the door. Not because she hadn't wanted him to stay, but because she'd heard the news about her mother and lost all ability to be any kind of decent company. "If this is your way of trying to make last night a regular thing, you don't—"

"That hadn't even crossed my mind." The muscles over his cheekbones stilled, and his color drained. "I mean, last night was amazing, and I did want to see you again, but no." His focus fell to the floor. "Seems I really do need a job."

She slouched in her vintage, brown leather office chair, none of this making any sense. "But you have money, right? I mean, you drive a Tesla and your watch is a Rolex, and"—she leaned in and squinted at his black hoodie—"I'm pretty sure that's a Ralph Lauren logo on your top there, buddy."

"I *was* loaded." His gaze reconnected with hers, before dipping to the ground again. "At least, until this morning."

"You've got to be shitting me!"

A pink tinge rose on his face, and the twist of his brow in turn twisted something within her gut. He looked utterly devastated, like someone had stolen his favorite shoes from right off his feet, or keyed his car, or like, all his money had disappeared overnight or something.

"Oh my God." The words slipped from her lips in a soft whisper. "You're not shitting me, are you?"

He shook his head.

She stood, genuine sorrow for him hitting her square in the chest. "What happened? No, wait, you don't have to tell me that."

For a split second, her body warred between throwing herself forward in an offer of a hug or staying put and simply unleashing yet more questions. Thankfully, her jaw knew better and remained shut.

"So." His weighty stare broke her avalanche of thoughts. Sure enough, he wasn't all too eager to be here asking for employment, but that direct stare said he needed her to wake-the-fuck up and focus on what he'd come here for. "Can I apply for that job now?"

She wanted to say no. Actually, *hell no*. She wanted him in her bed, not working in her bar. Plus, she never canoodled with staff, even though Max hadn't been staff when they'd canoodled.

And still, what stood before her now was the prospect of a mighty awkward work situation.

She took a deep breath and crossed her arms, her sky-blue dress crumpling thick cotton against her bust. Only his reluctant presence kept her from giving him nothing more than a cold, hard rejection.

The slow bob of his throat as he swallowed, the unblinking strain in his eyes, the last thing he wanted to do was stand here and ask her for help—that much was clear. Which made turning him down flat impossible, even for someone as no-bullshit as her.

Strain slipped from her shoulders, and she lowered them by a couple of inches. She couldn't help but imagine what it'd be like to go from being a god in her bedroom last night, to standing here before her asking for work.

The very least she could give him right now was a chance to prove himself.

"All right." She strode forward, then took a seat on the front edge of her desk. "Let's start with your experience. Have you ever worked at a bar?"

"I've been to many bars, does that count?" One corner of his lip ascended into a grimace, the look in his eye something akin to a puppy who'd been caught chewing a prized heirloom. "Dive bars… high-end luxury bars… international bars… Bars made out of ice…"

He scrubbed the front of his shaggy hair with the tips of his fingers, perhaps a nervous habit, and his grimace changed to an apologetic smile.

"No. None of that counts." She jutted her chin and paused. If this had been anyone else, she would have booted him from her office for being a smart ass by now. The fact that she didn't, brought instant stiffness to her back. "Do you know how to mix a drink?"

"Not really. I might own fancy cars and watches, but I'm not into fancy when it comes to drinks. I'm more of a beer and water guy, you know?"

She exhaled, a low growl traveling up her throat, one that rumbled and sent forth a warning.

Did Max really want her to help him or did he just want to waste her time? Surely a person in his situation wouldn't pick the playfully stupid approach over at least *trying* to prove some kind of suitability to work at her bar.

She'd assumed he'd be nothing like his rich, clueless friends—the ones who thought it was cool to flit through life without knowing a goddam thing about anything. Now he had her questioning her judgement. And unlike him, she'd started with less than nothing and worked doubly hard for all she had.

The last thing she should do was let him mess her around or trash her bar's reputation just to throw him an undeserved line.

"I don't care what you drink." She gave him her flattest tone, along with an equally flat stare. "You know, all my job applicants come with a Responsible Service of Alcohol accreditation as a bare minimum, and often a bunch more years of actual bar experience. Is my livelihood a joke to you or something?"

Oh no. Her ribs felt suddenly too tight for her lungs, and she worked hard not to lean forward. Maybe last night had been his rich guy version of "slumming it on the wrong side of the tracks".

But then he pitched a wounded expression, one that seemed to melt her skepticism all over again.

He stepped toward her.

"Look, I'm sorry." His voice was soft and smooth as butterscotch, and a little flutter replaced the churning in her tummy. "I'm not messing with you. I promise. I'm just screwing this up like I seem to do most things. I wouldn't be here if I didn't really need the help."

"You do understand I'm running a business here, not a charity?" She cleared her throat, her cheeks warm from the obvious gravel in her tone. Even in this weird-as-hell encounter, his near proximity had an effect on her. "I'm not going to hire someone with no ability to earn their keep. Besides, up until yesterday I didn't even know your name. So even though last night was fun and all, given what we did, you working here would be a terrible idea."

She looked him over with his blond waves and baggy hooded sweater, albeit designer. How different he appeared now from last night. Gone was his clean-cut shirt and scent of fresh mint and sandalwood. Still, his mussed-up appearance added an air of vulnerability, unearthing memories of him and her intertwined in her bedsheets.

And aside from the hot-as-hell sex, he'd been easy to talk to, and just hours earlier, she'd learned his help with The Creeper last night had spared her from certain torture and death.

Her chest constricted against a cascade of emotion, a new lump taking space in her throat. She wasn't ready to think too much on what the police had shared with her on the phone earlier. About The Creeper and his known violent history.

"I can't have you working behind the bar." Her voice held a rasp, and she prayed Max didn't notice.

His chin dipped, and he gave a quiet nod, like he understood. The fact he didn't argue produced an ache around her heart.

"Look, there's no way you'll be able to work the bar without upsetting my customers." She gave a heavy sigh, set to once more pay her dues. He'd helped her. He'd saved her. And even if he didn't know all the details, she wanted to thank him either way. "Much less my staff, but I can offer you another position, if you really are that desperate."

He snapped his chin back up, a new light entering his eyes. "Honestly, I'll take anything."

"Good." She pushed her weight off the desk, heading for her office door and gesturing for him to follow. "You do a four-week probation period as part of my clean-up crew, all going well, then your position here becomes official. And then. *Only* then. If you're consistent and fit in well with my staff, and you get your RSA accreditation, I just *might* consider letting you serve behind the bar. I hope you're ready because you start tonight."

Eleven

MAX PUSHED his wheelie bucket and mop through a heavy crimson curtain and into the cleaner's nook, a tiny area separated from the main action at The Ruby Room. He'd changed the bucket water not fifteen minutes ago and already it held a murky gray-brown color that made the mop head disappear at the bottom. The nose-wrinkling smell wafting from the surface was stale and bitter.

He peered down at his white-gold Rolex, not exactly fitting with his black, grime-stained cleaner's apron. And if that wasn't sign enough of his faded lifestyle, right about now, his plane to Ibiza would be coasting down the tarmac at Melbourne Airport, mere hours from sunshine and paradise. *Without him.*

He lowered his wrist and rested his chin atop the wooden mop handle, the sound of yet another dropped glass shattering what he'd hoped would be a few seconds of sulking peace.

Two hours of hellish mopping and he'd had no break from the stomach-churning stenches and the sweeping of broken glass, much less the customers who insisted on giving him their orders, even though waiting tables wasn't his job.

He let out a resigned sigh and grabbed his new friends—the

dustpan and brush—from a hook on the wall, his grimy water-filled bucket coming along for the ride out into the bar again.

He'd been warned to be quick with cleaning up spills, something about broken glass, patrons getting injured, blood everywhere—which he'd have to clean up—and the potential for lawsuits.

A wall of joyful chatter engulfed his re-entry, coupled with people perched on red velvet couches along the back wall. The Ruby Room's iconic ruby-colored chandelier hovered high and center, pear-drop crystals dangling above black glossy tables. A burlesque trio danced on stage—a curly haired redhead and a brunette woman, along with a stocky guy in a black sequined corset, all belting out a '70s diva number.

A girl seated a few tables down waved him over, her cherry-red bob swinging with her movements. She pointed down, indicating she'd been the one to drop the glass.

He nodded and wove his way through furniture and people, the flash of disco lights and loud music muddying his senses.

This time yesterday, he'd been one of these patrons, enjoying an evening with his friends and spending money without a second thought for how much actually remained in his bank account. *What a dream that had been!* Now he mopped floors, tinkering with the real chance he would lose his home.

The cherry-bob lady leaned forward in her seat, lips curled into an equally cherry-colored smile. "Well, aren't you a handsome one? Sorry about the mess."

The glint in her dark brown eyes, and the way she used them to glance down his body, said she wasn't at all sorry.

"It's fine," he mumbled. "Seems to happen a lot around here."

He crouched down and started sweeping broken glass into the dust pan, avoiding eye contact with Cherry Bob's fishnet covered calf, the one she not-so-subtly stuck out beside him, swinging her black stiletto-covered foot pretty much right under his nose.

"I'm from Adelaide. Only here for the weekend."

He peered up to Cherry Bob talking to him, her voice low and rough like maybe she smoked about ten packs of cigarettes a day. "Is that an accent you got there?"

"Yes."

He stood and passed the mop over the miscellaneous red puddle on the floor. Wine, maybe? No doubt Freya would be disappointed he couldn't identify which drink exactly. Then again, Freya would probably want him to play friendly with the customers, even though he just wanted to get through this night.

A stray piece of glass sat inches from the woman's foot, and he bent down to pick it up. That's when her cold fingers latched onto his jaw.

He jolted his attention up to Cherry Bob smiling down at him, her clammy fingers holding a stink that confirmed his theory of her probably being a ten-pack-a-day smoker.

"I have a little secret." Her eyes glinted again, like she assumed he cared to hear what her secret was. She leaned in closer, more cigarette stench, her lips way too close to his ear. "I've been watching you all night, and I broke that glass on purpose just to get you here. What do you think about that, honey?"

The nauseating smell of red wine—at least he got that bit right—and bitter nicotine had him reeling back, just as Cherry Bob aimed her lips at his.

A sharp tug at the hood of his sweater pulled him off-balance so his butt connected with the hard, polished floor.

"What the hell are you doing?" Freya bent over him, her eyes narrowed.

He stood, almost head-butting her in the process, before dusting his hands over the back of his pants.

"This lady here"—he stabbed his thumb toward Cherry Bob and held back an urge to dry retch—"was just about to jam her tongue down my throat."

A crosshatch of wrinkles spread across Freya's brow. "Are you looking to get fired on your first night?"

"What? Why would you fire me?" He turned and scowled at the woman who'd assaulted him. "It's not like I *wanted* her to kiss me."

The tension on Freya's face dropped. "Wait. What? You didn't?"

He shook his head.

Her expression turned hard again, though this time she shot a searing glare at Cherry Bob. "You. Get out."

Cherry Bob's mouth slipped open. Freya ignored her, waving over the security guard standing at the front entrance.

Cherry Bob mustn't have moved fast enough, because Freya hooked her hand under the woman's armpit and jerked her up, barking, "I said, *out!*"

The security guard moved Freya aside and took over with Cherry Bob, the cigarette-infused woman peering over at Max like she expected him to save her.

No freaking chance, lady!

He pressed his hand over his stomach, holding back a need to heave.

Freya turned to him, gaze narrowed like he was a puzzle she wanted to work out. "Are you okay? I'm really sorry I assumed…"

"I mean, yeah?" He took a second to consider the softer glow to her eyes, perhaps a sign of genuine concern. "Though I'm not sure your reaction just then was proportionate to the lady's offense."

Her raised shoulders contradicted any sense she might be amused. "Why? Because you're a guy? You think if any man in here tried to make out with one of my staff, male or female, it'd be cool if I just let it slide?"

The muscles on his face turned lax. Frankly, he'd never thought of unwanted sexual attention like that. In truth, he'd always figured that as a man, not a small one at that, he was supposed to handle himself or any woman who tried to accost him. Hell, women accosting men wasn't even a thing in the world he grew up in.

He was meant to just laugh that shit off, right?

Or parade the attention with pride, a man desired, a "man's man".

He'd certainly never had anyone step in and save him.

"You have a point." Now the churning in his tummy had less to do with Cherry Bob's smell and more to do with the boatloads of times he'd shrugged off similar unwelcome moments.

She reached out and grabbed his hand. "Damn right I have a point, but that's not the only reason I asked if you're okay. Looks like you've sliced your thumb on some glass while trying to escape the mouth leech."

He peered down at his hand. Sure enough, a thin trail of blood snaked its way down his wrist, the piece of glass still clasped between his fingers. Well, at least he was up-to-date with his tetanus shots, probably the only good thing about cutting his foot open on a piece of coral while surfing in Hawaii a few months ago.

Yeah, also another reason why I'm broke now!

Freya instructed a fellow staff member to take him back to the cleaner's nook and the first aid kit before she disappeared to do whatever it was bar owners did. Max had orders to get a plaster on his cut, then get right back to pushing his mop bucket around.

Though the cut itself was small, the stream of blood remained consistent. He hunched in a seat at the back, waiting for the blood to stop, his heartbeat heavy and a sense of loneliness taking over.

Though he appreciated Freya stepping in before, she hadn't offered to help patch him up, hadn't jumped at the chance at some alone time with him in the musty, dark cleaner's nook, which could totally transform into a romantic hiding spot if only for a few minutes.

Heck, she hadn't even thrown him a lifeline and bailed him out of mopping floors. She'd merely sent him on his way and gone back to work.

Thick-skinned. No-nonsense. Caring, but not the sort to dote. Maybe this was typical of her? He could just hear the words, "Suck it up and get on with the show" coming out of her mouth.

Maybe she had more in common with his brother Luke than she did him?

A familiar laugh broke through the nook's heavy curtain. A quick glance confirmed his suspicion; the laugh belonged to Adele Maslow, snuggled up against her long-term partner, Cedrick Pascal, at a nearby table.

Max slinked back. The bleeding on his thumb slowed enough for him to stick down the plaster. Adele was the second to last person he wanted seeing him in his new role as bar cleaner, with Cedrick being the absolute last. Adele came from a family of high-profile lawyers and surgeons, while Cedrick's father owned a century-old business, his surname synonymous with a well-known brand of preserved foods.

Also, Cedrick was a prick. A mean drunk. Everyone knew it. Even

Cedrick. He showed zero cares about hiding the fact, especially when it came to Max.

Not after Max dated Adele for a short time about a year ago, back when she'd tried to break away from Cedrick and his ham-fisted ways. Cedrick had taken a huge enough exception that he'd stalked and harassed her until she caved and went back to him.

Though sweet and maybe a little timid, Max had liked Adele, but not enough for a strong connection to ever grow. He hadn't pushed the issue when she'd ended things, though maybe he should have, since it seemed even money and a good education didn't spare someone from a bad relationship.

He twisted his watch to find he still had another forty-five minutes on the clock. Somehow, he'd have to survive his shift *and* avoid Cedrick, the douche lord of the century, who'd no doubt blab to everyone in their shared circles about Max's fall from grace.

He'd been so desperate to get the ball rolling on earning some money, he hadn't really considered this particular complication before asking Freya for work. If only she'd given him a job behind the bar, something semi-cool he could spin as an easy way to pick up women while hiding the fact he had money. A rich guy's eccentric idea of having fun.

His friends would have thought him a bonafide genius.

As it stood, there wasn't much he could say that would glorify mopping floors and collecting empty glasses. *Shit.* He really didn't want to go out there.

"What are you still doing in here?"

He blinked to find Freya staring at him. *Shit again!* There were genuine disadvantages to the height difference here, namely, that she had a knack for sneaking up on, or more like, *under* him.

She snapped the velvet curtain open wider. "We have ten minutes till closing and a bunch of empties on your side of the room. The tables are filthy, and Edward says you've been hiding back here since you sliced your finger something like twenty minutes ago. You need to get out there."

She grabbed the front of his black apron and dragged him a couple of yards forward, out into the bar, and to where his "friends" waited.

Twelve

"No! I'm not going out there." Max planted his feet and refused to move.

Freya stopped and turned to him, eyes blazing like she had a boatload of other things to do right now and wouldn't stand for his rebellion. "Fine then, you're fired."

His gaze skittered to the curtain again, the quiet seclusion so close but so far. He wanted to disappear again, but not as much as he wanted to keep his apartment. "Look, please don't fire me. It's just, there are some people out there I'd rather not see. People I haven't told about my situation yet."

The skin over her cheekbones eased, and a sudden laugh cracked past her lips. "And you want me to ask Ed to shoulder the entire floor, all so you can save some face?"

He gave a cringy sort of smile. "Would you?"

"*Pfft.* No." She jerked her chin back, expression twisting. "And what's with you? Do you not understand the subtleties of sarcasm? You can either get your butt out there and do the job you came here to do, or go home right now and deal with your financial woes without my help."

"You'd really fire me?"

"Dude. You think you'd be the first?" She barked out another incredulous laugh, head tilting back to display her glowing neck and that sun tattoo he loved. "Besides, this is a trial, remember? I haven't even hired you yet. And right now, you're letting a pack of judgmental assholes keep you from getting the job you practically begged me for a few hours ago. So yes, you have less than three-seconds to get back to work, or I'll give you the grace of slinking through our back exit at the expense of this job."

He darted his gaze around her face and narrowed his eyes, trying to decide how serious she was about kicking him to the curb after they'd spent last night all over each other.

"Right." She spun on her heel and took her first storming steps away from him.

"Wait." He thudded after her, wrapping a hand around her forearm, keeping her close. "You can't mean that."

"You haven't paid much attention to me or how I run The Ruby, have you?" She gave a slow shake of her head, her lips pressed in an expression he knew all too well. She was just another person on the long list of people he'd disappointed. "Go home, Max. You're not cut out for this place."

Despite what Freya said, his feet stayed rooted to the floor; for a multitude of reasons, he couldn't let her get rid of him so easily.

He'd be failing all over again. Something he'd done far too much of. Something he refused to do now. Also, he liked her and wasn't all that ready to burn this relationship for the likes of Cedrick Pascal.

He lifted his attention to the sea of people again. *Screw Cedrick.* He'd never liked the guy anyway, and Cedrick sure as death didn't like him either. Heck, maybe the opportunity to pound Max's reputation into the dirt would bring an actual, genuine smile to the asshole's sour and ugly face.

Either way, up until this point in his life, Max had blown far too many chances, which brought him to this predicament now. He couldn't afford to keep making the same mistakes.

"No." He stepped back into the cleaner's nook and grabbed a scuffed-up tray from a counter, then fronted up to Freya again. "I'm staying."

He pushed past her and went about collecting glasses, starting at the tables farthest from Adele and Cedrick. As brave as his snap decision might have been, he needed time to gather his courage. Or perhaps one small corner of his soul hoped the couple would leave before he got to their section.

Thankfully, because of his stalling in the cleaner's nook, a lot of empties needed collecting. His tray kept filling, and he made three trips back and forth between tables before he had no place left but Adele and Cedrick's table. The whole time, Freya stood in front of the cleaner's curtain, arms crossed and brow raised, as though she half expected he'd lose his nerve and run. Not an unreasonable expectation given the loud rush of blood roaring in his ears and the sweat prickling on the back of his neck.

For as long as he could, he pretended not to notice them, his face turned to some point across the room. And they didn't notice him either, not until his "non-looking" got the best of him and his hand fumbled, knocking over one of many beer bottles on their table. *Damn it.*

"Max?"

He'd already turned his back, set to flee to the next table, but Adele's light trill held him in place.

"Is that you?"

He squeezed his eyes shut, fingers straining around the edge of his tray. He could ignore her, move on, pretend he hadn't heard. But Adele had never been anything but kind, and he figured she probably had enough cold reality in her life just dealing with Cedrick.

He spun around and plastered on a smile.

"Oh hey, Adele. Oh, and Ceddie." He tried not to vomit in his mouth or throw the tray at the asshole's pinched face. "You're here too. How brilliant."

Adele's pale green stare took him in from top to bottom. "What are you doing?"

He let out a forced laugh, one that sounded like a choppy *ha-ha-ha,* just as his brain and mouth shorted, and the next lie slipped past his lips. "I'm. Ahh. I'm helping a friend."

To be honest, he hated lying, but a light tingle of relief zipped through his body at this lie. Maybe he could save face *and* keep his job all at the same time.

"Oh really?" Cedrick's voice was its usual bored drone. "Which friend?"

"Well, you probably haven't met *her*. Actually, I only met *her* last night." Max sent forth a wide smile, his emphasis on the word "her" an overt suggestion he only did this because a woman was involved.

"Hey, Max."

He jolted. Freya's stern voice was a solid smack to the back of his head.

She sidled up to him, her unimpressed stare pinned to his face. "The MC has already called for everyone to clear out. I'm not paying you to stand around holding my patrons up, so get these glasses to the bar, then hurry up and wipe down the tables. After that, you have chairs to stack and a final mop to do before you're good to go. Got it?"

Her lips curled, her not-so-subtle hint that she'd heard him use his connection to her to worm his way out of this uncomfortable exchange.

Cedrick looked from Max over to Freya, a rare light glinting in his eyes. "She's paying you?"

Freya gave Max a gentle punch in the arm and peered up at him with that same deranged smile. "Of course I'm paying him. The Ruby is an ethical employer. We certainly don't make anyone work for free or favors."

He narrowed a glare at her and bit the insides of his cheeks. She had good grounds to correct his insinuations, though lucky for her, he also had enough class not to point out that they *had* in fact slept together. But more than any of that, given the conversation from moments earlier, he was pissed she didn't back him up whatsoever.

He turned back to Adele's now gaping face and offered a light shrug, though his limbs felt heavy. He refused to stomach whatever snide-smug look Cedrick pinned his way. "The boss is right. I better get back to work."

Thirteen

MAX RESTED his hand on The Ruby Room's exit door, ready to leave a good hour after closing time. But a burning unease kept him from moving, a hard knot of emotion settling deep within his tummy, that emotion being one he so very rarely experienced. *Anger.*

Anger at his situation. Anger that his money was gone. Anger that he would likely lose his home, even though he'd had everything going for him and still screwed up.

But right now, his greatest anger lay with Freya.

He turned on his heel and brushed past the super tall security guard, Crystal.

"Hey, where are you going?" Her voice sailed across the venue, but he ignored her. "I'm trying to lock up here."

He didn't care. All he cared about was charging through the door marked EMPLOYEES ONLY and up a short flight of stairs where a single fuchsia door waited. Freya's office.

He barged right in, since any niceties would be wasted on a woman who, not an hour earlier, had smiled as she'd thrown him into a social bonfire.

She stood ahead in the arms of a tall, bronze-haired man, his fingertips caressing her jawline.

Max startled, the knot in his tummy turning into a lead-filled balloon, one that burst and sent shards of disappointment in all directions.

Maybe he should have knocked.

She turned her attention to him, before turning back to the man holding her, her hand squeezing his navy shirt-covered arm. "Go. I'll see you tomorrow."

The guy narrowed his brown gaze at Max. "You sure?"

She gave a light smile and nodded. "I'll be fine."

Well, at least that made one of them.

The guy's stare burned into Max as he passed; since Max was in his own bad mood, he had no problems returning the dude's venom.

The door clicked closed, and he nudged his head toward where the other guy exited. "What was that?"

"None of your business." Freya spun toward her desk and went about flicking off a couple of lamps. "What do you want, anyway?"

He had no place feeling jealous or possessive. They'd spent one night together and made no promises, but in light of all he'd lost today, his fading hopes over Freya just added to the sting.

He glanced past her fuchsia painted office, with its giant Picasso and Frida Kahlo prints, and over to the scene outside her double windows, white street lights disrupting the black night sky. The subdued atmosphere deepened his loneliness and offered the sense that this day and his run of bad news would simply never end.

"What you did out there wasn't cool." He turned back to her, his earlier anger not enough to stop his heart from shrinking.

"No, what I did out there was a stroke of genius, and you should count yourself lucky that I'm so forgiving." She punctuated her statement with a stiff clench of her jaw. "You implied to one of my regular customers that I'm paying you in sexual favors, or at the very least, you're working here in the hopes of receiving sexual favors. *That's* what's not cool, Max."

The mild heat in his chest turned into a sharp prickle, one that worked its way up his neck and into his face. He could have pointed out he'd already gotten "into her pants", but that was too crass, so he took another tack. A highly immature, blame-fueled one.

"I played along so you could lose that creep last night. You could have helped me when I needed it, too."

"What did you want me to do, dry hump you on the dance floor?" She snatched up her purse from atop a filing cabinet, an embroidered black silk-looking thing with bamboo handles, and began throwing things from her desk into it.

"Cut me some slack, maybe?" He strode forward. She wasn't even looking at him. "Heck, you even threw me right back to work after I sliced open my thumb."

"It's hardly 'right back to work' if you hid in the cleaner's nook for a good portion of your shift." She thrust her chin up, gracing him with a glare. "And did you stop to think about how your rumor-slinging tonight might affect my business's reputation, much less my personal safety? For someone so willing to bring up your heroics last night, you sure are quick to undo your good deed. And for what? Just to impress a couple who don't seem to care all that much about you, anyway."

He scoffed, a distinct and totally uncharacteristic stiffness entering his tone. "Well, you made sure there was no chance of that. So, thanks."

He turned to leave.

"Really?"

He spun back around. "Yes. Really."

She lifted a brow. "Really?"

"What are you getting at here?"

"As far as I can tell, I'm the *only* one helping you right now." She strode closer, honey-brown eyes blazing as though at any moment they might ignite like glowing molten gold and lock him in with some kind of enchanting spell.

And truth be told, it was impossible not to stand here alone with her and not think about what it had been to spend an entire night in her bed.

"I have help." The words sounded weak, even to his ears.

"Right, but not enough to stop you from coming here in search of a job? And I helped you, didn't I? I offered you a chance at employment, a decision you've made me question numerous times already, by the way."

She stopped just shy of actually touching him, even though she stabbed a finger forward. He yearned to have her hands on him all over again, even in retaliation. Even though he'd seen another man holding her just moments ago.

What is this madness? What has she done to me?

He opened his mouth ready to apologize, but he didn't know if he actually meant it or if his raging hormones merely held him hostage. Then again, this day wouldn't be so bad if he got to end it buried deep inside her.

Her gaze danced about his face, her posture and expression softer now, like she had dropped the boss-lady act and slipped into being the woman who'd taken him home last night.

"You realize most normal people don't get to just dip out of their job, don't you? That a non-emergency room accident doesn't result in an instant day off? Most of us don't have the luxury of hiding when someone we know enters our place of employment. We own it. We get on with our job. We have no other choice. Besides, your social set has been frequenting this bar since it opened five years ago. You can't tell me you didn't think you'd get a job here and never bump into someone you know."

A tiny smile curled the crimson corners of her delicate but teasing mouth, like holding a grudge didn't come all that naturally to her.

He dropped his attention to the floor, wanting to believe that something about him drew out her good nature, but not quite arrogant enough to truly accept that.

"Actually, that's exactly what happened. I was in shock over losing everything, and I just kind of raced to the first friendly face I knew might be hiring."

Hell, even when I don't look at her, my mouth with its stupid words won't play cool.

He gave a shrug and tried not to cringe. Her shoulders sank, and she stared at him a moment longer before turning away to lean against her plum-draped window frame.

The look she shot him was wide and incredulous, like she either couldn't believe someone could be so impulsive and shortsighted, or that the vulnerability in his mistake stunned her a little. Maybe both.

Eventually, a deep sigh fell from her, and she crossed her arms over her chest. "Can you see how what you did out there might make me question your character?"

A beat passed before he gave her a reluctant nod. Right about now, he felt as worthy as a blot of mud marring her dainty sky-blue ballet flats.

"Max?" Her gaze held him, unwavering, like maybe she wasn't all that done with her questions. "What is it about mopping floors that you find so shameful?"

He took an impulsive step forward, only to stop in his tracks. "I don't, it's ju—"

"Have you been frequenting my bar all this time, silently judging my floor staff? Perhaps their job, as necessary as it is, makes them inferior, somehow?"

His spine snapped to an involuntary straight position, a harsh coldness zipping down his arms. "What? No! I—"

"Then why hide from your friends?"

He parted his lips and tried to force an answer, but nothing came.

Her gaze dropped to the ground, as though she gave up on him having an adequate reply, probably a good thing since he still didn't have one. "Some friends you have if they'd ditch you for falling on hard times. *They're* supposed to offer you help, not some woman you spent one night with and who just happens to own a bar."

Her dark eyelashes flicked up, her knowing stare slamming into him; so hard, he could practically feel a solid indent forming in the center of his ribcage. She didn't seem annoyed at helping him. No. But she had succeeded in summing up his social support—or lack thereof —to a T.

Yes, he had family, and they'd helped him in the past.

But even they had limits and were sick of his shit.

Miro. Well, he was a genuine friend. Really, he was. But not one Max would ever ask for a bailout. Especially when he didn't trust his ability to pay anyone back.

And everyone else? Well, the best he could call them was entertainment, fun as long as the drinks flowed and the cash kept coming. Though, the one thing he could bet money on was that his exchange with Cedrick would come back to bite him at some point and probably soon.

"I'd rather work for my money."

And that much was the truth. At least then, if he failed to come up with any decent funds, he'd only be disappointing himself. This time, anyway.

"Max?" Her voice pulled him back to her again, husky and low, and way too compassionate for what he deserved. "I don't know how you lost all your money, and it's not my place to ask, but as a business owner, the prospect of going bust is a risk most of us juggle every day. I'm the last to hold it against you, so you want to know what I would do?"

He nodded, somehow believing what she had to say would be the most useful thing he'd heard all day.

"I'd go home. Give my ego a little time to heal. Then get back up and learn to find some pride in where I am now." Her throat bobbed, her pause suggesting she maybe needed a second to consider her next words. "You know. I've been where you are. Not in the sense that I've lost all my money, but that I had none to begin with. You have to dig yourself out of the hole you've fallen into, do you understand? Even if that means mopping floors and taking shit from people who know you. And while you're at it, as long as you're keeping up your end of the bargain, you've got a place here at my bar."

Her soft smile now offered the same kind of uncomplicated acceptance he'd found in her bed last night.

His heart kicked, and a dull pain spread beneath his ribcage, somehow buoyed and ashamed with how much his trampled spirit clutched at her offer of having somewhere and someone to rely on. That maybe he wasn't so alone. At least while he mopped floors, anyway.

"Thank you." He offered a wary smile.

If not for the dude he'd seen her with earlier, he might have stepped closer. Not so much because he begrudged her life away from him, but because she'd pointed to his arrogance and entitlement. Maybe working on that meant not presuming every encounter with her would lead to intimacy.

Plus, she had a point about him having a lot to think about. Trying to make things happen with her would be a bad idea. And didn't he have years of bad ideas to atone for?

Gone were his days of assuming everything would work out no matter what risks he took. He'd taken risks. Gotten too comfortable. Now his future lay more uncertain than ever.

As much as he wanted to believe he'd already hit rock bottom, a whisper rebounded within his head, one that said things could always get worse.

Fourteen

GIDEON FABER WAS one of the most attractive men Freya had ever met. With his thick caramel waves, tawny eyes, and full, European lips, he was downright gorgeous, and he knew it.

But Gideon had more going for him than just being beautiful. He was also her best friend, and maybe more than that, he was also one of Australia's top cabaret performers.

No matter what persona he wore—man, woman, or something else entirely—he rarely failed to garner a double take from those who encountered him. For the longest time, she'd lived in a weird kind of jealousy and awe, ever since he'd used his natural free-spirit to guide her from her dark early beginnings.

The Ruby Room's success in its first few months could also be attributed to his involvement, and once again, she counted on his immeasurable talent to lead her bar through the Live Wire Festival.

Now, she scowled at Gideon in his sky-high stilettos, certain she'd have zero chance of walking in them, much less keeping up with the two equally perfect female dancers either side of him, shaking and singing before the urban-chic rehearsal room mirror. Just the way he belted along to the horn-heavy music and filled out his tiny black booty shorts made her want to be him when she grew up.

The music stopped, and right on cue, so did Gideon and his dancers. Freya brought her hands together in an excited clap. Gideon strutted over, while the two dancers rushed to their gym bags in the corner, like they had somewhere else to be.

"Hey, Frizzle!" He winked and nudged her with a hip, Frizzle being his nickname for her. A play on the days she hadn't been so skilled at taming her curls, curl-taming yet another thing Gideon had helped her with. "Finally not too busy to talk to your old friend, huh?"

"Sorry about last night." She lifted her arms and wrapped them around her friend, hoping to goodness he wouldn't read too much into Max's interruption in her office. "Work dramas."

"Oh, forget about it. I'm just glad I finally got my hug." He squeezed her tighter, patting her on the back. "Missed you, Sweet Cheeks."

She laughed, and tears prickled the inner corners of her eyes. They stood there for a long time, swaying and laughing in the firm embrace, before she finally pulled back to get a better look at him. "Tell me about the Europe tour. I can see you've been working on your tan."

He threw back his head and closed his eyes with a sigh, just as the final dancer left.

"The shopping, the fashion, the nightlife, the shows, the beaches, the food"—he patted his washboard tummy as if he'd gained some weight, which was nowhere near the case—"heaven. The whole damn continent was heaven."

"And Prague?" She reached up and cupped her hands to his face, sending forth her biggest smile. "Amazing, right?"

"An art nouveau lover's fantasy." He reached down from his six-foot-two height, plus heels, and cupped her cheeks back. "But my goodness, I'm glad to see you again."

He rubbed his nose to hers. She laughed, so glad to have him back.

"Come on." She pulled him toward his white sports bag, with its hard-to-miss Chanel logo. "I assume you've got something other than booty shorts in there. Let's get you changed and go for that coffee."

He went about digging in his bag. "Yes, I have more than booty shorts, and why wait for coffee? There's nothing stopping us from chatting while I change."

"Actually, you're right, and there's something I did need to clear with you first." She joined him in the bag digging, though she riffled through her own giant, yellow, cotton handbag. "I have the flyers for your stint at The Ruby Room for you to approve. Helena, my event manager, had someone put them together."

He paused, wiping off the dusky rose-pink lipstick he often said helped him feel in character, even during rehearsals. "Oh, great. Give us a look."

She handed him a large white envelope. "If you like these, we'll do some minor tweaking and produce larger posters for around the bar and nearby alleyways."

He tugged off his thick false lashes, as if that would help him see better, and slid his gaze over the poster, its glossy, black layout accentuating the magenta font and a central photo of him in his full-drag glory.

His brows tensed for the shortest second, before a mega-watt smile broke across his mouth. "I love it. Especially the line, *'Come for the eye-candy, stay for the showwomanship'*. That's me in a nutshell, right?"

"Really? You love the flyer?" She gave him a sidelong stare. Gideon Faber almost never simply loved something. His exacting standards were a huge reason for his success.

He handed back the envelope, then ripped off his skin-tight black singlet and replaced it with a less-sweaty white one, his impeccable six-pack abs just one more perfect thing about him. "The flyer is fine, Sweet Cheeks."

He pushed his shorts down and then rolled his fishnets off, kicking them with precision into his open bag on the floor. "Though I hope you finally fixed The Ruby's manky old stage. That thing is a death wish."

He smiled at her from over his shoulder, fastening his pleated gray slacks.

She let out a growl and sank back. She should have known better than to get too comfortable with his praise. "I have some tradesmen booked to pull up the boards in two weeks. We've even closed the bar for a day to get it done."

"Brilliant. I'm not breaking my ankle in front of my home crowd. I don't even care who you are or how long we've been friends, I'll sue your ass. You hear me?"

She let out a laugh. "You're the genius who named their show, 'Shockwave'. Maybe a broken ankle would help the show live up to its name."

He snapped his attention away from his image in the giant rehearsal room mirror and on to her. "You know I don't need help in that department. You think I can't deliver the goods?"

"Maybe I should be more concerned you will?" She dipped her chin and gave him a look of mock suspicion.

"Damn right." He turned back to the mirror and used his long fingers to run styling product through his thick curls. "The Ruby won't know what hit it."

To be fair, in an odd way, his ever-present pressure forced her to keep her own business in order. Gideon had been the first person to ever expect anything much of her.

For so long, she'd thought herself insignificant and incapable. A shadow to her mother's criticisms.

Why would Freya ever try when everything she did was wrong?

For some inexplicable reason, a mental image of Max popped into her head, one of him holding the mop at work, refusing to step out and face his friends. As much as she could relate to how he felt, she frowned and shoved the thought away.

Gideon had changed how she felt about herself. A survivor of his own critics. He'd worked his literal butt off earning his place into a highly competitive performance degree, then built an incomparable reputation in the industry. And through it all, through high school to now, he'd taken her along with him.

She owed him, even if he never demanded repayment, and the least she could do was give him a great show every time he graced her venue. Because every time he did grace her venue, the crowds packed The Ruby Room just to see him. Festival lure or not, his shows sold out fast, though this time the festival did add extra pressure.

Gideon gave a dramatic turn in front of the mirror, checking out his gray pleated pants and loose white shirt with the first two buttons undone. He looked every bit a carefree and classic English gentleman, even though as a pre-teen, he'd escaped the refugee camps fresh from the Bosnian War, minus any English.

"All right, let's go." He swept up his bag from the floor.

She followed him down the dark staircase and into a side street leading to Chapel Street, one of Melbourne's major café hotspots.

"So—" She paused, using the advantage of being behind him as he entered the busy flow of foot traffic. "I… umm… I saw my mother again."

He stopped, just as a young woman striding toward him almost slammed face-first into his chest. He ignored her and spun around, eyes wide and focused on Freya. "What? You did *what?* Why would you do that?"

She stiffened her spine, ready to pretend she'd made peace with her decision, when in reality, the tense interaction with her mother still played on a loop in her brain. "I didn't really have any other choice. She's in a bad way."

"To hell with that. Or should I say, to hell with her? Don't tell me you can't remember how things turned out the last time you reconnected with that woman."

Yes. She did remember. How she'd sought her mother out again, expecting… what? Maybe some kind of remorse for the hell she'd inflicted, only to have to listen to a stubborn monologue about her mother being a blameless victim.

That stubbornness had sent Freya down a spiral of apathy, her old mode of survival kicking in, followed by a phase of soul-wrenching depression.

But she'd matured since then. She'd learned to use a detached perspective to view people, events, and various attitudes. At the very least, whatever her frail mother had to pitch at her now would never come close to eclipsing what she'd done to Freya as a child.

She swallowed at the strain growing within her throat. "Yeah well, either way, this is the last time. I can handle one last time."

Gideon hooked an arm over her and patted her hand, guiding her through the open double doors to an expansive café with large, gray-scale artworks decorating the back wall. "You mean, she's in a bad way, as in, she's dying?"

She plonked herself into a seat opposite him, nodding her silent confirmation.

"Wow." He paused, a reflective sigh breaking from him as he stared at her. "And just your luck, Clay isn't around to help. Your mum never made any secret of him being her golden child."

Golden child. A big, fat understatement.

Her mother had downright abused and neglected Freya, while worshipping Clay.

The overt favoritism obvious to her, even as a child, and she'd spent her entire younger years lost, unloved, and wondering why her mother had ever even had her.

And it wasn't as if she could just ask her mother why. Kerry Branner was the master of giving no straight answers, especially when the question meant holding her accountable in any sort of way.

"Yeah." She gave a hollow laugh. "On the golden child count alone, Clay deserves to be the one dealing with this mess. But as much as our relationship isn't the best, I can't blame him solely for where he is now."

Gideon toyed with the lid on a short glass jar filled with light-brown crystals of raw sugar. "And what exactly will 'dealing with this mess' entail for you?"

"Helping with final decisions if needed, organizing a funeral home, tying up lose financial ends, selling her house."

"Oh, please don't tell me you're about to organize a lovely send off for that mad witch." Gideon's face took on an uncharacteristic hardness, while she honed her lifelong skill of internalizing her dislike for her mother. "I can't imagine her having any friends who'd want to show up, much less you standing out front of an empty funeral home, sharing sweet memories that sure don't exist."

She peered down at her forefinger drawing small, invisible circles on the white table top, her heart straining because she didn't see her mother as a "mad witch", even though she maybe should.

Gideon was right. Chances were, her mother didn't have any friends. The fact that she didn't, and that her life had never expanded beyond the same cage of mistrust and fear she'd grown up in, only tightened the vice-like band around Freya's heart.

Her mother had endured things no child should endure, but worse, she'd tried to force that same existence onto Freya.

"I probably do owe her a visit." She mumbled the words, maybe out of a misplaced desire to make up for her mum's lack of friends. *Who knew?* She sure didn't.

"You don't owe her shit, and you know it." Gideon stabbed a finger her way. "Don't you start feeling bad, now she's the one in the hospital bed. I bet she didn't even ask how you were when she saw you."

Pain burrowed deeper into her chest because Gideon had called it; her mother hadn't asked anything meaningful. She'd just hacked and complained, and as usual, Freya's life and choices were never good enough.

She raised her hand, intent on rubbing at her sternum, only to think twice about making her pain all that visible to Gideon; so, she pushed her hands onto her lap, nails digging sharp and distracting points of pain into her palms.

"I know, it was just a turn of phrase." She veered her gaze, searching for any nearby waitstaff, anyone who might make eye contact long enough to bail her out of this conversation. "Is it time to talk about something else yet?"

She didn't like this topic, but he knew her whole story, and she didn't want to lie to a friend. Not with what would be coming up in her life. *Her mother's death.* He'd find out eventually, anyway.

Gideon didn't speak right away, which drew her attention back to him and his head tilted to one side, golden brown stare perusing her face. "Oh, honey, her problems aren't your problems, you know that, right? I just want to hear you'll look after you first."

"I know. I know." She took a deep breath and leaned back in her chair. "It probably doesn't make much sense to me either, but I just can't leave her to die alone."

"I think if you dig deep enough, you know exactly why you don't just give up on her." He sent a pinched, pitying look her way. "Still that little girl waiting for Mumma to be less messed up. For her to care."

Well, mothers are supposed to care. Aren't they?

And what if they didn't? What did that say about the child?

Her stomach lurched, but she ticked one corner of her lip up, still acting like nothing about her situation hurt. "I guess some dreams never go away."

"Well, speaking of dreams"—he reached out and pressed a hand over hers, as if he saw her pain and chose to make good on the topic change—"I hope your ruby chandelier is in top shape. I have big plans for that thing for the show."

She spluttered out a tight laugh and gave him a side glare; even for Gideon, the comment on her club's semi-famous chandelier seemed an odd thing to say.

"Why does my chandelier have to be in top shape? Please don't tell me you plan on swinging from it?"

"Ha!" He rolled his eyes and gave another snort of laughter. "Like that ancient roof would support my weight. No, just like the rest of the world, you're going to have to wait until the show to see what I have planned."

Fifteen

MAX ADJUSTED his tie and climbed the stone stairs stretching between two old columns that led to a set of ominous black doors. The Morris mansion loomed giant as ever with its large stone bricks. Others walked ahead of him and into the great foyer, the family's annual charity ball already in full swing.

But as ridiculously glamorous as this setting was, something felt off.

Maybe it was just his fidgeting, coupled with the hard sensation nestled in his belly since long before he handed his car over to the valet.

In the foyer, he swept his gaze over the white-marble double staircase and gilded handrails, his thoughts snagging on how someone usually would have spotted him by now and approached to say hello.

"Max." Diana Morris, the reigning monarch to the Morris fortune, glided over, her pale pink sheath dress floating in her wake. "So unexpected to see you."

He gave a small cautious nod. "Yes, I should be on holiday, but there was a change of plans."

She lifted her chin before her lips pulled into a graceful smile, one that only slightly accentuated the wrinkles over her cheekbones. For the most part, women in her social set weren't allowed to age, something Max never understood, but he put Diana to be somewhere around her mid-fifties.

"Yes. That's right." She extended a hand and shifted side-on to let him pass, the strain in her smile hard to miss. "Very well, then. I'll have the staff seat you at Antonio Fiorei's table. As I recall, you two got along quite well at last year's event."

"Thank you." He moved past, but not without catching Diana's tense gaze holding on him for a moment too long.

He spotted Fiorei's table soon enough, and waited for the staff to add an extra table setting, before wandering over.

"Hey, Max." Antonio Fiorei held up his beer glass in his version of a wave; the nine other guests at the table all fell silent. "Been a while, hasn't it?"

Max huffed out a laugh, a portion of strain slipping from his shoulders, though he did peer down at his clothes. Surely, they hadn't gone out of style in the mere week since he'd become broke?

"Not since November and Jackson Morelli's thirtieth birthday. Ingot Nightclub, as I recall." He ran a hand over the front of his shirt. Maybe the others could tell he'd done his own ironing?

Antonio offered a knowing grin. "That was a hell of a night. Though I don't expect you'd remember much since you got so tanked, we had to fold you into one of the cars and have a driver ferry you home. You always were a wild one."

Truth be told, Antonio was right. Max didn't remember much about that night… Or many nights out, really.

He sat at the table now, all gazes still pinned on him and every one silent. For a moment there, he had a compulsion to vow he'd changed, but even that felt like admitting defeat, as though his situation had won out and his nights of fun and no consequences were forever over.

Besides, he hadn't come here to advertise his problems, even though his peers might notice he wasn't buying any drinks. Alcohol was usually covered at events like this, but the proceeds from tonight's bar were meant to go to a charity, so everyone was expected to drink and spend up big—something he couldn't afford to do.

Heck, one reason for his showing up was that he'd already paid for his ticket months ago, and a meal *was* included in the price, so one less thing to add to his list of bills for this week.

And maybe Freya had a point. These people were meant to be his friends. Educated, philanthropic, worldly. Surely his bank balance wasn't the only admission price into their lives?

He passed his attention over the table and made eye contact with Sadie Williams and the deep blush darkening her narrow cheeks, before she spoke. "Is it true?"

A collective "shhh" broke across the table, and the girl next to Sadie gave her a light elbowing in the ribcage.

So, there it was. Everyone *did* know.

Sadie gnawed into her lower lip. "I'm sorry. It's just that Cedrick said he saw you mopping floors at The Ruby Room, and I thought… I thought maybe that was just him being a salty dickbag, you know. Especially since that night when he threatened to kill you cos you had the nuts to go on a few dates with Adele and everything." She gazed around the table, cringing in awkward apology to the others. "Surely he's lying about your money though, right?"

For the briefest time, she and Max held a silent stare. Sadie was a good fifteen years younger and still had a lot of maturing to do—not that he could talk. Either way, her question now seemed more a genuine need to check in on him than pure and hollow curiosity.

Still, a cold wave washed over his body, and he did his best to hold his head up high as if his lack of funds didn't worry him. Maybe if he kept up that facade, he'd somehow recover his money and manage to keep his friends in the meantime. "Yeah, it's true."

Sadie's expression sank, and her gaze fell from him, skittering to the side, while her straight blond bangs covered whatever reaction flashed across her gray eyes. For the next hour or so, her gaze failed to meet with his again, as did many of the others around the table.

He excused himself after dinner and escaped to the courtyard, needing fresh air and a break from the tension.

His world had just shrunk.

"Don't take this the wrong way." Antonio pulled up alongside him and pressed a hand to Max's shoulder, like he meant to console him; though given how this evening was going, Max couldn't be all that sure anymore. "But these events are pricey and maybe your time would be better spent getting your affairs together. No one in here knows what to say to you. No one here wants to cause you any embarrassment. Heck, the charity auction is about to start, and we both know you won't be bidding on anything. Wouldn't it be easier if you just left?"

Max frowned, holding back from pointing out he'd paid for tonight's ticket months ago, back when he had money, so his being here cost him nothing new. "That's it? After years of knowing each other, I'm booted?"

"No mate, nothing like that." Antonio staggered out a laugh. "We all want to see you back on your feet. What I mean is, talk to your numbers guy, or whatever, and once you're back on track, come and regale us with how you did it. I'm sure being here doesn't feel all that good to you right now."

He stared at Antonio and worked against a compulsion to tell him to "fuck right off", even though something like that really wasn't his style, no matter how out of line a person's words or actions might be.

Antonio had been born into money. He had no idea what he talked about. In his world, failure was impossible, and there would always be plenty of money to bail him out, no matter how badly he screwed up. Hell, the only time anyone in a family like his ever claimed bankruptcy was when they wanted to fold a business without paying their debts.

Money was a game to them.

Not the difference between having a home or not.

And maybe Max's situation wasn't as bad as most, but he'd at least grown up in a world where something like poverty waited only a few missteps away.

Then again, maybe Max *did* need to take the hint and leave.

Maybe he no longer belonged and needed to let this place and the people inside it go.

But where would he go?

To the apartment he was set to lose? No. He didn't want to go there. Not alone, anyway.

He wanted somewhere he could escape to. Somewhere he felt accepted.

Only one place came to mind, but whether he'd be welcome was another issue.

Only one way to find out.

He patted Antonio on the upper arm, putting the man out of his misery, and accepting the truth. When it came to these people, he no longer belonged, and he would have to deal with his losses alone.

"I'll see you around."

Though Antonio's shoulders sank, the hard lines on his face eased. Max turned away, his world off-kilter.

He strode through the mansion, past the tight gathering of happy people, and down the outside steps. The arching black gates loomed ahead, and he waited for the valet to return with his car, all while wrestling with an image embedded in his mind from the last time he'd spoken to Freya. The image of another man holding her in her office.

Her social life shouldn't have mattered. She wore her free-spirit clear enough for anyone to see, and unlike him, she knew who she was. Far be it from him to expect her to alter her life over one encounter, even if something more drew him to her than simple base attraction—the obvious difference between her and him.

She'd never in a million years let the Antonios of the world hold her back or bother her.

So maybe Max was right to feel something for her. To need more of that. *More of her.*

Because heaven knew, right about now, he didn't have much, and he needed to get out of the rut he was in.

Freya's elbows dug into her desk's turquoise timber top, her fingertips pressed over her closed eyelids. Loud jazz music clanged from The Ruby Room downstairs, clashing symbols and piano-heavy rhythms so different from the fat bass and club bangers played at the bars she'd once worked at. Though she'd long ago learned how to block out loud sounds, the day's exhaustion had set in, and she fought to stay awake.

"You look wrecked."

She pulled her hands from her eyes, blinking against the assault of lights in her office, not taking note of who spoke to her.

Nope, still too bright.

She returned her hands to her eyes, splitting her fingers slightly to buy her time to adjust. "I had a brainstorming session with Gideon earlier. We came up with more ways to outshine the other venues in this year's festival. I've spent the rest of the day researching and implementing those ideas. I want us to make a splash, you know?"

Empty silence followed her answer, and it was then that she took a second to really look at who stood before her, instead of just assuming it was one of her managers.

A beautiful, blond surfer dude waited at the end of her desk, his fists jammed in his pockets, his irises a stormy gray. The mere look of him held her next breath hostage.

"Who's Gideon?" His lips pressed into a hard line.

She frowned. "He's our star performer for the festival."

"Is that all?" The stiffness held in his jaw. "Is he the same guy I saw touching you the other day?"

She jerked her chin back and then barked out a laugh. Was Max pissed? Jealous?

"That's still none of your business."

"We slept together."

"So?"

He opened his mouth, as if ready to protest, but then he closed his lips just as quickly in a sort of nonverbal, "Never mind."

"Look"—she let out a sigh, her brain too fried to continue this inane debate—"you weren't helping me cheat on anyone, if that's what brought you here on your night off."

She'd run from one disastrous, long-term relationship already, one involving five years of emotional and psychological manipulation because she'd been too messed up from her shitty childhood to expect any better.

A good chunk of her twenties had been lost to just learning she could do better alone. *And she had.* She wasn't doing that again. Not ever.

That's not to say she held a grudge against men. Her best friend was a man, and the man standing before her now proved she very much appreciated them on a physical level. What she hated was commitment and the prospect of losing even just the tiniest bit of herself to any one person. She wanted freedom more than she wanted another relationship.

She took a moment to look Max over—to notice his tailored, navy blue shirt with white detail on the collar and his fitted dove gray pants —so much dressier than the jeans and hoodie he usually wore to mop the club's floors.

He looked like the man she'd passed in the months before they'd ever even spoken a single word to each other. The man who'd saved her, then come back to her home long enough for her to make love to him, though with one marked difference.

"Are you done working?" His ragged tone spoke volumes yet again, as did the shadows under his eyes and the raw vulnerability flowing off him.

"Max, are you okay?"

He stared, barely blinking, his stillness making the hairs at the back of her neck prickle. "I asked you a question first."

"Fine. Yes, I'm about to head home." She stood, but didn't yet round her desk. "Now you answer my question. Are you okay? You look—"

"Don't go home. Come back to my place instead." His hyper-focused gaze didn't shift off her, and he squared his shoulders, as if bracing for rejection. Meanwhile, cheerful music busted through the floorboards from downstairs, only adding to the disquiet.

"Why?"

"I don't know." He released another heavy breath and stared at the ceiling. "Maybe because I'll probably lose the place soon enough, and you might as well come and see it."

A pitchy, deranged laugh broke free of her, and she glanced at the blue-framed clock on the wall behind him, with its painted, retro black cat. "It's past midnight and you want me to come to your place to appraise your decor?"

His face paled from fatigue or stress, or maybe both, like perhaps something had happened tonight. Either way, it took him an age to answer.

"Freya. Don't make me beg."

She wanted to laugh again at his dejected tone, as though a gorgeous man like Max really would get down on his knees and beg her to come home with him. But the sadness in his eyes pleaded to her in a different way—a way she simply couldn't mock.

He begged her not to play obtuse, to put him out of his misery with an answer either way. And she knew that look. Knew what it was to feel down. Knew what he *really* asked for. And maybe with all the things happening in her life, he had the right idea, that tonight neither of them needed to be alone.

She grabbed her sand-colored purse from beside her and tossed the long strap over her shoulder, rounding the desk and striding toward him.

"Okay, but"—she smiled, trying to lighten the mood—"just promise me you won't fall in love."

Sixteen

FREYA TURNED at the click of Max's apartment door closing behind her. He'd already spent the elevator ride up undoing buttons down the back of her dress, and now, the crimson polka dot material hit the carpet with a light thud.

Between Max devouring her lips and tugging away at the silk scarf she used as a head band, she laughed at her incoming weak joke. "I can't believe they cut off your electricity already. It's so dark in here, how am I supposed to fulfill my promise to check out your decor?"

"Shush, you." His tongue lashed hers, and she tried not to moan as he spoke again. "Things aren't that bad yet, but I can switch on the lights if that's what you're into."

She cupped his face and kissed him back, shaking her head.

Truth be told, she'd half forgotten how good he was at this whole "getting it on" thing. *And, holy fuck!* She'd forgotten how damn solid his body was pressed against hers.

Even as he guided her in a backward march through a doorway she presumed led to his bedroom, she wanted to melt into him, the space between her thighs bursting to life like an out-of-control fire.

Her back cooled at the kiss of crisp silk sheets suddenly beneath her. Seconds later, his naked torso pressed to hers, his weight a welcome reminder of what was to come.

"You're beautiful." He kissed the side of her neck.

"Umm… thanks?"

She tried not to frown into the dark, his touch arousing.

The kisses continued, and he whispered against the shell of her ear. "Like you don't already know you're beautiful."

This time she smiled. With her short stature and rounded curves, even the general lack of women like her on any mainstream cover didn't obscure her agreement that Max was right. She did know.

She loved the way she looked and the feeling of being alive, and strong, and able to sense every touch this man unleashed on her body. Her confidence wasn't one-hundred-percent bullet proof, but she'd begun to believe her act, her bravado, something adopted to help her get by in the world.

People liked her better when nothing seemed wrong, when she put on a good show, which meant they also asked fewer questions.

"Okay then, rather than tell me." She arched her neck, hinting his next kisses should extend there. "You really should show me."

He obliged with the throat kisses and hummed at her directive, a man willing to accept a challenge. And even as he did, even as he entered her and gave her just what she wanted, she couldn't keep from directing the play.

At times, she asked him to slow so she could savor the feeling of him inside her; at others, she demanded more when she wanted the thrill of him working at her pleasure. Harder. Faster. She relished being the sexually assertive one in this pairing. And bless his heart, Max seemed to relish it too.

His long fingers brushed her outer thighs, his thumbs hooking beneath her knees and pushing her legs higher so that he buried himself deeper within her. She sunk into the pillowy duvet, delighting in his increased thrusts, her breaths ragged along with his.

He wasn't like the others, intimidated or judgmental when it came to an insatiable woman. A woman unwilling to waste time suppressing her desires. *No.* His gaze fused with hers, and he studied her, as if taking in something only he could see. She felt free. Excited. Affirmed.

If only his life wasn't a mess. If only she wasn't allergic to relationships.

Actually, scratch that.

She liked being allergic to relationships. Her apprehension kept her life consistent, easy, trouble free, though she would miss Max when all of this ended.

She lashed her hands out so her fingers locked behind his neck, and she pulled him close, savoring the hotness of him—not just his beautiful aesthetic, but his literal hotness—the burn of his skin against hers and the heat of him within her.

His thrusts intensified, as though he lived for her reaction to his touch. She let go, giving in to what he wanted, allowing her peak to rise so that one pleasurable wave engulfed another. The swell of satisfied need shot through her body, and her arousal broke in a series of soft moans and uninhibited pleas for more.

He responded each time, driving into her with impossible force, his usually restrained strength now unbridled. She pulled him down and seized his mouth with hers, his pace unbroken when he did reach his own climax.

Soon after, the room filled with nothing more than the sounds of panting breaths as he collapsed forward, burying his face in her hair. Something about his near silence conveyed more than just a man who'd found pleasure. Like he'd searched her out in need of an emotional release and found it.

Blood rushed her body, rumbling and pounding in her ears, while something light and totally worth ignoring danced within her chest.

Joy. Maybe?

Max rolled and positioned himself beside her. Again came the silence, so she turned to him, her heart clenching at his pupils dilated and focused on the ceiling, only the smallest sliver of cerulean visible.

He turned to her, the action hinting that he sensed her concern, while the look on his face made her stomach sink. Even the room's limited light didn't obscure the sheen to his eyes, his whites tinged a pale pink. The thick line denting the space between his brows indicated a man overwhelmed and in need of comfort—but too afraid to ask. A man without an anchor and in need of someone to hold him through the turbulent weather.

She didn't want to be that someone, but her heart pulled rank, just as it did every time she saw the cracks growing across another person's soul.

She'd been where Max was now, many times alone, a child with no one to share the weight pressing on her tiny shoulders. So yes, her heart pulled rank. Even as her brain yelled for her not to get involved.

Her life had its own shadows to chase away, and yet, she rolled to her side and rested her hand on the furnace that was his bare chest.

The sharp rise and fall didn't belong to a man sated and unwinding. His untamed heartbeat pulsed through his ribcage and into her hand. And of course, her mouth pulled rank too, betraying her better sense and crossing the healthy space she'd put between them. All because she shuffled close enough to see the water gathering in his eyes.

She pressed her lips to his high cheekbone and whispered a sappy affirmation she knew better than to offer. One she'd wished to hear in her dark hours. Words he too probably needed to hear.

"You're going to be okay."

He gave a small nod, and his Adam's apple bobbed with a sharp swallow. Though he remained silent, she hoped he caught the subtext in her statement.

Nothing lasted forever, not even the bad stuff, even when things got so hard that it was impossible to see through to the other side. And as much as she didn't want to tie herself to this man, she did want him to be okay.

Seventeen

FREYA WOKE to the moon shining in her eyes. Okay, not the literal moon, but a lamp about half the size of her head that did a convincing impression of looking like the moon, gray shadows, craters, and all.

Now, she blinked at the lamp's "mooniness", those shadows and craters unnoticed last night when Max switched the thing on in passing, with her focus too busy ogling his beautiful nakedness.

She glared at a split in the curtains and the stinging sunlight creeping in, that sunlight aiding the moon in bathing the room in brightness. Years of working the bar scene meant she had a hate-hate relationship with early starts.

"Good morning."

She sucked in a breath and snapped her attention to Max smiling at her from the doorway. "Holy shit. You're awake?"

His wide grin grew and melted a small degree of rigidity in her body, even though his glittering blue eyes betrayed one poor and unfortunate truth.

Max was a morning person.

Her gaze slid from his face to the breathtaking view of toned pecs and perfectly naked abs above a pair of teal-blue board shorts. "You're too chipper for a Saturday morning, and why are you out of this bed?"

He laughed and strode over, taking a seat next to her on the bed's edge. "I wake early. Old habit."

She grumbled. She would ask about that old habit, but only after she caught up on more hours of sleep. Wanting to block the light, she pulled the bed cover over her face.

"I made breakfast." Max tugged the sheet down.

"Sleep first. Food later. Hang on a minute"—she gave up her attempt to wrangle the cover off Max, and for the second time in this incredibly short conversation surprise made her abandon sleep—"you cook?"

"If you call scrambled eggs on toast cooking." His smile made her skin go all tingly and alive, like he saw something in this moment that she couldn't.

That should have been her cue to drag on her clothes and get the hell out of his apartment. For some unexplainable reason, despite all his shortcomings of early morning wake-ups and all, she couldn't stay annoyed at him, much less leave.

Bailing on someone as likable as Max was like kicking a sweet-fluffy kitten, something she just would never do. Maybe his coming to her last night had something to do with her softening to him. He'd clearly been going through something. But the fact he picked her, of all people, again, should have sent her packing.

There wasn't any making sense of this, so she sat up and put on a dramatic groan. If they ever did this again, she'd make it clear that sleep-ins were her jam, and *no one*, not even Mr. Irresistible over here, messed with her sleep.

She nodded to the little moon, failing to recall any other time she'd seen anything similar in a grown person's bedroom. "What's with the nightlight?"

He shrugged, his smile easing to something wistful. "It reminds me of being a child again. Not because it's a nightlight but because it's a moon, and I spent way too much time sleeping under the stars."

She frowned, unable to identify with that memory.

He worked his attention over her face, as if maybe her confusion showed. "I mean, who wouldn't want to bring the moon inside with them?"

Who wouldn't, indeed?

She smiled at the innocence in his rhetorical question. "I'm going to take a not-so-wild stab here and guess you were a camping kid?"

He pressed his hand over hers on the bedspread, his palm and fingers so much longer than her own admittedly small digits. "Only the very second the weather warmed up back in Scarborough. I have a brother and sister, and we lived near the forest. If my dad was too slow to bring us out there, we'd take matters into our own hands and pitch a tent in our yard."

She caught the renewed light in Max's eyes, and a tight band squeezed around her chest.

"Your dad sounds like a great guy."

Whereas she'd barely known her dad.

Still, the mere stroke of Max's thumb over her hand sent a soothing warmth through her body. At least there was that.

"Yeah, he was." Max's gaze dropped from hers.

Was?

Her muscles locked, and she slipped her hand from his, fingers now pressed over her mouth. "Oh shit, I'm sorry."

He shook his head. "Anyway, Luke and I would sneak out to the forest on our own sometimes. Sophie was too chicken to join us half the time, but we still had fun."

She raised a brow at the sudden redirection, but let the change in subject go. He wasn't her boyfriend and she didn't need to delve into his problems, and he didn't need to tell her everything.

He stood, taking her hand with him. "Come have breakfast. You look like someone who needs coffee first thing in the morning. Besides, I have something exciting to tell you."

She wrangled her hand free long enough to drag a sheet off the bed and wrap it around herself, all the while grumbling because he'd not only gotten her up, but he'd also gotten her coffee-fueled "type" correct.

The moment she reached the bedroom door, she stopped, her mind freezing on her first glimpse of Max's apartment in full daylight.

To her immediate right stood a black stone kitchen island, with white embossed cabinetry behind. Four giant, bronze, hanging lanterns dangled over the counter, and ahead of that stood a ten-seater table, complete with a huge crystal vase filled with lush tropical flowers.

To the kitchen's left, a round black glass coffee table took up a reasonable amount of space in the huge living room, positioned in front of a giant white, L-shaped, leather sofa.

If her jaw didn't already hang open, it might as well have detached and fallen off the moment she focused on the wall-to-wall windows and the balcony outside.

Except, balcony was a gross understatement.

A wall of greenery backed an expansive red-wood terrace, banana lounges surrounding a small swimming pool, and a tall rusted-metal abstract sculpture nearby. And then there was the spa and slate stone tiles. Dark, woven chairs gave the terrace's other side a more intimate contrast, complete with an outdoor dining area comprised of Moroccan lanterns and a glass and bronze table.

She took a few silent steps forward, allowing the view to draw her in, even more than the terrace. Cool blue morning sky reached down, making contact with a teal Port Phillip Bay below, the ocean stretching out in calm, sparkling waves.

Melbourne could be so many different things depending on who and where the city was being witnessed from. Bustling and grimy. Sleek and professional. Boisterous and festive. But right now, all she saw was tranquility.

"Holy hell, Max." She took a few more steps and touched a finger to the cold glass window, not brave enough to splay her whole hand out and ruin his pristine windows with her handprint. "No wonder you're busting ass to keep this place."

Soft footsteps padded behind her, and soon, his warm body pressed to her back, hands sweeping around her waist, before he turned her to face him. "Yeah, about that, as much as I enjoy busting ass at The Ruby Room, I have another idea."

"You're leaving me already?"

Her stomach sank, even though she'd always figured he'd find something better.

Just not this quick.

"Ha! I wish." His cheeks creased either side of his full grin. "No, just something to add to my workload. Something more along the lines of my passions."

He led her forward, toward the kitchen; her gaze caught on a glass staircase along the living room's back wall.

Holy mother fruitcake, there's a whole other level to this place.

She squeezed her eyes shut for a second, reminding herself to stay on topic. "Let me guess, since you're a morning person, you want to be a professional alarm clock?"

"No, though the early morning thing does have something to do with what I'm passionate about." He deposited her on one of the four bar stools and then wandered around the counter. "Before I did the tech business thing, I was set on a career as an open water swimmer. Granted, it would never make me much money, but I loved it, and I want to return to it."

"Aren't you, like, thirty-seven?" She paused to drag her attention over his immaculate body, one part of the whole swimmer story checking out. "Wouldn't that make you too ol—"

"Old?" He narrowed his eyes at her like she was a bit slow in the head or something. "And I have a bung shoulder, yes. But I'm not looking to compete, I'm looking to coach."

She tipped back her head, rolling her eyes at the ceiling and feeling like a total idiot. "Right. I should have figured you meant coaching."

"Let's just blame the lack of caffeine."

"Thanks. I appreciate your understanding." She waited while he went about pulling cups out of a top cabinet. "Okay, so talk me through what becoming a swim coach entails."

"Well, from what I gather, there's an online component and two full days of training. I also need to do a first aid course and get a working-with-children check. I'll start with teaching smaller kids first and take it from there."

"Do you have the money to get all of that done?" She jutted out her chin, just as he grabbed a carton of milk from the fridge. "I'm dairy intolerant, by the way. I like my coffee strong and black."

"One black coming up." He gave her a wink, then pressed a button on his coffee machine, his voice rising over the whirring noise. "And if you mean, do I have money to spare, that's a definite no, but sometimes you've gotta spend money to make money, right?"

"Right. Why did you ditch the swimming for tech, anyway?"

He slid a tall glass filled with liquid black gold her way. She took a first sip and tried not to groan at the deep, bitter, wonderfulness.

"It wasn't by choice." He shrugged, leaning one hip against the counter opposite her, his own white coffee in his hand. "I got a shoulder injury falling off a cliff."

She choked on coffee and slammed a hand over her mouth, trying not to splutter all over his beautiful counter. "You fell off a cliff and survived?"

He gave a slow nod. "All one-hundred or so feet. Totally my brother's fault, though I don't like to remind him."

"Holy shit!" She stared at his shoulder and the jagged, raised scar running across it. "I guess that explains your scar."

His attention fell to the counter, and any light in his expression dropped, too.

She offered a smile, even though he couldn't see it. "This is where I make you feel better by admitting I think scars are hella sexy."

His gaze rose. "Really?"

She gave a steady nod, her heart pounding with just how much she wanted to breach the counter and press her lips to that scar, maybe rekindle a re-enactment of what they'd shared last night.

His mouth curled at the corners, yet another spot she wanted to kiss. "Good thing I *did* survive, then."

She peered down at her coffee and a vague reflection of her frowning face mirrored back at her on the shiny surface. "How did you fall off a cliff and live to tell the tale, anyway?"

"My brother, Luke, was going through something at the time, struggling with re-joining the normal world after his military stint. He asked me to come rock climbing on a day when conditions weren't exactly great." He rounded the counter and took a seat beside her. A low tug pulled within her gut, one that made her want to lean over and kiss him, to distract from her rising sympathy. "And after the cliff face gave way, I just happened to land on a stretch of earth without any rocks. The fall smashed my shoulder, but I lived. I was lucky and unlucky all in one."

He rested his elbow to the counter and took hold of her wrist, rubbing his thumb over her pulse and sending an instant and delicious tingling sensation throughout her entire body.

She didn't know what to do, except to watch his hand stroke her wrist while she contemplated why on earth anyone would go rock climbing to begin with, much less anywhere near some pointy-ass rocks.

"What do you think about my swim coach idea?"

"Will it pay enough to save your apartment?"

He drew her hand toward him and kissed her wrist, the gesture sending a surge of electricity down her spine. "Probably not, but it might tide me over until I can figure out something more permanent."

They watched each other for the longest time, sipping coffee through the silence. A part of her wanted to point out that many normal people worked jobs they didn't love just to keep a roof over their heads, that maybe losing his multi-million dollar "roof" wouldn't be all that disastrous. But then, maybe her version of bad wasn't the same as his version of bad, and it wasn't her place to judge the series of shock changes he'd been through.

Her stomach growled, a reminder she hadn't eaten yet. Before she could open her mouth to ask him to feed her, his lingering blue stare caught her off-guard.

Once again, the innocence in his eyes struck her, and her thoughts switched to what he'd told her about his outdoorsy childhood. How he'd developed a love for ocean swimming, participated in rock climbing—not the controlled, indoor, abseiling type—but the actual "someone could fall and break bones" sort.

His life was so different from hers. His childhood alone was light years away, simply because he'd had both parents, though she suspected he'd enjoyed way more than that.

He'd had forests, and moonlit nights, and siblings who seemed to mostly get along; meanwhile, she'd endured lonely nights in hospital beds and a miserable home to return to when she did recover.

Even if her life was mostly awesome these days, the sinking feeling in her belly reminded her of her recent misfortune of being lumped with her mother, of Gideon's warning about having an association with that woman.

The sinking in her belly turned into a hot, bubbling sensation, one that prodded at her anger. Anger that her childhood had been so fucking miserable, that both parents had taken advantage of her vulnerability, wasting the magic of her younger years while making her feel so small and unimportant.

And instead of merely raging, she'd taken revenge and become everything those two staunch Catholics hated. Everything they'd said she couldn't be. Unique. Independent. Brazen.

There'd been her bartending, her friendship with Gideon, all her solo travels to dangerous and exotic countries, her tattoos, her unwillingness to settle down, and the scores of men she invited into her bed.

She brought her focus back to Max and surrendered to her sudden need to break free once again, perhaps what she needed in order to deal with all the new stuff complicating her life.

"Take me camping."

Max laughed, but she answered him with silence.

His exuberant grin slipped. "What? You're not serious, are you?"

Eighteen

TWO WEEKS PASSED, and in that time, Max completed his online work and two days of practical swim coach training. He'd also obtained a Working With Children check card. Now he waded in the warm waters at Little Sharkie's Swim Center, a school a few minutes' walk from his apartment. His uniform consisted of an unmissable bright red swim shirt, complete with a giant, smiling, cartoon shark over his chest.

Like the other two trainees either side of him in the pool, this was his fourth session today; but unlike his fellow instructors, he didn't look fresh out of high school. In fact, he looked truly ancient and totally out of place; though, at least he could count life experience as an advantage.

Little Sharkie's had been willing to fast-track his teacher training in light of his competition past. With any luck, they would bump him from babies' classes to training the more advanced children over time.

So now, he hung back with his peers in the section designated for babies and toddlers, the lead instructor, Melissa, out front waving baby-laden parents into the pool.

He tried to smile and wave too, tried to give the impression he was here simply because he loved swimming and working with children, not because he really needed the cash and would lose his home if he didn't find more ways to make some money.

A stack of utility bills waited on his kitchen counter, adding to his mounting expenses, and as predicted, he wouldn't have a whole lot of money left over from his deal with Luke.

So, while he truly *did* love swimming and had never really analyzed his feelings about kids, the dull ache in his chest made him wonder if the whole swim coach thing really was the best idea.

Melissa explained to the parents that he and the other trainees were there to observe but would help out when needed. Unlike at The Ruby Room, he was expected to interact with people here, and even just smiling and waving made his nerves prickle.

Smiling and waving would lead to talking, and he had a way of stuffing that up, especially when paired with the pressure to keep things professional. After all, his runaway actions had cost Tiluma a major investor and caused his exit as the Chief Technical Officer. People had quit over his involvement, and his stupid ideas had almost destroyed the entire company.

If he couldn't hold it together in an adult environment, what chance did he have with a bunch of parents and children? No doubt, he'd end up offending someone.

Class started, and the parents held their children at chest level in a circle. Melissa sang a version of "Wheels on the Bus", instructing the parents to dip their babies in and out of the water, encouraging them to splash or blow bubbles on the surface. Next came counting to three, then dumping cups of water over the babies' heads, all while saying, "blink" in an attempt to train the babies to close their eyes when submerged.

Much shrieking followed, and by this point, Max's face hurt from his fake smile. One kid in particular was not loving the class. He appeared to be around eighteen months, and things didn't improve when the same boy's dad thrust him into Max's hands, citing a need to take the boy's older brother to the bathroom.

Max's mouth hung open as the dad waded toward a four-year-old doing a cross-legged wriggle on the pool's edge, the scrunch-faced toddler in Max's arms escalating from shrieking into slapping Max's chest in clear terror.

He tried to join the class in the dad's absence but had no idea what to do to calm the kid lumped onto him, so he followed his instincts and made a little *sh-sh-shhh* sound.

The shrieking stopped, and the blond-headed toddler stared gape-mouthed into Max's eyes, as if fascinated with his unfamiliar face, as well as the shushing. Well, at least until the little blighter widened his eyes, perhaps finally clocking that his dad was gone.

The kid let out his biggest screech yet and swung a fast right hook into Max's chin. Max reeled back, pain radiating from his jaw to the rest of his face.

Despite his young age, the toddler weighed about as much as a small bulldog and had the meaty build to match. The strength of his punch suggested he had a promising future in swimming. Or shot put. Or ring fighting…

Max wanted to rub at his still-throbbing jaw but couldn't because of the gigantic toddler in his arms.

"Max, would you and Alfie be the first to go through the arch?" Melissa smiled sweetly, though the strain of her cheeks told him to focus and get his shit together.

She held a large, flexible flotation board, about the size of a small mattress, against the pool's edge until it bent upward in an arch. From watching previous classes, he knew he'd have to walk backward through the arch, floating Alfie on his back, all while Melissa sprinkled water from a toy watering can onto the child's upturned face.

"Sure can." Max glanced at the other parents, doing the expected thing and hooking his fingers under Alfie's armpits, ready to lean him back so his head rested on Max's shoulder.

Except the kid seemed to know what was coming, because he flailed around, gripping at Max's shirt and scratching at whatever exposed skin he could dig his little talons into. It was a near miracle Alfie didn't draw blood, which would have forced Max out of the pool, though that would mean an instant escape.

So much for Alfie's bright swimming career.

A mum with tight red curls leaned closer and whispered, "Alfie hates floating on his back. The best his dad manages is to cuddle him and walk him through the arch instead."

Max nodded his thanks for the advice, before doing just that and turning Alfie in for a cuddle.

The toddler stopped beating Max up, opting to push away with his chubby arms, his head flopping back, like he decided Max stank of trash and garlic—or maybe garlic-infused trash. Either way, Max had no idea what thoughts ran through this kid's brain, except he was glad when they finally made it through the arch.

Alfie snapped out of his flop pose and swung his massive head forward like an airborne boulder, his forehead cracking into Max's nose.

Instant agony seared through Max's face, and he stumbled back, almost tossing the child in the air but catching himself just before he did that.

He pried a hand free and clutched at his nose, certain there'd be blood. Okay, no blood, but a strong pressure built in his sinuses, and before he could stop, a loud sneeze broke free.

Alfie shrieked, startling Max. Mostly because, for once, this shriek involved laughter.

"Oh." Max smiled at Alfie. "You like that, huh?"

Alfie tipped his head forward, attempting another head-butt.

Max ducked out of the way and gave Alfie a pretend sneeze instead.

More laugh-shrieking. Max kept sneezing and Alfie kept laughing —so much so he didn't notice when Max hooked his fingers under the boy's armpits and maneuvered him onto his back.

Every time Alfie looked around, threatening to cry, Max simply sneezed.

They got through the arch a second time, and all the other parents smiled in silence, as though cautious any cheers might break the magic Max and Alfie had going.

Max passed Alfie through the arch again and again, and eventually, Alfie didn't need the sneezes to distract him. He just simply floated, his head supported on Max's shoulder and Max's hands around the boy's ribcage. Melissa even sprinkled water on the toddler's face, and he merely gave an appropriate giggle, spraying the droplets that landed on his lips with a noisy *"brrr."*

Alfie's dad re-entered the water, and he patted Max on the shoulder, his expression lifted in a big smile. "That was amazing. I've been trying to get him to float on his back for months."

Max handed Alfie over, unexpectedly sad to let him go. "I guess I took a beating, and he decided I deserved a little pity."

Alfie's dad laughed, giving the kid a playful nudge on the chin. "That sounds just like Alfie."

Melissa threw Max two thumbs-up and moved the group onto a new exercise. For the first time ever in a professional setting, he enjoyed the light sensation of having not messed up.

After the class ended, he took a quick shower and got changed, soon heading to the exit to find Freya waiting for him. For once, she didn't wear one of her flare-dresses and instead donned a pair of sweat pants. Lumped at her feet was a huge camping bag.

Nineteen

Freya trudged over the wet ground, the tall gumtrees around her emitting a smoky-damp scent, the earthy smell from the soil strong and strangely calming.

She turned to Max beside her. "Is it true that male kangaroos can be really territorial and attack anyone who crosses their path?"

"I don't know." He shrugged, his breaths a light pant from the effort of lugging the majority of their stuff. "You're the Aussie, you tell me."

She tugged her backpack higher onto her shoulder and walked farther in silence.

The Ruby Room would be closed for a couple of days while her promised stage repairs occurred. Meanwhile, Max would be exposing her to the supposed joys of camping. Though given the current conversation, she wasn't so sure this whole camping thing was such a good idea after all.

"So, ah, tell me again why your brother has a spare block of bushland in Roseford?"

Max's eyes squinted against the glare from the pale gray clouds. "It's not a block per se, more like… an estate. Impressive, right? There's a main house and a smaller cabin just down the road from where we parked."

A flash of lightness spread through her body. "Ooh, does that mean we can spend the rest of the night under an actual roof if I pike out of this whole 'sleeping under the stars' business?"

Then again, Luke had already done so much to accommodate her camping dreams, lending them the use of these grounds, as well as his four-wheel drive since Max's Tesla probably wouldn't cut it with all the rough roads and needing to be charged and all. Maybe seeking to use Luke's house would be pushing her luck.

Max gave her a sidelong stare, his brow pressed into a straight line, as if to say, "You're joking, right?"

No, actually, she wasn't.

Just because she'd grown up in Australia didn't mean the bush didn't scare the absolute hell out of her. If not for the fact that nine out of the world's top ten most venomous snakes lived here, then because the venomous spiders weren't much better. And then there were those ill-tempered kangaroos.

And if not for the snakes and spiders and kangaroos, then for the creepy-as-fuck local folklore, from ghosts to indigenous bush spirits who gobbled up children who ventured too close to the rivers.

And if not for snakes, spiders, kangaroos, and freaky-ass ghosts, then because ever since she'd blurted out her desire to go camping, she'd doubted whether Max was the right man for the job.

Not because she didn't trust him to wrestle a snake or kangaroo for her, but because there was something indefinable about her connection with him. Something that made her believe this trip wouldn't end well. If for no other reason than they were at different points in their lives, and perhaps it would be safer to keep their relationship purely casual.

I should have just stayed in the city.

She turned to him again, with his backpack on his shoulders and a long, foldable tent strapped atop that pack. He also held a duffel with supplies in one hand and a rolled-up mattress in the other; his face tilted down, shoulders rounded, his shaggy blond waves spilling over his eyes.

"You know." She smiled as she spoke, her heart surging at the ambition of what she planned to admit. "I caught the end of that swim class you were in."

His head flicked up, his gaze locking to hers. "Oh, yeah?"

She let her smile grow, recalling his quiet air of vulnerability just seconds ago. "You did really well with that gigantor toddler."

He let out a laugh. "The scratches on my shoulders from that 'gigantor toddler' tell a different story. My nose is still recovering from his headbutt, too."

"Well, I don't see any bruises, so all's well that ends well."

A laugh bubbled through her, and she thought it best to let him know the truth of her observation. Ever since he'd come to her for a job, self-doubt seemed to be his default emotion, and she wanted to give him something to be proud of.

"I mean, for a second there I was sure you would pitch the kid across the pool, but you recovered well and won him over. Max, you have a knack. You made that kid adore you."

Really? Just the kid?

Shut up brain, just shut up!

She made a point of watching Max, his attention still on the ground, though she swore his posture straightened just a little.

"Thanks."

"I mean." She toyed with her ring, the one with the swirling silver and deep-set ruby, unable to hold back a joke at his expense. "He also looked like you, so that was weird."

He turned to her with a quizzical look. "Weird? How?"

"Well, it was like a freaky glimpse into your future."

He shook his head as though he didn't understand.

She groaned, sorry she'd said anything. Suddenly the joke seemed on her. "As in, if you ever had a kid, they'd look a lot like the one you were tossing about today. In fact, they'd probably act like the one you were holding, too. No doubt you were a knockdown, drag out toddler back in the day."

A new light entered his eyes, his expression lifting along with his smile. "I wish I remembered that far back, but you're probably right. Just like that kid, I had an older brother to rough house with, too."

The sounds of a rushing river, made fat from the recent rain, grew louder, and he swung his attention forward, his long strides making it hard for her to keep up. "And what were you like as a child?"

Her muscles seized for the briefest moment before she forced them to relax, and her well-tuned ability to save face kicked in.

She dug out a wicked tone. "Trust me, you wouldn't want to know."

Max laughed, hopefully fooled into thinking her statement had more to do with her getting up to all kinds of childhood silliness, and not because she'd been too terrified to engage in much childish *anything*.

The only upside to all this talk about children was that he hadn't yet grilled her about whether she wanted any. For some reason, she decided he wouldn't like her answer.

He stopped and dropped his duffel bag to the ground, the river bed about twenty feet away. "Right, this looks like a good spot to set up."

She peered about her, unable to find a full breath.

There were no signs of civilization nearby. She had no idea what a "good spot" looked like. All she had was her limited trust in the man beside her and that he'd get her through the night in the wilderness alive.

She let go of her bag, and it made a dull thud at her feet, her silence a sign of something she rarely gave willingly. Compliance.

Over the next few hours, Freya endured a crash course in outdoor living, and to her credit, she adapted well enough. She helped Max set up the tent, which wasn't all that hard since the thing pretty much popped up the second it was pulled out of its bag. And since there'd been rain, he insisted on trekking to the main house for dry firewood and kindling.

Of course, she flat out refused to let him go alone, not when she'd have to stay at the tent on her own. So, she followed him, making a concerted effort not to stray more than a couple of meters away, lest some snake or kangaroo jump out at her, or worse, a snake-flinging kangaroo. *Ekk!*

She shuddered at that possibility now, the flickering campfire before her lighting up the night, her belly full from the sausages and chili beans Max had cooked. He'd even gone to the effort of bringing a bag of marshmallows so she could have her first ever campfire toasted marshmallow on a stick… Not that she'd let on it was her first.

Her initial attempt fell into the fire, her second burned to an inedible crisp, but she got the hang of toasting marshmallows by the third try—the hot, sticky treat a comforting contrast to her cold, murky surrounds. She didn't even mind that Max switched between laughter and soft lingering stares throughout her entire awkward experience.

"It's probably about time we got some sleep." He slapped at a mosquito perched on his bare forearm, but the wily insect escaped. "What do you think?"

She nodded, silently refusing to move until he did.

With night here, and this being an unfamiliar and isolated location, her hands had already turned clammy. Getting a full and easy breath proved impossible. "Do we just leave the fire on?"

He turned for the tent. "Yeah. It'll burn itself out."

She shot up and chased after him, wondering if he noticed her extra clingy reactions.

Once inside the tent, he switched on a dim battery-powered lantern, which helped to slow her heartbeat a little. Not enough to quell her dashed hopes over not finding the peace she'd expected within the tent's cozy confines.

Max lay down and held his blue wool blanket open for her. She didn't waste time scrambling in next to him, his arms soon encircling her again; her racing heart slowed another degree.

He switched the tent lantern off, and her pulse shot to an instant gallop. Slow moments passed, while she tried to find calm, but the silence and darkness suffocated. Her skin prickled at every unidentifiable sound from outside.

She cleared her throat, deciding the best remedy for silence was talking.

"Have you ever noticed how in space sci-fi TV shows, no one ever wears shorts?"

She barely recognized the stiff and hollow tone she used, but just like her clinging, hopefully Max didn't notice.

He slid his hand to her tummy and rubbed a spot just above her belly button. The gesture should have comforted, but for some reason she found herself stifling a need to shiver. "What do you mean?"

"Like"—she shifted against him a little, trying to play casual—"no matter how warm it is on these other planets, no matter how advanced these supposed space travelers are meant to be, they haven't worked out how to make themselves comfortable on a hot day. What's with all the turtle-neck sweaters and pants? It's pretty much neck-to-toe clothes everywhere."

Max chuckled against her ear, the soft rumble producing the smallest bloom of warmth within her. "Maybe they evolved some kind of internal cooling system. Or their full-length clothes are made of some advanced cooling fabric?"

She blinked into the darkness. So much for her stalling. In one quick statement, he'd killed her attempt at keeping him awake.

"I don't want to have children."

The words shot from her lips before she could stop them. Where the statement came from, she had no idea.

She scrunched her face and mumbled a frustrated, "fuck."

In her hurry to think of something else to say, she'd picked the one conversation she didn't want to have, much less with someone she most definitely didn't want to have kids with, largely because he wasn't anything more than her current, casual sleeping partner.

"Ahhh…" Max pressed his fingers to her arm and tugged back a little, rolling her so he could talk to her face-to-face, even though the tent was pitch black inside.

She locked her muscles, refusing to move.

"Why are you telling me this?"

She blinked into the darkness and shook her head. "I don't know. Forget I said anything."

"Freya." He nudged at her arm again. "I didn't want to say anything, but you've been jittery all day, and you're acting even weirder now. Are you scared of the dark or something?"

Oh hell, he *had* noticed. Now she'd have to threaten to break his legs, so he wouldn't tell everyone at The Ruby that she was a huge wimp.

She shook her head again, denying her fear, the pillow beneath her rustling, just as a human-meets-animal screech broke through the night.

She sat bolt upright. Her blood rushed fast in her veins like it wanted out, all while a sharp pain grew in the center of her chest, making her want to cry from sheer, overwhelming terror.

Maybe more than most people, she hated being afraid. She'd had enough fear to last her five lifetimes, and she couldn't bear this, couldn't bear the powerlessness and the sense of some unknown danger just waiting to hurt her.

Max crawled forward and reached for the tent zip, the one leading to the outside world where vicious night creatures stalked and roamed. "It's probably just a possum. I'll go outside and have a look, if—"

"No. Don't," she yelled, lunging after him, her fingers latching to the back of his t-shirt while she pulled him back.

In her head, some mythical river beast with lion's feet and pointy bull horns waited out there ready to gore Max's guts out. And when that beast was done with him, well, it'd no doubt turn its beady, red eyes on her.

"Please. Just. Don't go out there, okay? Turn the damn lantern back on and don't you dare leave me here alone."

Twenty

FEAR RAN like ice water through Freya's veins, and her high-pitched scream for Max to stay reverberated through the tent, unrecognizable from any tone she'd used before. Worse still, she had no idea where this fear came from, only that this uncontrollable environment did not agree with her.

"Freya, what's wrong?"

Max's question made her skin outright burn, while sweat trickled down her back. She wanted to answer, but her thoughts refused to slow long enough for her to find a reply. Even just the idea of telling him her real problem made her tongue dry and her words dissipate.

The lantern came back on, and Max sat beside it. As much as the light soothed her, it surely also made the fear on her face even more visible, too.

There'd be no way to cover this up. She would be forced to admit to being a victim of her emotions.

"Freya?" His tone held a husky edge, one that opened a pit in her belly and rocked her resistance even further.

She slammed her eyes shut, pressing her hands to her face. "I've never done this before, okay? This whole camping thing. I really wanted to enjoy it, but I... I don't know why. It's just too overwhelming and weird, and that overwhelm is playing mind games with me."

"Okay."

His voice slowed, so soft and gentle, and something light fluttered in her tummy. Whatever that fluttering was, it pulled her nerves closer to snapping, like maybe she'd handle it better if he just called her a wimp and told her to suck it up and go to sleep.

"We don't have to stay. We can head back to the hous—"

"No." She waved her hands out in front of her, subjecting this poor man to yet more erratic behavior. *Damn it.* Why couldn't she get her body and mind to calm the fuck down? For someone who dealt with feral drunk people on a regular basis, her current meltdown didn't make much sense. "No. I'm not going out there again and neither are you, got it? You stay here. Right here."

Not only did she not want something to happen to him—like an encounter with a lion-footed, bullhorn beast—but she figured she'd probably self-combust from pure terror if she stepped outside and tried to trek to the house.

And even if she did give up and go back to the house, there'd still be the awkward drive home tomorrow. She couldn't pike out and let fear win, even if that meant holding Max to ransom in this tent.

She turned to him. "I'm such a fucking idiot. I'm so sorry."

His gaze shifted about her face, like he worked double-time to understand her. "Everyone gets scared some—"

"No. No. You can't honestly say my reaction right now is normal." And sure thing, she didn't deserve his understanding because, even as she spoke, she struggled to control her wildly animated hands, as though the active movement kept her from flipping out completely.

"Well, no, I gu—"

"Because while little kid Max Tindall was off pitching tents and getting over his fear of night creatures, I was... I was..." She paused a second and a cold shiver ran down her spine. "Let's just say I wasn't doing that."

His pupils grew into expansive black pools surrounded by cerulean blue; a picture of innocence, or maybe ignorance, since he'd lived a charmed life far different from hers. "What do you mean?"

His innocent-ignorance had her teeth clenching, and a renewed heat seared through her chilled veins. "As a kid, I never went camping, okay? Hell, I barely even made it to school."

His jaw went slack, and his cheeks hollowed as a result. She swore the color drained from his skin, while his unblinking stare seemed to say, "I hear you, but I don't understand."

A growl formed in her throat, and she shot to standing, as much as one could stand in a small tent. So really, she just hunched, while hot tears stung the back of her eyes.

"Fuuucck!" She pressed her face into the nook of her arm, damned if she cried now, resorting to the next best thing that would keep her from tears. *Swearing.*

"Fuck. Fuck… Fuck. Fuck. Fuck."

She spun around to find Max's mouth even more agape, his attention darting around the tent and giving the impression he wanted to be anywhere but here.

"I'm sorry. This is only getting worse." She smacked her palm to her forehead over and over again, waiting for a clear thought to surface.

Should I tell him about what happened to me? What would I lose if I did? What would I gain?

Nothing. The answer was nothing.

Speaking up was a bloody stupid idea.

She gave Max her direct stare, certain of one thing amongst all this havoc. "I'm not talking. You don't deserve the misery of my sob story."

"Well, that's a bit harsh." He tucked his chin in and frowned, his inquisitive stare making her feel as though even just alluding to her tragic backstory made her look erratic. "Besides, maybe now that you are talking, I want to know whatever it is you don't want to tell me."

Stillness took her over, and her hands dropped to either side. The reality of this conversation and why she didn't want to have it hit her.

"It'll change things between us."

Her voice sounded small even to her ears. She couldn't seem to pry her attention from the beautiful man seated before her, his expression open, and his whole demeanor way too quiet and accepting of her rant. "What if I promise not to let it?"

Her adrenaline from earlier fled, and her knees turned weak. She plonked down onto the air-filled mattress.

"I don't think that's possible. You'll backtrack away, or the truth will kill pretty much all excitement in this relationship. You'll start acting weird and feeling sorry for me. Or you'll get all strange and mushy, or worse, the second things aren't going well, you'll use the truth to hurt me."

Her gaze fell to the blue wool blanket all crumpled in the space between them, her thoughts sticking on the times she'd experienced every one of those scenarios. One of so many reasons why she rarely talked about her childhood.

"I'd like to think I wouldn't do any of that." He dropped his attention to the same blue blanket she'd been eyeing, his hands resting on his knees like he took a second to think. "I don't know what I'm dealing with here. You know, I'm fine with you not telling me." He peered up at her, a tiny smile curling his lips. "I understand."

His barely perceptible smile lingered, which only seemed to deepen the ensuing silence. She crossed her arms over her chest, and her muscles stiffened from the uncertainty of what to do or say next.

The silence should have helped. While it did buy her a minute to think without suffering through further bouts of verbal diarrhea, the lack of sound coiled the growing tension within her tighter and tighter.

Maybe she didn't owe him an explanation.

No, not maybe. She *definitely* didn't owe him one.

Her past struggles weren't just difficult to retell, they were downright exhausting.

Traumatic.

But then, he'd seen her rant and rave and accepted both. He handled her nonsensical reaction way better than she expected.

Maybe he would be different from most people…

After all, he'd let her drag him all the way out to the bush, just so she could enjoy this one normal thing pretty much every other kid experienced. Only she wasn't enjoying herself, and certainly not in any kind of normal way.

And now, the poor guy just sat there with a twisted smile, a tortured soul unsure of the reasons for his torture.

She threw her hands into the air and released a growl. "Okay. Fine. I'll tell you, but if you can't handle this in any kind of decent way, we're off, okay? You go back to being an employee at the bar. We definitely don't keep sleeping together. And we never, *ever* speak of this again. Understand?"

Twenty-One

Freya waited as Max sat taller and his eyes brightened, offering her a quick nod to continue, to share the details of her past and the reasons for her fear right now. His swift reaction hinted relief because she'd decided to trust him, but she wasn't quite done with setting her rules.

"Regardless of what you think of me next, you can never tell anyone a word of what I'm about to say. Got it?"

He gave another easy nod.

She eyed him a beat longer, no burning suspicions creeping in. So, she crossed her legs beneath her and readied to tell her story.

"I've never been camping because I was too busy just trying to survive my childhood." She scowled down at her red-tipped fingers caressing the wool blanket. "There was my mum and her issues, and then there were the years I spent in and out of hospital."

Max shifted in front of her, but she refused to look at him.

"Wait. You were sick?"

She shrugged like what she had to say meant nothing these days, but then she couldn't make eye contact, so maybe that was one massive lie. "Sort of. My dad left us when I was six and my little brother, Clay, was three. He left to be with another woman, and my mother blamed us more than she did herself. And I, being a girl, bore the brunt of that blame. My mother was raised to believe that girls were always the lesser of two options, an expensive burden, so of course she doted on my brother."

Wind howled outside the tent, flapping and pushing the walls in slight arcs toward her. She paused her story to flick her gaze at the rippling fabric, her stomach giving a sick flutter.

"Clay, he got the best of everything, while I was lucky to get whatever was left. I don't recall Mum ever freely giving me a single genuine hug, much less buying me clothes that weren't already well-aged from a second-hand shop. Meanwhile, Clay got all the brand new, branded stuff. And as often as she could, she pitted Clay and I against each other. School grades, popularity, looks, sports... You name it. Everything except chores, which were all mine, because boys don't need to know how to clean a dish or do a load of laundry, right?"

"Freya."

Max's voice dipped, but she frowned, glaring down at her nails again.

"Mum's temper had always been wild and unpredictable, and I'd already learned to moderate my behavior based on what mood she woke up in—play if she was happy, run and hide in a cupboard if she wasn't. And mostly, she wasn't. But something truly broke in her after my dad left. The shame consumed her so much she couldn't even admit to what happened, that he'd found someone else, so she deflected all that anger onto her children. Or should I say, me? Dad's leaving was all my fault."

She took a second to peer up at Max, at the two deep lines scoring the gap between his brows, his stare unwavering. She wanted to crawl forward, to land in his arms, but then she'd have no hope of finishing what she had to say, so she cleared her throat and pressed on.

"I recognized from an early age that Mum was damaged, but after Dad left, it was less about her inherent need to dominate and more about her reports of constant poor health. All she ever talked about to other adults was her doctor's visits and how she was dying. I don't know, maybe that just deflected her having to talk about the divorce. As messed up as our relationship already was, because of my mum's unwillingness to shelter me from her medical stuff, I developed a genuine fear that at any point I could lose the only parent left to me.

"I mean, sure, sometimes we'd get to visit Dad, but still, those years came with the sense that at any moment my mother could die, and my world would come crashing down. I lived on permanent edge. Except back then, I never accounted for how important my dad's occasional presence was. Not until I was ten, and he and his new wife died in a car accident."

Max parted his lips and then closed them again, as if he wanted to say something but thought better of it. She gifted him a few seconds of her direct attention.

"It's okay, you don't have to come up with anything insightful."

She smiled at him, and his shoulders sank by an inch or two, like maybe he appreciated her observation over his struggle to find the right thing to say at times.

"Anyway, after that, the wheels truly did fall off my childhood. Mum knew she had all the power and control over my life, and very little accountability. There'd be few close relatives to interfere or check in with us."

She paused to take a big breath and close her eyes, a dull ache growing in her chest, those old memories pressing on her shoulders. Only the outside river sounds and Max's mere presence brought her any calm.

"I don't understand." His gentle tone cut her like a sharp blade. "What did she do?"

Freya opened her eyes and went back to staring at the blanket, fingertips shifting the tiny, soft fibers while she weighed up how much to reveal.

Whatever she did say wouldn't come easy, and pangs of pain and humiliation clawed at her insides, reminding her of all she'd endured and escaped.

Not that someone with a story like mine ever truly escapes.

There were all the lies she'd been raised to believe. The ones about herself. That she was unlovable and the source of everything bad in her mother's life.

Those lies bubbled up to haunt her, doing their worst on the days she felt her lowest, and sometimes on good days, when a hard-won victory could fill her mouth with bitterness and the dreadful sense that she might one day return to her old hell.

No good experience felt real, not for long, anyway. And the scars she sought to cover sat exposed for all to see.

And then there were the times she wished she had a different story.

That she had a family like Max's.

One with two loving parents and siblings on equal footing.

The kind of family that acknowledged each other's specialness. That each person mattered.

The kind of family that went on camping trips.

She tugged at her black woolen sweater sleeves and pulled them over her hands, releasing those aching thoughts.

"I started getting sick. Just like my mum, but worse." Her tummy churned, maybe a form of muscle memory from her days of unrelenting illness, or maybe the roil of pure shame over how bad things had been, much less having to relive that story now. "I couldn't keep my food down most days, started losing weight. Sometimes I'd throw fevers, and this would go on for weeks and months at a time."

Her focus broke at a small screech coming from outside, perhaps some kind of bush rodent. Max reached out a hand and patted her knee, his thumb stroking warm circles through her cotton leggings.

For the sake of getting on with her story, she decided to let this screech go.

"This all lasted two years, and no one could figure it out. I just kept getting sicker and sicker, and new symptoms would appear. All in all, I looked skeletal and lacked energy, I barely ever made it to school. Not that my absence mattered much. I'd lost all my friends from poor attendance, and as someone entering their teens, the gray and bony look took a sledgehammer to my confidence. I didn't feel attractive. I wasn't social. I was behind academically. Even when there were phases where I'd be fine, I still had nothing and no place I belonged.

"Home was depressing, school was a place to feel stupid, ugly, and lonely. Though strangely enough, during that time, my mum's happiness improved. Clay would be at school, and it would be just me and her at my hospital appointments. She was super doting, and when it came to her, it felt to me like the sun had finally come out from behind a cloud. For that short time, she really seemed to care. I thought that maybe—just maybe—she really did love me."

She gave a tight laugh down toward Max's hand on her knee. "I guess, what with her losing her support payments after Dad's death, only for my illness to gather extra help from charities and government payments for her as my carer, she no longer had to continue her job as a dental assistant. So for that reason alone, I gave her a lot to love."

Her grim smile slipped, and she replaced it with a deep frown. "At one point, I saw her talking to the hospital chaplain. She was dabbing at her eyes with a tissue and making plans for my funeral arrangements. You know, what coffin to pick, which funeral home to use…"

A sharp pain stirred within her, and she snapped her gaze back to Max again, needing to break from that memory, only for his pure physical beauty and undivided attention to rip a hole through her all over again.

"Before I tell you anything more, you should know about my mother's childhood. She grew up in an isolated, rural area during the fifties where the abuse she encountered was easy to hide." She cringed to herself, that same shifting pain in her turning even more distinct. That a child could be born into the life her mother had. "She was beaten regularly, left hungry, her education patchy at best since she'd been mostly taken out of school to work on her parents' farm. Again, because she was a girl, no one saw a point in her having an education. She had eight other siblings, and although she was put to work at an early age, she was also just another mouth to feed.

"I've done a lot of reading up on psychology over the years, trying to understand everything that happened. One thing I've learned is that children's brains can be like cement, and you only have so long before their idea of 'normal' is set forever. Neither of my mother's parents held or kissed her. No one told her she was loved. From the moment she was born, she had no chance. Abuse and neglect were her normal, and her parents slowly but surely destroyed her spirit. I think about that little girl. I think about her a lot. Someone so small and in need of help, only for that help to arrive far too late."

Max's hand tightened around her knee, bringing her attention back to him. His open expression said that he hung on her every word.

"Freya, what are you telling me?"

"That when I say my *grandparents*, I mean the ones who adopted my mother, not my piece-of-shit biological ones who sent her and three other siblings to an orphanage when she was thirteen. That by the time she was adopted, the damage was done. That those same adoptive parents, the ones I consider my real grandparents, were the ones who saved me, too."

Twenty-Two

Freya took a deep inhale and tried to use that breath to cushion the hollow sensation opening up inside her, the fire's strong, smoky scent permeating the tent walls and filling her senses. She wanted to stop talking, to keep the rest of her story to herself, but speaking about her past was too rare and validating, the pressure of what she constantly carried easing a little inside.

"That being said, long before I was born, my grandparents had stepped right out of my mother's life. She'd taken a toll on them too, and they really only managed a few occasional visits, and by occasional, like, every few years. And one of those visits fell around about the time I turned twelve."

She peered down, twisting the blue blanket laid out beneath her, that twisting somehow representative of how she felt about that day; her attempt at distraction not enough to make her forget Max's presence, as though she never needed to see him to feel him nearby.

"I guess they must have taken one look at me in my bed and suspected something I hadn't, because my grandad kept my mum busy in the kitchen, while my grandma talked to me alone in my room. I was old enough to notice the leading questions she kept asking: Whether my mother was giving me anything the doctors didn't know of, whether my mother hit me or had maybe scared me into covering for any lies. At the time, I denied everything because truly I'd never witnessed anything outside of my mother's usual yelling and mean-spiritedness. And again, I got more attention compared to my earlier years, so in a messed-up way, I thought my life had improved."

The muscles in her throat grew thick, and the heavy and familiar sense of shame over that day crept in. How she'd been so protective of her mother. How she'd been annoyed at her grandmother's persistence and what she implied…

"And even if those questions did make me think twice, I'd never known any other kind of love. And though I now know what my mother gave me wasn't actual love, at the time, I loved her fiercely enough to not want to let go of the more even-keeled mother I'd gained while I'd been sick. I simply figured she thrived away from her former job and, as my caregiver, that was what our relationship had needed all along."

"You were like a seed in need of water."

She flicked her gaze up to catch his softened smile, one that bent at the corners, not exactly happy with where this was going, but offering support all the same.

"Your mother essentially left you outside, in need of rain, so of course you drank up whatever she gave you."

She pulled her focus off him and back to the blanket, trying hard not to blink because his words cut her to the core and gathered tears in her eyes. Max Tindall wasn't meant to be insightful, but here he was, absolutely right.

She'd so wanted to believe her mother's heart had changed. That she'd really come to love and care for her daughter. That her sole motivation hadn't been the sympathy and attention she received as the mother of a seriously sick child.

But sympathy and attention *were* love to her mother, a woman who'd received neither, as well as no love.

And while a young Freya had thought her days of being ignored and discarded had ended, that belief had proved near fatally wrong.

"Anyway." She cleared her throat, wanting to get through her story, somehow feeling lighter and more damaged at the same time. "For the next two weeks, I made sure not to eat the food my mum prepared for me. I snacked on crackers hidden at the back of my wardrobe and snuck raw vegetables from the fridge into my room. I ate all those when she wasn't looking. Of the food she did prepare, I'd just pretend to feel too sick to eat, or I'd only take meals in my room where I could later flush them down the toilet under the guise of having thrown up. Some meals I secretly buried at the bottom of our trash can."

A jagged laugh broke from her lips. "I started to improve after the first week, and by the second week I felt pretty much normal, all while I pretended to feel as bad as ever. And then one Wednesday, my mum left for her usual trip to take Clay to school, her weekly shopping trip always after that. I knew she'd be gone for a while and searched the house until I found a mortar and pestle tucked in the back of a top kitchen cupboard. Nestled in the bowl was a blister-pack still half-full of pills."

The hard muscle over Max's cheekbones fell, and his posture deflated right along with them. "Freya. She was poisoning you? I can't—"

Believe it?

She held up a hand, shaking her head. "Please, I know, but let me finish. This story gets worse before it gets better."

Despite the forewarning, she still didn't want his sympathy. Still felt small and insignificant every time that day entered her mind.

She'd been a child. One who hadn't known better, and still, she felt shame.

"I didn't see her walk in behind me. I was too busy reading the pill packet, trying so hard to memorize the bloody long name, when the stool I was standing on gave way beneath me. Well, 'gave way' isn't the right term, more like my mum kicked the stool out from under my feet."

She lifted her hand and rubbed a spot within her hair, where the ancient tile counter had cleaved into her head a couple of inches from her hairline.

"I lay on the ground, blood gushing from my head, but she didn't care. Every lie she'd sold to the world about my illness had just unraveled. I'd ruined that lie for her, and so she flew into an intense rage. She beat me with closed fists while I was down, blows landing on my ribs and tummy, like even in her rage she knew not to leave injuries in any visible areas. I tried to curl into a ball, to make myself small. I was so stunned, and I struggled to breathe. I couldn't even find the space to cry."

A tremor took over her hand, and not from the cold, though she pressed her fingertips to her cheek so she might ease the shaking.

"She… she just kept yelling about how I'd ruined everything. How I'd destroyed her life just by being born. I was nothing to her but the money my fake illness brought in. Her words and her rage hurt more than the blows. That rage terrified me, and I can still remember the foam forming at the corners of her mouth as she yelled and yelled."

Freya stopped to catch her breath, to allow a moment for those last words to sink in. *Again.*

"I thought she'd kill me."

"Freya. Take another second." Max scrambled forward, pausing a moment to grab a flask of water from beside the bed, which he then unscrewed and extended her way. "Here, drink."

She accepted the flask and sipped at the cool water, the strain in her body lightening if only just a little. Her gaze fell to Max, and the painful shiver playing havoc with her nerves turned to a warm and settled appreciation.

"Are you okay to continue?" His pinched gaze skated over her face, cheeks slack in clear concern. "You can stop if this is too much."

He reached out, as if about to cup her cheek; but she caught his hand, having reached the limit of sweet gestures she could take right now.

"Just as quickly as my mother had flipped into a rage, she stopped and fell to her knees on the floor before me. She started shaking her head over and over, rambling and rationalizing everything she'd just done. How seeing me up on the stool had scared her. How now I had a choice. I could destroy our family, destroy the money I brought in, or I could continue to play along, and everything could go on as normal.

"She stared at me, the pill packet in her hand, and that's when an explosion went off where my heart should have been. Like something finally broke inside. Something I'd spent years attempting to hold together. I started sobbing then, so hard, I couldn't stop. The jerking added more pain to my already bruised ribs, and the tears fell so fat and fast down my cheeks, watery pools formed on the beige linoleum floor. It was this suspended moment of just her and me, and of course, the choice she expected me to make."

Twenty-Three

Freya couldn't blame Max for the ashen hue overrunning his cheeks, his pupils wide like he absorbed every word but struggled to believe any of it. She wasn't the kind to wear her heart on her sleeve—had built her life around fun and quirkiness—on being the epitome of lavish femininity and independence with nothing dry or serious to drag her down. So of course, her grim confession didn't fit with the woman he knew.

The rustle of leaves rushed from outside the tent, the tall and spindly mountain ash gumtrees emitting their dark scent, while cicadas chirped in all directions.

She gave a shrug and recalled her mother sitting across from her in that kitchen, her hard stare cold, unmoving, and demanding an answer —Freya could keep the pills and her guaranteed sickness a secret, or rat her mother out and tear her family apart, along with her mother's happiness.

Freya squeezed her fingers around Max's larger palm and forced herself to maintain eye contact, once more owning the decision she'd made all those years ago. "I chose the pills."

Max sucked in a low breath, his pale cheeks somehow paling even more.

She'd given the answer he didn't want, but it was her truth, and since she still sat here alive and well, her story clearly wasn't over.

He scrubbed a hand over his face. "I'm not sure I want to hear what happens next, but I know I need to, anyway."

She frowned and nodded. Perhaps more than his desire to know what happened, she wanted to finish what she'd started.

"Aside from dealing with the wound on my head and the agony from the beating, Mum made me take some pills. The vomiting and weakness started within the hour, and not long after that, I couldn't stay upright. So, she called an ambulance, and I lay on the couch while we waited. The whole time, she paced the living room, rambling about the story we'd use to explain my cuts and bruises—something about me feeling sick and fainting and falling down some stairs. Our house didn't have any stairs, but whatever, right?"

She gave a wobbly laugh, but Max just blinked, seemingly frozen in a state of shock. She went on, hoping to put him out of his misery.

"Anyway, at some point she looked at me with this flat stare and demanded I remember how many pills she'd given me. I didn't know. I'd numbly swallowed whatever she'd passed me. It was then she mumbled something about the pills not usually working so quickly, and maybe she'd given me too many."

Max's jaw dropped open, and his hand tightened around hers. She couldn't tell if he offered support or needed it.

Her hand clenched his right back, the action also helping to keep her from touching the small scar near her hairline again. A scar almost no one ever noticed since she covered it with her thick hair and signature headbands. Occasionally, she'd had to answer to those who did notice, always providing a fake story about needing surgery as a child.

But even now, the hot prickling through her body and sinking in her belly reminded her she'd never forget the moment she thought her life really over.

Sure, with her years of precarious health, there'd been many such moments. But it was one thing to face death at the hands of a slow and nondiscriminatory illness, and another at the hands of the woman who'd brought her into the world in the first place.

Mothers were meant to protect and nurture. To love without condition. *Not Freya's.* Her twelve-year-old self had just registered that her mother had never once loved her.

And that's when she came to think of her mum as less "Mum" and more "Kerry". Just a woman. Not a mother. And a fundamentally broken woman at that. Irreparably damaged. Even though Freya would spend years hoping that one day, maybe, just maybe, her mother would develop the ability to care. To love.

That day, watching Kerry rant and pace, Freya made her first ever truly selfish decision. *She would save herself.*

"The doctors and nurses were waiting for us when we got to the hospital. A few already knew me from all my past visits, so soon enough, I had my own bay in the pediatrics emergency ward, my mum glued to my side giving her award-winning rendition of a devastated mother. Of course, she was really just following to make sure I played along."

Freya pulled her hand from Max's and wrapped her arms around her waist, missing his touch, but needing space to get out the rest of what she had to say.

"I peered up at her, weak and in excruciating pain, and she had the balls to say, 'You'll be okay, darling. Mummy will make sure you'll be okay.' And something about that made me so angry, that I might die without anyone knowing what had really happened, that I could never rely on her telling the truth. I started to imagine my funeral and my mother using my death to garner more attention. She'd turn my memory into a farce. I had never been the rebellious type, always sweet and stupidly trusting, but right then I knew, if nothing else, I couldn't give her that final win."

Max's brows rose and a small light entered his expression. "So, you outed her?"

"My mum was busy filling in forms in the waiting area just outside my bay. A nurse I'd met before held my hand, trying to attach some kind of monitor, and I just came right out and whispered, 'Keep my mum away. She's poisoning me. This whole time she's been poisoning me.' I remember the pause, the way the nurse's expression turned slack. I hoped she'd believe me; that she'd understand. That she'd help. My whole life up until then had involved no one caring enough to make any real difference to my shitty existence."

She paused and gripped her hands around her ribcage even tighter, holding back a swell of emotion, one that took up space in her chest and threatened to break out in the form of an untamed cry.

"But this one time, this one time when I needed it most, that nurse squeezed my hand and gave me the softest smile, one that said she would keep me safe."

Her eyes prickled now, and she forced a deep inhalation, her breath shaky and undoubtedly betraying fragility. That nurse had cared enough to kick-start the beginning of Freya's life free from abuse.

"Everything happened so quickly after that. The nurse whispered something to another nurse, who went on to keep my mother busy until security, and then the police, came to take her away. At some point that same day, she confessed to what she'd given me. I later learned the police had threatened to add a murder charge to her list of offenses if I didn't live. I've had lots of therapy since, but one thing that helps is to think of all the people who gathered around me that day, the hospital staff, police. When I eventually recovered, my grandparents took in me and my brother. We didn't have to go into the system."

"And what happened to your mother?"

"She was given a diagnosis of what used to be called *Munchausen by Proxy*, likely influenced by her troubled childhood. The newer name for her condition is now *Factitious Disorder Imposed Upon Another*, but me, I prefer to call it medical child abuse."

"And did she go to prison for what she did?"

"No." She shook her head, Max's shoulders sinking like that wasn't the answer he wanted. "She avoided the maximum prison term in exchange for four years of good behavior and extensive psychological treatments."

The bulk of her story now told, for the longest time, Max merely stared at her, his face mostly still, as though he took time to process everything she'd said. To be fair, she'd shared one hell of a long and harrowing story.

He frowned, his gaze dipping to her hands still around her waist. "Did you ever see your mum again after that?"

She compressed one corner of her lip and gave a small shake of her head. "Her contact with us after that was heavily supervised and mostly only via phone. After the first six months, I guess the novelty wore off, and she'd maybe call once a year."

He nodded, his energy in the tent's close confines so still and quiet. "I can't imagine what living out that childhood must have been like for you, much less sharing it again now. Thank you."

"I don't usually like to tell anyone." The whispered admission slipped free without much thought, and she slumped back, hands releasing from around her. "Sometimes I'm not all that sure if the benefit of talking is worth the cost of dredging up those memories. I was taught I was the problem. My dad left. My mum was a nightmare. I spent years out of touch with my peers, wasting away in my sick bed. I believed there had to be something I couldn't see, something intrinsically wrong with me. Something to make me deserving of the hell I lived. I thought of myself as truly unlovable. And telling others, having them reject me because of my past, only made that unlovability more real."

"Please tell me you don't believe that any more."

She frowned down at her lap. How to explain?

She'd done all the work she possibly could, attended countless mental health appointments and improved greatly, but in the real world, not all honesty was rewarded with kindness. Rejection was a punishment unto itself. One that ingrained the hurtful things she'd been raised to believe.

"I *used* to tell people." She refocused on Max's pinched and imploring stare, feeling impossibly alone sitting within touching distance of him, fighting a desire to lean in and curl up in his arms. "I haven't for years, not since I learned that some less-than-brilliant people will use my past against me. I'd try to bring up an issue I had with them, and they'd use my trauma to label me oversensitive, like my past made me imagine problems that didn't exist, when I was really just asking for some basic respect."

The base of her throat swelled and turned her voice into a rough whisper. "Or worse, when people assume survivors of abuse are forever doomed to become abusers themselves, as if all the hard work I put in counted for nothing. Sometimes the unpredictable reactions just aren't worth getting into it with others, you know?"

Max's beautiful blue stare held hers for a while, and the strain across his face slipped away. He sat with his hand draped over his bent knee, those long fingertips pointed to the ground. "And why are you going there with me?"

His question sent an electrified shock through her veins, maybe because her "going there with him" surprised her, too.

Or maybe she'd hoped to get through this lengthy talk without analyzing her motivations at all.

She bent her head and took a few seconds for herself. As much as she wanted to think of Max as perfect, as much as she wanted to believe his life had thus far been immaculate and easy, that wasn't true.

She saw his everyday self-criticism, his struggle to figure out what exactly made him so passive, and his attempts to pull himself from the consequences of his passivity. She'd also witnessed others discard him and the resulting disappointment.

One key attribute shone above all else.

The *real* reason she liked having him around and why she'd just "gone there" with him.

"Because as much as you think you're a screwup"—a wobbly smile tugged at her lips, and the rigid strain pulling at her chest ebbed to a melting, warm sensation, one that brushed away her ability to restrain any praise—"you're not mean, Max. There's not a mean bone in your body, and to me, that's worth so much more than anything else not working in your life."

Twenty~Four

MAX CLAMPED HIS TEETH TOGETHER, fighting his jaw's instinctive need to drop open. Meanwhile, Freya's lips parted, as though she too hadn't expected to say those words.

Her comment about him not having a mean bone in his body stood out as the most significant thing he'd heard about himself in as long as he could remember. The first compliment he sort of believed, one that acknowledged something inherent to his personality, transcending his money, reputation, and his current problems.

What she offered was a raft he could cling to. His first taste of *purpose.*

The only problem? He wasn't all that used to people saying nice things about him. At least, not things that weren't about his looks or his money, both of which he'd done nothing to earn.

He took in the details of Freya's golden-brown eyes, now a burnt treacle color against the lantern's dim light. Her kind words echoed in his head, and the one truth he'd held onto throughout her tragic story fell from him.

"I don't know how anyone could be mean to you."

Her muscles pulled taut for a few seconds, before falling slack, her unblinking stare pinned on him in stunned silence, before a sharp wave of broken laughter escaped her.

She turned from him, seeming to hide from his scrutiny, her flaxen curls obscuring whatever expression marked her face.

A dull ache grew low in his stomach, an ache that spelled hope over pain, suggesting he might have inadvertently reciprocated her gift of saying something she needed to hear, even if she too didn't know how to handle it.

"Thank you." She returned her attention to him, her voice a husky whisper, the whites of her eyes pink-tinged, and her lips bent in a frown, despite her words of gratitude. "The thing about abuse is, it doesn't end when the abuser leaves your life. That's just the start, and there are constant small reminders. Someone says something that's innocent to them but painful for you, or maybe an interaction doesn't go so well and scrubs at your damaged self-worth like a new abrasion over an old scar. And sometimes, even happy moments are drowned under a sense of looming dread."

Her fine-boned hand lay flat atop the dark blue blanket, her painted nails glinting in a contradictory happy shade of red.

He shifted forward and dared to hold her hand again, not all that sure if he offered comfort to himself or to her, only that his awe over her personal strength held him trapped.

"Do you mind if I ask you something else?" He gave an easy smile, hoping to lighten the mood and wanting to help her at the same time. Even if she did seem more than perfectly capable of helping herself. Even if he doubted his own level of grit to handle the intensity this woman carried with her, day in and day out. "I have a hunch, though my hunches do have a reputation of being way off target."

Not only that, he also had a justified reputation for screwing up important conversations. But she'd trusted him and voiced her struggle to talk about her ordeal, and he wanted to offer her some kind relief for sharing her story. He rubbed his thumb over the back of her hand, savoring the silkiness, until she gave a quick nod.

"That sense of looming dread you mentioned"—the muscles around his throat clenched, but he pressed on all the same—"has that been hanging around a lot lately? Is that why this whole camping trip has you spooked?"

Her gaze dropped from his. "Yeah. I guess."

"Has something happened?" He thought back to the first night she'd approached him. "Was it that creeper we dodged outside the bar? Has that experience set you off, maybe?"

"No. At least, I don't think so." She shook her head. "Though maybe at any other time he might have, this has more to do with that morning after you first came to my house. That call I got before I sent you away, was about my mum. She's sick. Dying actually. And I'm the one in charge of tying up all her loose ends."

"You still speak to your mother?"

"No, not really." She released a sigh and pushed her hair from her face, lifting her posture as she did so. "I've tried for a different outcome with her over the years, but each time, it's like holding my hand over an open flame and expecting it not to burn. I know this doesn't make much sense to most people, but I have a lot of guilt about escaping and taking my brother with me. About being the one who well and truly busted our family up. About surviving. About having a better life than her and Clay. I don't want to feel that way, but I do. Mum knows this, and she loves to poke at my guilt, laying the criticisms thick every chance she gets."

His brow turned heavy, and he frowned at Freya. "You didn't 'bust your family up'. *She* did."

Freya rubbed her palm over her forehead and squeezed her eyes shut. "I know. I know. There's not a lot that's logical about this. My only two comforts are that I'm not the only child of abuse to grow up confused, and at least my mum won't be around too much longer to continue this vicious cycle."

He waited until her attention returned to him. "I'm trying to understand. Why put yourself through it all again?"

"Because what was done to her was, to a different extent, done to me and because of that…" She rolled her eyes, her expression more sad than sarcastic. "I understand her."

He wanted to ask her to explain further, though he already had a small hint of what she referred to. So, he stayed quiet, allowing room for her to offer what she wished.

Her attention stayed on him for a beat longer, and she dropped a heavy sigh, shifting in her spot, as if to get comfortable to unleash her reasoning.

"Look, it's the irony of abuse, okay? The crushing of another person's spirit until they believe all the things the abuser imparts. No matter what age or background, no one is immune, as much as some of us would like to believe we are. Manipulation is what my mother does best, what she was inadvertently programmed to do to survive. So was I. Though maybe I turned out differently because I had access to people outside of my messed-up family, at school and in the hospital. I had glimpses of what 'normal' meant away from hearing I was *less*. Less than my brother. Less than my peers. Worth no more than a fortnightly government payment and the attention my mother could get from parading my misery. And want to know the most fucked up thing about all of that?"

She lifted a brow, as if assessing his focus, before her expression faltered and crumbled altogether. "An abused child will love their parents despite the abuse. Any hate is turned in on themselves. The abuse is all their fault. They are not good enough for kindness and love. And those beliefs filled my mum's childhood. They're what she passed on to me. She took her hurt and hurt me, all the while believing my life was an improvement on what she'd had.

"I've experienced first-hand how someone like her is created. And I sit somewhere between wanting to punish her for what she did, and acknowledging she has a mental illness she didn't ask for. Even if it sounds to others like I'm making excuses. Where I sit is my choice. What I know for certain is, she doesn't know any other way, and maybe, the only difference between us is that her experience broke her and mine didn't."

Max's heartbeat plodded under the weight of his inability to know what to do with her words; meanwhile, the muscles over her face hardened, and she spoke again. "Max, unless you've lived this for yourself, you really can't know."

His stomach sank, and the dark truth of that statement pulled him under, a genuine ache surrounding his heart.

He *didn't* know. Which made him want to beat his chest and promise to strip away the layers of confusion and contradiction blanketing this otherwise steadfast woman. To save her.

But she wouldn't want that, would she?

To have someone take on her burdens. To surrender her control.

The least he could do was check she'd be okay.

He pressed on a strained smile and lowered his voice, hoping his tone would match the level of care she deserved. "Have you got anyone looking after you while all of this is happening?"

She remained silent for a while, her focus landing on some far-off point beyond the tent's close confines. "My best friend Gideon knows, but I don't need anyone looking after me. It's not fair to lump my wellbeing onto my friends when I can pay a professional to listen to me if I'm feeling overwhelmed. To be honest, therapy has been the single most useful thing I learned to lean on after they first took me from my mother. I'm lucky to have access to basic mental health care." Her gaze landed on him again, and she gave a light smile. "I'm at a point now where I think I can compartmentalize my relationship with her and dust off any venom she spits my way during the short moments I have to see her."

And still, in spite of her statement, the precariousness of her situation with her mother had his spine stiffening. Like one misdirected push would send that whole relationship tumbling down, and more alarmingly, taking Freya's wellbeing with it.

He schooled his face as much as he could, working hard not to betray skepticism over whether she truly believed even half of what she said. Could she hear the level of mental gymnastics she performed in order to justify her contact with her mother?

Then again, she *had* explained this was one of those things only someone on the inside could understand. As much as he wanted to jump to her defense, he most definitely wasn't "on the inside" when it came to Freya or her past.

"You're right." He took a steadying breath, resigned to giving her the next best thing he could offer outside of his unwanted advice. "It's no one's place to tell you how to handle this, but if you do need someone to look out for you, to help you in any way, you can count on me."

Her stare burrowed into him, her lips curling slightly at the corners. "And who's looking out for you, Max?"

"What do you mean?"

"I mean, you've got a heck of a lot happening in your life, too, and I don't see many people jumping in to help."

He let go of her hand and slumped back, quashing a hot swell of anger over the truth in her observation.

"The problem is, I've had too many people looking out for me, which is ironically why some of the main players in my life have stepped back."

"No person is an island though, right?" Her stare held firmer than ever, as though she analyzed his every nuance, bringing a wave of electricity to his skin. "You need *someone*."

He scoffed, dipping his chin in an expression he hoped denoted sarcasm. "Are you volunteering?"

She threw back her head and gave her first genuine laugh in way too long, the throaty richness bringing levity to his dampened spirits. "Definitely not, but maybe the *real* problem with you is that you've had people helping in the wrong way."

It was his turn to laugh now, though the sound had a decidedly taut delivery. "And you've burned way too much energy analyzing what's *wrong* with me."

Despite his half-hearted jab, her eyes glittered with good humor— the sort of humor that came from years of working at a bar and learning not to take people's shit-talking too seriously. To that extent, maybe he did need to believe her when she said she knew how to compartmentalize her dealings with her mother.

"Don't flatter yourself. I'm just good at reading people."

He smiled, not for a second doubting her claim.

Unlike him, this woman had the art of *"knowing thy self"* down to a precise skill. "Is that your way of saying you have psychic powers? Because *that* would be very useful to my situation right about now."

Her shoulders shook with a chuckle. "Yeah, I wish. I'd use those powers on my own problems first."

"You sure? Because if you could just slip me this week's lottery numbers before I drop you off tomorrow…"

She laughed again, deeper now, and grabbed a pillow from atop the camping mattress, throwing it at him.

"God, I'm exhausted." She lay down, soon tucking the pillow she hadn't thrown under her head. "We've been talking forever, and I feel like my eyes are going to fall out."

He opened his mouth, meaning to point out how her eyes dangling from their sockets wouldn't exactly be her most attractive look, that she was the reason they'd been talking forever. But then she peered over and patted the empty spot on the bed beside her, drying his words.

He crawled on over, the thrown pillow in his hand. He settled next to her, and she shifted closer, tucking herself against him so that her head rested on his shoulder.

In that moment, with the smallest hint of humor-induced tears in the corners of her eyes, and in the wake of her painfully honest story, something within his world stopped.

He took a minute to figure out what.

Maybe it was the constant whirring sense he might get things wrong.

Maybe it was the nonstop race of his heart whenever this woman was close.

Or maybe the never-ending knowledge she had her life so much more together than him.

He could never hope to measure up, but in that brief second, he also knew one undeniable fact. He'd succeeded at *something*. For one fleeting moment, he'd made her feel better, been someone she trusted enough to confide in. Added value to her life.

She blinked up at him and pressed her palm flat to his chest as though she heard every one of his thoughts and wanted to reply.

"You have something missing in here, Max. Most people have figured that part out. But your unease, it didn't start in your heart. It only exists because there's something off-kilter in your head."

As much as he wanted to pry his eyes from her, to rein in his wild thundering pulse, his voice was what ultimately ran from him in a raspy and way too serious tone. "So, you're saying I'm not right in the head?"

"Your head works fine, Max, or at least your brain does, and though you seem to have decided otherwise, you're not inherently lazy. What I mean is, there's a sadness buried inside you, and until you figure out where that sadness comes from, you won't get rid of that lost feeling."

His focus lingered on the finer details of her small and alluring lips. She was probably right about his buried sadness and how it was the root to all his issues, but as much as he should have zoomed in on her big reveal, his mind snagged on something else entirely.

On just how much she recognized parts of him no one else did.

"I'm really lucky to have met you." His voice came out strong and way more certain than he expected, maybe because he meant every word.

She was his silver lining in what remained an extra-horrid period in his life.

He crossed an arm over his body and ran the pad of his thumb over her cheekbone, his forefinger brushing away one of her silken ringlets. "Up until now, I've been plodding through life, but you're one of the few people to demand I lift my game without being condescending. Somehow, your approach makes me want to do better, Freya. It's like you know me better than I know myself."

Her gaze dipped to his collarbone, and a slow smile crept across her face. "Maybe that's because we share something in common. We're both stuck in less-than-perfect situations right now."

He kept stroking her cheek, admiring the way the lantern's warm-yellow glow added extra radiance to her skin. "I don't need my life to be perfect to know we might just be perfect for each other."

"Max..." She all but whispered his name, and her attention flicked back to him. "This is what I meant about certain conversations changing everything. You promised me that wouldn't happen."

His lip tugged at one corner, and he gave what was likely a bitter, lopsided smile. Though his heart shrank from her rebuff, the dull pain in his chest wasn't enough to keep him from wanting to prove her wrong.

Besides, the intimacy in this tent had him feeling bold.

"What you told me about your past hasn't changed *everything* for me, it only changes how much I know about you. Your past doesn't change what I like about you most, which is who you are right *now*. I like your laugh. The way you don't make excuses for anyone, especially me. How, when I stuff up, your jaw gets all stiff, like you want to throw me into heavy traffic, even though you still give me a chance to get things right the next time."

She gave him a sidelong glare, new light entering her eyes, like maybe he'd given her a pleasant surprise.

He took her new lightness as a chance to move his fingers down her face, to that stubborn jawline of hers. The one that spoke volumes of what went on in her head.

"You had no reason to give me a job at The Ruby Room, but you did anyway. You helped me because you knew I needed help. And for some reason, you accept me as the lolloping fool that I am."

He gave a soft chuckle, hoping to provide at least a glimpse of what he saw every time he spent time with her. "I don't think you appreciate how rare your brand of acceptance is, or how much it means to me. What's more amazing is how you continued to accept me after you learned I was broke, even though you barely knew me. I'm not the brightest man ever; I know you could do better than me, I get it. But I am smart enough to acknowledge my gratitude for you. I'll *always* be thankful for you, Freya. I'll never forget how, when my life turned into a steaming mess, you were the one who cared enough to be there for me."

Twenty-Five

BY THE TIME Freya crawled from the tent the next morning, the sun and azure sky hit her with a glare that stung her eyes. She squinted at a frying pan beside the newly re-built fire, the savory scent of fresh cooked bacon and eggs being what had pulled her from the tent in the first place.

She perched on a toppled log also beside the fire; wary over being alone with no sign of Max nearby.

A high-pitched screech came from high up in the trees. Try as she did, she couldn't see much, though she knew enough to recognize that the call belonged to a cockatoo.

Then again, bugger the bird, all she really wanted was Max.

Her heartbeat picked up pace, and she peered behind her, shrinking at the idea of having to venture too far from the tent in search of him. A loud snap came from up ahead, and she flinched, her startled focus landing on an overgrown clump of trees.

"Good sleep?"

Max stepped out of the clump.

The snapping sound must have been him treading on a fallen branch.

She swore under her breath and stiffened her expression, wanting to hide any not-too-happy glower. Then again, she could at least be grateful that Max stood before her and not some giant, murderous kangaroo.

She gave him a weak nod and tried to forget how her crippling fear last night had led to an outpouring of her life story, followed by hours of fitful sleep in his arms. No sex required, no need to prove there was nothing wrong with her in light of her past. All this, despite previous bad experiences divulging to others, much less deep conversations generally being off-limits in casual relationships such as this one.

Stop it! He's just a nice guy, and we had a nice conversation. It's no big deal.

Right. Maybe that screaming voice in her head had a point. Best not to overthink this.

He bent to the fire and went about serving bacon and eggs on a white, tin plate. "I made food for you. It's still warm."

Her stomach churned in spite of her hunger, the day's gathering heat not enough to keep her from tugging her khaki jacket closed over her chest. Even as she reached for the plate, she pressed her tongue to the roof of her mouth, stemming a new rise of emotion.

"Thank you." She cleared her throat, refusing to look directly at him. "My first ever fire-cooked breakfast."

And he'd let her sleep in. Hadn't prodded her awake so he could get some early morning attention. He'd merely woken when he wanted to, and made food.

Simple.

But she wasn't used to simple.

She took a nearby fork and began picking at her breakfast, her thoughts nagging her to hurry up and eat so they could end this whole camping thing and go home.

Maybe she'd been wrong to share so much of herself.

Maybe she'd ruined the one good thing they had going for them, casual sex with no touchy-feely emotions swirling in-between.

Besides, he might have handled her story well enough last night, but Max still had so much soul-searching to do. It wasn't right for her to stick him with a potential sense of duty to stand by her.

Maybe his words of adoration last night only supported her idea he might be needlessly attached.

Don't lie. I'm scared he'll hate what he sees and then abandon or control me, just like the others… mother, father, pretty much every boyfriend…

She shoved a piece of bacon into her mouth and chewed with way too much enthusiasm. Max sat on the log beside her, elbows resting on his knees and his attention burning into the side of her face from her periphery.

His stare made her skin sting and her mind race. *What was he thinking?* He liked to play the fool, but there was a certain intuition there, one not even he seemed to know he possessed.

"I got a bit bored waiting for you to wake up." She turned at his voice, one corner of his lip hiked in a bashful grimace. "So, I made you something."

She tried not to choke. "The food wasn't enough?"

He chuckled and reached behind him, pulling out a bundle of brown twigs and white twine, his forefinger hooking on a loop, before the whole bundle fell and dangled from his fingertip.

The crisscross of knots and twigs resembled a five-pointed star.

A tight giggle broke free, and she extended a hand to tap the star so it spun in the air in front of her. "Thank you. I can hang it on my front door to ward off evil spirits."

And still, there was something so childlike about his gesture, which only added to the guilt already pressing on her ribcage.

"I was aiming for a Christmas tree ornament." Max's wonky smile grew. "But whatever works for you."

He handed the star over, and to her surprise, she clutched the bundle of sticks against her unnecessary jacket.

His gaze lingered on her hand for a moment too long, and a flood of conflicted emotions grew within her. She turned her attention to the campfire, the lack of new wood reducing the whole thing to little more than a pile of hot glowing embers.

"When do we head home?" She pressed her lips together, regretting the question.

"I thought we'd go for a walk first."

"I know you're Mr. Fitness and all"—she gave a light-hearted shrug, hoping to dampen his pain—"but I actually enjoy doing nothing on my days off. I'll pass on the walk."

"Okay, well, we could just pull out a blanket and spend some quiet time by the river." He jutted his chin toward the tent. "I noticed you brought a book with you. Why not kick back and make the most of being out in nature?"

She stared at the embers backed by a tranquil bush and the river, and tried to remember the last time she'd just "kicked back".

With all the chaos of festival planning, her mum on her death bed, and whatever the heck this thing was with Max, maybe delaying her re-entry into the real world wasn't such a bad idea.

"And if I were to pull up a blanket and read my book"—she sent a playful scowl his way—"can you promise there won't be any overly friendly snakes trying to cuddle up to me?"

"Do I count as a snake?"

"Hey." She kicked a plume of dry dirt his way. "I'm serious here, I need to know I won't become some creature's new chew toy."

He gave a sly grin, his crystalline eyes sending sparks across the space that illuminated her grim mood. "I don't know how Australian snakes select their chew toys, so I can't promise anything, but if it'll make you feel better, I'm happy to keep an eye out while you get a few pages in."

"I can live with that." She shifted her plate off her lap and placed it on the ground, before dusting her hands against the rough spun denim of her jeans.

"Good." Max stood and headed toward the tent. "In the meantime, I'll try not to get in the way of your time with 'Taming Mister Trouble'."

She sputtered and coughed, pounding a closed fist at her chest.

"Jesus… Max." She coughed again, pain shooting through the base of her throat. "You've been gawking at my books?"

"Just one book." He held the tent flap open and laughed, deep wrinkles scoring the corners of his eyes, which only served to make him even more annoyingly attractive, despite his mocking. "Have you seen the cover? Abs galore and the guy's zipper is wide open. There's no way I wouldn't have noticed that."

Her belly shook with new laughter, her next words hard to form. "Screw you. Why are you checking out some guy's abs and open zipper, anyway?"

She picked up a handful of dirt and tossed it at him. He shielded his eyes with his forearm, then disappeared into the tent, his laughter still painfully clear even from inside.

"My masculinity isn't so weak that I can't acknowledge a fit-looking dude when I see one." He stepped out, the blue blanket from last night tucked under his armpit. "Actually, I'm so confident with my masculine prowess, I'd be happy to borrow the book from you when you're done."

She fisted another hunk of dirt and threw it at his back. He hunched, laughing again and deflecting the small explosion of dust and tiny stones.

"Leave the blanket. I'll set up for myself. Just go. I'm banishing you to the tent."

"But you need me to ward away the bitey snakes, remember?"

She shook her head in a slow and calculating way. "Not if you're going to shame my reading choices."

"Actually, I love your reading choices, especially if they mean changing your mind about heading home."

His attention lingered on her again, but she couldn't for the life of her figure out why.

Or maybe she just didn't want to.

The heavy silence following all that laughter, the pointed way his pupils narrowed and trained on her, held a certain grave significance that caused her heart genuine pain.

He turned away and spread the blanket out on the ground, soon abandoning it and taking himself to the riverside. Meanwhile, her mind worked over what had just happened.

Laughing with him had been so easy.

And his jokes at her expense didn't sting like the backhanded criticisms her mother, or any other man she'd dated, flung her way.

Maybe some of those criticisms had been her fault. Maybe she had a broken barometer for sensing who was good and who would hurt her, so she'd made a few misjudgments when it came to picking who she allowed in her life. Either way, she'd come to a point where she'd given up. On everyone. Except the couple of people who'd proven time and time again they wouldn't hurt her.

And now there was Max.

With his jokes about her and her reading material, his kindness and gratitude over the chances she'd given him, the fact they could talk, and that their times together were always just plain fun.

She rubbed the heel of her hand over her sternum, embracing the dull ache, as she tried to massage hard at a niggling unease.

The truth skirted the edge of her mind. Even as she got up and went into the tent in search of her book. Even as she found her book and stepped back outside, settling down on the blanket, the bright day failing to offer any extra comfort.

If anything, the sight of Max standing with his back to her—a giant gray gumtree to his left and the brown rushing river ahead, meters from his feet—only increased the tight sensation deep within her gut.

She couldn't just sit here. Couldn't ignore what was happening to her. So, she stood, the thick, dry tall-grass crunching under her feet while she trudged toward him.

Honestly, she should have just sat her ass back down on the blanket and opened her stupid book, but she moved forward all the same. At least until he spun around and a wide silence stretched between them.

"There's more to us, isn't there?" She jolted at her own words and prepared to deliver an unequivocal denial of what she'd just said, only to snap her mouth shut because she simply couldn't do it. *Not to him.* Not to a man who'd only ever worn his heart on his sleeve.

A muscle twitched at his jaw. On any other man the reaction might have intimidated, but on Max it only gave insight into the raw emotions circling within him. "And you don't like that, do you?"

Once again, she was incapable of lying, so she did the only thing she could do and gave a tiny nod. "Neither of us are in the right place."

"I know."

She allowed the silence to take over once again. He advanced, bringing his body mere inches from hers. "I just want our time together. That's enough for me."

He lashed out a hand and pulled her to him. Before she knew what was happening, his lips met hers. He unleashed on her a lingering, sweet kiss, so slow and gentle, he made it impossible to miss the suggestion of things she'd always figured weren't for her.

What it would be to have someone fall for her. Really fall for her.

To have them consumed with her every detail, and her with his…

A small chuckle worked past her lips, and she broke loose of his hold, mostly because she refused to fall for her ridiculous thoughts.

A shadow of a smile drew at Max's lips, and his eyes glinted with the welcome return of his trademark mischief. "Can Mister Trouble do that?"

She gave a small laugh and shook her head. "Not even close."

His eyes glinted again, this time with seemingly genuine pride.

"Come with me then." He slid his palm down her arm and hooked his fingers with hers. "Reading is cancelled. I'm giving you a few new positive associations with tents."

Max steered Luke's four-wheel drive off the country road and into the heavy flow of suburban traffic, Freya silent in the passenger seat beside him, her attention lost somewhere through her rain-covered window.

He depressed his foot onto the accelerator, the car picking up speed on the wet road and keeping up with the other vehicles all around, his mind still toying with his time alone with her in the bush.

He frowned at her, and then refocused on the road. "What are you thinking?"

Personally, all he could think about was her tragic childhood and the sometimes confused, sometimes broken, sometimes overwhelmed looks she kept giving him all this morning.

He'd never been great at reading a room, but he sensed he'd gotten closer to her now than before they'd left for Roseford.

She gave him an easy smile, appearing totally relaxed and content, while he had to remind himself to keep watching the road.

"Actually, I was just wondering if we could go camping together again sometime. It's a pity the rain rolled in and forced us home early."

He laughed, chancing another quick glance her way. "Really? I could have sworn you were ready to bounce out of Roseford the moment you opened your eyes this morning."

What changed?

With the heavy pounding of rain on the car's windscreen, he wrung his hands over the leather steering wheel, waiting for her to say that *he* was the reason for her shifted opinions on camping. That the time with him meant something to her. That he stood out from any other man she'd ever dated, even if she insisted that this thing between them remained temporary.

He thought back to that first night he'd worked at The Ruby Room and the man who'd been holding Freya…

Oh hell, what if I'm still not the only one?

His nostrils flared. He tried not to glare at the road, even if his fingers hurt from clutching the steering wheel, and he battled against emotions he wished didn't exist. *Envy. Entitlement. Misery.*

"Max?"

He didn't answer right away, instead focusing on the silver hatchback ahead, all while pretending he didn't hang on her every word.

Even when he'd wanted more, he'd never had a relationship last longer than a few months, but his flighty relationship history wasn't enough to obscure the huge warning signs that putting too much importance on this woman would leave him broken-hearted.

His phone hung mounted on the windscreen, guiding him back to Melbourne and now ringing as if the tech gods heard his need for distraction.

He glanced at Freya again. "Do you mind if I put the call on speaker? It's Luke's wife, Agathe."

Freya shook her head, and he pressed a button in the car to answer the call. "Hey, Agathe, you're on speaker. What's up?"

"Oh, okay, no problem." There was a long pause, as if Agathe was stalling. "Do you happen to be near the airport? There's been a change of plans."

"We're maybe twenty minutes from there. Why? Did Sophie and Orlando's plane land early?"

"Yeah, like twelve hours early. Their stop in Abu Dhabi was

shuffled around, and they're waiting at Tullamarine Airport right now. Only, you've got Luke's car, which leaves only my car with Nova's giant child seat taking up a bunch of space in the back." Agathe gave a tight chuckle. "I don't think we'll be able to fit all the luggage, Sophie, and a big guy like Orlando. Rather than sending them over in a cab, it'd be so much nicer if one of us turned up."

"Right."

Max peered over at Freya, her hand pressed over her mouth, her complexion paled like a woman realizing she was minutes away from meeting her casual lover's family.

He wouldn't have borrowed Luke's car, except that it had so much more room than the Tesla for camping equipment and did better on rough country roads.

He mouthed the word, "Sorry," to her, but she swatted a hand. The situation wasn't ideal, but she'd obviously bear it either way.

"Can you do it?" Agathe's voice dipped with an air of uncertainty. "Can I let Sophie know you'll be right over to pick her up?"

Twenty-Six

FREYA HUNG BACK JUST BARELY inside Luke's South Melbourne home, her body jammed between Max and the front door, while she tried to be as invisible as possible.

Sophie ran out across the foyer's high-gloss floorboards and into Luke's open arms, a similar scene having played out less than an hour earlier when she'd first seen Max.

Sophie slipped out of Luke's hold, tears streaming down her face. Orlando, in all his beef-cakey glory, stepped forward to give Luke a strong slap on the back, thanking him for taking them on as guests since everything was up in the air with Max's place.

Freya switched focus to a little girl bouncing up and down, clearly excited with all the commotion and adding to it herself. This had to be Nova, Luke and Agathe's three-year-old daughter.

Freya had barely heard of Luke, and she'd only learned of Nova whilst listening to the conversation in the car ride over. Now she stood awkward in this home, her hands clasped at her elbows, a definite thickness coating her throat over how this happy reunion was totally foreign to her.

The Tindalls consisted of siblings and spouses genuinely excited to be together. A functional family, with a child loved and unafraid of her parents.

Orlando grabbed Nova and swung her around, the little girl squealing in delight as he informed her that the closest they'd ever come to meeting was when she lived in her mother's tummy, and that it was "so cool" to see her now.

Freya's heart hurt at the display of clear affection, and she struggled to pry her attention from the cozy scene, though she also didn't want to look like a total weirdo for staring.

The excitement ebbed, and everyone shuffled deeper into the house.

With its dark-brown polished floors and giant abstract paintings on the walls, the only two people not heading forward were her and a woman she assumed was Agathe—her wide grin and nearly onyx-colored eyes glinting at Freya.

"You must be Freya." She extended a hand. "I'm Agathe, and I'm sorry we highjacked your journey home."

Freya accepted the hand shake and opened her mouth, ready to say it wasn't a big deal, even if it kind of was, since she was way exhausted and hadn't had a warm shower since yesterday morning.

But then, Agathe tugged her hand, dragging her toward where the others sat, amidst a cluster of cream leather couches and armchairs. "Sit with us. You must be exhausted."

Freya closed her mouth, shocked at her uncharacteristic lack of words and that she allowed this woman to pull her into something she wasn't all that sure she wanted to be part of.

Sure, none of this impromptu meeting was Max's fault. Flight plans changed, Sophie and Orlando needed a ride from the airport. But none of that dulled the overriding sense that she didn't have a place in such an intimate setting.

She wasn't Max's girlfriend. She couldn't even call them firm friends. Or that their association would survive much past the physical stuff inevitably dying out.

Not that she necessarily wanted this relationship to survive past then. And she still remained the odd person out at this close family gathering.

Besides, what with her shitty childhood, she wasn't exactly experienced with how to handle displays of affection between loving family members, which only made this whole thing awkward as hell for her.

She dropped onto the end of a couch, the end closest to the front door, resigning herself to mostly just skirting the edge of this reunion until she could wrangle Max away long enough to get a ride home.

If only she didn't have so much stuff to haul from the camping trip, then she'd just excuse herself and catch a tram home. Maybe she could still call an Uber? All she had to do was ask someone to open Luke's car, and she could unload her stuff.

No. Just, no. That would be weird, and rude, and antisocial. I'll just sit quiet for a minute. They've already forgotten I'm here, anyway.

Agathe stepped in front of Freya again, a warm smile on her face. "I'm no bartender, so please don't expect too much in terms of drinks, but could I get you a glass of wine or something?"

A subtle heat spread over Freya's cheeks. Clearly, Agathe knew at least something about her, the part about her bar, which meant Max *had* mentioned her in some shape or form.

She and Max had just returned from a night camping together; no doubt everyone here had the wrong idea about just how involved this relationship was.

Max raised a brow at his sister-in-law. "Shouldn't you offer her tea? Isn't that your entire schtick?"

Freya frowned at Max, oblivious to what he meant.

"Oh, that's right, you don't know." He nodded to Agathe, with her bronze skin so flawless it almost hurt to look at her. "Miss Tea Obsessed here owns a tea shop in the city. She specializes in all things tea cups, teapots, and actual tea."

"No way." Freya turned to Agathe. "Not 'Pekoh Boo', near the corner of Elizabeth and Little Collins?"

Lightness entered Agathe's eyes, and she nodded.

Freya shifted her entire body to face her new acquaintance. "I stop by there every time I make it into the city. It's the cutest boutique in the area, and the tangerine and gold packaging is luxury in box form."

"Well then, next time you're in, ask the sales assistant for me. We also do wholesale orders if you're ever looking for something for the bar…" Agathe winked, then inclined her head to one side. "So, can I get you a tea after all?"

Freya ran her gaze over the room and let out a loud sigh. "Given that I went from the seclusion of the bush, to a giant family reunion of people I don't know, maybe a straight whiskey would make more sense."

Agathe cracked out a laugh, already turning away. "I'll hunt down some of Luke's nicer stuff and send out a family order for everyone to go easy on you."

Tendrils of warmth moved through Freya's body, and a portion of her doubt slipped away. Just because she'd had the exact opposite of a happy family, it wasn't fair to begrudge Max his. What's more, no one fluttered an eyelid at her presence. Both Sophie and Orlando, and now Agathe, had welcomed her. Maybe she needed to stop trying to find fault here.

She settled back, allowing her right shoulder to sink against Max, vowing to simply enjoy this glimpse at an untroubled family. Perhaps absorb some of the tranquility for herself, as well as the knowledge that people like this actually existed.

"How was the camping trip?"

She lifted her gaze to Luke, his moss-green stare on her.

She gave a shaky laugh, not really wanting to recount her near meltdown last night. "It was an adventure. That's for sure."

"Well, I have to hand it to Max." Luke jutted his chin at his brother. "I didn't expect you'd both come home in one piece."

"Ha. Ha." Max scowled at Luke, though the slight curl in his lips said the fake laughter was mostly playful. "I might not be G.I. Joe, like you, but I do well enough."

"G.I. Joe?" Freya glanced between the brothers. "What's that about?"

"Luke here did a few years of military service before becoming a CEO extraordinaire. And yes, he is the family's overachiever."

"And aren't you glad?" Luke grabbed a couch cushion and threw it at Max.

Max caught the cushion with a laugh, just as Luke snapped his mouth shut in a way that hinted he'd been about to remind Max of his struggles over the years. How Luke's help was the only thing keeping him afloat in that time.

Agathe swanned in between the brothers.

She rolled her eyes at Freya, extending a short glass with whiskey, a tray of nibbles in her other hand. "I'm sorry about these two. Brothers, right?"

Luke straightened and redirected his focus to Freya. "And what about you, do you have any siblings?"

"Don't answer that. It's a trap." This time Orlando intervened, his attention switching to Luke. "Vetting the potential new family members again, are we?"

Her heart beat faster, not liking the line about "potential new family members", still remaining quiet so she could hear what Luke would say next.

He shrugged, nothing more than a light smile on his face. "Does that sound like something I would do?"

Sophie flopped back in her seat on an adjacent couch and clapped her hand over her mouth as she laughed. "You mean you've forgotten how you gave Orlando a hard time when he and I first got together?"

"Well, look at him." Luke gestured to Orlando. "Doesn't he look like a guy deserving of a hard time?"

Freya peered over. Orlando, with his big frame and broad shoulders, golden skin, dark stubble, and a thick scar along the top corner of his forehead, looked rough and handsome all at once—a complete contrast to Sophie's sweet, bookish looks. Luke kind of had a point.

"I have a brother." The words flew from her mouth, perhaps because the mild tension in the air, particularly when it came to family discord, set her nerves on edge. "He's in prison."

Fuck! Did I really just say that?

Everyone's gaze switched to her, before looking to each other in dumbfounded silence. She couldn't quite meet Max's eyes; didn't want to read anything there that hinted at displeasure.

Nice first impression, genius!

Orlando reclined next to Sophie, his elbows raised on the couch's back, his beer bottle dangling loose from his fingers. "Yep. Told you it was a trap."

Luke nodded to her drink, a not-so-subtle suggestion she should take a sip.

"You know, I couldn't care less if it was." She let go of the tension in her shoulders and started on her drink, allowing the rich warmth to settle her. "I have no control over what other people do or what they think of me, my brother, and everyone in this room included."

Agathe sat next to her, her hand finding Freya's forearm. "Hey, you'll get no judgment here. I'll make sure of it."

"Thanks." Freya smiled at Agathe, then returned her attention to everyone at large. "But since imaginations have a way of doing more harm than good, I'm willing to explain what my brother did to get locked up."

"Freya. No." Max grabbed her hand, the one without the drink. "You don't have to."

"It's a simple story, and I have nothing to hide." She shrugged him off. "My brother, Clay, went to the States hoping to become a corporate big shot. But he's my mother's creature, idolized to the point of having to reflect everything she said he should be. Handsome. Rich. Popular. But the money wasn't coming in fast enough, not for the crowds he wanted to break into, so he turned to running online scams, which brought in the money sure enough. At least until he caught a four-year prison sentence."

"I bet there's more to *that* story."

"Luke!"

Agathe reached out and smacked his knee.

"No. I don't mean it like that." He squeezed his eyes shut and shook his head. "I mean, as much as we siblings have our squabbles, we still have a bunch of positive memories to lean on when times get tough. I'm not prying. I just figure, to have a brother and not really have a relationship with him, which is what I'm getting from her story, must be a hard thing to contend with."

Freya stared at Luke for a while, her cheeks slack, and her skin suddenly cold, like he'd traipsed through her brain and uprooted hidden emotions she made a point of hiding.

Even as the "loved" child, Clay still paid a price for their mother's brand of love. He'd been hyped up and deemed undeservedly special for nothing more than being born a boy. That love had destroyed his ability to develop his own self-image, leaving him to waste years trying to prove his mum's theories about him right.

He played a role. A role that damaged him in more ways than one.

And just like she understood their mother, Freya understood Clay, too. She just refused to hurt herself trying to maintain any kind of involved relationship with him.

She took a deep breath and directed her next question at Agathe. "Does Luke do that often?"

"You mean the psychoanalyzing thing?" She grabbed the nibbles plate and pushed it closer to Freya in some kind of peace offering. "You have no idea, but on a positive note, it usually means he likes you, or at least considers you a possible regular fixture in our lives."

Freya brought her glass higher, pressing its cool surface to her cheek, all while deliberating over whether she should break it to everyone that she and Max were only slightly more than fuck buddies.

Thankfully though, her phone rang, so she took herself a few meters from the group to answer the call.

"Hello?"

She didn't recognize the number calling, but the quick-fire response of a female voice had her staring dead-pan at the kaleidoscopic reds and yellows of an abstract painting up ahead.

She gave a numb, "Yes. I'll be there," and ended the call, her lightness from this morning completely gone. She turned a quick glance to the group of happy people behind her, her heart plummeting at the vision of something she'd never have.

As if sensing her change in mood, Max leapt from the couch and drew near, stopping just short of touching her. "What's wrong? You look gray."

"I need to go." Her throat swelled from the inside, and the audible rasp in her voice betrayed the rising tension in her body. "Mum's had a violent outburst in the hospital. The nurse said it's a normal, end-stage reaction. Something about toxins building in her brain, but they've had to sedate her. She's refusing to wear a hospital gown and wants her pajamas from home. I need to go to her house and retrieve her pajamas. Maybe then, they can settle her without more drugs."

Max ran his fingers through the scruff of his hair before he gave his family a quick glance. "I'll say goodbye to everyone here, and then I'll take you. Don't go alone, okay?"

"That would be a bad idea."

His brows slammed together, more insistent than offended. "No, it's not. You don't have a car, I do. You're already visibly tired, and it'll take you hours to get everything done without my help."

"That might be true." She crossed her arms over her chest. "But I'll manage all the same."

"I never questioned whether you could manage."

"I can't ask you to leave your family when they've only just arrived."

"You're not asking, I'm offering." He twisted his torso, nodding at Sophie and Orlando. "Look at those two, they look even more wrecked than you do. The quicker we get out of here, the quicker they can wrap up the pleasantries and get some showers and a nap. Heck, same goes for us. Besides, there's some hardworking nurses dealing with your cranky mum right now, just praying you'll hurry along and end their misery."

She narrowed her stare, allowing a burning silence to drag between them, but the mere sight of his kind, star-filled eyes shifted something.

Even as his gaze slipped from her and to the ground between them —a sign his conviction waned—she couldn't deny his reasons.

"Fine." She dropped her arms, already heading for the door. "But wherever we go, you wait outside."

Twenty-Seven

THE MOMENT MAX'S pristine Tesla pulled up to Freya's childhood home, Freya sank deeper into her seat, the house a tattered, old weatherboard in the thick of Melbourne's northern suburbs.

This house looked even worse than when she'd grown up there. Bad enough to call it a headache-inducing eyesore—the peeling paint an unappealing shade of custard yellow, the window frames and dented gutters a gag-worthy shamrock green. Even the exterior door appeared ready to fall off its hinges, while the fly wire hung loose, torn at one top corner.

As much as the sight made her queasy, staring at the house beat meeting Max's gaze, especially since they'd arrived to this decaying hovel fresh from Luke's lavish home. Even if she did trust Max not to judge her on her poor upbringing, she still couldn't understand why she'd agreed to let him witness this bleak part of her past.

"The thing is." She squinted at the quiet street ahead, at the lack of trees lining the grassy nature strip, her words a chance to delay the inevitable. "This is probably a shitty thing to say, but I can't help but second guess whether this errand is really just Mum manipulating the situation again. You know, she spent so many years using her health, and then mine, as leverage. I can't tell what's real and what's not anymore. I can't escape the idea that this is one final attempt to gauge what hoops she can get everyone to jump through before she drops."

Max frowned down at the steering wheel. "You think she'd go to the extreme of getting sedated, just to watch everyone dance to her tune?"

She let out a sigh, flopping her head back against the headrest. "Honestly? Yes. The woman drugged her own daughter just to fill a void, so…"

She eyed the Tesla's see-through roof while a long silence dragged out. She didn't need him to acknowledge her point to know that now neither of them knew what to make of this mission to collect pajamas.

Her resentment toward her mother grew in her abdomen, a hot, hard knot taking up space and bringing pain to her lower ribs. She closed her eyes, absorbing the ache, only for Max's long fingers to slide through hers rested on the center console.

"You sure you don't want me to come with you?"

The sweet gesture cooled her anger and made room for another, more frightening, emotion. *Affection.*

She sat bolt upright and pulled her hand away. "Fine, let's get this started."

Maybe if he came face-to-face with the evidence of her childhood, he'd get scared and stop messing with her long-term dream of being alone forever. The fact she'd caught Luke's lingering frown as Max ushered her out of his front door, like Luke too could see this relationship getting way out of hand, and that Freya would, sooner rather than later, crush Max's way-too-kind spirit.

She dug through her backpack and retrieved the keys she'd collected the last time she visited her mum at the hospital. Even as she exited the car, and Max followed, she found herself thankful for his silent and unquestioning compliance.

With every hurried step toward her mother's front door, her heart rate climbed, and a thin sweat clammed up her hands, forcing her to cling tighter to the keys, at least thankful she'd packed deodorant in her camping bag.

She stepped over the fat cracks on the veranda's concrete slab, refusing to make eye-contact with Max. When she tugged at the flimsy fly screen's thin metal handle, the springs made a sharp metallic *twang*.

The solid front door behind wasn't much better; the thing refused to budge open, and she had to jam a shoulder into the cream-painted wood before she finally stumbled in. The shambles of a small living room greeted her, sinking her mood deeper.

There was the cheap, blush vinyl couch, with shadows of hibiscus flowers embossed all over, the sand-colored carpet stained and uneven. Her trauma-loaded brain protested the imprinting of any more memories of this place.

So, she marched ahead and took a left into the short hallway, assuming Max would follow despite his uncharacteristic silence, her mind settling into some kind of blinkered, protective mode.

She came to her mother's bedroom at the end of the corridor, the bed still unmade and a collection of clothes strewn across the mattress and floor.

Her mum had never been all that neat, but this scene suggested she'd given up entirely. Maybe she'd figured this place was for her eyes only and that no one visited, so why bother?

Except right now it wasn't just her mother's eyes taking it all in, and all Freya could think about was how the state of this house embodied her mother's inner world.

Apathetic. Disorderly. Chaotic.

A chest of drawers along the room's back wall stood with most drawers still open. She strode in and made fast work of digging through each drawer, unearthing multiple pairs of pajamas.

She bundled the clothes in her hands and took a moment before turning around.

One day soon, she'd have to pack this house up, its mess and horrid memories filling each corner of each room. She'd have to enlist a real estate agent and sell the place, even though she preferred the idea of burning the entire goddamn house down, just erased from the earth altogether.

She turned and lifted her gaze to Max standing in the doorway, his long frame blocking the already limited light in the crammed space.

The look of him brought more pain to her heart, his continued silence still unnerving.

She marched forward and squeezed past him, her steps quick, but not quick enough to block out her heightened awareness or her imaginings of how this all looked to him.

The disarray. The lack of luxury. Her former life of decay, solitude, abuse, neglect. That people lived like this. That *she'd* lived like this...

God, my list of contrasts to his life don't end, do they?

The linoleum floors out in the corridor were a scuffed and depressing shade of beige, the whole thing printed in a pattern resembling fake tiles. Not even the thin plaster walls, in a misleading bright cool blue, hid the dented and bowed panels.

Still, she powered ahead, set on getting out of the place as fast as she could. Just two quick turns and she'd be back out on the veranda, reunited with the fresh air and the outside world's sweet civility.

Only another door lay straight ahead. The final obstacle. The door she'd ignored on her way in. The one leading to the kitchen.

Her feet came to a dead stop, and a heavy stone seemed to drag down on the inside of her stomach, all while a voice in her head screamed to turn right and get the hell out of there.

Staring back at her was the same, old, green table she'd eaten at multiple times a day for years, a significant amount of those meals poisoned. She took another step where dirty and crooked white tiles drew her in, her gaze falling to the stained brassy yellow sink along the left wall, a rickety, wooden breakfast stool beside the adjoining counter.

A wave of sickness rolled within her stomach and hit her with a painful vivid memory, one of a small, frail girl, pale and bony, her head full of ratty blond curls...

That girl balanced on the wooden stool—weak of body, but ultimately, not weak of mind—her bare feet stretched so that she stood on her tippy-toes, her wiry arms reaching high into the cupboards.

The girl shifted and adjusted, accommodating for the stool's uneven feet, but no amount of adjusting compensated for a cold-hearted mother determined to cover up her self-serving and evil schemes.

Freya's lungs drew a sudden sharp breath, and the memory collapsed like a weak house of cards, all while her skin prickled and her nails dug into her palms.

"Are you okay?" A pair of large hands pulled her in so that warmth soon lapped at her back. *Max.*

His voice delivered a gentle whisper, one that hurt her far more than his silence.

She closed her eyes, and emotion swelled in her chest, taking up too much space.

He'd caught more than a glimpse of what she'd lived through, and now he asked if she was okay, his concern not strong enough to quell the shame swallowing her whole. A shame that made her shoulders hunch and her cheeks burn.

She reopened her eyes and made room for a cooler, more collected, Freya to return. Sure, Max knew her story, and now he'd seen where she'd lived. If that didn't drive him away, meeting her mother would.

Kerry Branner's eyes crinkled at the corners, quite a feat given the woman was dying, the strain of her forced smile directed at the person she'd already deemed the most important in this room. *Max.*

Freya ground her molars together, dreading the inevitable questions to come.

"Thank you for the pajamas, honey." Even now, addressing Freya as "honey", a term of endearment her mother never used, all while neglecting to give her own daughter any direct eye contact. "Who is this handsome young man you've brought along with you?"

Max stepped forward, at least refraining from any reward laughter at her mother's attempt at charm. "I'm Max. I drove Freya here."

Her mother's attention slid down to his hand around Freya's. Sluggish and slow, she raised a brow, before finally focusing on Freya. "You never told me you had a boyfriend."

Freya did her best not to growl at the brightness in her mother's fake-nice tone, sending forth her own words on a flat delivery. "I heard they had to sedate you."

Her mother giggled and gave Max a weak shrug. "Oh, that. They don't understand what it's like in here. I only wanted a little comfort from home."

The giggle turned Freya's cheeks rigid, much less the not-so-subtle victim act she'd already witnessed far too much growing up.

There wasn't anything comfortable about her mother's home either, though any actual discomfort had more to do with the cold woman who lived there than the shambolic conditions or her mother's lack of funds.

Besides, her mother's glib response now, in light of Freya and Max's journey across town, only added more weight to the suspicion that this whole pajama fiasco was yet more manipulation.

Max tightened his grip on her hand, pulling her attention from her anger and onto the slow circles his thumb drew in the center of her palm. "Well, hopefully you're feeling much better now. Apologies for the quick visit, but we really should go—"

"Oh, such a sweet boy." Her mother purred over the gravel in her age-worn voice, though the hard set of her amber eyes failed to match her saccharine delivery. "Tell me how you met my Freya? You look so unlike someone I imagined my girl would date."

Freya glared at her mother, every muscle in her body clenching in protest. "You've never met anyone I've dated, and—"

Max squeezed her hand again, perhaps a reminder not to fall into her mother's trap. "I met Freya at her bar. You must be so proud to have such a successful daughter. She's excellent at what she does."

Kerry swatted a hand in Max's direction, her narrowed stare fusing on Freya. "I couldn't give her the best things growing up, but I did my job and gave her everything I had. I didn't raise soft children. I taught her the world is a hard place, and because of me, she knows how to survive, even if teaching her meant she abandoned me in the end." Kerry's eyes filled with frost, a frost that melted as she turned back to Max and gave an unconvincing shrug. "And you're right. Just look how she turned out."

Freya's shoulders sagged at her mother's reference to parenting as a "job".

If that were the case, her mother would have only ever made a great, sadistic army drill sergeant or maybe the heartless matron of an 1800s orphanage.

Not only did her mother take credit for how Freya had turned out, she also claimed "abandonment" while Freya quite literally stood staring her in the face, as death slowly but surely crept close.

No Clay in sight. Just Freya.

Here, right now.

Hand delivering pajamas, when she had every right to never look her mother's way again.

And the most ass-end-backward of all statements? That preparing Freya for a "hard world" counted when it was her mother who'd been the sole source of all that hardness.

"Anyway." Her mother spoke to Max now, again leaving Freya to think she should have just stayed in the damn car and let Max drop off the pajamas. "What's a man like you doing at her club? You don't look tattooed, drunk, or scruffy enough to be in that place."

Freya spat forth a manic laugh, her gaze lifting to Max's pinched expression.

Lucky for her mother, he jumped in and replied before she could. "Not that tattoos are any measure of a person, but I started out as a customer at The Ruby Room. Freya was kind enough to offer me a job when I really needed it."

"Well. Well." Her mother let out a croaky chuckle, ending on a spluttering cough. She turned her venom-filled gaze to Freya again, as if Max's value had just plummeted. "You're screwing the *help* then?"

Her mother popped the "p" in the word "help", then flung her head back into her pillow, a series of rattly laughs and coughs breaking forth.

Freya's spine turned rigid, and she bounced on her heels trying to work through an emotional onslaught. Anger. Shame. Anger again. Her mother found ways to make her feel small at every turn, always insinuating she'd been put together wrong—doomed to be a screwup, no matter what she achieved.

She quashed a desire to lash out, clinging to the distraction of the gray cityscape outside the hospital room window, mostly because lashing out would only feed her mother's habitual need to stir people's temper.

Freya wouldn't lower herself to unleashing on someone slumped at death's door, wouldn't waste her energy defending herself against a woman who would never be convinced to change—even though holding back felt like losing, like Freya sent forth the idea she didn't mind the disrespect.

Disrespect from a dying woman. There is that.

Yes. And her mother's impending death was one point of relief.

In the scheme of things, letting her mother have this one shallow win meant little. So, Freya forced a half-smile and let go of her clenching muscles, relief soon sweeping over her body. "It was something to see you today, Mum."

Her mother's laughter stopped, her silent stare holding Freya, as if she didn't know what to do with the lack of retaliation.

Despite the shitty meeting, and maybe because Freya had taken a bit of her power back, she leaned in and kissed her mother's forehead. "I love you."

From the outside, and in light of all the abuse, that statement seemed like a weird thing to say, but for all Freya knew, this would be the last time she'd see her mother.

Then there was Freya's other coping mechanism—seeing her mother for the tortured child she'd been, not the damaged woman she'd become.

Her mother ripped her attention from Freya and blinked out toward the window, her sudden quietness causing an ache in Freya's tummy.

This wasn't her first declaration of love to her mother, though she'd learned long ago never to expect the sentiment returned. The way she saw it, at least she tried. At least she could say that she didn't hold back and that she hadn't inherited her family's inability to show affection. And whatever her mother did with that affection was her own damn problem.

Freya turned to Max and nudged her head in the direction of the door, only for her mother's cracked and hollow voice to halt their exit.

"Love?"

Kerry continued to blink at the window, her stare soulless and the flickering movements of her eyelids picking up speed. "I don't know what that is. No one ever taught me."

Freya spun around, ready to leave; only Max tugged her back, a stern stare fixed on her mother. "Freya just did."

Twenty-Eight

Not quite ready to start the engine, Max paused behind the steering wheel, the hospital parking lot several levels high, densely packed, with sharp corners that would have made maneuvering even a small car a tight squeeze.

"This day just doesn't want to end." Freya scrubbed a hand over her face, the skin under her eyes darker than usual, her cheeks pale like the interaction with her mother had totally drained her.

"Come back to my place." He clenched his jaw, not having intended to speak his wishes out loud. Though on further reflection, he had zero regrets about the offer.

Freya didn't need to be alone tonight. Heck, neither did he, and he also didn't want to see her go.

"I can't." She spoke down to her lap, her voice muffled by her hands still over her face.

"Sure you can."

"No, I can't." She lifted her head, and the sad distance in her stare left him deflated. "You've done enough for me today. I'm sure you want a little time to yourself now."

He reached out and put his hand over hers, hoping she'd appreciate the extra support and connection. "I'll waste whatever time I have to myself, anyway. Come back to my place. Let me look after you. It'll be good for both of us."

He offered a weak smile, biting back an urge to say he'd found nothing likable about her mother, and that she'd been manipulative and mean. That he hated the toll the woman took on her daughter. Hated how Freya continued having anything to do with her mother, when even one short encounter zapped all signs of her innate happiness.

But this was Freya's life.

Her story.

He'd respect her desire to work through her mother's last days in her own way.

Her stare skittered around his face, her lower lip disappearing between her teeth as if she took a moment to weigh things up. "You sure? I mean, *I'm* not sure. Aren't we stepping beyond the whole casual limits of this relationship?"

"And spending a night in a tent together is something normal work colleagues do?" He allowed a short shot of laughter. "Look, I promise I won't overthink this if you don't."

The guarded sheen in her eyes melted. "Okay, fine. Let's do it."

He started the ignition. "Good, my house it is."

The late hour made the drive to his apartment a short one. He soon pushed open his front door, the heavy camping gear and bags clanging together over his shoulder.

"Feel free to throw your stuff in the washing machine first." He held the door open and side-stepped to make room for Freya to pass. "Unless you'd prefer a warm shower first?"

"More than you could know." She groaned, squeezing past him, her own giant bag trailing behind. "I've been dreaming about a shower for two days now."

He laughed and closed the door behind them, then took a few steps deeper into the apartment. A wave of cold air hit his face.

"Just a moment, I'll crank up the heat before you jump in. No one likes a cold bathroom."

Melbourne weather tended to shift through temperatures faster than a Formula One driver shifted gears—even at the tail end of summer—that and he made a habit of shutting down his climate system whenever he left his apartment for any extended time. His apartment's location at the edge of the bay only made the evening chill-factor worse.

He dumped his bags by the kitchen counter, then found the touchscreen control for his climate system. He fiddled around for a bit, but the usual start-up "beep" didn't come.

Freya sidled up to him, peering over his shoulder as much as someone significantly shorter could peer. "What do you have there?"

He frowned at the tablet and pressed the start button three more times. "Still trying to get the heat to work, but this thing is glitching out. I need a moment to restart the app."

Except, even when he did restart the app, over and over, nothing happened. He growled under his breath and restarted the whole device, the screen turning black.

He'd spent crazy money on the best climate system available, one that would heat and cool his apartment, whilst being as eco-friendly as possible—this system just one of many additions he'd gone literally broke installing.

Surely, a climate system that damn-well worked was the least he could expect for all the money he'd spent!

His skin tingled, and his heart rate picked up. The device finished rebooting, but no amount of app tinkering worked. To make matters worse, his funds sat dangerously low, so even with his work at The Ruby Room and the new swim instructor job, he probably wouldn't have enough cash to pay for repairs.

Freya tapped him on the shoulder, but he was too busy glaring at the tablet to look at her. "Hey, there's a note on the kitchen counter."

He continued stabbing wildly at the blank screen, the back of his neck prickling with sweat because he was sure his system was about a year out of warranty now. "Just read it out to me."

"You sure?"

"Yeah, go for it." He shook the tablet, as if that would get things working.

"Hey mate, thought you should know, seems your heater and air conditioner are on the fritz. Tom and Pats." She dropped the note to the counter and gave a light shrug, like she didn't understand the severity of that news. "Well, that sucks. Who are Tom and Pats?"

He ran a hand through his hair and headed back toward Freya, his face and fingers cold and void of blood. "Tom and Patricia. They're my cleaners."

Her eyelids flared. "You *still* have cleaners? Are you crazy?"

"It's highly likely," he mumbled, not exactly in the mood to have his poor life choices dragged out at this very moment. "I haven't found the heart to fire them."

He waited for Freya to spill with her tough "Boss Lady" advice, but she reached a hand out and stroked his arm. "Oh, Max."

He dropped the tablet onto the counter alongside Tom and Pat's note, not quite able to take her look of sympathy, even though he did appreciate it.

The problem about splashing out on expensive things was they weren't supposed to break all that often, but when they did, they were painfully expensive to repair.

He let go of a loud sigh and sank back on his heels. "This is probably going to set me back a couple of thousand."

"Do you even have a couple of thousand?"

"No. No, I definitely don't." He whispered an expletive, staring off into space. "This is embarrassing. I wanted to look after you, not freeze your ass off and bore you with my problems."

She drew closer, stroking his face, her touch undeservedly soft and warm. "I've bored you plenty with my problems this weekend. You're welcome to bore me with a few of yours."

Despite the warmth sweeping over his skin, he fell short of reminding her that her offer to share problems probably went beyond the casualness she insisted on maintaining in this relationship.

"Fine." She dropped her hand and released a sigh. "Maybe you having a few problems makes me feel normal about my own issues, okay?"

"Way to make this sound like a fair trade."

"It is a fair trade. Tell me, do you need help with your problems or not?"

"If you're offering to loan me money, then no. The whole point of my downfall is I'm supposed to claw my own way out. At least, that's what everyone keeps telling me."

She shrugged. "Well, yeah. They're kind of right."

He rubbed the heel of his palm against his chest and accepted her bitter truth.

One way or another, he'd find a way to keep his apartment, preferably without going broke or the place falling to pieces due to his inability to maintain repairs.

Freya leaned back against the counter behind her, though her gaze dropped to the floor. "And you don't need to worry about me tonight. You heard my mum, she built me tough. We didn't have heating or cooling growing up. This isn't something a thick sweater and some sweat pants can't fix."

She peered up from under her lashes and sent him a rueful smile— the sensually sweet look spreading heat through his belly. But in the next beat, his insides churned at the memory of her unkempt childhood home, its dilapidated, weatherboard exterior and thin plaster walls. There'd been nothing warm there. Not anything the world's most sumptuous woolen sweater could fix.

Comfort had been yet another thing lacking in her life, and the fact she'd been through so much, only to have more unpleasantness in his home, sent a sharp line of shame snaking through his body.

He stepped forward and dropped a hurried kiss to her lips—a kiss he hoped conveyed everything she didn't want him to say out loud.

That he wanted her to be his.

That he wanted to give her far more than what her past entailed.

But for any of that to happen, he needed to get his life together.

An easy task, right?

He pulled away, logic stinging him to the core, even as her mouth twisted up in a sly grin. "Well, there *is* another way to stay warm."

He paused a second, before quick laughter broke free. Trust Freya to take a bad moment and turn it into something else. *Something wicked.*

Her grin widened, and she kicked off her shoes, at the same time grabbing hold of his hands. "Come on. Let's check if the shower still works."

The playful trail of her voice, the new sparkle in her eyes, the high lift of her cheeks from her smile; he couldn't and didn't try to stop himself from getting to her again, from scooping her up with a light growl so he could transport her to the shower as suggested.

And even as he worried about how he'd fix his life, even as their clothes hit the pewter gray tile and their mouths meshed together in a series of deep and hungry kisses, his heart clenched at the knowledge she once again accepted him despite his shortfalls. Despite his dwindling money, shitty friends, and nonexistent heating.

Steamy water spilled from the shower down his back. He held her to the wall and entered her quickly, taking all the comfort she offered, accepting her ability to turn any sucky situation good. That as always, she wouldn't leave him to deal with his problems alone.

Twenty-Nine

THE RUBY ROOM buzzed with way more commotion and music than usual, quite a feat given this was a Wednesday morning, and the bar should have been closed.

But this was no normal Wednesday morning, and butterflies danced within Freya's tummy as she nursed a hot cup of golden chamomile tea and planted her feet under the small table to keep from wriggling. The reporter sitting across from her had a tall glass of local craft beer, the woman's near six-foot frame intimidating, even though she'd been nothing but kind.

"The Ruby Room is already a well-established underground live arts venue." The reporter leaned forward, her black cowboy hat shielding her eyes, her looming question hanging partway between Freya and the cell phone recording this conversation. "What prompted you to put The Ruby forward for the festival?"

Freya pondered the question, allowing her gaze to shift to the stage, not having to imagine Gideon up there since the dim houselights and open stage curtains showcased a bright spotlight shining right on him. His two dancers stood on either side, and they ran through an abridged dress rehearsal, a photographer snapping photos from ground level.

"Honestly?" She turned back to the reporter, conscious that whatever she replied would likely appear in one of Melbourne's most widely distributed newspapers ahead of Saturday night's first show. "The fact you use the word 'underground' is exactly why I'm doing this. I want to pull The Ruby Room out of the shadows and make live performance art accessible to all. I didn't grow up with much, and I understand what it's like to be locked out of certain experiences. That is why we partnered up with The Walk with Pride Foundation to raise money and awareness of their wonderful work. I want everyone to know The Ruby Room is a home for all. A place where everyone is accepted. A place that tries to be different, as well as make a difference."

"As someone who's been to a show here, I can definitely say The Ruby Room embraces all things avant-garde, while being a safe space for anyone who walks through the doors. And then there's you, an enigmatic and bold woman who runs this whole thing, which only makes a night at The Ruby even more exciting. Has starting and growing The Ruby been a long road? As a female business owner, do you find there are different pressures on you?"

"You mean, aside from certain people asking when I'll settle down and have some babies?" She gave the reporter a mock cringe, her thoughts switching to her mother and how no amount of success or work would ever be enough.

Maybe if Freya had forced her past relationships, the ones that weren't working, and gotten herself needlessly pregnant, maybe then her mother would be happy.

Another pitchy laugh broke free from her. *As if!*

A baby would only please her mother for all of two seconds before she found fault. So, Freya sure as hell didn't regret putting her uterus on permanent hiatus.

She straightened, having only partly answered the reporter's question.

"And yes, the road up until now has been long and grueling. I've been looked over for promotions or refused additional training simply because of my gender. Don't get me started on the colleagues or patrons who assume their drunkenness and your close proximity entitles them to grab or jeer. These hurdles put a lot of women off this industry, which is one reason why I started The Ruby. I stopped waiting for an invitation to get ahead and set my own place at the table. And wherever possible, I help those who have been in a similar situation."

A wide smile spread across the reporter's face. "Thank you. I have everything I need. I'll call if I need anything more, but in the meantime, our photographer will get a few shots of you when he's done with Mr. Faber." She tipped her chin to Freya's direct left. "Also, I think there's a gentleman here who wants your attention."

Freya thanked the already departing reporter and turned to Max looming over her left shoulder. She jolted at the sharp flex of his brow, as though she'd interrupted him in deep thought.

Her heart thundered, his attention making her insides burn in a *good* way, a way that made her feel like she'd been caught doing something she shouldn't.

"I wanted to double check the tables are positioned as you wanted them." His gaze slid over her body in a slow, up-and-down motion, his concentrated frown bending into a delighted grin. "Before I go to the effort of arranging all the chairs."

She gave the room a quick glance and nodded, then dropped her focus to his chest, not all that sure she should have invited him to help today.

Aside from juggling the reporter and photographer, she had staff prepping the bar for tonight's press and society preview—The Ruby's chance to gain early reviews before Saturday's first show—as well as providing something for the arts industry "who's who" to talk about.

Besides, since her camping weekend with Max, she'd kind of spent her days brooding and burying herself in work. Work she needed to do, what with the whole make-or-break festival drawing near, though perhaps an element of her busyness had something to do with running from her bubbling emotions.

But then again, Max did need the money, and she couldn't find it in her to deny him the chance of some extra work. The money wouldn't be near enough to fix his problems, but he'd still jumped at the offer of a double shift.

"If you don't mind…" She turned away from his frown, her eyes stinging at the glare of the returned house lights now Gideon was done with his rehearsal, all while she pretended her hands didn't burn with a need to touch Max. "The photographer needs me."

And she didn't touch him. She didn't even offer a smile. She merely mumbled something about the layout being good and then brushed toward the bar, denying any chance of anything "touchy feely" playing out at her place of work.

She didn't want any overly familiar exchanges of looks. No displays of affection.

Not here and especially not in front of her best friend or the press.

She ran her attention over the venue edged in crimson curtains and mirrored walls. A venue *she'd* created, despite her hellish childhood, the years it had taken for her to claw her way out and her soul to recover… And the myriad ways it still hadn't.

Gideon crossed the room and took a seat with the reporter, Freya still hanging back since the photographer fiddled with his camera.

In that brief pause, her mind slipped to a series of thoughts plaguing her from days ago. To the stuff she'd told Max.

There'd been her childhood abuse and her decision to take on her mother's current needs, and how maybe Freya's existence so far away from her horrific childhood made up one big reason why she'd agreed to help her mother.

She'd lost count of how many people had called her lucky over the years—because of her thriving business, or her carefree spirit—but what they didn't understand was that luck had little to do with anything she'd gained. Attributing her success to luck denied the hot coals she'd dragged herself over.

For her, freedom hadn't come without a cost. There'd been years of believing she wasn't good enough. That good things only came to those with a good start.

Those from a supportive family and no murky past.

Then she'd had to overcome the lies. That she was stupid and incapable. That she was still just little Freya, unlovable and born to bear the consequence of other people's neuroses.

For so long, her mother had guided Freya's internal dialogue, though the day Freya had spilled the truth to that nurse had changed everything. That day became the impetus to her own voice finally breaking through.

The Ruby Room *was* hers. *She'd* made this place. Not luck.

Her efforts afforded her a beautiful home in her favorite suburb and provided a steady income to scores of employees. The Ruby was a sanctuary for artists, staff, and patrons alike, especially those who didn't have anywhere else to go.

And The Ruby provided her most valued asset. *Freedom.*

Freedom from her past. Freedom from ever having to rely on anyone else. Because, despite her self-made reputation for having an unbreakable heart, her heart *wasn't* unbreakable.

It was more fragile than most.

Her heart knew pain and wanted nothing more to do with it. Her heart knew abandonment and betrayal, all on a literal and excruciating level. She would never, *ever* let herself be hurt like that again.

And so, she'd become a master of defenses and hid those defenses with an air of playfulness and deflection, just like so many other abuse survivors.

But oh, how those defenses were wonderful, soul-protecting things. They operated every moment of every day, squeezing her heart at any minor sign of impending disappointment.

And that was her problem with having Max around.

She could see herself falling for him. *Deeply. Completely.* And that fired more painful reactions, unleashing the prospect that her heart might never bounce back should things go wrong, and all because her instincts warned her of something else. Something downright undeniable.

Things *would* go wrong. This relationship would not work.

Not with the messy way he conducted his life. Not with how little he knew of himself. Not with her desperate need for consistency, despite her "fun and carefree" persona.

Even if Max wasn't moody or violent like her mother; even if his growing affection shone undeniably. Freya's stomach hollowed at the possibility of once again living on tenterhooks with someone else, which gave life to a special kind of anxiety. One she didn't want to address but would have to anyway… Sometimes, love really wasn't enough.

"What's with you and Mr. Cute Face?"

She blinked and tried not to appear shocked at Gideon standing before her. "Sorry, Cute Face, who?"

"The man I'm guessing you were just daydreaming about." Gideon dabbed at his forehead with a white sweat towel, stabbing his gaze toward Max. "Shouldn't you be drowning in thoughts of how to make my show shine brighter for the festival, if that's even possible? And don't play stupid with me, lady. Spill. Who's the hot blond fellow over there with the bed-ruffled hair? Why does he have you blushing like a Catholic school girl?"

She touched her knuckles to her cheeks, which had in fact gotten warmer at the reference to Max. "He just works here. And yes, he's admittedly attractive, but otherwise nothing worth mentioning."

"Well, I really only came over to get your feedback on the show, but since Mr. Cute Face 'isn't worth mentioning', I most definitely am going to need you to start mentioning."

Gideon crossed his arms and tapped his foot, waiting.

An awkward silence dragged out. Well, silent except for all the noise of furniture shifting about and Gideon tapping his brown Oxford on the black wood floor.

His unwavering stare said he wasn't moving on from this conversation, so she better get talking.

"Fine. I confess." She rolled her eyes in an impression of a bored teenager. "I climbed aboard Mr. Cute Face's train a couple of times, that's all. I mean, look at him, can you blame me?"

Gideon jerked his chin back, doing a poor job of suppressing a smirk. "Really now? What happened to your whole 'I don't mix business and pleasure' rule? How many dreamboat men have walked through The Ruby's doors, and you've never 'ridden their trains'?" He leaned way in now, eyes narrowing mere inches from her own. "Tell me, what's changed?"

She forced herself not to look away, even though her eyes stung, and she wanted so desperately to peek down at her shoes and escape this standoff.

Gideon might have spent way too much time over the years away from her, studying and then touring, but Goddess-damn-it, he knew her too flipping well.

"What do you want me to say?" She shrugged, keeping her small show of defeat low-key in the hopes it would be enough for him.

His smile softened just a little. "You like this one, don't you?"

The invitation for honesty coiled her muscles and brought nausea to her stomach.

"We're a bit more than friends with benefits, but still nothing more than friends. It's hard to explain." She crossed her arms and gave herself the treat of looking away and escaping Gideon's scrutiny for just one second.

"He knows. Doesn't he?"

She nodded, catching on that he meant Max knew about her past and mother now being ill.

"I let him meet her. I don't know why I did it, but I let him meet her."

Gideon's fingers curled over her shoulders, and he turned her to look at him again. "He met The Dragon?"

"You know I don't like it when you call her that."

And still, an unavoidable chuckle broke from her.

"*I* haven't even met The Dragon." Gideon pressed a hand to his chest in mock offense. "Sorry, I mean, Ms. Dragon."

She narrowed a silent glare at him. In truth, she'd never let him meet her mother because Kerry would take one look at Gideon and unleash untold cruelty on him based on his sexually. Gideon didn't deserve that. No one deserved that.

"What?" He raised his hands in a gesture of innocence. "The name fits. I mean, I'm sure a dragon would totally eat their young, which is only one step worse than what your mother—"

She squeezed her eyes shut, a wordless warning for him to just stop.

"Sorry." The apology prompted her to look at him again, while Gideon flung his sweat towel over his shoulder. "Okay, so tell me how the meeting with Mr. Cute Face and Mother went."

She dipped her chin and mumbled, "Not well."

"And let me guess, you thought you'd present this stunning tall drink of a man to Mama Dearest, and she'd finally give you some love in return?"

She opened her mouth, ready to tell Gideon to shove his theory, *that wasn't what she'd intended at all*, but then silence swallowed her reply.

She hadn't used Max to gain approval from her mother; rather, she'd wanted support *against* her mother, but Gideon would take any explanation as an admission of guilt and forever heckle her for using Max as mother-bait.

So, she cleared her throat and set about giving him nothing. "Anyway, so feedback on your show, it's brilliant. Thank you again for using The Ruby as your premiere venue."

She offered a giant, cheesy grin, daring him to return to the subject of her and Max.

"Of course, you know flattery will get you everywhere, including off the hook." Gideon gave her a side glare, his features brightening, as he jutted his chin toward the stage. "It looks like the photographer is ready for you. I'll let you go for now, but I'll need way more than flattery before I drop this whole Mr. Cute Face scandal."

Thirty

GIDEON'S SHOW began with a flash of blinding yellow light and a blast of jazz horns, but for the longest time, the man himself didn't appear. The audience mumbled. Why wasn't he on stage? Only the soft ding of a bicycle bell turned everyone's attention all the way to the back of the venue.

The curtain belonging to the cleaner's alcove flew wide open, and Gideon pushed through on the back of a bicycle; his outfit a super tight, aqua blue unitard. A bushy, horseshoe mustache overwhelmed his upper lip, and a white sweatband stretched over his forehead.

He pedaled through the crowd, spraying water from a drink bottle in all directions, yelling at the audience to get out of his way and to stop looking at him. Melbourne traffic had supposedly fucked him over, and now he was late, and everyone would know what he looked like without his makeup and heels.

Howls of laughter filled the room. The impact of his entrance was more amazing when he leapt to the stage and began his first song, his immaculate voice and instant stage presence cutting clear across the room.

In that moment, he proved without a doubt he'd never needed his innate beauty or the glam costumes to grab a crowd. Not even garish spandex and a hideous mustache obscured his talent.

Freya worked the bar, feverishly helping her staff fill the endless demand for champagne and red wine, all the while stealing glances at the show and trying not to ogle Max.

Max. As much as she tried, she couldn't wipe him from her mind. More to the point, as cruel as it seemed to push him away, doing so would be inevitable.

Even with someone who wasn't a great person, walking from a relationship was never easy. But Max was better than great; he was amazing. If not for a couple of fatal flaws, he'd be her perfect man. He didn't deserve the distance she had already put between them, using her work and the festival as an excuse to pull back.

Then again, leading him on wasn't right either.

She giggled at Gideon seated on a man's lap a few rows from the front, the man somewhere in his fifties with a gray-streaked red beard and a bunch of laugh lines creasing the corners of his eyes.

Gideon had changed from the aqua spandex to a short, under-bust corset and his iconic skin-tight booty shorts over black fishnets. His bike shoes were gone, too, and his signature black suede heels covered his feet. Now he rested cheek-to-cheek with the other man, crooning a sweet serenade into a cordless microphone.

Freya smiled at his unabashed freedom, at his effortless command over a room filled with been-there-done-that press and society notables, but even this wasn't Gideon's true self.

She'd grown up with him after all.

She knew his stage face when she saw it. His alter ego.

Together, they'd fought to figure out where they fit in the world. Her personal challenge all about sorting through her past and where to go next; Gideon's struggle spread over a series of things.

There'd been his fight for his place as an artist, made worse in a family and world set on devaluing art, despite the daily consumption of movies, music, and books.

Then there'd been his coming to terms with his sexuality and identity, the biggest tragedy being that he'd had anything to come to terms with. For some, acceptance was a given, while others, like Gideon, had no such luck.

He'd been forced to choose between buckling to the pressure of becoming something other than who he was, or developing a thicker skin, shedding family and friends who'd refused to make good on their promises of unconditional love.

And as much as Gideon had gotten tougher, he'd taken a real hit some years ago when the entire country engaged in an unnecessary survey on whether gay people could marry.

Bad enough there'd been a vote, but then so many in his community were left to process the huge betrayal of having forty percent of voters—people they interacted with on a daily basis—choose *against* something that had little-to-no impact on their lives.

And surprise, surprise. In the years following, the country hadn't collapsed, and life went on as normal.

"I'll have a scotch on the rocks."

She startled at the familiar rumble, her attention lifting to Max on the other side of the bar.

She gave him a side-glare, and his lips split into a mischievous grin. "As if I'm letting you drink when you're not even halfway through your second shift. Besides, you're more of a beer guy."

His blue eyes twinkled in the venue's golden light, and she swore her breath caught in response. "You've been watching what I drink?"

"Don't get too cocky." She busied herself wiping down a nonexistent spill on the polished black bar top. "I've poured drinks for as long as I've been legally allowed to. I have a mind for orders, and if you don't believe me, I can tell you what the lighting guy drinks."

His grin fell by a degree. "You mean I'm not special?"

"I mean, if you're looking for some kind of undying declaration while we're both working"—she flicked a curl from her eyes, dismissing her desire to prop him back up or comfort him—"it's not going to happen."

"Well then, I am working." He nudged his head toward the stage. "I'm here bothering you right now because the show is about to finish, and Gideon asked me to find you during his last song."

Her nerves fluttered into high alert. "What do I have to do with Gideon's last song?"

Just because she had a venue that hosted shows didn't mean she wanted to be *in* them.

"He told me to pass on a message."

She swore under her breath, her leg muscles jittery with a sudden need to run. "What's this message?"

Gideon danced across the stage, too busy being a star, while she calculated there was no way Gideon picked Max at random to be her messenger of bad news. He wanted to meddle. Or at least, invent a reason to talk to Max.

Max pointed a finger. "See that gold cord running along the wall back there?"

She spun around. A gold rope was, indeed, camouflaged amongst the equally gold-framed mirrors behind her. She turned back to Max, the heavy bass and brass in Gideon's song overly loud, the deep vibrations playing havoc on her insides. "What about it?"

Max's cheekbones lifted high, a man proud to be part of Gideon's shenanigans. "The music will slow at the very end of Gideon's song. He'll hold a really long note on the word 'love', and that's when you pull that rope."

"And what's supposed to happen?" She snapped her attention to the stage. There stood a solid chance she'd fuck this up for Gideon.

She narrowed her glare and tuned into the music—her glaring a nonsensical reaction to intense listening. The music slowed, and Gideon winked to her from across the room. Her eyelids flung wide. No doubt she looked like a terrified rabbit.

"Oh God, is this it?"

Max shook his head and held up a hand, gesturing for her to wait.

"*Looooooooooooooooooooooove.*"

Gideon's voice filled every corner of the venue, the crowd whooping in support of his perfect pitch and the high and prolonged execution of what he called "a money note". His ability to pull that sound off quite literally paid his bills.

Max nodded at Freya. She sucked in a breath and lunged back, pretty much falling over herself to pull the damn rope.

A shriek of excitement broke from the crowd. She turned just as an avalanche of fuchsia and electric blue sequins fell from an aqua silk canopy Gideon had stretched under the iconic ruby chandelier.

Three child-sized, inflatable bicycles floated from the fray of sequins, the crowd dusted in sparkle. The bikes bounced, audience members swatting them between each other, like a game.

Gideon melted away behind the velvet curtain, everyone in the crowd too busy to notice, his exit as enigmatic and as "Gideon" as an exit could get.

Max smiled, his eyes giving off a soft sheen, as though the crowd and commotion faded and all that mattered was her. "I guess Gideon thought I deserved advance warning since I'll be the one cleaning up the glitter bomb."

Her stomach clenched at how it felt to be the center of his attention, a man as beautiful and well-meaning as Max. In all her years, she'd never been one to attract beauty *or* goodwill, not without a decent amount of hard work on her part. Mostly people treated her more like an afterthought, and that said a lot about her headspace during the years just following her escape from her mother.

She'd surrounded herself with new people, but most of those new people still held too many similarities to the family she'd known, her sense of familiarity completely askew when it came to those people she allowed in her life. The themes of coldness and dysfunction repeated.

Gideon had been the only exception. One person to truly look out for her.

Even now.

So Max, with his sweet brand of innocence, had decided this whole rope-pulling spectacle was about Gideon's need to forecast mess, but Freya knew better. That wasn't the case at all. Gideon had wanted to meet Max. To vet him. To make sure he could be trusted with Freya's heart.

Points of warmth radiated through her chest. Her friend cared. Even after years of managing herself. And despite knowing her days with Max were severely numbered, his stare on her now forced her to consider what life would be like attached to someone like him.

Someone who noticed her.

Someone who cared about the smaller details like the cringe-worthy books she read or her aversion to dark tents. Someone who accepted her completely, from the tattoos on her body to the scars from her past.

And more than any of that, she questioned whether she had the stamina to *pick and stick* life with someone. Anyone.

That thought left her mind and a new one entered. The memory of her parents' disastrous marriage and how quickly people turned into monsters.

Would she one day turn into a monster like her mother? Would Max?

Because her experience of monsters was a real thing, something even the fictional type could not rival. Knowing what she did, how could she ever truly trust anyone?

"Max, maaate!"

The bellowed words yanked her focus toward a man standing yards away, his bloodshot eyes and flushed cheeks hinting he was drunk or perhaps even high.

Max pivoted and stared at the man, too, before turning back to her and whispering, "Why does my old crowd insist on following me?"

A smile tugged at her lips, and she couldn't resist her next comment. "They're not following you. You work where your old crowd hangs out, remember?"

"*Pfft*"—he swatted a hand—"details. Anyway, I'll fob this one off and get back to work. Catch you later."

He gave her a lazy salute and slunk away, but her years of dealing with nasty people reared up to warn her. One look at his friend's twisted sneer told her this particular guy wouldn't be easily "fobbed off".

Thirty-One

"Hey, Cedrick. Sorry, can't chat. Got to get back to work."

Max gave Cedrick an obligatory wave and brushed past, but not before catching the demented joy fading from the man's eyes.

Unwilling to pretend Cedrick was anyone he wanted to talk to, Max gave the equivalent of an internal shrug and headed for the cleaner's alcove.

Perhaps the biggest benefit of being booted from his former social circle was that he no longer had to pretend to like certain people. The farce was over. He had no money. Therefore, no value. Now he and his old "friends" could move on.

He grabbed the large broom from the farthest corner of the cleaner's alcove and went back out to the dance floor, detouring away from Cedrick.

Loud applause rolled across the room as he went about sweeping sequins, glad that less than a couple of hours remained of his long shift. He peered up to find Gideon prancing down the stage steps and into the crowd. He now wore an eye-catching, royal blue blazer embroidered with tiny gold stars, thrown over his plain black shirt and pants.

Max couldn't remember the last time he'd met someone so skilled at drawing attention, all while somehow maintaining so much class and mystery. Gideon's elegance made everyone want to be his friend—a funny observation coming from a man who'd lost almost all his friends.

Only the ones who never really counted.

Right, well, the loneliness still sucked, and as much as he knew nothing of performance art, a small portion of jealousy grabbed at him. He begrudged Gideon his natural born showmanship—the type that looked simple but that no normal mortal could achieve.

What Gideon did wasn't by any stretch easy. Max had watched the man rehearse, and he worked hard for his perfection, that work ethic and drive a puzzle to Max.

Why couldn't he just get his act together and be more like Gideon? What was with the constant aimlessness?

"You think you're too important to talk to your old friends?" A hand gripped Max's shoulder and spun him around. "Now that you're sweeping floors."

Cedrick smirked through an unfocused gaze.

Not wanting any trouble, especially not on an important night for Freya, Max turned away and went back to his work. "I saw Adele around here somewhere, why don't you guys just enjoy your night, okay?"

He eyeballed Adele standing by the bar, hoping she'd do something to draw her control-freak boyfriend away. Only, she just pressed her glass of complimentary champagne to her lips and averted her gaze to the floor, denting any idea she might one day find the courage to stand up to, or at least leave, Cedrick.

Since Max had forgotten to bring out the giant dust pan, he pushed the glittery pile of sequins across the floor with his broom and toward the cleaner's alcove, the task a legitimate reason to walk away.

By the time Max came out again, Cedrick seemed to have forgotten him. So, he hauled away another pan of glitter, then came back out to start clearing tables since the crowd had thinned out.

He passed Freya on his way to the kitchen to get an empty tray, a huge relieved smile on her face as she served out last drinks.

He sidled up to her and used his elbow to offer a nudge of

encouragement, even though what he really wanted to do was pull her into him and kiss her senseless. "Gideon was brilliant. I hope you're ready for The Ruby Room to be at capacity for the rest of its existence."

She slid a drink over to a patron, giving a little shoulder shimmy as she did. "I can't believe it. Now I've seen the show, I'm so excited for what the next two weeks will bring."

He waited for a pause between patrons, and for her to turn and look at him, before he spoke again. "I'm really happy for you, you know that? And I'm happy I could be part of that happiness, even in the tiniest way, such as sweeping your floors."

Her lips parted, and her stare lingered on his for some time, like maybe she hadn't experienced much of anyone being glad for her. For a microsecond, his thoughts revisited all that he'd learned about her childhood, but rather than pity what she'd endured, he felt pride.

She'd pulled through. Even as a child, she'd stood up for herself, forging ahead with her life—two things he still struggled with as a grown man. And somehow, he'd been lucky enough to meet her. To be part of her world. She'd confided in him. Included him. Surely, that meant something?

"So… err…" She blinked and shook her head, as though snapping out of a trance. "What's with your friend over there?"

She tipped her head toward Cedrick.

"To be honest. I have no idea. I'm counting down the seconds until he leaves, or we can at least close and I don't have to look at him anymore."

"Well." She gave a seemingly casual shrug, though the downward bend of her lips told a different story. "He keeps glaring at you, and he doesn't look all that sober. My guess is he's ready to cause trouble, so I'm seconds away from getting Crystal to boot him."

"You don't have to do that." Max backed away so they could both return to their work. "Cedrick and his crowd are regulars here, and I don't want his problem with me to get in the way of business for you. Let me handle him, okay?"

He winked at Freya, an untruthfully light gesture given the invisible weight pressing on his shoulders. He couldn't opt for his usual tactic of ignoring and avoiding the problem, since Cedrick seemed disinclined to go away, which meant Max needed a plan to deal with the guy. Again, not great, since Max had a zero-percent success rate at dealing with anything, much less people in tense situations.

He went about collecting a new tray of empty glasses, waiting for courage and a game plan to surface.

His tray was half-full by the time a wide palm hit him square between the shoulders, pushing him forward so he stumbled. He wobbled, trying to correct his position, every small effort consistently too late.

The glasses slid to the front of his tray, and as if by slow motion, toppled one by one over the edge. One by one, those glasses smashed to the hard wood floor. A high-pitched shattering filled the room.

Patrons gasped and leapt out of the way, a sudden clear circle opening up around him... Well, him and the man who'd done the pushing.

Cedrick.

Max peered down, first to the broken glass across a large expanse of empty floor, then to his shins, his long pants having saved his legs from an encounter with any flying shards.

But then he lifted his focus to a woman a yard away who hadn't been so lucky.

Blood dotted the yellow hem of her knee-length dress, and a steady red stream gushed from her knee. Her gaze darted around the room, only to land on him in a wide stare.

A cold prickle washed over his skin. He was meant to do something, but he stood frozen and unable to make sense of what had just happened. He glanced to his left and found Cedrick glaring back, the knuckle dragger having stooped to pulling innocent people into his grudge.

Max strode toward the woman, but the double thud of footfall followed.

Again, his world spun. He found himself wrenched back by his shirt until he caught sight of Cedrick for one brief second—a brief second before the man's meaty fist connected with Max's left cheekbone.

Holy shit!

A sickening crack filled his ears, and the crowd gasped again. Sharp pain sliced through his face, and he stumbled to the floor. Cedrick bounced on his heels, shaking his hand in the air, swearing, yelling… Something about his "broken fucking knuckles."

Maybe the cracking sound had come from Cedrick's hand more than Max's face?

Still, the only thing Max could really focus on was the way the room wobbled and his thoughts jumbled. Really, he had no focus at all, and his head bloody hurt! And still, he tried to push off the ground, not wanting to fight, but needing to stay upright so that Cedrick wouldn't get on top of him.

Cedrick wasn't much bigger, but he wasn't sober either, and there was no telling what a person in a bad state of mind might do. Plus, Max didn't want to leave The Ruby in the back of an ambulance.

"I don't know what your problem is." He held his palm to his throbbing cheekbone and clenched his eyes mostly shut to keep them from watering. "But you need to leave."

Crystal stepped in through a hollow in the crowd. "Actually, someone's called the police, and he's coming with me until they get here."

"Fuck you both." Spittle flew from Cedrick's mouth, his glassy stare holding Max. "And you don't tell me what to do. Do you think you can waltz on in and get what you want, *who* you want? No, you fucken' can't. You're just a piece-of-shit nobody. A sad, pathetic, broke-as-fuck loser!"

Well, Cedrick was still pissed about Max dating Adele for all of two minutes. That much was clear.

Crystal took a step forward, only for Cedrick to spin around and clamber onto a glossy black table, the ruby chandelier looming just above. Crystal's next step prompted him to kicked a beer-filled glass at her. She ducked out of the way, but glass and amber liquid exploded at her feet.

Screams cut from the crowd. Some yelled for Cedrick to get down. A few fled through the venue's front door, though most stood in wide-eyed morbid fascination. Meanwhile, Freya stood in a spot a few feet ahead of the bar, her mouth open, seemingly frozen.

Crystal kicked beer from the hem of her black jeans, using quick, shifting eye movements to signal for Max to help tackle Cedrick off the table.

Max nodded and ran forward, only for Cedrick to kick another glass.

This time, glass bounced off the floor and struck Max's shin, his pants no match against the projectile's velocity. Though pain radiated up his leg, he didn't have time to dwell on the ache since Cedrick jumped into the air, and in the most idiotic move ever, grabbed the chandelier's brass spokes.

A loud ripping sound cut through the space and a huge crack opened up in the white ceiling. The chandelier jolted. Cedrick held on, his face turning pale like he finally saw how asinine his plan was and didn't know what to do.

Plaster and paint fluttered down like tiny snowflakes, and once again, the chandelier moved, the whole thing dropping by a couple of inches.

Another rip split the air, and this time the entire chandelier fell, taking Cedrick down with it. His ass hit the table first, while the giant chandelier landed on top of him, the table legs snapping and then collapsing.

Dust sailed out in a billowy, white cloud from the epicenter of the fall and across the room, followed by eerie silence.

Max didn't dare breathe. He didn't move. Save for mumbling, "Is he still alive?"

Crystal lunged forward, soon tugging at the chandelier, only to stop. "Hang on a moment, are we even meant to move this thing?" She spun around, glass crunching under her shoes, as she stared at Max. "Won't that cause more damage?"

He'd only just completed a first aid course for his swim coaching job, so the information sat fresh in his head. The chandelier's wires were completely severed, so electrocution wasn't a risk.

"He doesn't seem impaled on anything, so we'll pull the chandelier off, but not move him in case of possible spinal injury."

Besides, copious amounts of glass lay all around and moving Cedrick might mean inadvertently slicing him up. That wasn't something Max wanted to do. Even if the guy had just caused everyone a world of pain.

Max stepped forward, half contemplating whether he could just give up now—go home and have a cup of tea—maybe leave the snot-nosed-bastard under the chandelier where he couldn't bother anyone anymore.

At the same time, his stomach churned at the dystopian vision surrounding them. The Ruby Room's gaping roof, the iconic chandelier a twisted mess atop Cedrick and a now scuffed-up floor.

Freya would have seen everything unfold. And yet he lacked the courage to turn and acknowledge her since he'd played a part in whatever heartbreak would come out of tonight.

He leaned down and wrapped each hand around one of the chandelier's brass spokes, nodding to Crystal to lift along with him. Though nowhere near as heavy as he expected, the chandelier groaned, and a hard tug freed Cedrick enough to have him rolling and shoving clear of his entrapment.

He soon sat coughing and spluttering, a tirade of swears coming between each involuntary noise. Spots of blood seeped through his silver gray shirt, his face a busted and weeping mess.

Even through the blood, Cedrick's glare turned glacial, and he pinned it to Adele standing nearby. "Did you film that? Did you fucking film that? I want a copy for my lawyer."

He made no attempt to rise from the floor, which made Max wonder if he actually could.

Cedrick stabbed a finger at Freya. "Your pathetic club is over, do you hear me? I'll sue you, and I'll fucking win. I'll have this place shut down."

Freya shuddered as though trying to awaken from this entire nightmare. "Has someone called an ambulance yet?"

One of the bartenders waved her hand from across the room, a phone pressed to her ear. "I'm on it. They're already on the way."

"Good thing the hospital is just down the road." Freya spoke in a dull mumble, as if a large part of her had already left the building.

Meanwhile, Cedrick became weirdly silent, his head lolling forward, the heel of his oxford pushing at a pile of red glass before him. There was something ironic about that image—a man, who moments earlier had kicked beer glasses with no regard for the damage he caused—now soaked in blood, the self-inflicted victim of the mother of all glassing incidents.

Freya's focus flicked to Max, her pupils dilated and jaw still loose. Heavy seconds dragged until slowly, but surely, the muscles over her brow hardened, and her eyes formed a razor-sharp scowl.

He'd promised to handle Cedrick, shutting down her offer to get Crystal to eject the guy long before he caused any problems. Now The Ruby Room lay in ruins, as did this monumental night. The entire festival was now likely a lost cause, too.

And of course, there was the bleeding woman and Cedrick's injuries, plus his threat of a lawsuit. Worst of all, the countless employees, performers, and technicians now out of a job with the bar in its current unworkable state.

There'd be no positive spin to bail Max out of *this* disaster. Nausea swirled in his gut. Guilt and yet more failure lay heavy on his heart.

The bartender from earlier sidled up to Freya, phone still in hand.

"Honey, there's a call for you." She extended the phone with a grimace. "Saint Vincent's Hospital. It's your mum. It sounds urgent."

Thirty-Two

FREYA'S HEART beat so hard and fast her chest hurt from the unstoppable effort, her muscles so weak they trembled and felt as if they were made of water. She sat in the passenger side of Max's car, wringing her hands, hating that she hated him right now, while still needing his help to get her the few blocks to the hospital since she wasn't anywhere near stable enough to make it there alone.

She opened and closed her hand, her elbows down to her fingers numb from the unforgiving adrenaline filling her muscles, and she tried to get back some sort of sensation. She didn't know what to think. *Couldn't* think. Her thoughts were out of control and incapable of slowing down.

Her mother's last moments loomed.

Heck, so did Freya's time with Max.

Or any man.

Regardless of what had just gone down at The Ruby, she couldn't see herself wanting to date for a long time. Something not easily defined was about to happen, something uncontrollable. No matter what, death waited for no man or woman, and her life balanced on the edge of a major change.

Her throat hurt from the labor of holding back tears. Her stomach held the heaviness of someone seconds from lunging off a bridge—even though she'd always imagined she'd feel nothing on the day her mother's reckoning finally rolled around.

The car stopped at a set of lights, and she gnawed at the inside of her cheek, her focus glued to the pedestrian crossing and a smiling couple walking hand-in-hand on the other side of the windshield.

To them, this was just an ordinary night. They had all the time in the world, and life held no hurry. But not for her. Certainly not for her mother.

She pressed the heel of her hand to her sternum and rubbed, the rapid beat of her heart refusing to abate. There were things she had to say. Things she'd held on to for far too long.

She'd tell her mother that although she could never forgive the abuse, she understood how she'd ended up the way she had. That wherever death took her next, she really did hope her mother would finally know peace from the hurt and hate gifted to her as a child.

If death were a fair place, perhaps her mother would get a replay. A new family. A new life free from abuse, neglect, and childhood trauma. A permanent escape from the war that had raged in her mind every day for decades.

And maybe one day Freya would get a new childhood too…

A tear spilled down her cheek, but she swept at it before Max could notice, breathing deep to still her runaway mind—a mind for some reason grappling with the concept of reincarnation.

What the heck is that about?

Just once, she wanted things to be okay. To think that maybe, just maybe, in her final moments with her mother, she could see a flash of something more than judgment and manipulation.

A sense of love. Apology. Acceptance…

Max's car plunged into a stretch of deep shadow, and she blinked at the concrete gray walls of a multi-level parking lot, one packed level flicking by after another level, an available spot seeming illusive.

She needed an escape from the rising panic that she wouldn't make it in time, so she rehearsed what she would say, all while questioning whether she could really execute this final conversation.

Then again, even if her mother failed to budge, at least she could say she'd tried her best, that she'd done all she could to fill in the final missing pieces and have the one talk she and her mother had never had.

Maybe she'd get closure, before the opportunity was lost forever.

Max parked, and she pulled at her door handle, her bag already slung over her shoulder.

She raced for the bank of elevators, leaving him to catch up—or not—because at this point, she didn't care.

Soon, she dashed across the asphalt to the hospital, then into another elevator, and up eleven floors to the palliative care unit, where she burst across the blue-carpeted corridor and right past the nurses' station.

Her breath exploded through her lips and cream-colored walls flickered by, her gaze darting from one door to the other until it landed on her mother's room number.

She bolted through an icy-blue curtain surrounding the only bed in the room. Her feet ground to a halt, her body jolting at the sight of a nurse—a woman in her forties, with short salt and pepper hair—standing over her mother, hand stroking her sandy-blond fringe, thumb rubbing tenderly at a forehead no longer quite so scored in wrinkles.

Freya's muscles turned rigid. There were no more monitors. No more drips. No needles feeding pain meds into her mother's arms. A rolled-up towel sat tucked under her mother's chin, keeping her slack jaw from falling open.

Freya's knees unlocked, and she forced a few tiny steps before she fell to the ground yards from the bed. Her attention locked on her mother's eyes.

Closed eyes.

Freya jerked her chin higher, catching sight of the nurse's lips pressed into a thin smile, one that conveyed sympathy and apology.

"I'm so sorry." The nurse held a soft tone, one that somehow sounded like glass shattering in a silent room. "She's gone."

Freya's body took over, and she stumbled the few steps to her mother's side, collapsing at the bed's pillow end, a great wail breaking free of her. The deep-within sound wasn't like anything she'd ever known herself capable of making. It embodied all-consuming grief and knowledge that an invisible cord had just been severed. The link between mother and daughter. A link that existed regardless of where the relationship stood.

She reached out and stroked her mother's forehead, the warmth in her skin still present as if her mother only slept. And now the tears came thick and fast. Tears she hadn't let herself cry in years, but which she worried would never stop.

Her tummy cramped, pained and hollow, as though someone had taken a shovel and scooped out her insides, and even as the tears fell, a new and more depressing understanding grew.

That this was the first time. *The only time*, she'd ever been able to touch her mother with any kind of tenderness, except for that ill-received kiss on her mother's forehead last time. The one chance she'd ever have to voice any of the thoughts that swirled within her mind for as long as she could remember.

"Oh, you poor woman." She leaned forward and pressed a kiss to her mother's head. No one would understand this. That *she* would feel sorry for her mother. Her abuser. Her tormenter. But no single journey through life was the same, and this was her particular mess to untangle. "I hope you know what peace is now."

Another sob broke out, along with more fat tears. She crumpled forward and rested her head on the thick hospital pillow beside her mother's. The room and everyone watching—the nurse, Max—all disappeared.

It was just Freya, her mother, and a heavy, uncontrollable grief.

That final conversation, the one she'd planned during the ride over, would never happen now. All she had was *this*. And the ability to touch her mother. Her *dead* mother. Along with the engulfing sense she was forever alone.

A filling breath forced its way into her lungs, as though she'd failed to breathe the entire time she'd been sobbing, which maybe wasn't all that untrue.

So, she sat back and took more breaths, dedicating herself to memorizing the details of her mother's face one last time. For once, Kerry Branner looked calm, her wrinkles eased, and her skin inexplicably glowing.

Even growing up, Freya noted the permanent creases between her mother's brow; her jaw always fused and strained. She'd wondered if her mother even had the ability to just let go.

As an adult, Freya knew different. Her mother had never had an easy moment in her entire life, the ghosts of her past continued to haunt, and that alone was something worth crying over.

Freya extended her arm and pressed her hand to the top of her mother's sternum, wishing her heart still beat in there. "You never had a chance, did you?"

Another wave of grief rose through her chest, culminating in another thick downpour of tears. They slid to her jawline, hitting her forearm, the room's cold air adding a chill.

Her mother's golden lashes extended down in their closed position, sprinkles of gray highlighting the rarity for Freya to really observe. Never once in her life had she felt comfortable enough to really look at her mother. At least, not in a way that didn't involve staring each other down.

She jerked back, the space between her shoulders taut, while a new heat flared in her belly. She swiped at her face with an open palm, sniffling, her eyes narrowed at her mother's peaceful face.

Except, now her expression appeared less restful, more mocking.

Amazing how a motionless face could still portray so many emotions.

When Freya had received the call to come to the hospital, she figured she'd have a few minutes alone with her mother before she passed away. But no. Her mother had blindsided her.

"You couldn't wait just a moment longer, could you?" She laughed and shook her head.

Am I really talking to a dead person?

And of course, her mother hadn't waited.

Even in this last thing, she denied Freya.

A daughter she'd never wanted and used all the same.

Fuck.

Freya rubbed at more tears. Even in death, her mother confused her.

Unlike any normal child from a normal family, this experience couldn't be as simple as knowing she was going to miss her mother. Just the fact that this moment hurt so much seemed truly unfair.

Why? Why do I care?

Because her life is just one giant pity, now isn't it?

A ruined childhood. A ruined child. A damaged woman who'd only known how to damage others. She'd passed her wound on to her children. A generational wound that dated who knew how far back and kept on giving, or more precisely, taking.

Nothing and no one could help Freya climb out of the hole she'd been born into.

No one would truly understand. Not even her brother.

She'd always been alone, her latest involvement with her mother an attempt to get the inflictor of her wounds to provide the healing, and that ploy had always been doomed to fail.

Maybe she'd brought this pain on herself.

Gone was any chance of an apology, any chance her mother might express any feelings of love. Freya would find no resolution here, that much was clear.

A large hand landed on her shoulder. She slammed her eyes shut and sucked in a breath. *Max.*

"Is there something I can help you with?"

His gentle tone made her want to fold forward into a ball, his kindness more jarring than if he'd been mad at her for shutting him out. She shook her head and withdrew any verbal response, continuing the sham of being mad, when she really just didn't want to hear her own grief-affected voice.

"I just spoke to the nurse." His strong fingers massaged her shoulder, and her heart sank. "The hospital needs to know which funeral home will be collecting her body tomorrow morning."

She tilted her head toward her handbag, which she'd thrown onto the ground on her way in. "There are papers in my bag. Can you call and tell them? I just... I can't..."

She sucked in another shuddering breath, rustling filling her ears. How was it possible to have so many layers of pain? Pain for her mother. Pain for herself. Pain at Max's presence.

She launched to her feet. "Wait."

She faced him for the first time since entering this hospital. She had no idea how much of her grief he'd witnessed, and she didn't really want to think about it. All she knew was that she was glad she hadn't been completely alone.

His attention snapped from the handbag and back to her, and within seconds, he stepped forward and wrapped his arms around her. She sank against him, burying her face in his black cotton shirt, the boozy scent of The Ruby Room and his cool mint cologne infiltrating the emotions already swallowing her whole.

A new set of claws dug into her heart. The pain of having someone take her weight, both literally and figuratively. This should be a relief, but for a broken woman like her, the support hurt more than she could handle. A sob tore from her, and she shook in his embrace, more tears spilling forth and soaking into his shirt.

And he just stood there, silent and holding her, as if he knew words couldn't help.

He held her for as long as she needed, until she took a step away and said, "Thank you."

The weak gratitude was the best she could muster. She slunk back and stared at the ceiling, the top of her head hurting from all the crying and having to process so much all at once.

The totality of her mother's life.

All the missed opportunities and wasted years.

The sheer lack of love.

And the coldest, hardest truth of all?

Sometimes, no matter what, there was no apology, no heartfelt goodbye, certainly no happy ever after.

While she'd been running for years, trying to escape her past, working double time to gain all she'd missed out on, her mother's death came as a brick wall telling her to stop and just be sad. To say goodbye to all the things she'd never had and the things she'd never wanted in the first place—the abuse, the permanent emotional scars.

She refocused on Max and his soft smile, his brows raised in an expression of hope, like maybe she might tell him the worst was over. But the pain in her head said the worst had just begun, and the ache in her heart would likely never leave.

"Come back as soon as you can." She paused, taking a second to appreciate her even voice that time, vowing that for once in her life she'd hit stop on the treadmill and finally step away. Things were going to change. "I want to go home."

Thirty-Three

A MIXTURE of gray and white filtered in as Max lay on the couch, blinking at the heavy floor-to-ceiling drapes in Freya's living room, the tiniest slip of light spilling in through a break in the center.

Having slept there overnight, he huffed out a sigh and interlaced his fingers over his belly trying not to breathe in the smell of clothes still worn since the beginning of his long bar shift yesterday morning.

Every so often, the light from the curtains flickered with the soft plod of people walking by in the street outside. People just starting their day. Occasionally, the plodding came with the sound of chatter, another reminder of just how long he'd lain here, awake and alone.

Last night, within seconds of arriving home, Freya ran upstairs, and he'd stayed in case she needed anything. In case she needed *him*.

So far, she hadn't.

He let out a groan and sat up, his head aching from sleep deprivation, his back sore from his night on the couch. A dull click came from upstairs, followed by the creak of floorboards. *She was awake.*

He shot up and made his way to the curtains, not wanting a dark, depressing room to greet her when she came downstairs.

"Oh, you're still here." Her tone croaked, flat on delivery.

He spun around, his ribs contracting painfully at the sight of her bare feet on the bottom step.

He slid his gaze up to her lopsided, white silk robe and her frizzy, misshapen hair. The unkempt look didn't bother him so much as the soullessness in her eyes, the surrounding skin red and puffy, her small and fragile stance adding to her overall shattered look. Like all the spark he loved about this woman had left.

He swallowed at the thick sensation in his throat and stepped forward. She slipped past him, veering to the right and into the kitchen.

"I wanted to make sure you'd be okay."

She poured herself a drink, an *actual* drink, tequila splashing around in a flare-rimmed shot glass at seven in the morning.

She pressed the glass to her lips and tipped back her head, gulping the straight liquor, before straightening and staring at him. "I'm not okay."

She poured another shot and tipped that one back too, catching his gaze as she placed the glass soundlessly to the white marble counter. "It's best you leave."

His mouth turned dry, her speech slow and calculated. Couldn't she just get angry and lash out at him? Give him something more than dull apathy? If she'd lost all spirit, then that meant he'd lost something else altogether. Something he still grappled to understand. Something irreplaceable.

He opened his mouth ready to speak, but his jaw just wavered and nothing came out.

His natural inclination in a bad situation was to find the sunny side, but this was way beyond a *bad* situation. Her bar had been trashed. Her mum was dead.

Maybe she was right.

Maybe she wasn't okay.

Maybe more went on in her mind than she let on.

He forced a smile, though the thick knot grew in his throat, his heartbeat drumming loud in his ears. "Is there anything you need me to do for you today?"

He paused, not sure he should mention The Ruby Room, though

the situation there needed urgent attention, too, largely because of him. "Anything you'd like me to handle at the bar?"

She dipped her chin, her fingers twisting the faceted shot glass so that a rainbow of reflective lights danced round the counter.

The prettiness of those lights did nothing to hide her numb reaction.

She shook her head, messy bed-curls flopping about her face. "Burn the bar for all I care. Your friend half-demolished the place, anyway. I don't have the energy to fix any damage before the festival tomorrow night." She lifted her chin, her red-tinged stare meeting his. "Leave me alone. Please."

The lower rim of her eyes glistened with burgeoning tears, and her pitchy tone drove a knife through his heart.

This wasn't Freya. His strong. Upbeat. Self-assured. Freya.

This was someone else entirely.

Or maybe it *was* her. Some long-buried version he only met now.

What he *did* know was that he wanted to bundle her in his arms and take her upstairs to bed. To hold her and kiss her until all signs of palpable pain melted.

He stepped forward, seeking to do just that. "Let me—"

She slammed her eyes shut, a tear breaking loose. "You might like people to clean up your messes, Max, but I don't. Go!"

Her voice reverberated around the room, casting a tight wire net around his heart, but leaving no doubt of just how much she meant what she said. When her eyes flung open again, the fire in her glare sucked the air straight out of his lungs. All he could manage was a numb nod, before turning for the front door.

His hurried steps didn't distract from the pain filling his chest. The pain of being discarded. Of having his flaws once more thrown in his face.

His association with Cedrick, however unwilling, meant he'd contributed to Freya's hurt, and for that alone, he'd never forgive himself.

He stepped outside and squinted at the bright morning light, the crisp breeze nipping at his cheeks. He stood on the wrong side of her closed door, breaths faster and harder than he could handle.

He leaned forward and placed his hands on his knees, the wild beating in his ribcage battling against the mad churn of his belly because maybe, just maybe, she'd finally had enough of him. And even though he'd never thought too deeply on their relationship, now that he did, he simply couldn't bear to lose her.

So, this is what heartbreak feels like.

That couldn't have been it, though. He and Freya had nothing more than a casual thing, right?

Wrong.

Multiple people had ditched him over the years, especially of late, but the thought of losing Freya overshadowed any fear of having no friends, money, or his apartment. Her sudden dismissal shone a giant spotlight on something he'd never known he wanted but now clearly needed. A sense of belonging. More precisely. Belonging to *her*.

He peeled away from the wall and strode toward his car, his phone lighting up with a message the moment he pulled it from his pocket. In fact, there were a number of missed calls and voice messages, all from the same number.

He slid into his car and settled behind the steering wheel, glowering at his screen and flipping through the messages.

He had no idea how this person—the last person he expected to be sending him a slew of sweary, demanding messages—had wrangled his number. But they had. And each message read more urgent and heavy-handed than the last.

Thirty-Four

Max pushed through The Ruby Room's doors, only to stop in his tracks. Apart from this not being somewhere he wanted to be right now, his pulse still ran high at having watched the spark fade from Freya's eyes, only for her to cast him out moments later.

And now *this*… The carnage from last night.

A massive pile of rubble and glass sat in the center of the bar's floor, and his mouth filled with a bitter taste at the sight of it. In the stark light of day, everything was so much worse. If not for Gideon's convincing that fixing the bar was the one and only chance for Max to make things right with Freya, he wouldn't be here.

"Oh, this isn't going to work." He tapped his forehead with his open palm, turning back to eye the door.

Not only was the chandelier shattered into a million tiny pieces, but the floor itself sported major dents and scratches. If he squinted hard enough, he was almost certain spots of Cedrick's blood still dotted the place, too.

His stomach churned, not only at the blood, but that Gideon had to be out of his mind to genuinely think he'd be putting on a show tomorrow night.

Gideon strode across the room from the cleaner's alcove, some stocky woman Max had never met keeping pace beside him. "Oh yes, it will work. I don't quit, and I certainly don't cancel shows. So, wipe that frown off your face and start with the positive thoughts, you got it?"

Gideon stopped a few paces away, his narrowed gaze tracking up and down Max's body. He made a show of sniffing the air.

"Holy Rollers!" He swatted at the air and made a show of coughing and spluttering. "You might be hot, but right now you stink like a moldy shoe."

The woman behind Gideon puffed out her cheeks, face turning a quick red, before she doubled forward in a fit of laughter.

Max peered down at his clothes, the ones he'd indeed been wearing since yesterday morning, all rumpled from sleeping on Freya's couch. "I haven't been home yet."

"Lucky for you I have more friends coming in to help." Gideon rolled his eyes. "I'll get someone to bring clothes. The bar has no showers, but I'm sure we can hunt down some soap. Just freshen up in a sink, or something; whatever it takes to put us all out of our misery."

Max gave a lopsided smile. Despite the dig at his unintended lack of personal hygiene, the more he spoke to Gideon, the more he liked the guy. At least he could take comfort that Freya had one decent friend, someone she could rely on since she'd kicked him to the curb.

"You really think we can do this?" He ran his fingers through the front of his hair, needing every last bit of hope he could get, no matter how hollow.

"That's what Cynthia's here for." Gideon gestured to the woman beside him. "She's a Jill-of-all-trades who can fix anything."

Cynthia shrugged and gave a sheepish wave, perhaps embarrassed about her loss of composure just moments ago. "It'll be a last-minute throw together, and we definitely won't get a replacement ruby chandelier in time, but I have an alternative plan that should work. Freya can always get the original fixed or replaced if she doesn't like what we do."

"Okaaaay." Max switched his gaze between Gideon and Cynthia, unsure how he felt about the whole "thrown together" aspect. "Where do we start?"

Cynthia cringed. "We can't do anything without money, and we're talking thousands of dollars of damage here. I need materials and plenty of extra help. I have some buddies who'll pop around for free though, so I guess that's a start, yeah?"

Gideon whipped his phone out of his pocket and waved it around. "I've started an online fundraiser and pitched in what personal money I can, but other than that, it's a waiting game until we have some cash flow. There's definitely not enough time to wait on the bar's insurance to come through, that's for sure."

"So, until the fundraiser money *maybe* eventuates, we do nothing?"

Gideon shrugged. "I mean, for now it's all about cleaning up the mess. And then I guess we see what money we have to work with in the hours to come."

"That's not good enough. Your show is tomorrow night."

"Well, if we're lucky and my fans and friends feel generous, we'll have the beginnings of something to work with by the end of today." Gideon lifted one corner of his lip, cramming his phone into his black pants pocket. "Maybe we can get stuck into something tomorrow morning."

"There's no way you'll get everything done in one morning." He turned to Cynthia, shaking his head. "The plaster won't be in time, right?"

Cynthia nodded. "I mean, there's a beam the chandelier will be bolted to, but it'll still be a tight call. I'd say we'll be applying paint right up until showtime."

His pulse climbed, the seed of a non-ideal notion taking root. "But if you get the money straight away, you can start straight away?"

Cynthia rubbed the back of her neck. "I don't see why not. I have people waiting to start today, just in case there's a miracle, but I don't see how the money will be here any earlier."

He glanced around the rubble-cluttered Ruby Room and drew in a deep breath, taking time to reconsider before committing his new intentions into words.

There wasn't much to consider. His next move had been decided the moment Cedrick ripped the ruby chandelier clean out of the ceiling, and the numerous moments since, when despair marked Freya's face.

A distinct strain bunched the muscles around his ribcage, the repercussions of what he was about to do sinking like a heavy stone in still water. Last night's disaster jeopardized Gideon's career, along with Freya's bar, and the multitude of people relying on it staying open.

This was the right thing to do. The only thing to do.

"I'll pay."

The tightness around his chest disappeared the second the words came out, and he sucked in an easy breath. He'd not only done the right thing, he'd done the *responsible* thing, which was so contrary to his nature he had the inexplicable desire to dance.

Gideon merely stared, though his light brown eyes glittered with understanding.

The desire to dance faded just as he remembered this move would cost him his apartment.

No matter what I do here, something sucky will happen.

Yes, that much was true, but he could deal with something sucky happening to him, something sucky that he'd brought on himself. Freya and Gideon, The Ruby Room, were innocent victims to his years of recklessness, of bad friendships, of ignoring multiple warnings on multiple fronts. Cedrick included.

Besides, the apartment had turned into a ball and chain around Max's neck—albeit a nicely designed, eco-friendly ball and chain—though not so much more than a glamorous arrangement of bricks and steel attached to a nice view.

From the desperate attempts to dodge calls from his bank, to taking on any job he could get, while trying to fix things he could no longer afford, he'd been so stressed just trying to keep the place. *This wasn't the way he wanted to live.*

Maybe it *was* time to move on, to downsize like he should have the moment he lost all his money.

Gideon pressed his fingertips to his lips and gave a playful shake of his head. "I'm not even going to ask if you want to reconsider. We're taking that offer and running, regardless."

Max reached into his back pocket and handed his credit card to

Gideon. "Go make all the calls you need and get this thing started. I'll wait around until you need me."

Gideon fanned himself with the credit card, his expression aglow like a man already making plans and on a mission. "Trust me, we have *a lot* of work to do, and you won't just be sitting around here looking pretty. While I'm busy calling around and spending your money, you better be making a few calls of your own. We need all the help we can get. That means getting any and all of your friends and family down here to lend a hand."

<h1 style="text-align:center">Thirty-Five</h1>

OVER THE NEXT FEW HOURS, a small army of people Max didn't know arrived at The Ruby Room to help. Miro found someone to take over at the café; Orlando, Sophie, and Agathe also came by. Luke still had to work at Tiluma but would swing past at the end of the day.

At least Max had some familiar people here, even if he hadn't found the courage to tell anyone about his run-in with Freya that morning. Also, true to his word, Gideon found someone to bring Max a change of clothes, though, much to everyone else's amusement, a button-up shirt in an eye-watering shade of tangerine wasn't what he'd expected.

The roof repairs were well under way since one of Miro's first jobs when he'd arrived in Australia had been as a painter. He knew a fair bit about patch up jobs and turned out to be Cynthia's best assistant.

Orlando, being a former firefighter and now a park ranger, took on the physical tasks of hefting heavy items to and from the work site. Sophie sat cross-legged on the floor with a pair of pliers, attaching new crystals sourced from one of Gideon's costume designer friends to the old chandelier's frame.

Cynthia called a rest break, and Miro fired up The Ruby Room's coffee machine, going so far as to take individual coffee orders. Max, having resigned himself to losing his apartment, threw financial caution to the wind and put in a phone order to a deli down the road to provide sandwiches for everyone.

Though the coming months would be a financial challenge, he had no regrets about lobbing money at getting The Ruby Room ready for tomorrow's show. His contribution made a pivotal difference, and the sea of smiling faces today confirmed he'd taken a wise risk.

Even if she didn't know it, Freya would still get her dream of being part of the festival, of being part of something bigger.

The sandwiches arrived, and he took one to the cobblestone alley behind the bar. He'd intended to have a quiet moment alone, except Gideon beat him to the idea and stood with a gold-rimmed, black coffee cup and saucer perched in one hand, a sideways glance pitched Max's way as he sipped. His cheeks were ashen, like maybe the effort of appearing chipper for his friends had finally worn him out.

Max leaned against the opposite wall, ripping at the white paper around his sandwich. "Not what you expected for the day before your big new show?"

Gideon's posture sank, his gaze searching the silver clouds. "Expending my precious voice on a million phone calls followed by hours of hard labor?" He dropped his attention back to Max. "No. Not exactly. But then we do all manner of extreme things for love, don't we?"

Max returned Gideon's stare, not entirely sure whether to read into what he'd said. Did he mean his love for performing? Or maybe his love for Freya as a friend?

Gideon raised a brow, a sudden lightness lifting his features in a way that suggested humor, or maybe that the statement about love was meant for Max. As in, Gideon thought Max loved Freya.

An invisible fist slammed into Max's gut, and he clenched his stomach muscles against that suggestion's hard truth. Freya had only hours ago booted him from her house. And his relationship with her had never been more than anything casual. He'd played a part in her bar getting trashed. Her mother had died. He didn't exactly stand in the best position for falling in love.

A small smile curled Gideon's lips, as if his verbal sucker punch had landed exactly as intended. "You still sure about what you did in there? You know, giving away your money? Freya told me you're working at the bar because you need the cash."

Max peered down at his sandwich, not sure he still wanted to eat. "What choice did I have?"

"You and I both know you could have done nothing."

Gideon took another slow sip of coffee, perhaps drawing out a chance for Max to think over that statement. But Gideon was right, only Max couldn't bring himself to admit anything regarding his feelings for Freya. Maybe because he knew it was way too late for any of that.

"What happened last night is partly my fault."

Gideon set down his cup and closed his eyes, letting out a loud sigh. "You know, I don't like wasting my voice on pointless conversations. It's not your fault that assholes exist in the world, so maybe you could cut the bullshit and start saying something we can both work with."

Heat flared in Max's belly, and his fingers tensed, no doubt leaving an imprint in his still uneaten sandwich. "Fine then. I had to do this for her."

"Well, now. That's a different story, isn't it?"

Max straightened, the muscles at his spine drawing taut along with his jaw. "You would have done the same."

Gideon shook his head in a slow, deliberate, somehow mocking movement. "Uh-uh. Similar, but not the same. Intention is everything, and you, sir, have very different intentions. But then, who you are and what you intend don't always sync up, do they?"

Max slumped against the wall. He'd always thought of himself as the fun guy. The sociable guy. The one who everything worked out for, no matter what. But here he stood with a nearly empty bank account and all but one of his old friends gone.

He bit into his sandwich and tore off a chunk, the deli meats and grilled vegetables tasteless in light of where his mind went. The woman he potentially loved wanted nothing to do with him.

"I can't remember the last time I had any idea what I wanted for my life, but this sure isn't it."

This day had been a total rollercoaster, what with this morning's devastation, then the joy of having so many hands on deck at the bar, and now this—a demoralizing education on just how lost he'd become.

Gideon's stare lingered, and the center of his forehead crinkled with tiny lines. "You know, I'd be willing to bet money that somewhere deep inside that pretty-boy brain of yours, you know exactly what you want to do. You're just too chicken-shit to do it."

Max jolted. "Sorry. What?"

"All these years and you've used money and distraction to avoid taking any real risk." Gideon took another sip from his coffee cup, smiling over the rim. "I've been around a while, you know. I've watched a lot of artists sit about waiting for 'inspiration', rather than just getting the bloody work done. You're no different. I can even guess why you do it."

Max frowned, doubting Gideon would know anything more than he did about the inner workings of his mind, mostly because he'd mulled over this exact problem for years and always came up empty.

Gideon lowered his cup into its saucer ever so slowly, seeming to enjoy the way-too-long pause. "You're afraid of starting something and failing, which is pretty cliché and boring really, so I'll do you one better. Given your failed career as a tech mogul, as well as who your brother is and that he *didn't* fail, my guess is you feel the need to justify your existence and your choices with how much potential money you might make. You've decided that since you can't have guaranteed huge success on anything, you just won't try."

Gideon quirked a brow, as if awaiting confirmation, even though everything else about his face said he'd already decided he was right.

Max frowned at his feet and the slate-gray cobblestones beneath, his churning stomach continuing an assault against this new revelation.

"I don't know if I ever quite thought of it that way." He peered back at Gideon and shrugged. "But maybe?"

"I'm right about the fear of failure, yes?"

Max took another bite of his sandwich, the flavor returning, and the tension in his body inexplicably lighter. "Yeah, I guess so. Something like that."

"Then my question to you is, given you're likely to lose everything anyway, what's stopping you now?"

Max paused mid-chew. "I don't know where to start."

Gideon rolled his eyes, though the upturn of his lips signaled he meant no insult. "You don't need to know the where, you just start. That's all there is to it." He stabbed his cup forward. "Let me ask you something. What do you think people said when I told them I wanted to be a performer?"

"I don't know. Congratulations?"

Gideon threw back his head and barked out a thick laugh. "You are a sweet one, but no. They laughed and said an arts degree was a one-way road to homelessness. Maybe the career I have now is an exception to the rule, but even if I had never made it on stage, there were always other options. I have never regretted my choice. Unlike so many people, at least I'll die knowing I got to discover who I am through chasing my dreams. So as much as the ridicule and abandonment hurt, I'm still the one who lives in this body day after day, not them. I decide where my story goes, no one else."

Gideon's expression hardened. "You take whatever start you can get, Max. You don't have to do things right the first time, but you do have to work your ass off to build a life you're willing to smile about on your deathbed. Your only other option is to live an existence you've let others bully you into." He paused and eased his shoulders down, lifting his hand in a resigned sort of gesture. "And if you really want some cheesy motivation, then do it for love."

Max nodded to the ground, this time not even trying to escape Gideon's assumptions about his feelings toward Freya. Truth be told, he wanted more than what they currently had, though they currently had nothing, so the bar was set mighty low.

"You're right." He raised his chin, for the first time in ages relaxed and not totally discordant with his own body. "Freya won't want a man who's not successful in some way."

Gideon burst into laughter again, tipping forward as much as a man could while holding a half cup of coffee. "What sort of hideous 1950s rhetoric is that? Do you even know Freya? Jesus… If you haven't already noticed, she's about the last person to care what's in your bank account and is an old hand at looking after herself. The question is, can you do the same? Do you have the ability to survive without expecting other people, *especially her,* to compensate for the unglamorous mess you're so tangled up in right now? Because I can tell you, like any person with her backstory, Freya sees your issues from miles away. She most definitely does not deserve to deal with yet another person's problems."

Max winced, heart retreating at Gideon's morsel of truth. From the sound of things, he and Freya wouldn't be a couple for a long while.

And at his current rate of success, probably never.

"You're right." His voice dragged thick past the tension in his throat. "I'm not happy with where I am. I'm coasting through life and fucking things up as I go. What's the point of wasting these years being miserable and going nowhere? I don't want to pretend I'm okay with that kind of aimlessness anymore. I want my life back. I want something to look forward to. To work toward. And *someone.*" He peered back at Gideon, delivering his next heartfelt truth. "I want Freya, but I just don't see that happening."

"Max." Gideon twisted his lips in an expression of deep thought. "I would love to tell you to go out there and get your woman, but I can't. Freya is my closest friend. My oldest friend. When she hurts, I hurt too. She needs a man who can take charge of his happiness, who walks his own path, and doesn't expect her to always lead. You and I both know that's not you, even though you want it to be. And while wanting is admirable, I need to ask…" He downed the last sip of his coffee, the flatness of his stare not making him appear all that hopeful. "Do you honestly think you can become that man for her?"

Thirty-Six

ANOTHER DAY PASSED, and Max pushed in the final chair at The Ruby Room. Gideon's show was due to start in four hours. He took himself to the farthest wall and ran his gaze over the space, the updated chandelier sporting less ruby glass and a little more rainbow.

For the first time in months, his skin tingled with excitement. The club's rushed repairs forced him to focus in a way that he hadn't managed in years. Not since his time as a competitive swimmer, staring down the challenge of a long-haul race, his perspective sharpened after Gideon's motivational talk.

Soon, Freya would be in to look over the repairs. He hadn't seen her since yesterday morning when she'd been a total wreck, demanding he leave. Though he wasn't stupid enough to think one day would change her mind altogether, maybe the club's quick renovation would lift her mood in some small way.

"Burn the bar down for all I care… Leave me alone. Please."

Those words knocked around in his head, and his lungs filled with a strained breath. He'd quite literally put everything into these repairs, but chances were, they'd mean nothing to her. Not after what she'd been through. Not when he'd contributed to making a bad situation worse.

But he'd needed to do something—anything—to increase her chances of finding happiness again, at least eventually, anyway.

So, he'd sacrificed the money he'd spent weeks saving and thrown his heart into the possibility that her outlook on the bar might change, that she might still want him around in some kind of way.

The club door creaked, and seconds later, she stepped through, her dazed stare tracking around the room, her cheeks pale, hair unkempt, and expression frozen on the room's center.

Gideon snapped the microphone into a stand on the stage, causing a loud pop through the speakers. She jolted, her lashes fluttering in rapid blinks, and her lips slipping open.

Gideon only now noticed his friend. In no time, he leaped off the two-meter stage and ran toward her, dodging a gauntlet of tables. Freya took two quick steps toward him, and he threw his arms around her.

Max's muscles turned weak at the sight, at Freya sagging into Gideon's embrace, her face buried against his neck.

There was something so intimate about the way they held each other, two people with a long history of supporting each other. He didn't deserve to feel jealous, but he did anyway, wanting desperately to be the one holding her, to sweep her up and hug away her pain.

Even if Gideon hadn't seen Freya since her mother had passed, and as unhealthy as Max's desire was, he still wanted to be her everything.

He closed his hands into fists and made himself stay put, watching the scene unfold, acknowledging Gideon's place as her comfort. For one, he'd never ruined her club. In fact, he'd only ever added to her success, standing alongside Freya throughout some of her worst years.

He also had his life together and had a heck of a lot more to offer than Max did.

Freya pulled away and said nothing.

He fought an urge to slink away and hide in the cleaner's alcove, far from where he'd have to witness yet more of his shortcomings when she finally did look at him.

But denial hadn't been his friend thus far, so he stayed and followed her line of sight to the new chandelier, no longer pure ruby since many of the lost or damaged original crystals had been painstakingly replaced to make a multi-colored chandelier.

The new chandelier wasn't inferior. It was an explosion of iridescent color. A surprising change fitting with the spirit of the pride charity the bar would raise money for during the festival.

But then, his opinion didn't matter anywhere near as much as hers, and right now, her unblinking gaze filled him with a weak ache.

At no point did her attention land on him, which brought up the possibility that she'd noticed him but wanted to keep her distance just like yesterday. And though he wanted to look away, to wallow in his heartache, he also refused to tear his attention from her.

Her focus remained latched to the rainbow chandelier, the skin under her eyes red and splotchy.

"It's nice. Thank you." Her husky, tattered voice traveled across the room.

She gave Gideon a tight smile, like she acknowledged the effort in getting the bar in shape but lacked the heart to dredge up any real excitement.

Gideon wrapped his arm around her shoulder and squeezed her in. "Honey, are you okay?"

She bit her lower lip and gave a quick shake of her head, wincing as though she might cry. "I'm sorry. I have to go."

She twisted out of his hold and rushed toward the door, disappearing behind the black tinted glass.

Max's legs took on a life of their own, and he bolted after her, only for Gideon to catch his elbow as he reached the door. "She's not well. Let her go."

He held Gideon's furrowed stare but said nothing, the man's brow twisting in an expression of concern more than a need to control anyone's actions.

And perhaps Max *was* better off letting her go. Nothing about his desire right now made any sense. But then, when had anything he'd ever done made sense, much less anything to do with Freya?

The tension in Gideon's hand eased, and he released his hold, stepping back with a resigned sigh, as if conceding to Max's need to speak with Freya. Max lunged forward and out the door, the stark contrast of afternoon sun making it momentarily hard to discern the world around him.

He turned from side to side, searching for her among a throng of daytime window shoppers, her distinctive blond curls glowing in the distance, across the entrance of a narrow laneway.

He called her name.

She paused, her weight shifting forward in the inertia of her abrupt stop.

He bound after her, barging between two women chatting shoulder-to-shoulder, despite Freya's head dipping as if she didn't want to have this encounter.

He caught up and positioned himself in front of her, delaying any attempt she might make to walk from him. Her gaze flicked up; the mischievous affection she often held in his presence gone like it had never been there to begin with.

"How much did you spend on the bar?"

"How do you know I paid?" He took in the details of her face, his stomach clenching at the fact that even her characteristic red lipstick was missing.

"Gideon sent me updates. I only saw them this morning, otherwise I would have told you to keep your money and asked everyone to go home."

"So why did you come today?"

"To see if I could." She jutted her chin. "And I did."

"And?"

"And what?" Her voice rose, and she threw her hands out to the side. "I felt nothing. Absolutely nothing. Is that what you want to hear?"

His throat closed up, and his own voice dropped to a whisper. "You know it's not."

A fellow pedestrian bumped into him, breaking his stare-off with Freya. He hooked his hand around her elbow and pulled her into the nearby laneway.

She huffed out a heavy breath, her shoulders slumping on the exhale. "Just tell me how much you spent. I'm paying you back. The bar's insurance will reimburse me, eventually."

"It doesn't matter." He stepped in, wanting to hold her but falling short out of the fear of breaching some unspoken boundary. "My contribution is about more than what's between you and me. Everyone at The Ruby deserves for the festival to go ahead, and so does Gideon. It's partly my fault they almost missed out. Count my money as an apology gift."

"I don't want gifts. I just want to go home." She squeezed her eyes shut and shook her head, a growl breaking from deep within her. "Look. Whatever. Forget it. I'll ask Gideon and repay you via your payroll bank details."

"And I'll return the money each and every time."

"No." She paused, and a small muscle ticked at the corner of her jaw. "I won't let you. Not with where this relationship is headed."

Taut muscles throughout his body turned slack, a sense of foreboding settling in. And even though he didn't really want to hear the answer to his next question, he asked anyway, needing the truth out all the same.

"And where exactly is this relationship headed?"

Thirty-Seven

"Nowhere, Max. This relationship is going nowhere." Freya dropped her gaze to his chest, not wanting to face the reality of what she was about to do to him. "We don't belong together."

"I know you said you don't want anything serious, but—"

She flinched at his words and glanced at his cheeks suddenly hollow and pale, his lips parted, as if he wanted to finish his thought but couldn't. Like he now recognized her aversion to the topic at hand.

Yet, barely a second of silence had passed before he replied, hinting that maybe he'd known this conversation was coming and had already planned his rebuttal.

So, she helped him out, making sure he would have no further doubts about what she wanted.

"You're right, I don't want anything serious. Actually, I don't want *anything*. I can't be in any kind of relationship right now. Do you understand? And… and it hurts just to look at you."

Her voice creaked, and now her eyes prickled. *Shit!*

She'd spent the last day bawling and hiding. The skin around her eyes still burned from the continuous outpouring of grief. She should have been done by now. The fact that she wasn't meant she really did need to get back to the painful solitude of her house. She couldn't do this whole "talking through their problems" thing. Not now. Not ever. Because to her mind, there was nothing to work through.

"Look." She compressed her lips into what hopefully looked like a regretful smile, once again burying the extent of her pain. "I know you feel guilty about the bar getting trashed, but I'm over it. You don't need to keep beating yourself up. You also don't deserve to be in the thick of whatever misery I'm in right now. And before you argue otherwise, let's be clear, I don't *want* you with me through this, either."

His attention darted about her face, and she cleared her throat, deciding to lay down the plan for how things would go now that she'd stomped out the romantic side of this relationship. She didn't want him trying to make her feel better. He had his own problems to sort through, and she couldn't deal with his circus as well as her own.

"If you think you can handle seeing me at The Ruby Room, I have no issues with you still working there. Otherwise, I understand if you want to work elsewhere."

Max's expression twisted. "That was the last thing on my mind. I don't understand. We're damn good together. Did I do something else wrong? Why are you dropping the axe on us?"

She ripped her attention from him and onto the bare, red brick wall to her right, her hand finding its way into her hair—hair she hadn't had the time nor care to style. She looked and felt like misery, and sure as hell didn't want to be standing around in public hurting a man who'd been kind to her in all ways that mattered.

"You know enough about my life to understand why there's not much good about what we have right now." She stared back at him, her voice rasping past her already raw throat. "I've got a lot of shit going on. As do you."

"I'm selling my apartment, so my life just got simpler. Please, let me help you."

He stepped toward her, but she backed away. "No."

"Why?"

"Your problems are much bigger than just selling your apartment."

He dipped his chin, attention falling to the ground, hard-to-miss sadness dimming those lake-blue eyes, adding yet more pain to her already overburdened load.

"Let's at least call this a break then." His gaze joined hers again, her tummy clenching and aching. "Until things settle for you, and I can take some time to sort myself out. Maybe then we can reconnect."

For a moment, she toyed with the idea of accepting his terms, but even a break wouldn't be enough to salvage this capsizing ship.

She let out a sigh and worked to piece together a coherent explanation. "Max, as much as I love my independence, I don't want to always be the strong one."

She caught sight of his wince. *Fuck.*

This conversation would only get worse, but for all he'd shared with her, she owed him a clear end to this relationship. She wouldn't take the ultimate coward's way out and simply fade from his life.

"Well before you and I hooked up, I decided I didn't need a man, not in any permanent way. I've been there, done that, and it didn't work. I'm at a stage now where I know *I*, on my own, am enough. I'm a woman with a past, Max, a woman who knows how to survive and thrive. *If* I ever do commit to someone again, I need to know he will add to the life I've already built for myself."

The frown on his face deepened. "You're saying I'm not enough."

She cringed. His description was harsh, but mostly true. Though she wanted otherwise, he wasn't enough, and dragging him into a relationship would hurt them both.

She stepped forward and looped her palm through his, his pain palpable through the tension in his fingers and the low tilt of his chin. All she could offer now was comfort and enough plain honesty to help him find his way without her.

"I never planned on meeting you, much less that you'd take up so much space in my life, but I'm glad you did." She gave him a weak smile and rubbed a thumb over his knuckles. "I don't want you to walk away today thinking I'm not grateful for our moments together. I am. More than you could ever know."

His jaw locked in a fixed position, a slight harshness filling his eyes. "So then tell me what you want from me and don't leave."

His plea filled the space under her ribcage, putting pressure on her next breath, so she tightened her grip on his hand, demanding that he understand.

"I need someone who can hold their own space away from me. I need someone with purpose and direction. Someone who can stand on his own two feet, so I don't have to worry about his survival, as well as mine. I don't want a one-sided love where I'm the only stable person keeping us together. And contrary to popular opinion, I don't want to be anyone's everything. The thing that keeps their world from imploding. I want to be an equal. Someone's something extra. And if I can't have all of that, I want nothing at all."

She stopped, feeling as though she'd said too much and not enough, like what she wanted didn't exist, as much as she'd come to learn she desperately wanted it to.

And wanted Max to be the one she spoke of, even though he clearly couldn't be.

"In other words." He loosened his hold around her hand, as if he too stepped away. Her heart kicked in protest, even though this was just what she'd asked for. "You want someone who's got everything I don't."

Exactly.

But at the same time, no.

She reached out, pulling him closer when she should have dragged herself farther away.

"If you could see yourself through my eyes, Max, you'd see an incredible light. You'd see the potential for everything I just described, and more. You'd know you are someone special to me, and that this hurts me as much as it hurts you. I don't let you go lightly. You've come to mean more than I ever expected. But I have to do this. I have to let you go. It's what's fair for both of us."

His muscles strained under her touch, hot and hard, a man rippling with wounded energy. "There's nothing fair here, and let's not pretend this is what I want, too."

Stiffness entered her body, and she let go of him. No matter how much she explained, all signs pointed to him not wanting to understand.

Maybe this wasn't the right time, but she had no other options. She wanted to leave knowing she'd at least tried to give him the closure he deserved.

"You and I both know you're more than a little lost right now, that me sticking around will just enable the same dependent behavior you've struggled with for years. I'll also be falling into my tendency to patch others up at my own expense. I can't date potential, Max."

Her voice competed against the bustle of foot traffic just yards away, even though she wished so much for quiet calm and control. "Believe me, I want you. And I want you to stay, Max. But I've learned my lesson too late with my mother. I won't make the same mistake with you. Sometimes the kindest thing to do is to walk away."

He jerked back, perhaps an outward expression of his internal pain, his mouth wavering before he found his words. "I've never felt for anyone what I feel for you."

A large group strolled past the alleyway's opening. She flicked her gaze toward the loud chatter of smiling people, repressing an urge to ask Max to expand on exactly what he felt for her.

In truth, she'd grown up in a house where survival depended on reading another person's mood, so Max didn't need to admit to anything. She understood within her bones what he meant.

His love showed in his fight for her now, his direct attention lighting a hyper-awareness in her own body. Getting him to speak on his feelings would only be cruel.

His gaze fell to his feet again, and his blond waves tumbled over his brow, obscuring his eyes and seeming to take him further away from her. "And the thought of you moving on to someone else… I know I have no right to limit you, but—"

"Trust me, I have no plans to replace you anytime soon."

The only thing she had to offer was this pathetic concession prize. For so many years, she'd considered herself a free woman, and now her heart shifted painfully at the idea of being with anyone else.

What have I done to myself? I'll have to move on one day, but how?

One day, yes, she would have to move on, but the emptiness inside of her said that wouldn't be for a very long time. Her heart had jumped from one kind of sorrow to another of late; she didn't need more complications or hurt.

When would she learn? She always did better alone.

Max moved closer, his fingers finding the side of her neck. "Walking away right now feels all wrong. You're hurting, Freya. You need me."

His thumb stroked her jawline, the depth of his stare prompting her to lean into his touch, even as she gave a small shake of her head. "Sometimes being alone is the perfect antidote."

It sure as hell hurts less, too.

She repressed the thought, afraid that pain would stir an inability to end this.

"I know you want to fix my life for me, and I appreciate the sentiment, but sometimes there's nothing to do but curl up in bed and cry it out. That's what I'll do, and I'll be okay. You know what I mean?"

A small line formed between his brows. "I'm not sure I do."

She frowned and trained her attention on the finer details of his face, his skin smooth and eyes relaxed in an open expression. "What did you do when your dad died? When that cliff fall ended your dreams? Don't tell me you never grieved. Everybody does."

"I don't know." He shrugged and offered a tight smile, the darting motion of his eyes hinting at evasion. "I just kept myself busy. Though, clearly not with anything all that productive."

He gave a stumbling laugh, and she shook her head at his deflection masked as humor. *A typical Max move.*

Even as his lips settled on an oblivious grin, a new thought took root in her mind. The reason for his aimlessness. Why he'd been so busy distracting himself with fun, money, and socializing and never dealt with the disasters that exploded all around him.

She pressed her hands to his cheeks, the pads of her fingers lingering over the soft prickliness of his stubble. "Sometimes those who laugh the most are the ones running the hardest and fastest from something."

He gave her a side stare. "I don't understand."

"It's just—" She bit her lower lip and second-guessed whether she should say something.

But the pieces fit.

And maybe. Just maybe. Her hunch would help him.

She slid her hand down and patted his chest, savoring the warmth —a warmth she would soon give up forever. "Max, have you ever considered that maybe you're depressed?"

Thirty-Eight

MAX STUMBLED BACK A STEP, so fast, he might as well have held his hand to a hot stove and not the softness of Freya's neck. He dropped his palm, his lips dragging heavy at the corners, no doubt sending forth one monster of a frown.

Have you ever considered that maybe you're depressed?

What an odd thing to say.

And in the middle of a breakup.

Besides, if it were true, shouldn't his supposed depression be another reason for her to stay?

Only if I plan on having the overly dependent relationship she just said she didn't want.

No. That's not what I want at all.

Her suggestion about his mental health knocked around in his head, the sounds of rushing traffic and pedestrians passing only adding to his confusion. He'd never considered that maybe there was more to his behavior than just him being him. Depressed? Was that true?

He opened his mouth, ready to scoff, to defend himself and insist that she was wrong. But maybe she wasn't.

He hadn't always been lazy. He'd had goals and a routine, and a ton of discipline and motivation—motivation that had taken him across oceans on the pure power of his own body.

The years after his accident hung over him like a black cloud, Luke's guilt the reason Tiluma had come about—a new project meant to pull Max out of his funk.

Except maybe he'd never risen from his low point. He'd just gotten better at hiding his pain.

His routine and motivation had transformed into impaired forward thinking and impulsiveness; the majority of his days spent living in a hard-to-clear fog, though at least those around him seemed less worried.

And what about his need to always have people around?

Well, maybe he'd learned he couldn't trust himself alone, because being alone meant thinking, and he didn't like the man he encountered when left with his thoughts.

Oh hell!

In his years as a distance swimmer, he'd spent long stretches alone —had loved the solitude of just him and the waves—a serene stillness he'd never experienced since.

My mind is never serene or still these days.

"Oh, now." He flicked his gaze back to Freya. "That's messed up." His cheeks turned cold and probably lacked color. "You might be right."

And even as the words left his mouth, an unfamiliar heat exploded in his belly. An angry heat—one that made him want to charge away and smash something—an uncontrolled energy so unfamiliar to him, he struggled to breathe.

Worlds of sound and sight sped impossibly fast around him. That expanding heat roared in his ears. It roared at Luke for his thoughtlessness, for pressuring Max into climbing that cliff in the first place. It roared at Max for never telling his brother how much he resented the unraveling of his plans. How that unraveling left him adrift, with years of hating himself for failing to recover in a way that Luke and everyone else saw fit.

And sure, they'd talked about the accident. He recognized Luke's remorse and that he'd been going through his own issues leading up to the accident. Maybe Max had deflected his real rage onto other things, perhaps offering Luke forgiveness long before he'd been ready to give it.

Freya stepped forward, her hand landing on his bicep. "Are you okay?"

"I'm not sure." A thousand little firecrackers went off inside his head, exploding at random intervals without any indication of when they would all stop. "What do I do about this?"

"Find the help you need, Max. Find a good therapist, a government-funded one if your money won't cover it, though I guess if you down-grade from your apartment, that won't be an issue." She gave a light squeeze of his arm, along with her gentle smile. "Simplify your life and take some time to figure yourself out. Once you do that, go about discovering what *you* want and where you want to go next."

Though her even tone hinted at wise advice, he struggled to take in much of it.

His fall from that cliff had stolen far more than just swimming. He'd lost the one thing he'd been unquestionably good at. *His dream. His passion.* His future disintegrated in one dumb move. And now he was losing Freya.

Seriously, how would he fix this?

All his friends had left. He had orders from Luke to sort his life out on his own this time. Even Miro had a family to look after and a business to run; he didn't deserve Max sulking around.

Max had been a mess for so long, with someone always around to lean on when things didn't work. With Freya stepping away, he had no one.

He bore his gaze into her and pleaded with his eyes, the gravity of his impending loneliness all too much.

He needed help. He needed someone. He needed *her*.

"Can I call you sometimes? Can we still meet, even just for a chat and nothing more?"

Her gentle smile slipped as did her hand. Still, he wasn't below looking and sounding desperate, much less asking the impossible.

"I'm sorry." Her chin trembled in a moment of prolonged silence. "I wish I could help you through this, but I'm not in a place to help anyone right now and would do you more harm than good."

He stared at her a moment, seeing her fragility, before breaking eye contact and taking a second to come to terms with this really being the end. He nodded at the ground repeatedly, a man truly losing his mind. And his home. And his first genuine shot at love.

"Max." She stepped closer, as though she sensed his dip in mood.

Where she normally smelled like sun-warmed mandarins, today only the soft musk of her skin minus any fragrance cut through, indicating again that she too wasn't operating as she normally did.

"I'm used to dealing with things alone, so please don't think for a second I don't care about you, it's just…" Her hand met with his arm again, and she remained silent until he lifted his gaze to her whiskey-gold eyes, the surrounding skin still dappled in a red reminder of her grief. "I don't think either of us needs any false hope. I can't give you the answers you're looking for. I can't do the healing and discovery work for you. You need to find your own place in life."

"But what if I've already found my place in life?" He hooked a hand around her, pressing his palm to her lower back. "What if *you're* my place and walking away is the worst decision for either of us?"

She startled, almost as if an electrical current ran through his touch. "That's not a healthy example of love. People leave. Things happen. All love fades eventually—"

"Maybe your examples of love, but not mine." He pulled her into him, grasping at his last chance to change her mind, to spare them the misery of going through their respective hardships minus the other's support. "My mum and my dad, Luke and Agathe, Sophie and Orlando, they all experienced love transforming and redirecting their lives for the better. Why not us too? Please. Don't leave, Freya. This isn't the only way forward."

Her stare pulled wide and searched his face, her lips parted in a hint she wanted to say something but didn't. She turned from him and took a few hurried steps toward the passing crowd at the end of the alleyway.

Perhaps this was her way of showing she could walk away at any given moment.

He reached out, only to stop. She'd already fled from his touch. Maybe his desperation would be yet another reason for her to say no, even if her demeanor said she'd already made up her mind to leave.

"Don't. Not like this."

He bounded after her, catching her elbow before she could exit the alleyway, throwing away his last desire to save face.

She swung around and stuck out her chin, a stubborn gesture that didn't hide the tears gathering in her eyes.

"You're making this harder than it needs to be." Her voice wobbled, the heat in her stare cooling. "Don't you understand? Sure, we gave each other moments of happiness, but as individuals, we're still one-hundred-percent responsible for our own contentment. Maybe the fact we see love so differently is a big flashing sign we were never going to work."

"Freya."

"No. Stop trying to convince me." Her pitchy tone spoke of pain more than anger. "I have to leave. I don't want to, but I have to."

An emptiness opened up deep within him, and his ability to reply dried on his tongue, an inescapable truth seeping in. She *did* have to leave, even when every fiber of his being pushed him to plead otherwise. He wanted this. Wanted *her*. When, for so very long, he hadn't wanted anything.

She'd become his only sense of purpose, the only sure thing in a world rapidly falling around him, but the tears in her eyes, the huskiness in her voice… She was right. He needed to stop.

For once in his life, he'd put someone else ahead of his need to escape a few difficult feelings.

And what a time to make that realization…

He took a half-step back and let his hand slip from her elbow. "I know, but first, there's something I want you to hear." He paused, trying to slow time down. Trying to memorize every small detail of a moment he'd hold dear until his dying day. "I—"

"No." She slammed her eyelids shut, a tear finally breaking free and spilling down her cheek. "Please don't say it."

He pressed his lips together, fulfilling her wish at great expense to himself.

This was as sweet a parting as they would get.

She flung herself forward, leaning her weight into him, her arms folding around his shoulders in a tight hug. And he wrapped his arms around her too, lifting her off the ground, giving his all to this embrace.

Her hands rose from his shoulders and landed on his cheeks, her lips finding his, as though they were made for him, even if this would be the last kiss they'd share.

And the kiss was everything.

Everything he'd ever wanted and by far not enough—hungry and impassioned—a rush of need and despair. For all his doubts about life, he had none in relation to Freya. And still, he would lose her, anyway.

Of course, she was the first to end the kiss. So, he lowered her to the ground, his heart rate slowing to a weak plod. She swiped at her eyes, and her lips twisted into a half-smile, a smile that somehow both acknowledged and denied the pain in that moment.

She spun away, her steps taking her closer to the main street and the throng of passersby, all while his insides ached, like she'd wrenched away some vital part of him.

He'd meant to whisper the following words, to keep them for himself, but as always, even this he fumbled, his voice rising louder than intended.

"I love you."

She stopped in her tracks and dipped her head low, her hand coming to rest on the wall beside her, her fingers curling into the red brick as though she fought his words and took a second to decide whether to respond.

In time, she turned her red-dappled face and gave him her anguished stare.

"I know."

Thirty~Nine

FREYA'S HAIR whipped her face, and her burnt-orange skirt flapped about her knees as she stood on the rocky outcrop. The start of Fall might have been evident in the sea's icy winds, but more than a week after her mother's death, that iciness matched today's bleak mood, and she appreciated the element's camaraderie.

A light-yellow cardboard box weighed heavy in her right hand, her mother's ashes nestled inside. There'd been no point in a funeral since Freya would be the only person in attendance.

She snapped her focus to Gideon. He reached out from beside her, wrapping his long fingers around her waist, holding her steady on the rocks and offering comfort. "Are you ready?"

Her throat pulled tight, her answer stalling, though she told herself the cold wind had swallowed her sound. "Just one minute more."

He gave an understanding nod and turned to the ocean with its glistening surface like a million twinkling lights. She pushed her gaze a little more to her right, to the sandy alcove pressed between another outcrop. A spot where she and her brother played as children in relative privacy, this particular beach a good hour and a half from where they'd lived.

Sometimes, *sometimes*, her mother had tried.

Even if those outings occurred only a handful of times, the briny smell and the lack of people took her back to one of the few magical moments in her childhood, the sea succeeding to tame even the savage beast within her mother.

Freya slammed her eyes shut and shook her head, wanting to break free of the memory. Those happier moments never lasted long.

Sometimes, even just the arrival home would result in her mother's strong, adult hands locked around Freya's tiny arms. There'd be nitpicking and blaming, screams in her face, her eyes scrunched closed to block out the tirade. It was as if her mother could only stomach so much peace before her demons grew too angry and retaliated.

A seagull cawed, and Freya leaned to her left so that her side met with Gideon's.

She sniffed, the salty air settling her nerves, though the cold wind made it impossible to hold back her tears, and her heart hitched at the stubborn hollow inside her from ending things with Max. At least she still had her best friend.

She'd come to this beach to release some of her feelings, to say goodbye to her mother, to let go as best she could. Maybe this wasn't the time to hold back on acknowledging just how much she hurt right now. That some things she would never truly recover from.

She could survive. Yes, that much was proven.

But certain scars became a permanent feature, and sometimes life threw up events that would never make sense—no matter how many times she rolled the same thoughts over and over within her mind.

Every breath now made her nostrils sting, and that sting affixed to the harsh memories threatening to hurt her anew—the pure evil of having her survival tied to someone whose purpose should have been to love and protect her.

All she'd received was years of neglect, pain, and shame.

And her mother knew what she'd done. Though how much she could control her actions was anyone's guess.

Freya had witnessed the cycle. The guilt, the apologies and pleading, those apologies making her search for her mother's softer side, giving birth to an obnoxious need to find a positive. For years afterward, she'd hated herself for even trying.

She peered down at her hand clenched around the yellow box, a lovely thing with silk lilac flowers on the outside and a matching ribbon. Everything sweet, and delicate, and feminine. Everything not her mother.

Freya hunched and tugged at the ribbon, willing all her hurt and the bitterness to go, attempting to replace it with something more productive. *Hope.*

For all she'd been through, she knew something her mother never had. She'd experienced peace, time and time again, and hope said peace would return some day. Maybe not for a while, but eventually.

She lifted the box's lid and already gray particles fluttered out. She raced against the wind, tipping the box upside-down and allowing the remnants of her mother's body to burst out into a plume across the sea.

Freya's life would be better. That was her vow to herself, and maybe to her mother.

Freya would be the last in her line. Whether she went on to have children didn't matter so much. She would not pass on her pain, even if that meant being alone forever.

The gray plume dissipated, her mother gone except for the reminder that actions and decisions mattered. They mattered a lot.

Freya would start over. She would pick herself up. And everything she did would grow bigger and better. Not just for her benefit, but for anyone who came to her in search of a livelihood or life, or simply a place to escape a world that often punished those who dared to break from their torments or to simply have a dream.

Max handed Miro the apartment's keycard and waited for him to embark on his trip out the door for more moving boxes. Meanwhile, Luke dropped something loud and metallic on the dining room floor, the sharp sound bouncing off the tile and down the hallway.

Max returned to the kitchen and made a hard right away from Luke, continuing the task of packing glassware.

"You're quiet today." Luke sat on the floor, a socket wrench in his hand—probably what he'd dropped moments earlier and now used to loosen the legs on the upturned dining table. "And something tells me your silence is about more than just the move."

Max lowered the glass in his hand to a box on the counter. "Because losing my home isn't demoralizing enough?"

The narrow of Luke's eyes seemed to question Max's blunt reply. "You have a point, it's just that—"

"Freya and I broke up."

He hadn't planned on blurting out that news, and now he pressed his jaw tight to keep from saying anything else unexpected.

There was so much he still didn't understand, and he hadn't told anyone about his last conversation with Freya, though Gideon's recent lack of any mention of her hinted he knew something had happened.

Luke lowered the wrench and straightened his stance, his full attention focused on Max. "I thought you two were just friends."

The man was a master of reading between the lines and making it near impossible to delude him. Max skittered his gaze to the glassware inside the box before him. He and Luke rarely talked about relationships, and nothing about this moment felt natural.

"We were just friends, and then at some point, we were more." He reached for another glass. "At least, that's what I think happened…"

He peered over to Luke shaking his head. "And let me guess, things got too serious, and everyone got their hearts broken?"

He gave a knowing smile, maybe because he'd experienced a similar breakup with Agathe, long before she'd become his wife. Not like that would be happening with Max and Freya.

"Yeah, something along those lines."

He didn't have the energy to tell his brother that two weeks had passed since his farewell from Freya, and maybe he'd been the one with the bigger broken heart. After all, he'd told her he loved her, while she'd left, not stopping to reciprocate.

And so, he'd worked the entire festival, really needing the money to pay for this move, while also not wanting to leave his co-workers short-staffed and in the lurch. At the same time, he constantly checked The Ruby Room's doors hoping to see Freya walk through them.

But not once had she shown up. Not once in all the nights her best friend, Gideon, performed—the show exceptional enough to whip up a kind of buzz never before seen at The Ruby Room.

She'd missed everything, and in turn, Max had missed her.

A long silence dragged, and the brothers pretended to be hard at work, but a hot, niggling sensation pulled at Max's focus. "You know, Freya mentioned something the last time we spoke, and it's bothered me ever since."

New wrinkles scored Luke's forehead. "Yeah?"

"She thinks my whole aimless thing started when I fell off that cliff."

Luke scoffed and returned to twisting the wrench. "Sure. You and I already knew that."

"It's more than that, though." His shoulders drew upward, and his throat felt tight, like he fought to keep his voice at a reasonable level, while very much wanting Luke to hear him out. "I've only now started to admit this to myself, but all these years, I've secretly resented you."

Luke peered up, eyes flared, and his spine snapped to a poker-straight position, as though Max had somehow punched him with his words.

But Max pressed on, vowing that if he didn't get this out, his buried rage would continue to eat away at him.

"We've never talked about this, but the fall from that cliff really bothered me. The actual fall. The belief that I would die. Then, there was the physical pain and the recovery, much less losing my swim career. All those years. All that training, pushing myself, working at something only to have it ripped away. All that effort wasted. Then trying to mentally return to where I was before all that happened…"

He frowned, the deepest part of this confession only now coming to him in the form of a sickening and cold shiver through his entire body. "I'm still nowhere near where I want to be. I still don't recognize my new life, even though it's been years, and I've tried everything I can to bury my feelings."

Max forced his gaze on Luke, even though he so wanted to look away and would almost certainly hurt his brother with his next brutal truth. "But denial and avoidance doesn't work, and if I'm truly honest, I'm miserable. And it's all because of you."

Luke sank back, and his shoulders rolled forward, his fingers curling tighter around the wrench. His stare fell to the floor, and he gave his head a small shake.

Max's face burned in the aftermath of his revelation, in watching his brother grapple with this new spin on the last years of their relationship.

He waited to hear what Luke had to say, whether he'd belittle this confession or try to deflect blame, and for some reason, the prolonged silence didn't seem to bode well.

Luke returned his direct stare to Max and pushed an incredulous sigh past his lips. "You know, I don't think I've ever been prouder of you than I am right now."

Max's chin jerked back of its own volition, and he gave his brother a side-glare, Luke's hushed tone and ensuing short, sharp laugh taking up space in the room.

"I've lost my home." He fought to make sense of his brother's reaction. "I've lost my woman, and I'm probably going to lose my job at the bar. My entire life is one big fucking disaster, and you're telling me you're proud?"

"Well. No." Luke leaned his elbow on his knee, the casual position portraying a level of acceptance Max hadn't expected. "But as much as you've said you've forgiven me in the past, it would be hard to bring this all up again now. And come to think of it, I always felt like you took the whole thing a little too well."

Luke lifted a hand and scrubbed at the stubble on his chin. "Look, I don't live in your head, but I can imagine how betrayed you must have felt back when you first fell off that cliff. And you're right, that fall was my fault. Everything about that day is one-hundred percent my fault. I can promise you I live with that guilt every day. I screwed up your life. Yet, because of how things panned out with Tiluma, I'm the one who's been laying down the rules, putting my foot down recently and attempting a tough-love approach. I'm the one who's had more of a chance to move on, both with my own issues at the time and the mess I created for you because of that." Luke's face drew in a pained expression. "Max, you deserve a good life, and I'm sorry I got in the way of that. I will do everything I can to help you. I only hope that someday you get to a place where you really do forgive me."

Max twisted a glass on the counter, a real smile tugging at his lips. "The thing is, to some extent, I already have forgiven you. It's just that, this whole thing with Freya and losing the house, I've had to look at my life through a different lens. I'm seeing things I never noticed before, while having to figure out what to do with these new discoveries about myself. So, I do forgive you, but I'm still mad at you. Does that make sense? And I won't be able to let go of that anger until I find a way to heal."

Luke nodded as though he understood, even if the strain across his jaw said he didn't totally love everything Max had to say. "Do you have any ideas on how you'll move forward?"

Max shook his head, still struggling to look Luke in the eye while admitting to how lost he'd become. "I'm way over my head here, and I don't think this is something I can fix on my own. I need help, Luke, professional help. I'm scared to imagine where I'll be in ten years if I continue down the path I'm on."

Luke frowned, turning the wrench in his hand. "You're right. This isn't something you have to fix alone. You have me and Agathe, Soph, and even Orlando's all right to talk to if you get him in a good mood." He lifted his attention, curling his lip at one corner and making light of Orlando's initial rough start in the family. "You're surrounded by people who want to see you succeed, even if succeeding is as big or small as getting out of bed each day and knowing that a lot of people love you. So, get all the help you need, we're here for you, and if there's anything you need from me especially, just ask."

That offer of help contradicted Luke's initial response to when Max first lost his money. Yet, as much as Max wanted to be pissed about the sudden change in attitude, Luke had been right to cut him off.

"Thanks for the offer." Max leaned against the counter, a quick lightness taking him over. He'd spent years hiding behind his brother's guilt, while Luke's over-compensating had stalled all progress. And even as Max's world disintegrated around him, he sensed that maybe something else waited just around the corner. The spark of a new idea.

All he had to do was sort out his mind so he could begin to unpack his future. Not a simple task, yes, but he had hope. And maybe that would be enough.

He returned his attention to Luke. "You know, I think getting help is something I need to do on my own."

"But if you're really not doing well…"

"I know." Max stared ahead, uncharacteristically silent, mulling over his situation.

While he appreciated the chance to open up, he wanted to prove to himself that he could, for once, be the one to put his life back together.

Luke returned to twisting the wrench over the bolts in the table, head shaking, as he released a soft chuckle. "You've made some hard decisions lately. I never thought the day would come where I'd see you sticking to them. It must have hurt a great deal to put this place up for sale, and all so you could help someone else out."

Luke stopped, sitting taller again. "And if that wasn't bad enough, I can't imagine how you must feel after letting Freya go."

Max set about adding more glasses to the boxes, but made sure to plaster on his flattest tone. "Actually, she let me go. But semantics, right?"

Luke's chuckle returned. "And somehow, for the first time in years, I'm not worried about what might happen to you next."

"Gee, thanks. I think."

Max pushed his chin higher and glared at his brother, whose eyes now glowed with clear humor.

"Hey, I'm not saying I don't care about you. Nothing could ever be further from the truth. I just see the changes you've already made, and I get a strong feeling you're going to be okay."

Forty

A YEAR and a half later

Freya slung her scarlet-embroidered handbag over her shoulder, the coin fringe tinkling as she passed through her office door and into the crowd at her new club. Sweat clammed up her bare collarbone, and her amethyst dress clung to her skin, the discomfort evermore noticeable since she ran late again. Gideon would no doubt chew her out.

She whizzed past the long bar, the air a mix of sweetness and astringency from the alcohol and juice cocktails. Various gargantuan gilded mirrors hung behind her rainbow-vested bar staff, the back wall dotted with black and white portraits of past and present burlesque stars.

And even as she raced, her body took on a life of its own, turning her toward tonight's manager, despite how ridiculous this final check would look.

She should have been on a tram already, speeding toward the stadium and a super rare Saturday night out to watch an even rarer concert. Besides, Gideon had a surprise for her, something he'd apparently been planning for a long time.

But her new venture was only two months old and a number of high-profile groups were booked to arrive soon, and so far, the bar hadn't yet done a night without her.

After the Live Wire Festival, more and more people had come to know about The Ruby Room. The place hadn't been the same, the smaller space struggling to keep up. And though The Ruby's makeshift rainbow chandelier had been replaced with a new ruby one, an idea had taken root.

She'd run with the rainbow idea and used the bump in success to expand her empire to a much bigger venue, one situated in the heart of the city; a place that held a bright mix of childish wonder, juxtaposed against the dark, adult glamor of nightly burlesque acts. The Rainbow Room.

And yes, a rainbow chandelier hung in the venue's center, a giant white unicorn reared with wings outspread atop a podium, the venue's walls coated in candy pink carpeting and bubble machines timed to go off throughout each night.

Vowing to work on her ability to trust her staff, she sidled up to her manager, his lips trembling from a barely restrained laugh. After a hectic year of setting up The Rainbow, she really did need to start enjoying her downtime again.

The manager flicked a hand and gestured for her to go, that he had everything under control. Her face heated, but she turned away, point taken.

She was running late now, so she took herself to the dark stretch of street outside and sent for an Uber, the time for a tram well and truly gone. Her only hope now was that the gods of rock and roll would be extra kind to her, and that Gideon wouldn't disown her for being so invested in her work.

Max sat in his home office, a small LED lamp lighting his desk along with the dusky gray of the fading sun through his window. His eyes now ached from the glare of his computer and the hours spent poring over designs.

Starting a business had been a million times harder than he'd expected, and funding the whole thing using money from his apartment sale, as well as two annual payouts from his Tiluma shares, only made the process even more stressful.

And rewarding.

He'd gained a boatload of new respect for Luke and all he'd achieved in the early days of Tiluma. Especially since he'd most recently taken Max under his wing and taught him all about money management, as well as given him a temporary after-hours cleaning job at Tiluma.

That job had allowed him to quit The Ruby Room without eating into his apartment money. He avoided facing his old co-workers and Freya, giving him space to work on rebuilding his life without his morale taking a further beating.

And as much as Freya's absence hurt him, he'd used his pain and solitude to undergo regular therapy, to develop ways to deal with the trauma of his fall all those years ago. Doubt still plagued him, but he now had tools to manage.

He'd crossed the line into becoming self-sufficient, learned ways to reframe his limiting thoughts. And his most important lesson? That as much as those around him liked to poke fun, they really did want the best for him. Heck, they *loved* him.

But the thing about depression, sometimes no amount of love could break through the fog clouding a person's outlook. So, he had zero regrets about seeking outside help because it had been what he needed.

Oh, and because of that, there was more. He had a new home. A small two-bedroom townhouse in Melbourne's south-east, nowhere near as expensive or sizable as his apartment, but still somewhere to rest his spirits. There was a small patch of grass in his yard, a place to lay, feel the cool earth against his body, and watch the clouds move across the sky.

Which brought him to here, leaning back in his office chair and scrubbing a hand over his face, his brain tired and his eyes dry from a long day's work. He slapped a hand over his laptop and closed the screen. Time to give up for the day.

He raised his arms high in the air, stretching, only for the clash of loud instruments to pull his attention down to his phone ringing on the desk. He groaned, hitting the speaker option, hoping it was a spam call over yet another work issue needing urgent attention on a Saturday night.

"Hello?"

He waited.

"It's time."

The reply came from a super low, heavily American-accented voice, one Max didn't recognize.

He scowled down at his phone. "Time for what? Who is this?"

"It's your fairy godfather. I'm here to make your wildest dreams come true."

What the hell?

He rolled his eyes, his head already throbbing from the toll of his workload without having to deal with weird prank calls.

"Okay. Bye."

"No, wait!"

His finger hovered over the red X button, but he paused because the accent had disappeared, and a decidedly more familiar Australian one had taken over.

"It's Gideon. Hear me out. I have a plan!"

By the time she raced up the top of the stadium's stairs, Freya's lungs burned and her sternum heaved with labored breaths. She paused before the doors to her section, the heavy music and cheers pulsing from the venue, the warmup band already begun. But Gideon wasn't anywhere to be found.

She peered at the time on her phone. *Damnit!*

She was later than she thought. He must have gotten sick of waiting and headed in without her.

No point calling him, given the deep boom and the stadium's walls vibrating around her. She'd just end up having to yell down the phone so Gideon could hear, and he'd yell back, probably annoying everyone around him in the process.

She shot off a quick text letting him know she'd arrived. Her phone pinged with a reply almost immediately.

GIDEON

Great to know. Just go straight to your seat.

She did as told, climbing down some steep stairs, then pushing her way through a long row of people on a lower tier. Of course her seat was smack-bang in the middle. Less expected, though, Gideon's seat was empty.

What gives?

She typed feverishly, taking a pause to have another swift peer around.

Where are YOU?

She plonked down on her seat and waited, hugging her bag even though a lot of people were already standing and dancing to the warmup act.

Granted, the band was brilliant, but she needed a minute to settle in, to breathe in the stadium's cold air, though she figured the temperature would rise soon enough given all the hot lights and people packed in.

Her phone lit up with another message.

Sorry. Forgot to tell you. I'm sick. Not going to make it, hun.

What on earth? Her mouth slipped open, and she stared at the screen. She might have said an expletive too, but with the mixture of noise and shock running through her head, she couldn't be sure of anything.

She growled at Gideon's perplexing text, then punched out another reply, relaying her scramble to get to this concert and asking him what the fuck was going on.

Her brows drew heavy. Maybe she should have gone for a more compassionate approach. Maybe asked whether he was okay or if he needed help, given his claim of being sick and all.

Either way, there was something strange definitely happening here.

Another message appeared on her phone:

> Let's just say, I took one for the team. Oh and… SURPRISE!

She slumped back in her seat, trying to work out what the hell this all meant.

Took one for the team? How? By not turning up to a show they'd both been looking forward to for years?

How did that benefit anyone?

Just as the warmup band finished their set, another expletive escaped her lips. She'd been dreaming of this night for so long, of seeing her favorite band, but never had she imagined she'd be here alone.

A hush took over the twenty-thousand-person venue, and her heart sank anew. She had no one to share the rising anticipation with—an anticipation that washed over the stadium like an electric charge—invisible and palpable all at once.

Her skin tingled, and the tiny hairs on her arms rose with the mood.

Screw it. I'm going to enjoy this night either way. Since when has being alone ever stopped me?

Never! That's when!

She nodded to herself and stood, lifting her chin and refusing to mope through the night. She'd made it to her first ever *Queen* concert, and no one—no one—was allowed to sulk through a Queen concert.

Her attention dropped to her right, everything about the empty seat beside her downright wrong, but then the venue plunged into darkness, and she lost all reason to worry.

Soon, lights exploded around her in short-sharp bursts; sounds bashed and clashed. She bounced in her spot, alternating between clapping her hands and raising a fist in the air, screaming a loud, "Woo hoo!" before looking to her right to see if the person across the empty chair showed the same excitement.

"Hi."

She startled, almost losing her balance, a man having taken up the now not-so-empty seat.

If he hadn't spoken, she would have assumed he wasn't real, that he'd materialized or was maybe a figment of her over-exhausted imagination. But his gentle tone was impossible to mistake. And those eyes. Those soft, crystalline blue eyes… they could belong to no one else.

The lights flicked off, only to explode once more. She jolted at the sound—the pull of her attention in two different directions. At him. At the stage. At *him* again.

Despite all odds, she wasn't hallucinating.

"Gideon said he didn't want you to go to the show alone." Max smiled at Freya, her pupils wide pools that betrayed her shock.

"So"—her mouth wavered for a moment before her gaze flicked to the stage and then back to him—"so he sent *you*?"

He fought an urge to step back, to leave her be, while questioning whether he should have let Gideon talk him into coming here in the first place.

"If you want, I can leave." He regretted the offer straight away. Leaving was the last thing he wanted to do.

She parted her lips, as though ready to say something, but then more lights flashed, and an even louder chorus of voices cut through the air.

Her gaze ripped from him and back to the stage, a giant white sheet covering the deeper part. There wasn't much to see.

Given her clear hesitation, he'd been right not to expect much from this night, and yet, hope still sprang eternal.

Maybe they'd healed enough to at least be friends.

What a lie.

I don't want friendship.

I also don't want to be rejected. Twice.

He stared at her. Just stared. Waiting for her attention to return to him, dazed that he got to share the same space with her again and dumbstruck over what to do next.

The music deepened, like the lower end of a piano or something. She glanced back at him, a sad frown dragging at her lips. Maybe she shared his confusion.

This time, when the music kicked up, the same distracting lights flashing in his eyes, she didn't turn away. Her stare held, her gaze shifting over his face.

They seemed trapped in a stalemate, so he dared to ask again, "Do you want me to leave?"

She pursed her raspberry-painted lips and gave a quick shake of her head, turning her whole body back toward the stage without a word.

He stood there, staring at her for the longest time, perhaps hoping for more, but she didn't give him anything.

He might have tried talking again, but the loud music made that near impossible. Besides, she loved Queen, and he wouldn't ruin this show for her, much less give her a reason to rescind his permission to stay.

The giant white sheet dropped from the stage, revealing the band. Queen.

Well, Queen minus Freddie Mercury, of course. Still, her lips curled ever so slightly, and her eyes glinted.

Standing beside her like a silent fool seemed suddenly worth her clear display of joy, much less that he got to share this experience with her. So, he smiled to himself, too. Maybe Gideon had banked on the forced close proximity and inability to have a conversation all along.

Max turned to the stage and vowed to just let things be.

He'd waited this long to see her again and spent months upon months learning to be okay with failure. Maybe this would be another exercise in dealing with uncertainty. What choice did he have? All he could do was wait and see where tonight took him.

Forty~One

THE CONCERT LIGHTS DIMMED, turning the entire stadium black; the crowd roared in a final goodbye. Freya had danced her way through the rockier songs, and tears ran down her cheeks through the sadder ones. There'd been no way Max hadn't noticed. And still, this night was so much more than expected.

At one point, she'd bumped her hip into him, attempting to get him to dance along with her. He hadn't, but his burst of laughter and the connection of his stare made her heart near explode, igniting an awareness of just how much she'd missed him.

But I broke his heart. Why is he even here?

The house lights came on, the sudden brightness breaking the concert's spell. She cleared her throat and turned to pick up her bag from her seat, not quite ready to make eye contact with Max again.

He walked ahead of her into the aisle, their pact of silence continuing until they got outside and into the cool night air.

Honestly, what were they supposed to say to each other? Where did she even begin?

Her chest hurt just standing near him. The wisest choice now would be to say nothing and let the past eighteen months of avoiding each other drag into eternity.

Her cheeks tingled, and the cool air brought a slight chill to her exposed collarbone. The beautiful man beside her, with his looming height and her working memory of what it was to make love to him, didn't at all ease those tingles or chills.

She glanced up to find his stare fixed on her as if he wasn't sure what to do now. Well, neither was she. Though a greater part of her wanted to disappear for at least a minute just to catch her breath in privacy.

Or maybe disappearing altogether was better.

But as always with Max, her body had other ideas, and she patted the large, over-stuffed bag on her shoulder.

"Gideon made me bring after-show snacks. I'm pretty sure he wants us to eat together." Shaky laughter broke past her lips, the low pain around her heart prodding a contrary desire to cry, one she stemmed by nodding to a low concrete wall a few steps away. "I'm willing to sit and indulge in his scheme, if you are?"

Max's gaze flicked to the wall, as though he needed a moment to decide whether that was what he actually wanted. A throng of people filed past, their bright chatter and screeches of excitement scraping sharp nails over her already heightened nerves.

She wasn't all that sure about her invitation to sit and eat together either, though maybe sitting and eating would be less weird than sharing an entire concert and a few laughs with this man, only to send him home without so much as a parting word.

"I…" His brows furrowed before he blinked and shook his head. "Sure. Why not?"

Old habits died hard, even if those habits hadn't been used for a solid eighteen months. Even as her shoulders dropped with released tension, she still fought an urge to reach out for his hand and lead him to the wall.

She ambled ahead, refusing to touch him, her steps loping and casual, like this whole thing didn't set her pulse to an aching gallop or that she hadn't spent the last year and a half in a state of painful curiosity over what he'd been up to. That curiosity now screamed at her to cut to the chase and ask him how he'd managed in all the time apart.

Oh, maybe I should just admit it. I want to know if he's been a wreck without me.

She took a seat on the wide wall, tucking her legs beneath her and trying to bury the memory of how messy she'd gotten in the wake of their breakup.

"How did Gideon rope you in, anyway?" She pulled her billowy dress over her knees, creating an excuse to avert her gaze.

"He sold me some story about being deathly ill and not wanting to send you to a rock concert alone." His easy tone tugged at her, making her attempts to look away impossible.

She smiled up instead, Max still standing over her, while she pretended the mere sight of him didn't suck the air right out of her lungs. "And you bought that story? Have you seen where I work? I think I can fend for myself."

Max laughed, and her own smile widened in response. "Well, the real clincher was his line about you dreaming of going to a Queen concert for as long as he could remember, and that he thought you should have someone to share the experience with."

She couldn't hold back and barked out a totally ungraceful laugh. "And so, calling my ex-boyfriend seemed like the best option?"

Her smile sank.

As much as Max had meant to her, she'd never even given him the honorific of being her boyfriend, though perhaps her mind had fallen back to him so many times over the years that *boyfriend* seemed far more fitting than *casual fling*.

He didn't seem to catch the pain in her expression, or if he did, he hid his awareness well as he sat on the wall beside her. "To be honest, I'm pretty sure Gideon wasn't calling me from his sick bed. I heard loud music, and I'm almost certain someone flushed a toilet in the background."

She spat out another laugh, willing a rogue tear to stay in her eye. "I bet he went out clubbing with friends and was calling you from the toilets."

An easy silence settled between them, and she twisted to dig around in her bag. "I'm surprised you didn't have anywhere else to go on a Saturday night."

Her face turned hot. Had she really just dropped a not-so-subtle attempt at finding out about his life these days?

Yes, she had.

Or is that, more precisely, who was in his life these days?

"There might be a lot about me that would surprise you." The added pause and the husky bend to his tone asked for her gaze to re-join his.

Her heart hitched, making her regret she'd even asked, that the hurt in his voice probably had a lot to do with her.

Oh God, please don't let his life be bad now.

She obliged and offered her attention, her heart rate kicking up another notch at that sad blue gaze connecting with hers.

"I was at home. Working. It's pretty much all I do at the moment."

The muscles in her face sagged, and his unwavering stare seemed to say, *Can't you see, I've changed?*

She went back to fidgeting, to pulling out food containers and placing them on the wall between them.

What did she hope might happen to him, anyway?

That he'd find his place in the world? Find direction and somewhere to focus his once wayward energy? That he'd found a woman who recognized how special he was? And even if he had changed, what did he expect her to do about it?

She pulled at the container lids, pretending everything about this situation was fine and dandy, telling herself to keep her emotions in check, otherwise she'd be swiping away tears.

Maybe she'd long ago recognized how special Max was, but she'd never done a damn thing about it. In fact, she'd flat out rejected him and left him in her dust. And here she was, her heart threatening to bolt out of her ribcage, her face near on fire, like she had the right to feel in any way possessive about him.

They'd never shared any sort of official relationship, his presence now probably having everything to do with his deep-rooted kindness. Besides, even if she did regret them not being together, she'd never regret her reasons for instigating the breakup.

So what if he'd evolved, maybe become everything she hoped he would be.

None of that meant she needed to change anything about the state of this relationship.

"I think I can relate. I've been locked down with work too." She gave him a weak smile and gestured to the food so he'd eat. "God, we both sound kind of pathetic. Two workaholics with no life, right?"

He reached for a cracker and returned her smile with a smaller one of his own. "You know, actually, this is the least pathetic I've felt in years. I like what I do now, even if I am on a short path to crashing and burning." His smile grew, and he nibbled on the cracker's edge, drawing her attention to his lips and how much she wished there wasn't so much literal and figurative space between them. "This is the closest I've come to taking a genuine stab at failure, and for some reason, it feels amazing."

Her eyes stung from staring at him. Or maybe it was the staring combined with not blinking. Everything about Max was the same. Those same arctic-blue eyes. The same ruffled golden waves. His lips with their subtle fullness.

But he had something else now. A glow. His eyes weren't just blue anymore, they shone with distinct brightness, like sunlight through sea glass.

"It's not the chance of failure that makes you feel amazing." The mumbled words found their own way out, and she distracted herself with passing him a grilled cheese sandwich wrapped in tin foil. "It's that you're trying. I mean, I'm glad you've found something you enjoy. What is your work these days, anyway?"

He shrugged; his gaze cast down to his long fingers toying with an edge of foil. "You're not going to believe this, but after I left The Ruby Room, I sold the apartment and used some of my spare cash to enroll in a year-long, intensive fashion design course."

She paused, halfway through unwrapping a sandwich, thanking goodness she hadn't already started chewing because she'd no doubt be choking right now. "You what? I don't think I ever got the impression you were *that* into fashion."

"I wasn't, but I've been into sustainable living for years, and that's where the fashion thing comes in." His smile resurfaced, vibrant and sparkling against the stadium lights. "By the way, your reaction is almost as good as the change itself."

She turned her hand in a repeated circle, gesturing for him to hurry up with his news. "Enough about me, how the heck does the rest of your story pan out?"

"Well, I ended up getting so into my design course, I graduated top of my class and decided to try my luck at producing a surf fashion line made completely from recycled materials."

He bit into his sandwich, his demeanor about a million times less ruffled than hers. "I'm still very new, so I have other designers helping me, but Luke taught me how to use the money I already had to bankroll the whole thing. The business is six months old, and I'm at the point where there's enough profit to pay myself a full-time wage, as well as hire virtual assistants to help with customer service and online marketing. Our next goal is to expand into activewear."

<hr>

"Holy shit!"

Freya's breathy tone ricocheted between them, and her mouth hung open. Max decided she searched for something more to say but couldn't find the words.

To be fair, he'd gotten used to that reaction from people who hadn't seen him in a while. "Bit of a surprise?"

"I mean, yeah." She blinked as if coming to her senses. "But when you put it like that, I guess the whole eco-fashion thing does make sense." Her eyes narrowed, like she inspected him anew, her gaze traveling down to his chest. He wondered what she saw.

Though he'd always held an unaffected air—the kind that came from denial—recently, he'd been told his brand of calmness had changed to the sort that came from someone who truly knew themselves. Maybe Freya saw that now, too, saw something more than his old jovial, surfer-guy act.

Because heaven help him, there was so much more to his accepting Gideon's challenge to show up tonight than the pretense of keeping her company.

"There were always hints you had an interest in that stuff, it's just" —her stare trained on him, like she took a second to come to terms with something—"I… I'm proud of you."

Her face relaxed, and she drew her posture up, the admission seeming to lighten something within her. He held her gaze for the longest time, feeling like a moth caught in candlelight—drawn to her, his twin flame.

Though she probably didn't see him in the same way.

She'd spent most of tonight averting her gaze. He'd been the one to bust in on her concert experience, so maybe she was just being nice, and whatever connection he sensed didn't exist.

Hey hero, whatever happened to "not fearing failure"?

Well, maybe his moth analogy wasn't far off the truth, but in a whole other way.

If he got too close, he risked being burned. Hadn't he done exactly that with her already, only to get epically dumped?

There was fearing failure, and then there was making an educated guess based on past experience.

But look at her, she's not turning me away now…

Maybe she's happy.

Maybe she wants the same things, too?

He drank in the warmth of her close proximity before time and reality ripped them apart again. "And what about you? What are you up to these days?"

"I… umm…" She swallowed, her eyes taking on a misty sheen.

Was she about to cry? Surely not.

"I have a new club. I mean, I still have The Ruby, but we've expanded."

He pitched one brow upward since he'd only ever seen her get emotional once before, and that had been in the wake of her mother's death.

Still, just in case, he tried to keep the mood light and offered a casual grin. "You mean, The Rainbow Room?"

Her forehead crinkled, her entire expression tensing into a focused scowl, like maybe she didn't totally love that he knew of The Rainbow Room. "You've been keeping tabs on me?"

Forty~Two

FREYA'S EYES prickled just looking at Max, her heart straining that she got to share a little more time with him. If that wasn't a big enough sign she most definitely cared… And then there was his mention of The Rainbow Room, an indication he too cared, at least enough to find out about her, anyway. And he'd turned up tonight, hadn't he?

Fuck her life.

Lord help her if he called her bluff. If he asked to rekindle what they'd had, how would she even respond to that?

My life is so different these days. So is his. Why am I still terrified of throwing myself into a relationship with him?

Because he'd want more than last time. He'd want a knock-down, drag-out, no-holds-barred kind of love. No more meaningless booty calls. Just intimacy, and promises, and a whole lot of other messy stuff she couldn't control.

And the worst part? He deserved all that and more.

Maybe she did too.

But her reasons for walking away from him had been all about what he lacked. Now she would be forced to look at what *she* lacked, and what she lacked was any kind of working knowledge or experience when it came to healthy, long-term relationships. Not counting her friendship with Gideon, of course.

"I'm sorry." She pressed her fingertips over her closed eyelids. "Things ended so abruptly between us, I guess I can't blame you for being curious."

"I wasn't keeping tabs." He frowned, breaking eye contact. "Enough people knew about us that some felt the need to tell me."

"It's fine."

She gnawed on her lower lip, fighting a desire to reveal the truth that she too had experienced moments of looking into his life. Like how, two weeks after the breakup, she'd spent an entire day clearing out her mother's rundown house. The sheer labor involved, the overbearing memories, the act of throwing so much of her mother away, had left her in desperate need of comfort.

Gideon was out of town with his show, and she'd been alone, so before she had a moment to take stock of her actions, she'd made it all the way to Max's apartment. Even gotten so far as pressing his buzzer numerous times, only to get no answer.

It wasn't until she returned to her car, despondent and more heartbroken than ever, that she saw the big *For Sale* sign.

He'd already moved. She'd missed him. And it was the act of catching herself digging through her handbag, seconds from calling him, that brought up the reality that she'd been about to drag him back into her orbit.

She'd used that moment to delete his number altogether, to sever all ties and all temptation to contact him again, to wise up to the truth that she needed to stop.

Her desperate clinging would only break her heart all over again.

An internal shudder worked through her core now, and she lifted her gaze back to Max. Reconnecting seemed like a nice idea, but maybe they'd be better off leaving things as they were.

"You seem well. I'm glad." She lowered her gaze and gave a weak smile, busying herself with the task of biting into her sandwich.

He chuckled, a light staccato not one-hundred-percent joy-filled. "Meanwhile, Freya Cortez continues on her road to greatness. Maybe we're both not so pathetic after all?"

She paused chewing and stared straight ahead, at the long journey of descending concrete stairs and the tall flag poles either side, banners flapping with adverts for future concerts. Even as she vied for mental distance, Max's lighthearted approach bore a hole through her defenses and made her want to hold on to him even more.

"Freya?" His lowered voice pulled her from her thoughts and onto his deep frown. "Are you okay?"

She swatted her hand through the air, dismissing his concern. "I'm fine. Just a lot happening right now. You know, work stuff."

"No." His shook his head, his overly focused stare offering no room for escape. "I mean, the last time I saw you, you'd lost your mother, and you were about as broken as a person could get. Are you *okay*?"

His emphasis on the word *okay* implied that she might fold over in a devastated mess. To be fair, anyone with her past could be forgiven for doing just that. Besides, he was right, she hadn't been a picture of mental stability in the days leading to their breakup, so maybe his concern now was somewhat warranted.

She lowered her sandwich to the foil wrapper in her lap and directed a smile his way. "Yeah, actually, I am. I'm good."

The lines on his face eased, and he tilted his head to one side, the slight curl of his lips hinting at delighted surprise. "Really?"

She cleared her throat and nodded, hoping he'd accept her reply as genuine honesty. "Yeah, really. I've had a long time to think since we last met, and even if there'd been time for my mum to offer the dying-hour apology I wanted, it wouldn't have been enough. A part of me would always question whether the apology was her way of hedging her bets. You know, easing her guilt before skipping off to wherever people like her go when they die?"

She shrugged and frowned down at her lap. "The only thing that might have truly helped was if she'd done a significant amount of work on herself long before she died. If she'd sought ongoing professional help and put in the hours to repair our relationship. I guess what you saw was me in the throes of realizing that was never going to happen."

His fingers slid along the concrete space between them, stopping just shy of reaching her hand, like he'd meant to comfort her but figured that was a bad idea. "That must have been a hard realization to come by."

"There's been a lot of hoops to jump through, and a lot of *ifs* and *buts*…" A ball of emotion took up space at the base of her throat, her voice raspy and hard to control. "I feel ridiculous now thinking back on how much I expected from my mother in those final months. I'd been on the right path, doing things my own way already, only to put my healing in the hands of my abuser.

"I should have trusted myself. Should have just admitted some relationships are complex, and it's possible to love someone and hate them at the same time. That it was okay to understand *why* she was the way she was, but still not be okay with her decisions. There were reasons for what she did to me, but none of those reasons made a valid excuse. So really, my mum's death threw one big fucking spanner in all the good work I'd done prior to her becoming ill, and it—"

Her voice cracked, and she slapped her hand over her mouth because there was no way Max hadn't heard her emotions rise up to overwhelm her.

"Freya?" He leaned in, the subtle movement imploring her to go on.

She took her hand from her lips. "It also means I might have been too quick to end things with you than I probably should have been."

His posture sagged, and he angled slightly away from her, his gaze searching her face in the prolonged silence.

Pretty much everyone from the concert had gone, which only left her with this giant wasteland of concrete pillars and some twinkling lights; the only sounds being the scuttling of leaves and the rustle of a few nearby seagulls scavenging for food. The whole scene built a haunting sense that she and Max might be the only two people left in the world.

His gaze dipped, as if he took a second to think, before a heavy sigh fell from him, and his stare captured hers once more. "You're the bravest person I know, Freya."

Her mouth slipped open. She'd expected his criticism, not a compliment.

"If I'd been truly honest with myself"—his hand slid forward again, this time succeeding in landing on top of hers—"I would have admitted that us being together wasn't doing either of us a whole lot of good, which means that you took the brunt and the blame when you did end things. And all during a time that would have been horrible for you already. And *that* makes you far wiser and braver than me. I can see that you want me to hate you, but I don't. Not at all."

Her insides gave an aching twist, her heart somewhere between swelling and shrinking at his words. With one hand, he complimented her wisdom and bravery, two traits she'd earned through blood and tears; with the other, he ripped away something she fast realized she still desperately wanted.

Him.

The truth was, despite what he believed, she *had* gotten a great deal of "good" from being with him. In fact, he'd been the first romantic partner to truly support her, to listen, to not ask her to dim her light so he could shine brighter.

He'd been gentle and sweet and obnoxiously positive—her soft place. Hell, most of their time together had been just plain old fun.

So yeah, hearing him say their relationship hadn't done much good took a pitchfork to her insides. That pitchfork stabbed holes right through the hope that *maybe* there was more to this catch up than stupid-old Gideon getting a big laugh at her expense.

"I… ahhh…" She tugged her hand away from his and went about shutting food containers and then stuffing them into her bag. She swore under her breath, tears gathering at the outer corners of her eyes. *Stupid woman.* "It's… it's getting late, and I have work in the morning. I should go."

She shot to her feet and gave him a lame half-wave goodbye.

He peered up at her—two great, thick lines digging trenches between his brows—gaze darting about her face like her reaction perplexed him. "Freya, what's wrong?"

"Nothing." She offered a tight smile, one that probably wasn't all that unbelievable what with her jittery movements and sudden inability to look any higher than his chest. "Nothing's wrong. You're right. There wasn't much good in what we had, and seeing you tonight, I should be thinking less about rekindling what we had and more about why I set you free to begin with."

Ouch!

She pressed her hand to her roiling stomach. The act of saying all of that made her want to pitch her barely digested sandwich. She hadn't meant to use such harsh words, but maybe harsh was what they needed.

He jumped up and drew in close. "Wait, what's happening here? Were you really hoping for a *rekindling*? Because right now you're walking away again, and I can't—"

She flapped her hands in front of her and spun away from him, tears beginning to spill while her nerves burned at the sense of teetering on the edge of something big. "I don't know, Max. I don't know."

She had a decision to make. The rest of her life with this man or complete nothing. Her wild reaction was all about her renewed chance to fuck up the only real and loving relationship to cross her path in her entire thirty-three years of existence, and still, things weren't as simple as picking between two options.

"All I know is, the reasons for us not being together still hold true. I still don't want to always be the strong one. I still can't take yet another person letting me down."

Max gripped her elbow and turned her to face him, and his mere touch and the act of making eye contact sent instant flutters throughout her body.

He isn't making walking away easy.

He pulled her closer, and despite her reservations, she allowed him to. "I wouldn't be here if I didn't in all honesty believe I've changed."

She squeezed her eyes shut, trying to shut him out, trying to keep her head clear. "I don't have it in me to find the hidden blessings in yet another bad relationship. I don't want to have to search for the lesson in something that's just plain broken. If losing my mother has taught me anything, it's that sometimes pain is just pain, and things just hurt. There's no rhyme or reason, no greater good." She shook free and pressed the back of her hand to her forehead. "I'm not even sure what I'm saying here."

"I think"—he took a side step so he stood directly in line with her, despite her constant turning away—"what you're trying to say is that you don't want me to flake out on you. That you want more than what we had last time."

She moved to speak, but he shook his head, indicating he wasn't finished.

"You want what happened with your mother to end with you." His voice held an urgent strain, like his life hung on his ability to convince her, even though his sheer lack of needing to convince her was what scared her most of all. "For you, that makes avoiding bad relationship choices even more critical. I get it."

"It's more than that. The need to get things right also puts a lot of pressure on whoever wants to be with me."

He narrowed his eyes, as if attempting to read her thoughts, before a slow smile lit his face. He lifted one hand to stroke her cheek, a cheek still hot with tears. "My parents raised me to believe that kindness costs nothing, Freya. And being kind to you is the easiest thing in the world. It's what you deserve. What you've always deserved, all along, despite how others treated you. Have I ever been unkind to you?"

Her chin wobbled with the emergence of a sad smile. She shook her head, distracting herself from the wave of emotion taking over.

He'd always been good to her, even when he'd been not-so-great to himself.

"Then let's start there. I have no intention of ever hurting you, and I hope you've seen enough to know that's not part of who I am."

Her gaze fused with his, and she held silent. Her reaction to his statement was easy. She couldn't envisage him ever mistreating her, couldn't even imagine him having a malicious thought or raising his voice. But the past was a shadow near impossible to step out from, and sometimes she saw monsters where they didn't exist.

But I still believe him. He's right; he's given me every reason to believe him.

With every encounter they'd ever shared, kindness had always been his default.

Not just with her, but with everyone.

How could she not give him a chance?

She took a deep breath and gave him a shaky nod, allowing her wayward smile to sneak through just a little. "Your parents did a good job with you."

His fingers connected with her chin, and he tilted her head so her line of sight matched his. "They did, which brings me back to why you're far braver and wiser than me."

His lips curled into a cheeky grin. He was stroking her ego, no doubt about it, but the hurt little girl in her needed the encouragement all the same.

"You developed your kindness, bravery, and smarts all on your own. You held so much pain, and yet you knew not to push it onto others. You're a special brand of person, Freya Cortez. Look at everything you've done so far. You're already the changed woman you wanted to be."

She tensed at the reminder of her mother and the unacceptable wounds inflicted on Freya year after year. "And you're not scared I'll turn into her?"

She'd been forced to carry a stigma she didn't deserve, so many people having distanced themselves, already labeling her a monster in the making. Why not Max too?

Because he's different.

"Can you imagine your mother, at any point in her life, being anything like you are now?" He raised a brow, point already made, but he had more to say. "You gave me a job when I had nothing. You gave me your personal time and affection when others ran. You've never yelled at me or insulted me, even after I made the dumbest mistakes."

"You mean like losing all your money?"

His lips curved into another smile. "Exactly. You couldn't be any further from your mother if you'd both come from different planets. Hell, you even broke both our hearts so we could each get our lives together. You did it for a greater good, and as much as I wanted to hate you for that, I couldn't. You achieved things with me others tried but failed to do. You saw the core of my issues when even I couldn't, and you forced me to heal the things that were holding me back."

"Well, then. You're welcome."

Despite her joke, his eyes held a focused stare, his cheeks lax in a somber expression. "No. Not yet. I'm not finished."

Her heart lurched. He was being way more philosophical and serious than she'd ever seen of him. Maybe he *had* changed.

"I know I've been indecisive, but I sure as hell know what I want now."

She quirked a brow, not used to this new and more direct version of Max. "And what's that?"

"I'm going to turn around in the next few seconds and leave for home. But when I do, I hope I won't be leaving alone."

He let go of her and stepped away, extending a hand for her to take, his forehead wrinkled in a silent question.

Would she take his hand? Would she go with him?

Forty-Three

FREYA STARED at Max's outstretched hand, everything around her seeming to pause and her world completely silent. She had a decision to make, less about whether she would take his hand, more about whether she could.

She lifted her focus to the warmth in his eyes, his expression pinched like his entire future rested on this moment. Maybe it did. Hers certainly would never be the same, no matter what she chose to do next. And still, with all the thoughts buzzing around in her head, her body was the one to make the decision for her, overriding years of careful and considered life choices.

She watched, powerless, as her hand rose and fingers extended, all too soon sliding home into the upward curve of his palm. Her feet moved, betraying logic, stepping her toward him.

"I can't tell if this is the best fucking decision I've ever made"—the statement fell from her in a rush of words and her heart drummed wild —"or the dumbest. So, start walking before I have any more time to think."

Max's lips split into a mega-watt smile, and he let loose with a soft chuckle. The sound worked its way through her chest and into her heart. The hard strained beating made her feel near ready to burst.

And the light in his gaze, cool in color but hot in every other way, made more tears well in her eyes and caused her laugh to escape too.

She was just so damn happy. Maybe stupidly so. She hadn't ever felt this carefree. The closest she could recall was that night in his apartment, after the heating died and they'd found other ways to keep warm.

But even now, she held back from kissing him because if she did that, they'd never leave this stadium. So, she took his lead and followed him down the long flight of stairs, all the way to the parking lot and his car.

Except, it wasn't his car. Not as she'd known it, anyway.

The Tesla was gone, the lavish vehicle traded for a more reasonably priced midnight-blue sedan, yet another hint of change, of the sacrifices he'd made to fund his newfound dreams.

The freeway lights soon flickered outside the car's windows, green overhead signs announcing each suburb as they passed. He'd clearly also moved much farther out from the city.

The knots in her stomach untangled more and more with each little sign of change, every one an indication she'd made the right choice in giving him a second chance.

Throughout the drive back to his place—wherever that was—they talked about the most mundane subjects. From the noisy cockatoo that had taken up residence amongst the red blossoms of a Firewheel tree outside her townhouse, to the massive dog who kept pooping on the nature strip outside his.

They laughed along the way, the whole casual exchange slipping them back in sync with each other, so contrary to the months upon months of no contact.

He stopped his car outside of a brown brick townhouse in the middle of suburbia and neither spoke as the locks clicked open on his doors. She should have felt nervous, but her heart pounded for a whole other reason. Pride surged through her since this man, who at their last exchange lived a shambled life, had come back for her. He'd worked hard to turn his life around, and now that work paid off in their favor.

He'd studied and excelled, then built a new business around a passion he'd struggled for so long to find. More than any of that, he'd dismantled the soul-destroying emotions that had torn them apart in the first place.

And somehow, she found the ability to accept him, to accept what would happen next.

She stepped out of the car, the night air still cool and filled with the sleeping suburb's relative silence. The short path up to his chestnut front door took seconds to cover, the stain across its indented panels slightly faded, indicating a well-lived-in house minus any true neglect.

From the outside, it looked like a *home*, modest and cozy, nowhere near as glamorous as his former apartment. This alone brought ease to her racing pulse.

Max pushed open the door, and they stood in his entryway, for a moment looking anywhere but at each other. To her left was a living room, one that blended with a kitchen; the entire area was small, with modern floating stairs scaling up the far wall.

"I know it's not what I used to have…"

She spun around to find his pupils wide in apology.

She pointed to her surroundings. "No. This is enough."

Her breaths drew tight at the notion he thought she might ever judge him for making a few difficult choices. Maybe others had, but not her. She'd come from far, far worse and understood he'd achieved something worthy of bragging. Not that Max ever bragged.

She fixed her stare right onto his and pulled him into her, making sure he understood too. "Max, this is *more* than enough."

The tension around his eyes eased, and an innate gleam returned before his lips crashed over hers, taking her by surprise.

Her bag slipped off her shoulder and fell to the ground. He swept her off her feet, his teeth nipping at her lower lip, as his long legs marched her across the room.

Stairs creaked beneath his footfall, and she held onto his shoulders for dear life, the living area's lights soon dimming as he entered his bedroom. He plonked her onto the bed and another giddy laugh broke from her lips, the ungraceful approach so very Max.

His laughter mingled with hers, and he pulled his shirt over his head, tossing it to the floor—yet more ungracefulness, though his slow crawl across the bed toward her caused any sound she might have made to disappear, her breath pausing for one quick beat.

He positioned his body over hers, covering her, as beautiful as ever, perhaps even more so because of the journey they'd endured to get to this point. Even in his absence, her affection for him grew, heart holding on no matter how much she tried to bury all her memories.

The sudden stillness of his face mirrored her emotions, like he knew the impact of this moment and how much it meant to her. This was more than any woman allowing him to fall in love with her. She was a survivor. One who knew how ugly the world could be. And that knowledge made all the difference. It raised the stakes for just how much trust she put in him now.

He leaned in so his lips met hers again, though a million times softer. His tongue caressed hers until she released an easy sigh and arched her body into his—this reunion everything luscious and luxurious—bringing her as close to floating as anyone could get, igniting a desire for him now… and fast.

His lips veered, trailing a maddening line of kisses to the side of her neck, his breath hot against her skin; and before she knew what was happening, his hand found her outer thigh, and he pulled away her panties.

Max smiled down at her, her dress's off-the-shoulder neckline the next to go. She wriggled, helping him slide the purple material down her body, all while extending her arms and tugging at his belt.

In seconds, his hungry kiss devoured her lips again, and he took her body with one swift thrust. She gasped, tensing around him, before curling her lips at the wondrous sense of connection. Maybe there would be time for slow and sweet later, but this time wouldn't be it.

He thrust into her again, unapologetic, demanding, her mind dizzying, while she didn't even attempt to stop her body's reaction.

"Max." Her voice came out soft, like a wish already answered.

She tightened her legs around his hips and dug her nails into the hard muscle at his back. There was more to come, and they were both set on making up for lost time, every one of her nerves catching light at having him inside her… and all around her… his body and heat claiming her over and over again.

An electrified thrill ran from her head to her toes, circling back, torturing her all over again. She laughed at the joy of it all. At having him again. At just how freaking good it was to feel him once more and hopefully forever.

None of this made sense. Not the building pressure or the trill of excitement spilling from her lips, but before she could control any of it, his movements grew faster still, and the pressure became too much. She threw back her head, muscles contracting, while a guttural moan exploded free of her.

She pulled him closer, wanting to feel everything, even though she feared she might black out from sheer exhilaration.

"Oh, Freya."

Her name fell from him with gentle endearment. He continued to bury himself within her until his body shook with his release. Her muscles eased, and she accepted him. *Accepted this.* That they were together now, and that from now on they would fight to *stay* together.

His climax eased and his head found a place at her neck, and he settled down beside her, his lips leaving yet more soft kisses on her skin. "Freya?"

She still floated from her release and his lingering touch, and she failed to find the energy to reply.

"Freya?"

She drew a sharp breath, forcing herself to look at him. "Hmm?"

His eyes glinted with his smile, like he might have something meaningful to say, only to utter, "If you had a choice—live on any planet, time travel, or know everything there was to know about everything—which would you choose?"

Her stare fused with the dark expanse of his ceiling. Before long, a rich wave of laughter broke past her lips.

He couldn't have given a more "Max" response to making love than that.

She shoved at his shoulder, still laughing. His cheeks lifted with a boyish grin.

"Time travel, you doofus." She leaned into him and rewarded his lovable silliness with a firm kiss.

Her life had been one sad and serious event after another. Maybe this man was just the light she needed.

He turned with his lingering smile, waiting for her to settle into the nook under his armpit. "Same. I would go back in time and see all the cool stuff we don't have anymore, then I'd go forward in time and find answers to stuff I want to understand." His eyes widened as though a new thought entered his mind. "Oh, and then I would go to a time with advanced space travel, so I could still tick living on another planet off my list."

She gave him a mock flat stare. "Except, it'd suck if you went ten years forward and found everyone was dead."

"Well, yeah." He frowned. "That *would* suck."

"Or you might succeed in visiting another planet." She shrugged and ticked one side of her lip upward. "Only to die at the hands of aliens who are smart enough to wear shorts in hot weather."

She pulled her mouth into an instant smile, while a slow chuckle reverberated through Max's chest. He too remembered that awkward camping trip where she'd tried to distract him with questions about nonsensical wardrobe choices in sci-fi shows.

His gaze caught hers now, and his fingertips combed loose curls away from her face, the rest of him falling still. "You know, I love you."

His low whisper, so intimate and sincere, traveled deep into her body and wrapped around her heart, giving life to a dull ache—an ache to last a lifetime because that's how long she'd wanted someone to say those words to her.

Though he *had* spoken those words before, only she'd been too broken from her mother's death to stay and say them back. Now things were different, her only fear being that life would find a way to take him from her once again.

I won't think like that. He's mine now. I won't ever let him go.

And so, she gave him a shaky smile, ran her fingers over the soft bristle of his cheek, and gave him the reply she'd so wanted to say the first time he'd uttered those words.

"Max, I love you too."

Epilogue

Three years later

"You don't usually hold these things during the day."

Max waited as Luke's attention broke to Nova bolting past, the little girl tearing through the busy beachside restaurant, while a heavily pregnant Agathe ambled after her.

"Much less encourage us to bring the kid." Luke turned back, sporting a bemused grin. "Come to think of it, where's Freya?"

Max dragged out the suspense and waved at Miro, bustling about in this, his new restaurant. He'd closed down his Port Melbourne café and moved to a bigger operation in the outer coastal suburbs.

The invites to this event had stated they'd be celebrating the launch of Max's company's new footwear line, but Miro knew otherwise.

An easy smile tugged at Max's lips, and he spun back to Luke, happy to continue the lie for a while longer. "Freya will be here any minute. She's caught up with work."

Sophie strolled past, also expecting, but not quite as pregnant as Agathe. Orlando trailed behind her, his fingers interlaced with hers.

They too headed outside to the restaurant's mini-boardwalk edging the sand.

The lightness of yet another secret prodded Max into patting Luke's shoulder, before excusing himself outside to meet the subdued heat of the late summer afternoon.

His feet scraped over the slightly faded wooden deck, and he turned toward the ocean before him, inhaling the briny air and awaiting his fate. A fate he'd instigated, only for Freya to join him the rest of the way.

They'd taken what they started three years ago and built something special. Together. The money from the sale of their respective townhouses had bought a larger home ten minutes down the road from where he stood now. A place for him to be near his beloved ocean and a haven for Freya away from the hustle of her busy city venues.

A place to raise a family.

A gasp broke from the restaurant's far corner. He spun around, his chest tingling with the fuzzy spread of excitement.

Two dancers burst from the kitchen doors dressed in skin-tight, black, mime outfits, only to prance through a gap in the crowd. He recognized the dancers from Freya's club, and though she'd mentioned she'd be making a grand entrance, he had no idea what she'd planned.

The dancers made it to the boardwalk and lowered a rucksack from over each of their shoulders, unceremoniously dumping the contents onto the deck with a loud metallic clang.

A pile of rose-gold-colored tubes lay at their feet, and they went about connecting the pieces together, occasionally stopping to prance before the gathering guests in a tangle of dramatic arm and leg movements. Perhaps their comical way of drawing out the building process.

The kitchen doors sprung open again, and two more dancers came out, Gideon positioned in the middle with a thick garland of bushy green foliage and pale pink roses draped over his shoulders, his midnight-blue velvet suit peeking out from underneath.

Subdued piano music spilled through the venue's speakers, and Gideon whipped out a cordless microphone from under his leafy plume. Before Max could register much of anything, Freya's best friend prowled toward him, singing Queen's "Somebody to Love".

The lyrics to the song weren't romantic at all, and a chuckle escaped him, but somehow Gideon sold the performance like only he could. By the time he made it to the boardwalk, the first two dancers had finished their construction—a rose-gold arch.

Gideon's dancers took the garland from his shoulders and draped it over the arch, and just about then, more gasps broke through the crowd—all Max and Freya's closest family, friends, and work colleagues.

This wasn't just any arch. This was a wedding arch.

The gasps turned to glee-filled shrieks, and Max's gut flip-flopped inside him. He didn't need to turn around to guess what had instigated the crowd's reaction, but he did, anyway.

Freya stood just inside the venue's main double doors, a shimmering blush silk dress flaring out from her waist, reaching down to just below her knee.

Her signature blond curls were swept up into a loose style with free locks of hair skimming her face, her hands wrapped around a white-and-pink bouquet.

She glided toward him, the slight tremble of her lower lip betraying uncharacteristic nerves. *Holy smokes.* The mere sight of her—dressed like that. *His* bride. Walking toward *him.* The muscles on his face fell slack, and his heart pounded faster than any of his swim races had ever required.

She stopped at his side, and together they turned toward their celebrant, Gideon.

Even though Max had always secretly wanted a wife, he'd never really expected to get a wedding day. He'd also never imagined the event galloping by quicker than he could process.

He caught Freya's quick glances at him, always capped with a coy smile. The voluminous lace on her dress hid the fact that she was three months pregnant, probably a good thing since they wanted *that* surprise to wait until after *this* surprise.

He reached out and wrapped his hands around hers, and before too long, they exchanged vows.

As much as this day meant everything to him, it meant even more to her. To trust him with the rest of her life, the words, "I do" falling from her lips and sending a jolt of joy-filled adrenaline through his body.

Tears gathered in her eyes, only to trickle down her cheeks, a shudder of laughter working past her lips, as though a heavy weight shifted off her. And maybe it did. Everything about this moment seemed so unlikely.

And as the words, "I do", fell from him too, the beat of his heart settled like one last puzzle piece finally slipping into place, where it always belonged.

A temperate wave of calm washed over him. Freya and his child would have a home a million times different to the one she'd grown up in. There'd be no shouting. No anger. No explosive rage. There'd be no name calling or manipulations. No fear. No pain. Just warmth and laughter and constant safety. A family open about their love for each other.

He might have lost all the things he'd thought he wanted, but he'd found so much more and all he needed with Freya—a woman who'd pushed herself through hell just to ensure she'd be the last of her line and the first to make a change.

THE END

GET A FREE NOVELLA AND EXCLUSIVE KATERINA SIMMS MATERIAL

Building relationships with my readers is one of the great joys of writing, it keeps me from turning into a robot! My newsletters are filled with information on new releases, cover reveals, sales, giveaways, and news relating to my series.
You also get a FREE download of my novella, Winter's Kiss!

To claim your copy simply go to the "Free Book" page on my website.

www.katerinasimms.com

THE HARLOW SERIES, BOOK 1

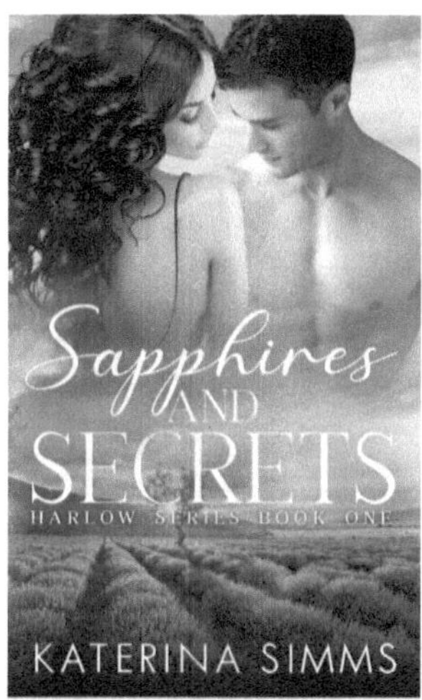

Forbidden love in a town where danger lurks at every corner.

Emilia Bonacci, introverted daughter of an overbearing jewelry tycoon. For one brief moment, she had it all. Now she's on the run from a family who wants to destroy her.

Small, charming, and picturesque. Harlow, Minnesota, seems like the perfect place to hide. Except a chance encounter throws her into the path of her forbidden first love…

Blaine Callaghan always had dreams of living in a big city, until he made the mistake of falling for Emilia. Her powerful family doomed him to exile in this small town, away from his family and future. Seeing her now unearths years of buried love and resentment. But this earth-shattering attraction is impossible to avoid.

Maybe they could be together this time. Except that anyone involved with Emilia will never be safe.

Sapphire and Secrets
(Sample)

CHAPTER ONE

Emilia squeezed her eyes shut, still too boneless with shock to move. The energy around her shifted, and her body wobbled back and forth, threatening to introduce her to the floor.

She sucked in a breath and vowed to treat this moment like ripping off a plaster, unpleasant but necessary. While her back remained to the room, she ached for an ability to teleport out of this nerve-shredding situation.

I could run again. I've already done that once this week.

No, she really couldn't, no matter how much she wanted to. She'd exhausted her funds running that first time. The least she could do now was dig out her courage and face her uninvited guest. She'd spent years faking pleasantness and could do it again.

She forced her eyes open and turned from the ugly olive-green wall ahead, shuffling her feet slowly beneath her. Harsh morning light poured from the open back door and stung her eyes; that light caused her to squint. All she could make out of her visitor was the silhouette of a long torso and strong-looking calves, a pair of weighty work boots, and…

The tradesman.

No, he's more than that. So much more.

He'd only said one word. Her name. It sailed upon his warm, rumbling tone and still somehow ricocheted within her brain, refusing to leave.

He took a small sidestep, the sun no longer obscuring her view. That view ripped at her heart and brought about a genuine pain. One that flowed from her chest and into her back, before a sharp shockwave shot through her muscles and burrowed that pain into her bones.

Oh yes, she recognized him. And recognition had her fearing her heart might fall out altogether and land with a bloody splat on the already disgusting wood floor.

Useless blasted heart. When have you done me any good?

Certainly *never* when it came to this man.

His pale green eyes, so familiar—as if ten years hadn't passed— they darkened to a deep chartreuse, his full lips tightening into a perfect frown. The ex who'd once lived in Minnesota. He *still* lived in Minnesota. Or at least, he'd moved back. Why?

Her pain intensified, prodding the idea that maybe she already knew why. His conflicted glower burned holes through her, seeming to confirm her theory; and still, nothing stopped his name from falling from her lips. "Blaine?"

Blaine. Despite the hard tug at her heart, it felt good to say his name. Maybe because she'd been forbidden from speaking it for over a decade. But saying his name, even just thinking it, should have been the last thing she wanted.

He was the beginning and end of her teenage rebellion. Nothing less than the end of her freedom as an adult... before her adulthood had even started.

Maybe I'm seeing ghosts. No. Not ghosts. Demons! Ghosts or demons would be better than this.

Not that there'd ever been anything bad about him. No, the complete opposite. Though his presence now proved once again that hell had, and still did, exist.

"Emilia."

Her name fell from his mouth, another full and unwavering statement, like he didn't need to bother posing her identity as a question. Like whatever glance he'd had of her earlier provided enough proof.

Like he'd never forgotten.

Of course not. He's etched on my soul forever, and maybe I'm etched on his...

That thought alone stole her next breath from her lungs. So, she did the one thing most likely to spare her from collapsing. *She ran.* Literally ran. Though not in a true straight line, which meant she cracked a shoulder into the vomit-colored door frame, the thing exacting revenge for her earlier thoughts on its ugliness.

Pain shot through her shoulder and down her back, but none of that mattered. She kept running until she reached the bathroom Frank had shown her minutes before.

She snapped the locks shut and sank to the cold tile floor in an attempt to catch her breath.

"You are to stay away from that Irish boy. I won't hear the name 'Blaine' in this house ever again. Do you understand?"

Her head ached from a rush of adrenaline, her father's voice haunting her.

His thick Italian accent rang in her ears as if he'd spoken those words just yesterday. Stupid girl. She should have listened. Should have played by the rules and played her part. The great Vittorio Bonacci had designs for her life, and far be it from her to stray from that plan.

Still, even as she'd done as her dad decreed, time and a wedding hadn't faded anything. Blaine Callaghan remained the old flame she couldn't extinguish.

Her tiny bathroom lights blinked, almost like they protested at having to do their job, but that blinking gave enough distraction to snap her from her tailspin of thoughts.

She couldn't stay curled on the floor forever. Besides, she'd caused enough of a scene already. Frank waited for her in the kitchen, and she had a new reputation to build. Coming across as flighty and irrational wouldn't do.

She gathered the energy to hook her hand to the bathroom counter and pull herself up. Her earlier vow to forget the past lay in tatters, but that didn't mean she had to fall apart. At least, not outwardly, anyway.

The mirror above the sink revealed a pitiful reflection, one that made her tummy churn anew. She'd been living in her car for the last few days, so she shouldn't have expected much. But her high bun lay in a frazzled mess, and loose curls stuck to her clammy forehead. Her left cheek was smeared in black dust from the fireplace. Worst still, the front of her light-colored outfit had somehow collected wayward soot, and she straight-up looked like a maimed creature from a C-grade zombie movie.

She took a steadying breath, pushed aside her overwhelming desire to cower on the floor again, and turned the tap on so she could run her shaking fingers beneath the cold flow.

She'd go out there and face the two men, and she'd do it with the confidence befitting a normal twenty-eight-year-old woman. One who hadn't hightailed it minutes earlier. One stronger than the scared shadow of a woman who'd left LA.

Her entire life thus far was a blur of numb acceptance that the men around her could dictate her destiny. *Again, stupid girl.* Maybe she'd had no other choice, but she couldn't afford to be that girl any longer.

She splashed handfuls of cold water over her face, removing the black marks while willing her nerves to settle. No towels hung in here yet, so she ran her sleeve over her wet skin, the classless gesture so far from her days as a big-city socialite.

Next, she lifted her posture and tidied her hair; anything to avoid looking like a woman who'd just flipped her lid. She'd make something out of this sucky situation. *She had to.* The cottage was *hers. Her* sanctuary. *Her* new beginning. Decrepit as this place was, she wouldn't let yet another man keep her from the independence she so desperately wanted.

Uncertainty nipped at her heels, and still, she pried the bathroom door open a crack and waited for a beat, sussing out the hallway before marching onward to the kitchen, where a giant metal box sat on the floor. The lid lay open, a bunch of workman's thingies visible inside.

Thingies? Tools, Scatterbrain, they're called tools...

Yes. Right. Tools!

Blaine's back was to her, his arms outstretched while he measured the overhead cabinets. He hadn't noticed her in the room, or if he did, he ignored her. And bless her soul, an effervescent tingling spread through her torso, the ease with which he worked and carried himself taking instant effect.

His distinct masculine form, the khaki work shirt pulled over well-defined shoulders—the stretched fit highlighting a steady interplay of taut muscles beneath light fabric. This was as close to a religious experience as she'd had since… Well, since the last time she'd seen him more than a decade ago. And the fact that he did still affect her didn't bode well.

He'd been nineteen back then—still gorgeous, with a heart of gold—but now he had to be closer to thirty-one. It should have been impossible for Blaine Callaghan to get more attractive, but his broader build and steadier stance took him to full-scale Adonis status. Just being in the same room as him made her knees want to liquefy beneath her.

A sudden jolt of shame rocketed up her spine. She'd only just left her awful marriage. Admiring another man's bulging biceps felt wrong. Not that Anthony had any bulging biceps to admire.

Maybe the view would be good for her. Might help her move on. She didn't owe Anthony anything, after all.

Good idea, Genius. Move on? Maybe one day, but not with this guy. It's not like the last encounter with Blaine didn't end in disaster or anything…

The grind of someone clearing their throat snapped her attention away from admiring "the view." *Frank.* Oh right, Frank was here! He'd tucked himself in the farthest corner, which made him downright invisible compared to "the view."

The older man raised a brow, suggesting he'd caught every second of her sightseeing. "Seems you two know each other, then?"

Blaine slowly lowered his arms and turned, his gaze training on her like he, too, wanted an explanation. She refused to offer him one. The past was strictly off-limits.

"I wouldn't go that far." She nodded at the cabinets. "So, what's the verdict?"

A muscle on Blaine's jaw ticked, and he narrowed his eyes as if to say, *Are you really going to pretend we're strangers?*

She skittered her gaze from his because, yes, yes she was. Maybe her lie annoyed him, but it was a lie she would tell either way, even though a part of her wanted to mouth the words, "I'm sorry. I'm so, so sorry."

"Frank already let me know what he needs." Blaine's easy rumble washed over her and set her heart to flutter as if she was the only one unsettled with this surprise reunion. "I'll take these measurements back to the workshop and put something together over the next couple of weeks."

She turned to Frank and offered a sweet smile, hoping he'd be her salvation. "Seems I'm lucky to have Frank and Maureen as landlords."

"Yeah, they're good people." Blaine's voice dragged her gaze back to his steely stare and the muscle in his jaw still twitching away. His rigidity made no secret of questioning whether *she* was "good people."

To be fair, the way things had ended, she didn't blame him.

But what really turned her insides to water was how the color of his eyes retained the same ocean-green flecked with gold. Even though the years had turned his expression more reflective and soul-baring, a tight wariness indicated he had zero patience for her need to save face or her submissive compliance. A submissive compliance that had hurt them in more ways than one.

Where once he'd looked at her with wide and hopeful wonder, now, hard lines and a clenched jaw took over. She let her vision fall to the scuffed floor, the swirling, honeyed pattern on the wood a weak distraction from the heat engulfing her face. If only she'd been stronger back then.

She lifted her chin and gestured at the house. "Seems I have my work cut out for me here."

He glided his attention over her dirt-stained sweater. "Seems you've made a solid start."

More heat rushed to her face, and she questioned the presence of a barely noticeable smirk tugging the corners of his mouth. That smirk softened the hard planes of his face, and that softness, the subtle yet somehow unescapable welcome, clenched a tight fist around her heart, hinting that maybe a mutual spark still existed.

Her treacherous lips wobbled, but she clamped her teeth over her lower lip, holding back the rebellious glint of joy. Given the moment's uncertainty, given the past, given the show she'd made of denying they had one, joy had no place here.

As if he'd heard her thoughts on joy, Blaine's gaze trekked down to her right hand; a frown taking over before his stare slammed into hers.

Sharp iciness grew throughout her body, and she was quick to tug her sleeve over her hand. Not quick enough. He'd seen the scrapes on her knuckles, knuckles already blue with bruises. Her hands still ached every time she clenched her fingers.

At least Blaine didn't question those bruises out loud, though she would need to find a way to keep him at a distance. Maybe she'd call Frank later and ask if he could warn her next time Blaine would be over. She'd find a way to stay out of the cottage, and then she wouldn't have to see him. Or maybe there was someone else in town who could take over the job…

Frank stepped toward her, a set of keys hanging from his fingers. "These belong to you now."

He dropped the keys into her palm, and she frowned down at the silver, jagged edges. A symbol of her new home, even though she didn't even have a bed yet.

"Thanks." She lifted her gaze and scanned the room. No table. Or chairs. Or even a couch in her dusty living room. "Could you recommend a furniture shop around here?"

"Oh ya, that's easy." Frank gave a choked and bumpy kind of laugh before reaching out and giving Blaine a solid but friendly clap on the back. "He's not just the best carpenter in Harlow, but his shop is also the *only* place to get any furniture around these parts."

Buy link: katerinasimms.com/sapphires-secrets/
Or use this QR CODE:

Also by Katerina Simms

The Love at Last Series:

The Last Heartbeat — Love at Last, Book 1

The Last Place You Look — Love at Last, Book 2

The Last in Line — Love at Last, Book 3

The Harlow Series:

Sapphires and Secrets — The Harlow Series, Book 1

Secret Surrender — The Harlow Series, Book 2

Second Hand Secrets – The Harlow Series, Book 3

Small Town Secrets – The Harlow Series, Book 4

For latest releases, go to:

https://katerinasimms.com/books

About the Author

Katerina Simms is a contemporary romance author, RWA Emerald Award finest, and International North Street Book Prize semi-finalist. She was born on a sunny Mediterranean island, only to move to the weather-challenged suburbs of Melbourne, Australia.

Tea addict, nature lover, and terrible gardener, Katerina's novels feature vivid modern settings and heart-stirring characters, punctuated with the occasional good laugh. Her romances skirt the edges of women's fiction, and her favorite tropes are opposites attract, slow burn, and heat with heart.

www.katerinasimms.com

Acknowledgments

I have loved writing the *Love at Last* series and I just know I will always look back on these books with extra special memories. Not only was this series my first set of published full-length novels, but I wrote these books in those magical years when my babies were still actual babies. I've poured so much of myself into these pages, and none more so than in *The Last in Line*.

Like Freya, as a child, I spent a decent amount of time in hospital. So much of her story is my story. While neither of my parents subjected me to medical abuse, I did grow up in a dysfunctional home where one parent suffered mental health issues that resulted in abuse.

Freya's struggle to tie up loose ends with her mother is something many abuse survivors experience. We wade through understanding that a person's mental wounds can cripple the ability to control abusive behavior, all whilst balancing an awareness that no one is obligated to endure or excuse mistreatment. No matter what an abuser insists.

But not everything about this book is doom and gloom for me. I really enjoyed setting this series in my much beloved city of Melbourne, Australia. I don't mention this often, but I have a degree in Performance Art and spent my twenties as a busy live performer. I knew the Melbourne arts and Burlesque scene well; and my goodness, those were some fun years!

The unique characters I met and the different social circles I skirted have left such beautiful marks on my life. So, put two and two together, and of course, you can see where Gideon, and Freya's Ruby Room, began.

Because of this, my first thanks goes to my city and the people in it.

For generally treating me so well, and being so weird and wonderful, and such a big inspiration. I always say, there's a place for every kind of person in this city. If you ever get a chance to visit, you simply must.

My next thanks goes once again to my friend Amanda, for allowing me to use her professional knowledge on a number of medical and accident-based moments in this story. She's always so patient with me. And as usual, I take full responsibility for any messed up truths on this front.

Special mentions as always go to my editor Chris Hall of The Editing Hall, my proofreader extraordinaire (and fellow romance author) Jen Katemi, and my cover designer Sarah Paige of Opium House. I'm so thankful to have such a reliable team behind my work.

Thank you to my sanity saving writing groups: the MRWG or Melbourne Romance Writers Guild, RWA Australia, and extra special brunch buddies The Romantic Elephants. This writing gig is solitary enough, and after months of pandemic isolation, seeing everyone again has been a much needed breath of fresh air.

And of course, a HUGE thank you to my readers, fans, newsletter subscribers, and reviewers. Every time you buy a book and support authors like myself, you become a much appreciated patron of the arts. Your support extends far beyond the financial. All the emails and messages, and lovely reviews, they feed our souls and keep our imaginary worlds turning.

Thank you, Everyone. I mean it.

Lots of love. Always.

X Katerina

How About A Review?

Authors love reviews, and good ones help us make a living, and thus write more books! If you've enjoyed this book, please consider leaving a review on Goodreads or your retailer of choice. Just a line or two would make a wonderful difference!

Eternally grateful,

Katerina Simms